Wicked Normal

By Lauren Courcelle

Lauren Courcelle

Published by Lauren Courcelle – 2012

To Dad -
who has always
loved and believed in me,
unconditionally...
(and always will!)

prologue

Happily Ever After...

And they lived happily ever after...

Okay, if you're thinking that means it's the end of the story then you better close this book, put it back on the shelf, and go find yourself a fairy tale to believe in.

For me, those words, "happily ever after," signify just the beginning. Although it is where most stories end, that's because writers typically aren't clever enough to write the happy stuff. Surely intelligent readers prefer books about the times after the happy beginnings, as indeed, most of one's life is actually the happily ever after. Maybe I *am* extremely lucky, but I've always known life to be happy because I am living in my parents' happily ever after.

Okay, so perhaps I am a little different. It's taken me quite a long time to begin to accept it, but I am at least now considering that I might have some rather unique qualities. I still can't help but believe that I'm wicked normal, just like everyone else, and despite the accusations of my jealous haters, I am not a monster. Honestly, I don't want to be anyone except who I am: Persephone Smith. I'm just a happy, young lady living her happily ever after, on her way to her eventual soulmate who will *not* be a prince. I mean, have you seen the eligible princes out there? Blech. No, thank you. I want an awesome hunk who loves me and is perfect for me. Mom taught me that there's no use in looking for someone who is perfect, because people aren't perfect, but instead to find someone who is just right for me.

Mom married Dad because he was perfect for her. According to her rendition of their love story, way back before I was born, my father was a member of UR My QTπ, a boyband that was very popular at the time. Although Mom tells endless stories about going to UR My QTπ concerts and crazy run-ins with band members, fans, and security, it only proves that she was their number one fan, not that she actually married a popstar. That's ridiculous! That doesn't happen in real life. It's a crazy fantasy dream that you'd read about in some mindless novel you'd save for a trip to the beach!

Undeniably, Dad is a marvelous singer, and shockingly, he sure knows how to dance. At my cousin's wedding, he not only led the train but he did this crazy dance with a chair and a hat that had everyone cheering! And well, I guess my dad must be pretty cute for an old guy because I have noticed ladies batting their eyes, giggling, and blushing around him. What's really cool is that he is unfazed by such attention and only ever notices my mom. It's true love. And well, a boyband guy, who used to sing onstage with thousands of girls screaming at him, wouldn't know true love, would he?

Alright, so Dad *is* pretty perfect - but Mom's pretty perfect, too, so I guess that's why they're made for each other. Now don't get me wrong. I certainly don't want to marry Dad! Yuck! No way! I just gotta find whoever is perfect for me. And okay, I confess, there's no rush because I am only nine years old, so I don't need to cast the role of soulmate *just* yet.

I genuinely love to spend time with the 'Rental Units, also known as my parents or 'Rents, and they are my true best friends and confidants because I know they'll always love me unconditionally! Since my happiness brings them happiness, they do everything within their powers to allow me to have a carefree, joyful, perfect childhood. Spoiled rotten? Without a doubt! It's one of the perks of being an only child! Dad works a lot and is the breadwinner for our family. Mom teaches first grade at my school, Saint Bart's, because she loves teaching little kids and gets free tuition for me. When I was younger, she used to stay at home with me, but that's not to say we're rich. We don't live in a mansion. We don't have servants. If Dad had *actually* been a member of UR My QTπ, surely we'd have all of those things plus paparazzi and security, but our life is perfectly normal.

Now, having spent a large portion of my formative years interacting primarily with adults, I tend to be rather mature for my age. I use an extensive vocabulary and derive tremendous pleasure in confusing imbeciles with my multisyllabic musings. And let's face it, if you typically use properly placed gigantuous words, nobody is certain when you misuse them or invent them every now and then.

Despite my advanced skills in socializing with grown-ups, the 'Rental Units think I need to have more interactions with other kids, particularly girls, who are my own age. I've moaned and groaned that I'm far too old for prearranged playdates, so for two weeks each August, Mom and Dad send me to Birch Bog Day Camp. It's an all-girl camp, but that's okay because with only a couple of exceptions, usually my friends are boys. I've loved going to Birch Bog each of the past two summers because I simply love day camp! Love it! We go swimming and hiking and do cool art projects, and perhaps the best thing is that every night I get to be home with my parents.

Well... usually. See, Birch Bog Day Camp is for campers entering first through fifth grades. For older campers, it becomes simply Birch Bog Camp – an overnight camp. As a transitional step, on the final Thursday of the two week session, the day camp has a special overnight for its campers who are entering fifth grade. So guess what summer I'm up to... yeah, I'm going to be a fifth grader this fall. Ugh, I am not so sure about this overnight business. Sleeping under the stars? With like bugs and bears? What are they thinking? Even Mom says her idea of roughing it is a four-star hotel that doesn't have twenty-four hour room service... and she's right!

But I can do anything for one night, right? *Right*?

Ohhhh, why do I have a terrible gut feeling that camp this year is going to be pure and utter torture? Cue big, dramatic sigh.

chapter one

Birch Bog Day Camp

Y et, on the morning of the first day of camp, I could only think of all of the reasons why I *love* camp – the bus ride, singing songs, the flag ceremony each morning and afternoon, the arts and crafts, the pool – and my bubbling excitement suppressed all of my negative thoughts! With my trusty plaid backpack expertly stuffed by Mom with everything I could ever possibly need, I bolted from the car the moment I saw the yellow school bus arrive to take us to Birch Bog. Mom and I exchanged hugs, kisses, and loving farewells, and I boarded the bus.

As we pulled away, Mom waved goodbye, yelling, "Have fun!" and I waved back. The counselors-in-training, otherwise known as CITs, started our singing that would continue for the entire ride. I've always loved to sing so what better way is there to kick off each and every camp day but with a sing-along!? We sang the whole gamut of traditional camp songs. Oddly, I have no idea how long the ride to Birch Bog actually is because it goes by so fast when we're singing!

When we rounded into the camp's long driveway, we were emphatically getting into one of our favorite songs. It makes fun of the counselors, and we were all belting it out at full volume just as the bus came to a stop at Birch Bog Camp. Needless to say the counselors heard us coming, and they were visibly not happy about our song choice. We all reported to the Horseshoe Green for the flag ceremony to open camp for our session of summer 2009. The senior campers, who were high school students who stayed overnight for the entire summer, presented the flag. After the Pledge and announcements the counselors called each of our names to divvy us up into our groups.

My counselors looked like absolute grouches. The older one, named Traci, had blonde hair and looked maybe in her twenties. The younger one, with maple syrup colored curly hair, looked like a college kid and went by the camp name of "Gilly." How on earth grown-ups who work with kids could be so grumpy is beyond me! They looked as if we were seriously cramping their style. Surely they're paid to deal with us... so they needed to just deal!

They led us to our cabin, Cabin Six, and we sat in a big circle to think up a camp name for our group. Honestly, I can't stand when girls whine and pout and get all melodramatic to get their way. The girls in my cabin unfortunately epitomized this behavior. Ugh. Personally, I thought our cabin should be aptly named, the Obnoxious Twits, but I didn't figure *that* would be well received, so I didn't suggest it. Eventually we agreed to be "Glittering Trillium," even though in my opinion it's a ridiculous name. Trilliums are a perfectly fine kind of flower found in Vermont, but there's nothing glittering about them. At any rate, we made a big "Glittering Trillium" banner and decorated it to represent the girls of Cabin Six.

After that we ate snack and went for a hike. The counselors seemed to be in some huge rush. "Come on, you klutzy campers!" Traci yelled. I didn't understand why they were in such a hurry. They were stuck with us for the whole day, whether they liked it or not, and speeding through activities wouldn't actually make the constant element of time progress at a quicker pace.

"Get a move on, you lazy little girls!" Gilly encouraged. If we were supposed to be motivated by insults, it worked because their rudeness provoked me to protest their behaviors by intentionally stepping ever so slightly more slowly.

Although some people say that they feel like they are going in circles in life, we literally were. They had us hiking on some long, circling trail that led us back to exactly where we had started, just in time for lunch. As we ate, Traci, Gilly, and the other counselors actually stole parts of the campers' lunches, right off of the picnic tables! Luckily, my lunch was hidden in my backpack, and thankfully, they didn't grab my peanut butter and jelly sandwich out of my hands.

At the end of lunch, Glittering Trillium got very excited with anticipation of what would come as soon as we waited our mandatory twenty minutes after eating... swimming! There's no way our grouchy, thieving, insulting counselors could ruin swimming! The Birch Bog Lagoon, as the pool was called, had always been a centerpiece at camp. Sparkling blue and clear, no other experience at Birch Bog remotely compared to swim times at the lagoon. Sure, ever since the beginning of time, there has been the legend of Boggy, the swamp monster of the deep end, but because the pool was always *so* pristine, Boggy seemed like a preposterous scare tactic simply to ensure campers wouldn't go near his "hideout," located conveniently under the slide that was strictly off-limits.

All decked out and ready for the first swim of camp, Traci and Gilly paraded us to the pool and I simply couldn't believe my eyes! This summer, the pool was of a color that could certainly be home to a huge, scary creature from the deep. The water was covered in a revoltingly disgusting, grotesque green slime! Yuck! To make matters worse, our cruel counselors actually *forced* us to swim in the potential cesspool, whether we wanted to or not, cackling wildly at us while they stayed dry onshore! As I waded carefully so as to allow the green slime the least possible contact with my skin, I couldn't help but wonder what had happened to the Birch Bog Day Camp I had been to each of the last two years? The counselors had always been so fun, energetic, friendly, kind, and supportive! They would have never made us endure swim time in the Green Slime Lagoon! Birch Bog had become the worst camp *ever*!

I was so relieved for the closing flag ceremony that day. I didn't sing on the way home... I just watched the trees and landmarks and broke into a full smile when I saw Mom waiting for me by her car.

I ran to her and received a big hug. "How was your day?" she asked.

"I'll tell you in the car," I explained, heading to the passenger's side.

One of the best things about my relationship with Mom is being able to tell her absolutely everything. I know that's shunned at my age, but I can't help myself. My parents have my back no matter what, so why wouldn't I let them in on the details of my life? Besides, pouring everything off my chest about my awful day at camp made me feel much better, and when I heard Mom's plan for what I should do if ever such a day should occur again, I hit the hay that night feeling as though I could surely handle another day at Birch Bog Camp. Let's just say Traci and Gilly had better behave themselves, and well, thank goodness for secret backpack pockets that are just the right size for a cell phone with the 'Rents on speed dial!

However, despite the pep talks and preparations, when the school bus actually pulled in the next morning to bring us campers back to Birch Bog, I had a clear-cut moment of trepidation and remained seated in the car.

"With the exception of yesterday, you've always loved going to camp," Mom reminded me, "and if it's too bad today, you know what to do..."

"Yes, Mom," I gulped. I was filled with dread because Mom was not reading my reluctance and offering to let me stay home. Apparently I would, indeed, be facing the appalling 2009 version of Birch Bog for a second day.

"Today will be better," she reassured me.

"Are you sure?" I looked up at her.

"Say it and it will be," she firmly asserted to me. "And worse comes to worse, if you're completely miserable, call me and I'll come get you."

"Today will be a great day at camp, Mom," I obliged, smirking.

"And so it will be, my Little Dragon! I love you… have fun!" she said with a hug and a kiss.

"I love you, too, and I will…" I said with complete determination that I would.

When I boarded the bus my heart was aflutter with nerves, but the feeling passed when the CITs selected *me* to choose which song to sing first. To keep the positive energy going, I picked "Good Ol' Birch Bog" and looked out the window to wave to Mom with a smile.

After our usual, bumpy, song-filled ride, we arrived at camp and Traci and Gilly greeted us with smiles and enthusiasm. It was Glittering Trillium's turn to be the color guard and raise the flag. During announcements, Sandy, one of the head counselors, stressed that the only phone permitted on the premises was in the Main Cabin and that the Mess Hall, the Main Cabin, and the telephone were strictly off-limits to campers.

I just had to snicker. First, these counselors must have been living in the 1990s if they actually believed for a millisecond that the majority of the girls didn't have cell phones hidden in their backpacks. Second, is there any way for grown-ups to make something more enticing than to make it forbidden? In my two plus summers at Birch Bog, I had never even thought of going into the Main Cabin, but with such an emphasis on the off-limits nature of it, even *my* curiosity was now piqued.

14

Sandy heard me and asked what I found so funny, and well, I'm an honest person, so I shared the part of it I could reveal... right there in the Horseshoe Green in front of everybody...

"When adults make something "off-limits," that simply makes kids want to do it exponentially more," I admitted. The rest of the campers giggled as Sandy reddened, flustered.

I will *never* understand why grown-ups ask questions they don't actually want answered. Sandy promptly escorted me away, and I was immediately assigned to the consequence of latrine duty. "Latrine duty" is the fancy Birch Bog way of saying "cleaning the bathroom," except we don't have toilets or running water. The latrine is a glorified multi-seat outhouse. Now, I just have to inquire as to the legality of assigning children to clean the latrine. Being forced to clean? With no running water? Without pay? Are we absolutely, positively certain that this isn't illegal?

Oddly, as completely disgusting as the task was, I enjoyed my time away from Glittering Trillium, Traci, and Gilly. Maybe it's because I knew they were all off swimming at the Green Slime Lagoon, or maybe it's because I actually enjoy time by myself so I can think.

Despite my dawdling at making the latrine sparkling clean, which it was, when I was done, surprisingly, not a single person had come to check in on me. Perhaps they had simply forgotten about me, or maybe Boggy had finally eaten the invaders of his lagoon! At any rate, being finished with my punishment, I headed over to the pool area to see if Glittering Trillium was still there.

That's when I spotted the ambulance. I saw that one of the lifeguard chairs had snapped in half and that the chair portion was in the middle of the shallow end of the Green Slime Lagoon! I rushed over to Gabby, my assigned buddy for Glittering Trillium's buddy system, to get the scoop.

"Gabby, what happened?" I inquired.

"Like oh my gaw! Didn't you see it? Where were you?" Gabby blurted in a tizzy.

As much as I wanted to make a flip comment about the irony of having a buddy that didn't know where I was, in the event of an actual emergency, I circumvented that temptation and pressed onward. "I was assigned to latrine duty," I said in a calm tone that contrasted significantly from Gabby's excitability.

"Oh my gaw! You should've been here! It was so loud and so scary! And she looked so gross! All slimy and green and we thought she was dead!" Gabby wigged out.

"Who?" I asked.

"Sandy!" she revealed.

I used a great amount of effort to contort my face to reflect the expression that I imagined should be shown in such a circumstance. The woman who had assigned me to latrine duty had almost just been killed in a freak accident at the Green Slime Lagoon. As my face was hopefully exhibiting an acceptable amount of shock and horror, my mind was busily thinking, "How soon 'til we can nickname Sandy, 'Slimey'?" as it's uber apropos for the newly-crowned Queen of the Green Slime Lagoon. I decided it wasn't the best time to mention the idea though, as people were crying and visibly shaken.

"She's gonna be okay, right?" I asked aloud, and a cute, green eyed, dark haired, young paramedic, reassured me that Sandy was very lucky to have been saved by her coworkers so fast. That emerald-eyed hunk then jumped into the driver's seat and drove the ambulance and Slime- I mean, Sandy away.

As the other campers got their eardrops and changed into their clothes, I was glad that nobody was paying attention to me because it provided me ample time to collect my thoughts without interruption. No matter how many times it happened, the realization that one's thoughts had actually transpired was always a little disconcerting. See, nothing I had just seen at the Green Slime Lagoon was shocking to me, as I had already witnessed the whole scene in my mind while cleaning the latrine! Coincidence? Psychic abilities? I don't know. All I know is that throughout my life, it's always just how it has been, and that I desperately hope that I am not, in actuality, causing the events to occur.

Traci and Gilly decided that our art project for the day should be "Get Well" cards for Sandy. I found a piece of green construction paper and some blue glitter and made a slimy looking creation on my card reading, "So glad you're gonna be okay!" On the inside I wrote "The latrine is sparkling!" using a silver glitter marker to write "sparkling." I thought my card was cool.

After arts and crafts we had lunch, and then we had a hike to a pond where we looked for salamanders and pollywogs. I'm not sure what they expected us to do if we found any, cuz we didn't have buckets and I'm certainly not grabbing them with my bare hands. Blech! Luckily, I only saw some minnows swimming in the pond.

The rest of the week passed swiftly without further incidents, although swimming would be forbidden until the accident scene was cleaned up and the lifeguard chair was replaced. Traci and Gilly remained on my ever-growing list of least favorite camp counselors, but they mellowed out a little to become nearly tolerable. We did some fun arts and crafts, outdoors, and teambuilding activities, and amazingly, I somehow survived the week with no more instances of latrine duty!

On Friday, we learned that Sandy was recuperating at home, but she hadn't yet recovered sufficiently to return to camp. You surely can tell that I'm simply heartbroken at Birch Bog's loss of a tremendous asset of a head counselor. Insert eye roll here.

chapter two

The Trouble With Fairy

So Monday morning brought about the return of the big yellow bus. "Ready for another week of camp?" Mom asked.

"It wasn't really so terrible last week after Slimey got what was coming to her," I smiled.

"Persephone! You know how I feel about that sort of talk," Mom said sternly.

"But isn't it weird that I thought about the lifeguard chair breaking and Sandy flying into the pool and having to be dragged out and the other counselors giving her mouth to mouth and -"

"Did you see her being okay in the end?" Mom interrupted.

"Of course, Mom, just like you tell me... always end thoughts happily, just in case," I grinned.

"Believe me, you don't want to mess with Karma," she warned.

"I know, Mom, cuz Karma's a -"

"Don't say it."

I giggled. Mom frequently panicked that I was going to blurt out words that warranted a bar of soap as a consequence, but such talk really wasn't my style. With my breadth of vocabulary I certainly needn't ever resort to the short little words that ignoramuses use to express themselves in an inappropriate fashion.

"Mom, I was gonna say, 'Karma's always coming back at you threefold.'"

"Thattagirl," she smiled and ruffled my hair. "Now go have a great day at camp!"

Monday was a sunny day and Traci and Gilly greeted Glittering Trillium excitedly with mention of a special two day project. It started with a hike into the forest. We got to a clearing and sat in a circle to listen as Gilly told us about the forest fairies, explaining that our project would be making fairy houses that they could stay in. Apparently, legend has it that the forest fairies leave a payment or reward for the night's lodging.

Fairies? Seriously? I'm nine. Every nine year old knows that fairies, as in lots of little fairies flying around, are a preposterously untrue concept. Maybe people see fireflies and make up stories or something, but other than the Tooth Fairy and the few oversized "fairies" you might run into at theme parks, fairies do not exist.

But, the idea of decorating a tree stump to be an in-the-wild dollhouse created solely by me, sounded like a truly fun way to pass a couple of hours. Obviously the "fairy's payment" would be some sort of treat from the counselors, so bring it on! I'm in!

I got completely lost in my own little interior decorating world, completely decking out the natural, humble abode. I had bits of bark as a couch and a fern as carpeting and the master bedroom had a black-eyed Susan as a bed with Queen Anne's lace as the comforter. I was still adding details and furnishings long after my cabin was playing duck, duck, goose in the clearing. When Traci announced we had five minutes before we would be heading back to camp for lunch, I put the finishing touches on the staircase to the fairy house balcony and completed it all just in time.

On our walk back to camp, our counselors told us that we'd check on our fairy houses the next day after lunch. So on Tuesday we all gobbled our food quickly in anticipation of hiking back and checking to see what the "fairies" had left us. But that was when Traci and Gilly pulled the mean trick of making us do our chores before the hike back, and Glittering Trillium's chore that day was latrine duty! I may not know what I want to be when I grow up, but I do know that I don't want to clean bathrooms or latrines. Blech! Gross! However, with the incentive of returning to the fairy houses and seeing what rewards awaited us, we sped right through cleaning that latrine!

We hiked back through the woods and reached the clearing, scattering to our individual creations. Shouts of joy filled the air as each camper found her candy payment. When I walked to my fairy house to collect my reward, I was completely shocked that there was no candy. There was no payment at all!

"Must be the fairy staying in my place hasn't left yet," I mumbled to myself. I contemplated telling the counselors, figuring if they had put the candy in the fairy houses, they'd likely just give me my owed sweet, but before I could tell them, my buddy, Gabby, saw my long face and rushed to me.

"What's wrong?" Gabby asked.

"I didn't get anything in my fairy house," I answered.

"What? How's that possible? The fairies left everyone a piece of candy to pay for the nice place to stay."

"I guess no fairies stayed in my accommodations," I surmised.

"Huh?" Gabby looked truly confused.

"I mean, the counselors probably didn't notice my fairy house," I explained.

"What? Why would the counselors need to see it? It's the fairies who left the candy," Gabby debated.

Apparently I am the only camper in Glittering Trillium who doesn't actually believe in these forest fairies. "Wow, you truly think fairies brought us candy?" I asked. "Must be they're in cahoots with the Tooth Fairy, giving us sugar to rot out our teeth." I chuckled and shook my head at the absurdity of believing that fairies would've stayed in these fairy house creations.

"I don't like you, Persephone. You're not my best friend anymore!" Gabby announced, pouting with tears welling as she ran off to tattle to the counselors.

I rolled my eyes and sighed. Whiney tattletales annoy me. Oh well, I knew I was in for some sort of ridiculous and undeserved consequence, but at least I knew it would not be latrine duty.

Gabby's mood changed completely as she was tattling on me. As she led the counselors over to me, she was skipping and smiling. Seriously, where do they find girls like her? I glanced again at my

22

fairy house. "What on earth?" I asked aloud, but out of earshot, as I reached for a beautiful crystal that was in the "bedroom." It most definitely hadn't been there before. I picked it up and quickly slid it into my pocket as the confrontation commenced.

"Gabby tells us you were mean to her just now," Traci began.

"I used my words," I explained. "What more can I do?"

"You owe her an apology."

"I actually would only owe her an apology if I did something wrong. There's honestly nothing legally or morally wrong with expressing one's opinion about the presentation of pieces of candy as a payment for the fictional lodging of forest fairies," I explained.

At this time I overheard Gilly whisper to Traci, "I didn't even see her house thingy over here."

Traci glared at her and turned to me with a forced smile, "Did you get something special in *your* fairy house?"

"Actually, I did," I answered.

"You did?" the two counselors said in unison.

"You told *me* you didn't get any candy!" Gabby raised her voice in that sing-song way that only those children, who must cause scenes to command attention because they're so dreadfully missable under normal circumstances, know how to do.

"I didn't *get* any candy," I calmly stated.

"Well either you did or you didn't," Traci said, threateningly.

"She didn't," Gilly whispered before receiving Traci's elbow in her abdomen in an effort to silence her.

"I got this," I suggested, pulling the crystal from my pocket. It was clear and sparkled in the palm of my hand.

"Hey guys, look what she got," Gabby summoned the other campers 'round.

"Wow, it's a diamond!" one exclaimed, reaching for it.

"Why'd she get a diamond?" another inquired.

"I want a diamond too," a Diva-in-training pouted... and wait for it... cue tears and hissy fit.

All my cabinmates were squawking at once and my counselors were beyond ill-equipped to deal with the ruckus. So I closed my fingers around the crystal tightly and yelled to get them to be quiet. "You guys... you guyyys!!" I didn't hesitate as soon as they quieted down, "You all believe in fairies, right?"

"Right!" the entire cabin agreed.

"Well, before today, I didn't," I admitted.

"You what?" Ms. Diva gasped.

"Told you so," Gabby smugly gloated.

"So why do you get the diamond?" a jealous voice pried.

"First, it's not a diamond," I reassured them.

"How do you know that?" Ms. Diva inquired.

"A diamond this size is worth like a million dollars! You can't believe fairies fly around with millions of dollars on their backs, right?" I reasoned with them.

"Leprechauns put pots of gold at the end of rainbows," the jealous voice retorted, "so why wouldn't fairies carry expensive diamonds with them?"

"Well, why do *you* get the sparkling non-diamond while we got candy, you fairy hater?" a tall girl asked, pushing to the front.

"It's a gesture to convince me that I was wrong about fairies," I concluded. "Since you already believed in fairies, you got candy and you were perfectly happy, but since I'd think candy is simply a hoax, the fairies left me something a little more... fairy-like... than candy."

"Fine, I don't believe in fairies either!" Ms. Diva announced, and one by one every member of Glittering Trillium, except me, followed suit.

Then the campers insisted that we needed to go to the arts and crafts building to make posters to show that Glittering Trillium no longer believed in fairies. They decided to bring the signs back to the clearing so we could stage a protest by having a sit-in right there, so the fairies would see. Now I couldn't help but roll my eyes at the whole plan, for if they really didn't believe in fairies, their protest was completely futile, as there would be no one there to see it. But I realized I couldn't join them because... well... where *did* the crystal come from? The only rational answer is... But fairies *aren't* a rational answer at all!

During the protest, I kept myself busy by using my new crystal to look at flowers in the clearing. I liked the way the blossoms looked with the distortion caused by the refraction of the sunlight through the crystal. When I came back to the reality of where I was, I glanced over at the girls who were now holding hands in their circle singing, "We don't believe in fairies, we don't believe they're true, cuz fairies are supposed to grant wishes, but what have they done for you?"

"Make them stop already," I groaned. "Can't they just have pretty rocks, too?" I held the crystal towards the sun over my head and twirled in the cascade of little twinkles of prismatic light that showered around me. A vision of the campers with colored rocks in their hands flashed in my mind. At the same time, I suddenly noticed that the blazing sun was instantly and unexpectedly, completely, obscured by ominous, dark storm clouds.

"Hey guys, you might wanna check your fairy houses again, cuz those fairies you don't believe in may have returned..." I suggested. The girls stopped their protest mid-chorus and ran to their respective houses, as I felt a storm-preceding wind come up suddenly. Squeals alerted me that the girls had certainly found something in their fairy houses that met their approval. The commotion when they returned to the circle was an explosion of shrill young female voices.

"Mine's pink!"

"I got a yellow one!"

"This here they call emerald," Ms. Diva commented with a green stone in her hand.

As the girls showed their finds, I noticed they weren't jewels or crystals, but smooth, polished, rocks. But the girls were happy.

"What else did you find?" Traci asked with a smile.

"More candy!" the girls exclaimed waving their candy and rocks in the air. Gilly looked triumphant that her campers had found the pieces of candy, but then she noticed I was standing away from the jubilation.

"Persephone, why didn't you check your fairy house again?" she asked, eyeing me suspiciously.

"I didn't figure there'd be anything there," I said frankly.

"C'mon, we're checking," she demanded, taking me by the hand and pulling me over to the tree stump.

To my utmost surprise, there was a smooth teal rock and two pieces of candy on the "balcony."

"Hey, thanks!" I said to Gilly.

"For what?" she asked, seemingly slightly confused.

"For actually finding my fairy house this time," I grinned.

"I should be thanking you," she whispered, "for ensuring that they believe in fairies forever! That crystal and pretty rock thing was brilliant! You should be a CIT next year!"

"Um, but I didn't give them the rocks," I began.

"Sure ya didn't... the fairies did... just like the fairies gave out the candy?" she baited.

"But I really didn't!"

"You lie very well, Persephone. Perhaps a little too well, but I'll forgive you for lying to me this time because the rock thing was simply genius!" she ruffled my hair.

"Thanks, I guess?" I said trepidatiously. "But I don't lie."

We were interrupted by a loud rumble of thunder. I looked up and saw the sky was now completely pitch black with threatening clouds. The girls screamed and the counselors headed us into the woods back to camp. The wind was gusting and the loud thunder rattled the ground under our feet. Considering we've always been told not to be near trees in a thunderstorm, I was more than a little terrified to be running through the woods, but there truly wasn't another option. I could hear raindrops smacking the canopy, but somehow we stayed remarkably dry.

When we reached the edge of the woods we discovered there was no way to get across the Horseshoe Green to the arts and crafts building without a soaking. However, we had no other choice but to make a break for it. You've never seen nine and ten year old girls and two camp counselors move so fast! I daresay we *almost* ran between the raindrops, but unfortunately we couldn't, and we got completely drenched.

The arts and crafts building's door had barely closed behind us when golf ball sized hail started pelting the ground. We all breathed a huge sigh of relief at our impeccable timing.

Still dripping, Traci and Gilly relayed the fairy house story to the other counselors and Glittering Trillium shared the story with the other campers. Gabby ran up to me to show off her orange rock, asking what color rock I got. When I showed her my teal rock she boasted that her rock was better than mine, and I didn't have the heart to tell her that nobody would ever pick orange over teal, cuz I knew I needn't stoop to her level.

Mia, the sole head counselor now that Slimey was still out recuperating, thought we should make our rocks into necklaces to promote the bond of the members of Glittering Trillium. So, until it was time to head home, we wrapped our rocks in wire and hung them from satin cords, exhibiting our treasures around our necks.

Back in town, when it was time to get off the bus, the other girls of Cabin Six ran to their families to show off their necklaces and tell the stories of the fairies. I walked calmly, remaining quiet and feeling distant, as I was still trying to sort through the day's events. How did those polished rocks get into the fairy houses? Where did that really horrible storm come from, on a day that was forecasted to be gorgeous? Why was there a crystal in my fairy house? I was completely distracted by my thoughts, and answers to my questions were not coming to me.

"Ooh, I like your necklace!" Mom excitedly stated when I got to the car.

"Thanks," I said, "it turned out pretty cool."

"You made that?" Mom asked.

"Of course, Mom," I said, rolling my eyes, "you taught me how to make jewelry."

"Ohhh yeah, that's right," she replied with a smirk. "Well you must have paid close attention because that's a nice necklace."

"You want it?" I asked, reaching around to the back of my neck to remove it.

"No... what's wrong?" Mom sensed.

"Nothing."

"Bologna."

I huffed a huffy sigh. Mom knows me too well. "I'm fine," I stalled.

"Good, but what's on your mind?" she pressed. We started driving away from the pick-up location. Mom allowed the silence to hang, but she was very clearly not letting me drop the issue at hand.

"What kind of crystal is this?" I asked her, pulling the crystal from my pocket.

"It looks like quartz," she identified apprehensively. "Where did you get that? Was it rocks and minerals day?"

I explained the events of the day going into great detail about the fairy houses. "So Mom, do you believe in fairies?" I asked.

"Persephone, grown-ups aren't supposed to believe in fairies," she replied.

"You didn't answer my question, Mom."

"Of course there are fairies," she verbally tiptoed, "you know... like the Tooth Fairy... and... uh, well, yeah, the Tooth Fairy."

"Obviously there's the Tooth Fairy but aside from the Tooth Fairy, are there fairies?" I persisted.

"What do you think?" she asked. Leave it to Mom to put the question back on me.

"Well, I thought fairies were poppycock," I explained.

"Poppycock?" Mom laughed, "People still use 'poppycock' these days?"

"Most people don't, but I do, Mom," I defended. "You know how I feel about going along with the crowd."

"Yeah, and sometimes I wish for you, Kiddo, that the apple fell further from the tree," Mom blushed. Mom has never been a woman who cares about fitting in with the crowd. She'd rather be right and standing out from everyone else than be wrong and blending into the mix.

"You love me just the way I am," I giggled.

"Yes, but life would be easier for you if you were more of an undefined follower like most of your peers," she dreamed.

"I wouldn't want life to be simple, Mom," I reassured. "I want fun and adventure and originality and fame and-"

"You don't need fame to be happy, my Little Dragon," Mom cautioned.

"Would you have met Dad if he wasn't in UR My QTπ?" I prodded, albeit halfheartedly, as I truthfully cannot believe my normal and down-to-earth father was ever a popstar.

"It was actually more difficult to meet your dad *because* he was famous, Persephone," she clarified. "Have you ever tried to circumvent security to get to a celebrity? It's not easy. Thank goodness I'm stubborn or you and I wouldn't be having this discussion right now."

As we pulled into our driveway, I realized Mom had completely diverted my attention away from fairies. "Mom," I whined. "You still didn't answer about fairies," I reminded as she turned the car off.

"Oh, right," she smirked, "you thought fairies were poppycock, but then your fairy house inexplicably presented a quartz crystal?"

"Exactly!" I exclaimed, astonished at her spot-on summary.

"When I was your age, we made fairy houses at my day camp, too," she started. "The counselors didn't see where I built my fairy house, but they checked in with each of the other kids about their locations. The rest of the kids got candy, but I didn't. I wasn't surprised, but I admit I was disappointed because it seemed that it was the counselors' job to ensure we *all* got 'rewarded' for our efforts."

"Your counselors didn't give you candy either?" I asked, astonished.

"Nope, I got absolutely nothing despite having spent hours making a wicked, far out, groovy, hip bachelorette pad," Mom said, butchering bad lingo from before her time in an unsuccessful attempt to give the impression that she was super old.

31

"Mommmm..." I cawed at her in that multisyllabic way of saying single syllable words that somehow offspring can only do to their parents.

"Come on inside and let's get dinner ready," she suggested, vacating the car.

"So, you don't believe in fairies?" I concluded, following her into the house.

"To prove or disprove this fairy house controversy, Kiddo," Mom brainstormed, "since the rain has let up, how about while I'm making dinner, you go make another fairy house. Since I'm busy in the kitchen, I won't see where you make it, and since Dad's still at work, he won't see either. Tomorrow before camp you can go check it to see if there's a surprise."

"That's a great idea, Mom! If something is there tomorrow, it can only mean there *are* fairies!" I hesitated. Did I really want to know if fairies were real? The double edge of information is that once you know something, you can't unknow it. Could I handle the truth about fairies forever?

"Well, what are you waiting for?" Mom prompted.

"I'll check in every few minutes, Mom, so you'll know I'm okay," I reassured, determined to build the fairy house in the backyard so that Mom couldn't see me from the kitchen window.

"You are safe in your own yard, my Little Dragon," she reminded me. "We *do* live in Vermont and it's still a fairly safe place to be!"

"What state is that in?" I jested, laughing, on my way out the door. At my house, we have an ongoing joke about geography and

32

Vermont. For whatever reason, the average Flatlander out there has absolutely no concept of where Vermont is! You don't know how many times we've fielded the "What state is that in?" question asked legitimately by someone who doesn't even know that Vermont is one of the fifty states! Mom has often retold a story about a time when she was shopping in New Jersey as a teenager and one of the locals asked her if Vermont was near Pennsylvania. She agreed to that proximity, as it's closer to Pennsylvania than say... Hawaii. So, if you are completely oblivious to the fact that Vermont is a state, I'll tell you Vermont is near Maryland. I know it's not really *near* Maryland, but if you're not of an intelligence level to know that Vermont *is* a state, then I really and truly do not want you ever coming here. If by chance you know Vermont is a state, but aren't so great with precise placement, due to it always being attached to other states in jigsaw puzzles, Vermont is one of the six New England states. Apparently even being familiar with New England doesn't help *some* folks with the associated geography, as one time Mom ran into a band in Boston, Massachusetts, which is only about four hours away, who asked her if Vermont was in Canada! Come to think of it, I really hope that band wasn't UR My QTπ!

I found a good spot in our backyard and made my second ever fairy house. I really didn't know what to expect. I still couldn't suggest a rational reason why a quartz crystal would appear in my fairy house at Birch Bog. Where did the colored rocks come from for the girls of Glittering Trillium? Did I will them there? Were there actual fairies? Why did the violent storm come out of nowhere? The cloudless skies had been so blue and clear literally minutes before I had groaned about my cabinmates. Maybe I could attribute all of it to my favorite excuse in life... coincidence.

At dinner, I was still having a hard time letting go of the events of the day. "Dad, do you believe in fairies?" I asked at a completely random moment.

Dad snarfed his milk. "Fairies? Like..."

"Like the Tooth Fairy, dear," Mom explained.

"You don't believe in the Tooth Fairy anymore, Squirt?" Dad asked, "Guess you won't be getting anymore visits from-"

"NO! I don't mean the Tooth Fairy!" I interrupted, stopping him fast. "I totally believe in the Tooth Fairy! I mean, like you know, little winged creatures that fly around in the woods sorts of fairies."

"Oh, *that* type of fairy," he pondered. "You know, I've never seen one."

"But that doesn't mean they don't exist, because sometimes things exist that we don't see," Mom interjected.

"Like what?" I asked, putting her on the spot.

"Air," she stated in a very first grade teacher way.

"Love," Dad chimed in.

"But fairies wouldn't be invisible, like air and love," I wondered aloud, "so why doesn't anyone see them?"

"I bet they're exceptional at hiding," Dad hypothesized, "because otherwise people might take advantage of fairies for their special powers."

"Wait, fairies have special powers?" I asked, intrigued.

"Oh, so *now* you believe fairies are real?" Mom pressed.

"I don't know anymore," I surrendered. "I think there's a good chance we'll find out in the morning, though."

chapter three

Completely Unexpected

You might think I would've slept horribly in anticipation of finding out whether or not there would be a gift from the fairies awaiting me at sunrise. If I wasn't so exhausted, maybe that would have been how the night went, but I slept like a log. When I woke, I didn't even remember that I had built a fairy house in our backyard. Dad was already awake and reading the *City Times* in the dining room when I sauntered sleepily in.

"How'd you sleep, Squirt?" Dad inquired, a note of excitement in his voice.

"Fine," I said skeptically, not comprehending his excitement.

"Have you checked yet?"

"Checked what?" I asked, groggy and confused.

"To see if the fairies visited?" he hinted.

I perked up at the sudden memory of having built a fairy house yesterday in our backyard. "I totally forgot!" Still donning my PJs, I ran to the kitchen door to go outside.

"Put some shoes on!" Mom yelled from goodness knows which room of the house.

Thankfully, my well-worn teal flip-flops were right by the door. The strap wasn't even between my toes before I was hurrying onto the porch, down the stairs, and straight to the location of the fairy house. The dewy grass soaked my feet, chilling them incredibly, and I realized it would've been far wiser to have worn a closed-toe shoe, but I didn't turn back now. As I reached my destination, I knelt down to inspect the makeshift fairy dwelling, my bare knees landing in the pine needles under the tree where I had built it. The rose bloom I had used as a sofa had wilted since last evening. The corner of the moss that had been carefully placed as a comforter on the bed was turned back in such a neat manner that I was reminded I still needed to make my own bed. Looking at the fairy house's bathroom brought me right back to the backyard though, as there was something in the bathroom that I had not put there. As I leaned around to see if it was safe to reach for the unknown item, my nose was almost touching the trunk of the tree. I determined it was some sort of rock, so I reached in and pulled out a soft pink colored crystal. I caught a glimpse of something else that seemed to have been with the beautiful stone, so I reached in again, with a shaking hand, as I couldn't tell what it was. It was transparent but there was bright pink on it. It felt like paper, but it was indeed clear with an etched, scalloped border, and the pink markings I had seen were words in a ridiculously perfect penmanship reading, "Merci beaucoup! - Rosette"

"Did you find something?" Mom asked, slightly behind me.

"Um... I can't explain this..." I whispered as I rose to my feet and turned to see my mother in her bathrobe, beaming beside my smirking father in his t-shirt and sweats with his arm around her. I held the pink crystal in one hand and the... *note?* ... in my other hand. I noticed that both of their jaws dropped at the same time and to such a degree that I knew, beyond a shadow of a doubt, that neither of them was responsible for my findings. They turned to look at one another in a somewhat accusatory manner, as if to simultaneously ask, "Did *you* do that?" I already had my answer though, as it was obvious from their genuine reactions. "No, it wasn't either of you," I spoke as an answer to their eying of one another.

I feebly put one foot in front of the other to cross the ten foot grassy span between us. "What does this say?" I held the note out to them. "It doesn't appear to be in English."

"It is French for 'Thank you very much,'" Mom's voice shook as she responded, "and appears to be signed by... Rosette."

"So a fairy named Rosette stayed here last night?" I hypothesized.

"Well, your Mom *does* know French," Dad said with a nervous chuckle that revealed that he was washing his hands clean of the whole situation.

"What kind of crystal is this one, Mom?" I inquired, holding the pink stone nearer to her face.

"That's a rose quartz," she identified without hesitation. "I have a necklace with a rose quartz crystal on it. My mom bought it for me when I was fifteen years old. It has the power of love."

"Look out, Squirt! Looks like love may be coming your way soon!" Dad teased.

"Daaa-ad!" I said in that multisyllabic offspring-only way of saying a father's name that infers an eye roll without needing to move one's pupils at all. "I'm only nine, I'm not finding true love YET!"

"You're almost ten," Dad reminded.

"Dad!! I am only nine! I mean, wait, wow, no, you're right, I'm nine and a half!" With all the fairy and crazy camp adventures I had completely forgotten that my half birthday was this past Friday! Rats! I have *always* celebrated my half birthdays! I couldn't believe this one had slipped by me, unnoticed!

"Are you going to have a fairy party for your tenth birthday?" Dad chuckled. This time I didn't need to imply rolling my eyes, as I simply rolled them. Then, I realized that Mom had been silent, and she looked pale.

"Mom, are you okay?" I asked.

"Honestly," she started, "I didn't expect that you'd find anything this morning."

"Ah-ha!" I exclaimed. "You do *not* believe in fairies!" I accused.

"Kiddo, I don't know if any of us can say *that* after what has happened here today," Mom uttered with a fearful look in her eyes. My Dad hugged her and held her, smiling reassuringly at me.

"I don't understand how this is a bad thing, Mom," I pressed. "Fairies are good, right?"

"Your new friend, Rosette, seems like a good fairy," she said, turning towards me and forcing the corners of her mouth upwards. "So I don't want you to worry about it."

"So, you believe there are bad fairies, too, then?" I deduced. Mom didn't answer.

"Squirt, you better get ready for camp," Dad urged, breaking the uncomfortable silence. "After all, today *is* the last day of day camp," he reminded.

"Wait, what? It's only Wednesday!" I quickly calculated. "Camp goes until the end of the week!"

"Yes, but tomorrow night is the big overnight!" he corrected. "So you'll be at *overnight* camp tomorrow!" he said with a grin.

"Oh, right, overnight camp," I repeated. I had almost forgotten about *that*, too. I had just about enough already on my plate, with the discovery of fairies and with school starting in less than three weeks, and so I really wasn't so sure I could handle the added stress of being overnight at camp, with those mean counselors and ding batty cabinmates, under the stars with mosquitoes and moose and bears, and being away from home, and –

"Just go get ready for today, Kiddo," Mom guided me, with a hand on my shoulder and fully realizing I was completely frozen in an overwhelmed state. "All this excitement had better not make you late for the bus."

I ran back into the house, tracking dew and bits of cut grass and pine needles in with me. Setting the rose quartz crystal and note on the counter, I kicked off my flip-flops randomly across the kitchen – yeah, my 'Rents were *so* not going to appreciate that – sending some of the bits of clingy earth airborne with the shoes. I scurried to the shower where the warmth soothed away the physical ickiness associated with kneeling on the ground in the early morning. I realized in forty-eight hours I would be waking on exactly the same sort of icky ground, albeit in a sleeping bag, but still very much exposed to the reality of nature and the elements all around me. I stayed an additional minute in the shower hoping to absorb an extra layer of warmth to store for Friday morning, but as soon as my teeth began chattering when I shut off the spraying stream, I knew my efforts were to no avail.

I heard a gentle knock on my bedroom door as I threw on clothes that would suffice for the day. "Kiddo, if you don't want to go to camp today, you don't have to go," Mom's voice offered.

"I don't want to go," I responded, as I brushed out my wet, snarled, hair.

"Oh, Persephone! Stop being such a wimp and get your tail in gear already!" Dad chastised from the other side of the door.

"If she doesn't want to go," Mom started.

"She'll go! She's Persephone Smith! We Smiths don't miss the last day of day camp just because of fairies!" Dad delivered in a pep talk manner.

"Well, Wallingford Smith, *you* are going to be late for work because you're all caught up in this fairy business yourself this morning!" Mom quieted him.

I laughed. Mom and Dad never actually fight. They sometimes rag on each other, tease one another, joke around with a little bit of venom, but their love is so strong that it's never a fight. Sometimes they don't agree, but ultimately they respect one another and their right to disagree and they move on. My friends have made it crystal clear that such a harmonious home life is ridiculously rare, but it's all I have ever known, and so it's what I've come to expect by whoever is fortunate enough to be my future husband. But I'm nine and a half years old, so despite the rose quartz and talk of marriage, I will *not* be getting married anytime soon.

"Alright, since you're apparently going to camp today, let's go, Persephone!" Mom encouraged, calling from the stairs.

I made it to the bus stop just in the knick of time. Mom was still in her bathrobe, but she stayed in the car so that nobody noticed. The bus ride was uneventful. We sang the same songs we had sung every day before. Each summer by the middle of the second week of camp I wondered why they didn't teach us a new song or two, but the songs were the same every year. We arrived at Birch Bog and the counselors led us to the Horseshoe Green where it was the youngest group's turn to present the flag. It's always a bit nerve-racking when the little ones try to unfold the flag and raise it without it touching the ground, so anytime they're the color guard, we big kids remain ready to dive in and save the flag from an accidental brush with the earth. This year's youngest campers did a surprisingly nice job though, so none of us had to save the day.

During announcements, things turned away from the norm. Traci commandeered the Announcements Stick because she had a "very important announcement." She started by describing what it means to be a friend. "A friend is someone who will do anything that they can to make life for the people they know a little bit more

42

enjoyable. They never hurt the hearts, souls, imaginations, dreams, ideas, or bodies of those they care about. They respect, trust, and accept their friends the way that they are and as they grow into the people they become. They are honest, supportive, and nurturing..."

Speaking of honesty, truthfully, I was so beyond bored at this point that I feared I would keel over in a momentary lapse of slumber. Yet, she continued on... and on. Believe me when I say I'm doing you a gigantic favor by chopping out the rest of her spiel and rejoining her announcement when she got to the good part!

"Here at Birch Bog Camp, we're *all* friends, but yesterday one friend showed a side of herself that went far above and beyond any description of friendship that I could share with you today," Traci continued prattling on, "and due to the amazing degree of friendship demonstrated, Persephone Smith is hereby awarded with this year's 'Best Friend' Award!"

Thunderous applause echoed and I felt my whole cabin jump on top of me in a burying pile. Wait, *me*? I'm the Best Friend of Birch Bog Camp 2009? Seriously? Hot diggity dog! I was very excited – not that my excitement was easily seen at the bottom of the melee of arms and legs. When they dug me out of the pile, Traci presented me with a handshake and a certificate, and we posed for a picture.

It wasn't until much later that I pondered what precisely had I done to deserve the award. Sure, I was nice to everyone. Why else would they assign Gabby as my buddy for *every* day of camp? Her vacillating moods and drama queen tendencies would crush the weaker campers like bugs! Maybe I got the Best Friend award because I can handle any person that I meet. I might not love them as

43

a best friend, but I can respect them as a human being, no matter how deplorable they are. I know to just smile and treat them as I would want to be treated. When that doesn't work, I mumble sarcastic musings under my breath and make sure they don't understand them. If they hear me *and* understand the sarcasm, well then I make a run for the nearest safe adult!

During crafts that afternoon, Gilly took me aside to shed light on the true reason I was the Best Friend of 2009. "I am still in disbelief as to how you pulled off getting those tumbled rocks in each of the girls' fairy houses like that," she admitted with an inexplicable awe.

"It wasn't me," I vehemently denied.

"Sure, it wasn't," she said in a way that made it clear she didn't believe a word of what I was saying. "So, it was the *fairies*, right?"

I didn't appreciate her mocking tone. "Look," I said as calmly as I could, "I was just as flabbergasted as anyone else that suddenly there were rocks in the fairy houses. I have no explanation as to where my quartz crystal or the rainbow of smooth rocks came from. I knew you did the candy, but I didn't do the rocks."

"Well, *I* am not responsible for the candy," she lied.

"You're lying," I looked at her with a very untrusting glare. "Just because you say something doesn't make it true."

"That saying works both ways, Persephone," she defended.

"The unfortunate error in your logic is that I am *actually* an honest person," I bragged, triumphantly, "so, when I say something, it's always the truth."

Gilly looked stung by my words. "I oughta make you clean the latrine for the way you're speaking to me," she attacked, "but I'll let it slide because you were mighty generous yesterday in giving away your rock collection to your fellow campers to win back their belief in fairies." I looked at her incredulously, but without words, as I really didn't want her to change her mind and assign me to latrine duty again. "Obviously in your backpack, you had one of those souvenir pouches of tumbled rocks, and while the girls were protesting fairies, you snuck to each of their fairy houses to put a rock in, to look like fairies had been there!" She was winding up, rather than winding down, and I knew I still had to hear quite an explanation before she'd finish. "You were the one who told them to go look again in the houses. You were the one who wasn't protesting that you didn't believe in fairies. You were the only one who didn't scream and jump around when you saw what was *in* the fairy houses."

"I was perfectly happy with my quartz crystal, cuz it's way better than the colored rocks," I interrupted. "Plus, I don't get riled up very easily."

"Persephone, I am *so*, so sorry, that I didn't give you a piece of candy initially when the fairy houses were made. I honestly didn't know that you even had a fairy house over there. I did not mean to leave you out of the fun."

"Apology accepted," I said in a futile effort to silence her so I could get back to making my wildflower crown in peace.

"To *not* get a piece of candy and yet to still have the brainstorm to pull a crystal from your pocket – what did you call it? Quartz? – a quartz from your pocket, just to pretend you got something at all, so as to fool the other campers into believing there are actually fairies so they wouldn't know *I* was really the one who put the candy in their fairy houses, was simply genius!"

"You *do* realize that I didn't do any of that," I tried to interject, but she just prattled on.

"Surrrre ya didn't!" She punched me in the arm in that gentle way that people do when they're acting like they're especially good friends with an inside joke. I didn't appreciate her chumminess. "Everything got crazy when the girls got greedy and decided to protest fairies, but they completely believed your 'I didn't believe in fairies so they gave me something special' story – which, by the way, was awesome to come up with on the spot like that to explain why you got something different. I so wouldn't have ever thought of something like that."

As much as I didn't believe this Gilly girl could be honest if her life depended on it, I had no trouble in nodding in agreement that she would have *never* had the brainpower to come up with a believable explanation as to why the fairies had brought me something other than a piece of candy.

"Their little protest idea would never have gotten them what they wanted though, because fairies really do not exist and so no little twinkly flying critters were bringing them rocks. In fact, we'd probably still be sitting there if you hadn't shared your rock collection with everyone."

"We would've come in when it rained," I corrected.

"The way the girls were so fired up and waiting for their rewards? I doubt that," she responded.

I noticed the other campers were finishing up their wildflower crowns and realized I wouldn't actually get to make one, because Gilly had taken up too much of my time. What is up with inconsiderate grown-ups who just don't understand that whatever they're spouting off has absolutely no pertinence whatsoever to the person they're speaking at? This whole spiel was more about her insecurities as a camp counselor than about my success as a camper!

"Anyways, that's why I felt that you deserved to win the award," she finally concluded.

"*You* nominated me?" I asked in disbelief.

"Yes," she confessed, smiling. "You went so far above and beyond what any reasonable person would do to make sure that the rest of your cabin would believe in fairies! I mean, after what happened yesterday, I know that us counselors are even practically convinced that fairies exist! Like they obviously do *not* exist, but you almost had us believing!"

"Fairies do exist," I whispered uncomfortably, looking down as I spoke and shifting my weight from one leg to the other.

"Okay, okay, fairies exist," she muttered with a wink. "Oh, that's right, I never know who is listening."

"You do never know when someone is listening," I agreed, looking up at her.

"I so meant what I said when I told you that you should be a CIT next summer," she said, ruffling my hair playfully.

"Um, we'll see about that," I hedged, hoping our conversation was done.

And at long last, it was.

47

chapter four

Coincidence or Vision?

M y eyes were saucers as the sun rose that Thursday. I had been awake for hours and the winks of sleep I did manage to get were anything but restful. Now, I was accustomed to colorful dreams that woke me in the night, but last night's dreams had a common, disturbing, thread... they all occurred at nighttime at Birch Bog Camp!

I won't say I'm afraid of the dark, but you'll surely agree with me that it is far easier for bad things to cloak themselves in darkness than in broad daylight. I haven't ever seen Birch Bog at night, so I can only imagine how creepy much of it must appear. If my dreams are any indicator, the grounds of Birch Bog Day Camp become, after dark, a setting more terrifying than an abandoned funhouse in one of those horror movies our parents won't let us watch.

It's impossible for marshmallows to pop like popcorn, isn't it? My mind raced with imagery from the night's slideshow of horror.

"Wake up, Squirt," my dad spoke softly with his signature rat-a-tat knock on my bedroom door. "Is everything alright?" he asked, clearly having noticed my expression as I lay motionless, staring towards the ceiling.

"I'm... I'm here... I mean, I'm awake," I stammered.

"What's the matter?" he inquired as he floated over and sat on the end of my bed with heartfelt concern.

"I have a really bad feeling about this," I hinted.

"Would you like to talk to Mom about it?" he offered.

"No, Dad, I love you. I'll tell you," I paused, "if I can explain it."

"I'm here for you, talk to me," he said protectively.

"I've never been away from you and Mom overnight before," I started.

"That's not true," he interrupted. "You've stayed overnight with Grampy and Grammy and Grandpa and Grandma before."

"That doesn't count, Dad," I defended. "They're my family. They have to love me."

"So you're scared to be away from your family overnight?" he summarized, breathing a sigh of relief. "That's completely normal, Squirt! Your fellow campers are all feeling that anxiety right now. The counselors will anticipate your nervousness and make it extra fun so you won't even have time to think about it. Stop worrying."

"Thanks, Dad," I smiled, grateful to have a dad who loves me so much, but painfully aware that he just didn't get it. That's exactly when he shocked me.

"What else is worrying you about tonight?" he asked uneasily.

"Um... well... what if I do something?" I asked.

"What do you mean?" he inquired, clearly hoping my elaboration would provide a hint as to what I was talking about.

"Well, you know how if I think things they happen, right?"

"That's just coincidence," he quickly reassured. "Don't worry about it."

"What if it's not?"

"It is."

"Even if you keep insisting, it won't necessarily make it true."

"You have lots of thoughts, and they don't all happen. The ones that do are just coincidence."

"Hmm... maybe you're right," I considered.

"Of course I'm right, I'm your father," he said proudly.

I realized I still hadn't moved from the position in which he had found me, and I daresay I hadn't yet blinked either. He was surely right about the correlation between thoughts and life's events – it *had* to be coincidence. I had tons of thoughts and they didn't all happen. I decided to test out the theory by thinking of a million dollars appearing right there on the bed, right then. And guess what happened next! One million times the amount of money that had been on the bed was now on the bed! Insert shocked expression.

Just in case anyone's thinking, "Wow! She's rich!" dial it back a notch, as *any* number times zero still equals zero. If you don't believe me, ask any teacher or equally smart other grown-up.

"Dad, is there a million dollars on the bed?" I asked, not wanting to move a muscle and confirm for myself.

50

"Did you *think* of a million dollars appearing on your bed just now?" he asked with a chuckle.

"Yep," I admitted, ashamed.

"Coincidentally, there's," he spoke with a guarded enthusiasm. His pause prompted my curiosity and I couldn't help but look at him, still wide-eyed. "There's a million tickle bugs on the bed!" he exclaimed with a chuckle, pouncing at me with "tickle fingers."

I screamed and laughed as I tried to get away from his tickle fingers. He unfortunately caught hold of my feet as I kicked the blankets off, and the tickle fingers were rather relentless on my arches. I hooted and hollered from the agony of the merciless tickling.

"What *is* going on in here?" Mom asked from the doorway.

"A million tickle bugs!" Dad answered, still torturing my feet.

"Oh, well if that's all," she said, walking away.

"Mom!" I struggled to speak between fits of laughter and screaming. "Mom, save me!"

"I'll save you from the million tickle bugs!" Mom exclaimed, rushing to my aid and foiling my nemesis's tickle fingers by tickling him! "Take that!" I daresay that Mom must know every ticklish spot on Dad, cuz he couldn't keep hold of my feet for long once her tickle attack began! Soon they were tickle-torturing each other and I was free to escape my bedroom and make a break for the shower.

"Thanks, Mom!" I shouted as I made a run for it.

"She's getting away!" Dad exclaimed. "And it's all your fault! Tickle bugs attack!"

I could hear their happy commotion even as I jumped in the shower. They're pretty silly for grown-ups, but it's fun.

They were back to being typical adults when I got to the kitchen for breakfast. "Are you feeling better now?" Mom asked. I looked at Dad and back to Mom, understanding fully that anything I say to one parent is told to the other, as they keep no secrets whatsoever from each other.

"I had bad dreams about the overnight," I blurted, having skirted the reason for my worry long enough.

"Dreams are your dad's department," Mom announced, apparently passing me off to Dad, before leaving the kitchen.

"What does she mean by that?" I asked.

"That Mom and I take on different parts of raising you, Squirt, and bad dreams that get you this fired up are my specialty," he calmly grinned. "So what's up?"

"Okay," I started cautiously, "So you think the connection between my thoughts and what transpires is coincidence, right?"

"Complete coincidence," he reiterated.

"Well, have you had dreams that come true?" I asked.

"Sure," he deflected, "I dreamed about your mom and she married me and we're living happily ever after."

"I don't mean daydreams, Dad," I defended, "I meant have you ever been asleep and dreamt something and it happened just like you saw in the dream?"

"Um..." he stalled, "yeah, you could certainly say that. That's kinda why your mom wants me in charge of the parenting section called 'Dreams and Nightmares.'" I instantly appreciated that Mom wasn't just passing me off but was hoping to allow me a surprisingly expert opinion on the topic. I would never peg Dad as being in touch with his dreams, much less well aware that he dreams things that come true. "So, what happened in your dream?" he asked.

I told him all the still-too-vivid details of the horrific scenes that had robbed me of a good night's sleep. He looked rather upset by my descriptions, but he clearly was determined to keep a strong countenance through every detail.

"Persephone, if you ever find yourself in a real life déjà vu of a bad dream, consciously change a detail of the scene. Picture what you did next in the dream and do just the opposite. Turn an object so it isn't situated the same as in your dream. If you change a detail, your dream won't come true," he advised.

I thought about the nightmare, trying to find details that could be changed, if such a situation arose in real life. "But what if what occurs as a result of the change is actually worse?" I astutely asked.

"Uh… um… well… you're not supposed to think of that, Squirt," he revealed with a smirk. "Yeah, I so don't have an answer for that."

"So much for letting him give you a successful little pep talk," Mom chastised with a gentle laugh as she reentered the kitchen.

"Well, what would you tell her?" he half-snapped at her.

"What's her question?" she asked, leaning against the counter.

"What does she do if she has a bad dream, realizes it's happening in real life, and changes a detail only to find the modification makes the situation take a dramatically worse turn?"

"Easy," she said, "speak aloud what you want to happen."

53

"Oh, so that's back to *your* department," he noted with a sigh and left the kitchen to finish getting ready for work.

"Thanks for the advice, Dad!" I called after him. Then I looked at Mom and asked, "So what do I say if I need to change the events?"

"First and foremost, always say good things," she began.

"Oh, like think good thoughts?" I connected.

"Yes, but even more importantly," she corrected, "you must always say only good outcomes."

"So, if someone is going to hurt me, I can say, 'Don't hurt me,' and I'll be okay?" I guessed.

"You'd be better off with, 'You will not hurt me,' or better still, 'May you find compassion, peace, and happiness in your heart, now!'" she explained with a distant look.

"I would never think of that," I said with an awe that *anyone* would have the frame of mind to come up with those words under intense pressure.

"It takes practice," she admitted, smiling.

"Practice?" I asked, "How does one practice such things?"

"In your everyday life, anytime things get rough, think up something to say to diffuse the situation," she suggested.

"I'll keep that in mind," I pondered.

"Oh, and try to remember that you should resist the urge to request things," she explained.

"Like I can't make a Christmas list anymore?" I asked, dejected.

"Noooo, not like that," she laughed, "more like 'Give me lots of money!'"

I gasped, "But Mom, you just said it!"

"Which brings us to the topic of how to make what you say actually occur," she started, "because you've said lots of things that didn't happen, right?"

"Dad said when my thoughts and life's events are the same that it's completely coincidental, so it's the same with words, right?"

"Not exactly," Mom explained, "Your thoughts mirroring life *is* coincidental, but when you speak from every pore and fiber of your heart and soul, that's when you'll undoubtedly find your words have immeasurable power."

"Like when I was frustrated the other day at camp and said, 'Why can't they all have rocks?' and they all got rocks?"

"Um..." Mom looked concerned that I had drawn that connection, "Yep, actually, exactly like that."

I gasped, "But Mom, I asked for something! I didn't know the rules and I asked for something!"

"And what happened when you asked?" she nudged calmly.

"We all got rocks," I remembered.

"And what not so nice thing happened simultaneously?" she pressed.

In my mind I replayed the moments around the discovery of the rocks in the fairy houses. I thought hard. "OH! The out-of-nowhere storm clouds and thunderstorm with heavy rain and hail!" I exclaimed, delighted and terrified.

"Yep," she affirmed in her teacher voice, "see, Persephone, that is why I implore of you not to ever request things, or at least to never ask for something without making a sacrifice or else you'll have to endure whatever sacrifice the universe chooses to take."

"A sacrifice?" I gulped. "I am not going to kill things!"

"Good, because killing isn't an acceptable sacrifice," Mom expressed, relieved. "A sacrifice is just when you give something up in exchange for something worthy of it."

"So, if I give a dollar to charity I can ask for something?" I thought aloud.

"It's absolutely better to not request things, so you don't have to calculate the value of the sacrifice needed." She gave me a look that made it clear she wasn't sure I was ready for this whole little talk.

"Thanks, Mom," I tried to reassure her.

"Just remember," she started.

"Only say good things," I finished.

"Exactly."

I really wanted to know what would happen if I said bad things, but I knew if I asked I'd probably cause Mom heart failure as she definitely wasn't ready for that conversation... yet. So I'll have to wait until I'm older to ask Mom about that. I just hope I don't mistakenly say something bad in the meantime.

chapter five

Birch Bog After Dark

Mom helped me carry all my gear to the big, yellow, Birch Bog, school bus, as it takes having more than two hands to successfully carry a sleeping bag, backpack, overnight bag, and kitchen sink onto a bus. Okay, scratch the kitchen sink, but no matter how you slice it, it's a lot of loot. She handed my stuff to the CIT who was onboard helping those of us who are new to the overnight camp experience get our gear to where it needed to go. Although I was due to get onto the bus, I took a few steps back, allowing other campers to board.

"I can't do this," I shook.

"You're going to be fine," Mom reassured with a hug. "Besides, you can do anything for one night, right? Right?"

I held onto her but didn't answer the question. By no means did I care one iota if the other girls thought of me as some big baby who didn't want to leave her mother and father for a night. The only opinions that matter to me are the ones of my loved ones, not some foolish girls who I wouldn't ever see again. "Can't we just call this whole thing off?" I pleaded, still holding her tightly.

"I wish I could go instead," Mom revealed, trying to trick me into changing my mind. But I'm onto her reverse psychology. Soon she would make this overnight thing sound wicked tempting.

"It's okay with me if we trade places, Mom," I gleefully hinted, "but you won't much like the girls in my cabin *or* my counselors."

As if on cue, just then Gabby walked by, overhearing my statement. She huffed loudly and threw her nose in the air, in an apparently thwarted attempt to upset me by snubbing me. She boarded the bus, waving and throwing a kiss to her mother, before taking a seat next to Ms. Diva. Then she spoke loudly about how ridiculous it is that some children are such big chickens that they can't even go to overnight camp. Surely that was meant for my benefit, but it amused me more than anything.

"That's Gabby, I presume?" Mom asked.

"I couldn't have described her better, could I have, Mom?"

"I think you might've been a little kind with the degree of wretchedness with which you painted her," she said with a smirk.

"Mom, one moment you're telling me I can only say nice things, and then you're telling me I'm not mean enough about my cabinmates," I joked back. "Really, you can't have it both ways."

"I suppose not," she concluded. She pulled me tighter and gave me a kiss on the cheek to end our hug. "You better get on the bus, Kiddo," she led, "I can't wait to hear all about your adventures when I see you tomorrow."

58

"Do I have to only say nice things *then*?" I asked, letting go of the hug. "Or can I be honest about the people and events of camp?"

"Well, since tomorrow *is* the last day of camp, when I pick you up, you can be completely honest," Mom laughed, "but only in re-telling me the stories! You need to remember to –"

"Only say nice things, yeah, got it!" I interrupted.

"I was going to say, 'Have a blast!'" she corrected. "Oh, and eat a nicely roasted marshmallow for me!"

"They're going to have marshmallows?" I said with a mix of excitement and horror, as one of the props from my dream was apparently going to be on the scene of the overnight.

"Check your backpack when you get there and make sure to bring them to your counselors!"

"Okay..." I said begrudgingly. "I love you, Mom!"

"I love you, too! Have fun!" She leaned in for one more hug.

"I will try," I gave in.

Bus ride, singing songs, flag ceremony, and announcements were all the usual. It felt like an ordinary day of day camp. We carried our gear to our cabin, though the plan was to sleep outside under the stars in the "Great Space," if the weather allowed. As it turns out, every camper had brought one of the ingredients for s'mores, as requested per the camp, so we handed those items over to Traci and Gilly. The day resumed with more normal activities. The pool had reopened, so we went swimming in the Green Slime Lagoon, ate snack, and did a neat large-as-life arts and crafts project where we traced one another on big butcher block paper and then decorated our "person" with magazine pictures and drawings to represent the things that make us unique.

My big paper doll had red hair and rosy cheeks, teal eyes (even though I don't *have* teal eyes), and was wearing hot pink lipstick (even though Mom won't let me wear makeup). I gave her a purple sneaker and a green sneaker to represent the favorite colors of Mom and Dad and to show that they are a part of every step I make, everywhere I go. I drew her wearing a really fun plaid flannel shirt, because I like colors and plaid is fun to draw *and* because I love flannel. Of course she was wearing overalls because overalls are the best clothing invention ever! I was looking at her triumphantly when the counselors came over and told me what they thought.

"You were supposed to cut out pictures from the magazines that show things about yourself," Traci scolded.

"I've never seen you wear plaid," Gilly mocked.

"Oh, I am not done yet," I snapped, "I was planning to add the magazine pictures next."

"Well, you *are* done because it's time for lunch *now*," Traci corrected. "Glittering Trillium, we're heading to the Great Space for a picnic lunch."

I'm sure that the concept of a picnic lunch was supposed to excite us tremendously, but frankly, we ate every lunch at the Great Space. I was blown away by how ridiculously normal this day was going! There hadn't been even a mention of the overnight. There weren't any hints as to exciting events that would be occurring after dark. It was just so absolutely ordinary. After lunch we went for a hike, and the counselors brought canned corn and had us "go fishing" in the brook. Basically, we just tossed corn in the brook trying to attract fish. When that was deemed completely pointless we all followed the brook to the pond and threw the corn, piece by piece, into the water. We actually saw some fish come and nibble the corn. It's always pretty cool to see creatures up close but in their own natural environments.

When Traci and Gilly lined us up to hike back to camp, they told us we'd return just in time for the afternoon flag ceremony, but afterwards, instead of heading to the bus, we would go to our cabin. Apparently the typical camp day would soon be abruptly ending.

At the closing flag ceremony, we were surprised by a very special guest, Slimey! I mean, Sandy! She was back, albeit of limited capacity, to stay with us for our big sleepover under the stars.

As I watched the younger day campers bound off to the bus, I was so tempted to just skirt along with them and sneak aboard. I was 98% certain that nobody would notice and 100% sure that nobody would care. I just had to let my feet follow right along with those other campers... but I watched them board the bus and I was still standing on the Horseshoe Green. The bus pulled away and yet I remained... at Birch Bog Camp, and apparently would be there... overnight.

The transformation after the bus left was nearly magical in its immediacy. Our only means of escape having vanished, the head counselors, Slimey & Mia, and the counselors of the younger campers joined Traci and Gilly and cackled with laughter and inside jokes that included inappropriate language. To say they were acting like we weren't even there would be an understatement. One of the counselors, Julie, who doesn't usually work with our group looked over at us, then said something to Traci and Gilly. They made gestures that made it abundantly clear that they were quite finished working with us for the day, so Counselor Julie laughed and yelled over to us, "Listen up, Brats, go get your swim junk and using the buddy system, go swimming!" with a mocked enthusiasm that made it crystal clear that they were trying to get rid of us for awhile. "When you're done swimming, it'll be time for the cookout and s'mores! Now, *GET!*"

Glittering Trillium cheered at the extra swim time and scurried towards the cabin, each grabbing her buddy's hand along the way. Gabby nearly swept me off my feet with her rapturous joy at the news. "*COME ON!!*" she exclaimed, dragging me by the hand as though my arm was a leash. We were changed into our swim gear quicker than a magician does a trick.

I most definitely didn't want to go swimming in the Green Slime Lagoon at that hour. It was blanketed in shade and I could not see the bottom, even in the shallow end. Gabby and I were the first to arrive at the pool, but I refused to go in, as there were no lifeguards on duty, there were no adults anywhere in sight, and there were no responsible adults within probably a thirty mile radius. Gabby didn't care in the slightest that I wouldn't go swimming. She splashed right in, relishing in the utter bliss of having the entire lagoon to herself. I sat on the dry land, keeping an eye on her, because that's what buddies are supposed to do. The rest of Glittering Trillium arrived soon and joined her in the murky water. After they had been swimming for probably ten minutes, they stopped moving around so much and started whispering back and forth. I caught some of their words and connected them to understand that they were eyeballing the twisty slide at the deep end of the pool that was absolutely, unequivocally off-limits according to Birch Bog Camp's spoken rules. Of course, we all know what happened next.

Water was thrown onto the slide and the caravan of campers pushed and shoved to get to the front of the line at the ladder. One by one they broke the rule and had a blast on the slide landing in the water with huge splashes. I knew we'd *all* get in trouble, even though I wasn't swimming, but I didn't care, as I don't have any respect for those counselors, and I knew, after tomorrow, I'd never have to see them again.

I lay back on the grass and watched the clouds in the sky. They soon began turning beautiful colors. I saw fluffy pink clouds, billowing peach clouds, and whispering yellow clouds, and then I noticed the sky was turning colors, too. The vibrant magentas, deep violets, and fiery oranges contrasted breathtakingly with the disappearing blue sky. I was so wrapped up in the beauty of the afternoon sky that I didn't notice how late it was getting. I realized it was exceptionally quiet and I sat up. It was dark. Not pitch black, but dusky dark. I squinted at the slide and the pool, but there was no one there. I stood up and looked around me, 360 degrees, but there was nobody anywhere in sight. I was alone.

"So much for the buddy system," I said under my breath, wondering how horrible the punishment from the counselors would be. The only thing creepier than the Green Slime Lagoon is the Green Slime Lagoon at night! I hadn't *really* considered that the legend of

Boggy could be true, but after seeing the lagoon at dusk, it wouldn't surprise me if there *are* creatures who call it home, and I wholeheartedly suspect they may be those species the scientists are searching for as a link in evolution.

I broke into a sudden sprint back to the cabin. I figured I may as well get some comfortable clothes on... and to have the secret cell phone in my backpack, near me. Arriving back at Cabin Six, I grabbed my clothes to get changed up, but nobody was there either, and there was no trace of discarded swim gear.

The silence of a cabin at a camp in the woods at night when there's no other humans visible, or apparently within earshot, is deafening and awfully spooky! I changed into my clothes right there, packing away my still dry swimwear. I debated as to where I should go next. Would it be better to locate my disappeared cabinmates, or to find Traci and Gilly, or should I just go sit by the Green Slime Lagoon, as that was the last place we had been authorized to be? I didn't have to ponder long as I heard a single set of footsteps on the cabin's stairs.

"Heyyyy, ya back from swimmin?" the counselor of the second-youngest group, whose name I didn't know, asked.

"I didn't actually swim," I replied honestly.

"I don't blame you, that pool is nassssty!" she hissed with an unguarded smile. "Where's your buddy?" she inquired.

"I don't know," I answered.

"What kind of buddy leaves their buddy at the Birch Bog Lagoon alone?" she scolded with a toothy smile and laugh.

"Apparently *my* buddy?" I replied.

"But *you* are the one who isn't at the pool," she pointed out.

"I left the lagoon after my buddy and the rest of Glittering Trillium disappeared from the pool," I shared.

"The Brats aren't at the pool?"

"You thought I'd abandon my buddy?"

"Oh, that's right, you're the 'Best Friend of Birch Bog 2009,' so you would *never* do something like that," she said with a sarcasm so thick that I started wondering if *any* of Birch Bog's counselors believed in anything about this place whatsoever. She then said some things that made it clear that we needed to go get the other counselors and find the missing "Brats." She stomped over to the Great Space where the other counselors were tending the bonfire and dancing to music that was coming from little speakers attached to an mp3 player.

"Where are the rest of the little dears?" Traci sneered.

"She says they weren't at the lagoon anymore," the counselor who had walked over with me mockingly whined.

"Where are they, Persephone?" Traci asked in a tone that made it clear she thought we were all in cahoots playing some prank on the counselors.

"I have no idea," I trembled.

"Take us to where you last saw them," she demanded. I led her, Julie, Gilly, Mia, the counselor whose name I didn't know, and Sandy, who was seemingly in charge of this debacle of an overnight adventure, back to the Green Slime Lagoon. I felt an awful wave of guilt as Sandy came upon the scene of her near-death experience, but I pushed the thoughts from my head, reminding myself that any

65

resemblance between my thoughts and what happens in life is merely coincidence. I repeated the word "coincidence" a few times in my head, for effect.

"They were sliding on the slide into the deep end," I pointed.

"They were WHAT?" the counselors all asked in unison.

"I was sitting over here, because I didn't want to swim, and they were lined up here." I ran to each position as I said "here," so as to provide them as full of a visual image as possible. "I leaned back and was watching the clouds, and when I sat up, they were gone."

I noticed the counselors were all staring at the water of the lagoon. They had petrified looks on their faces. Julie shook her head and broke the silence. "You don't really believe there's a swamp monster in the Birch Bog Lagoon, do you?" she asked the other counselors. They didn't reply but simply continued staring at the water which was far too dark to allow anyone to see anything.

"A swamp monster?" I repeated. "Are you referring to Boggy? That's preposterous! He's just a legend – a myth, a scare story, he's not real!" I ran alongside them with a playful bounce hoping they'd get the hint that they were *really* freaking me out and come back to a reality-based explanation for where the other girls might be.

Sandy turned to me. "How did *you* know not to go swimming?" she asked.

"I think the green slime in the lagoon is disgusting," I admitted, frankly. "We already went swimming once today, I didn't see any reason to go in again, particularly without adult supervision."

"We were watching you," Gilly defended.

"If you were watching us, where are the girls?" I muttered.

"Watch it, or I'll throw you in!" Gilly charged at me.

"We don't have time for this," Sandy grabbed her to keep her from reaching me. "There's a lost cabin of campers, minus one, and we have no leads as to where they might be! Did you hear them say *anything* about where they would go or if they had any hidden agenda of plans for the evening?"

All eyes were on me, but I really didn't have *any* ideas. "I'm sorry, but I'm not really close to the girls, so they don't tell me what they're thinking," I admitted. I couldn't help but see the irony that the Best Friend of Birch Bog 2009 truthfully did not have a single friend *at* Birch Bog Camp. I hoped they would find everyone soon because I was getting hungry and it was getting wicked dark. "I can't imagine that they would go somewhere they haven't been before," I hypothesized, knowing what a bunch of chickens my fellow campers were.

The counselors split into pairs to go looking for Glittering Trillium. That obviously left me to my own devices, so I went back to the Great Space where there was at least a bonfire to light the surroundings. The other counselors back at the bonfire looked puzzled to see me return alone and I noticed cell phones were whipped out and apparently calls were being made to the counselors in the search parties. "Well, kid, whatever your name is, you can help me bring the dinner to the bonfire," the counselor with black hair said. "Come with me!" she exclaimed as she headed towards the Mess Hall.

I followed, not quite sure what I should be doing at the moment and not exactly having a better idea than to just do what they said, as long as it wasn't something that would harm me. When we got to the Mess Hall, she flipped on the lights and I was temporarily blinded by the brightness. The Mess Hall was one of the off-limits buildings, so I had no idea what it would be like! Do you realize that the Mess Hall wasn't messy at all? It was so very neat and tidy!

"Yeah, you're right, kid, whatever your name is, we should just wait here until the search parties return," she explained, even though I truly had not spoken a word since arriving back at the bonfire. She whipped out her cell phone and was checking a website or texting or something... she was certainly not being a very counselorish counselor. "You want a soda?" she asked, standing and heading to the kitchen. "I'm having one, you want one? Of course you want one!" She brought me back the same thing she was drinking. I was so hungry that I figured drinking a soda would tide me over for the duration of this waiting time.

I went through a variety of awkward positions trying to find a comfortable way to wait on one of the hard, wooden, Mess Hall benches. While I was shifting and readjusting, the black-haired counselor who didn't know my name was on the phone talking to someone. I couldn't help but overhear the conversation, as she wasn't monitoring her volume at all. Of course being a phone conversation, I could only hear one side, but I could make sense of it pretty quickly.

"I can't believe she's back either," she paused, "I was *sure* that she would be at least out for the rest of the summer." She nodded and made sounds of agreement with the phone, "Right? I mean, what kind of freak takes a header out of the lifeguard chair, gets knocked out cold in the pool, and actually bothers to come back?"

Luckily she wasn't looking at me because my jaw dropped, and if she had seen that reaction she would've been aware that I was eavesdropping. But she was oblivious to my existence, so she continued on, even more incriminatingly. "I'm glad that the chair snapped, because I had definitely caused enough damage that if she had *seen* it she would've never sat in it, and it would've been obvious that it was tampered with," she brazenly boasted. "I know, right? Who doesn't notice that only one leg remains slightly in tact on a lifeguard chair? Maybe if she wasn't so caught up in simply being Sandy she'd have noticed, but no chance of that, the fool!"

My stomach dropped with a strange excitement because indeed I was absolutely *not* responsible for what had happened to Sandy! It felt like a threefold slap of Karma that I would be situated to eavesdrop in on this phone conversation! I couldn't believe I was hearing this counselor confess the morbid details to *someone*, but at the same time, it truly bothered me that one of Birch Bog Camp's counselors could be so remorselessly hurtful to another person! Did this counselor try to *kill* Slimey? Why on earth would she go through such an elaborate scheme to get rid of the head counselor? The confession continued but it grew increasingly twisted and when she wandered into the kitchen I tuned out.

I had finished the soda and although lounging on a hard, wooden, Mess Hall bench, I was nodding off when the black-haired counselor gave me a nudge because it was time to go back to the Great Space. "Come on kid, whatever your name is, we gotta bring the food for the cookout!" She handed me the hot dogs, the buns, the chocolate, the marshmallows, and the graham crackers to carry across the green. It wasn't until we were outside again that I realized just how much time had truly passed, as there wasn't a hint in the sky of any daylight at all. It was black and I could see the stars. "If you look careful tonight, kid, whatever your name is, you will be able to see the Perseid meteor shower! Tons of shooting stars - like one per minute!"

"Wow, really?" I wondered aloud.

"Wow, you actually *can* talk!" she exclaimed. We hurried the food to the Great Space where the rest of Glittering Trillium was setting up their overnight gear while the counselors were evidently giving them an earful about their disappearance. "Alright, here's the food, I'm gonna take the quiet kid here over to the cabin so she can get her stuff," the black-haired counselor explained. "Don't eat 'til we get back!"

We didn't talk all the way to the cabin, and when we got there, I grabbed all of my stuff and juggled it just fine by myself this time. I don't know why it had been so difficult to carry my own stuff when I was getting on the bus this morning. The others hadn't started eating when we got back to the Great Space, so I quickly set up my sleeping bag and sat down on it waiting to eat just like all the other girls.

Once I had caught up, Traci and Gilly finally gave the okay for Glittering Trillium to eat. We roasted hot dogs on sticks. Needless to say most of the hot dogs wound up falling into the fire, and most of the sticks wound up ablaze, provoking screams and cooking sticks being thrown into the fire. I was awfully tempted to just eat my hot dog raw, not because I actually like raw hot dogs but solely because I was famished! And well, I'm sort of accident prone and didn't want to lose my dinner to the bonfire like just about all of my cohorts had done. But somehow, miraculously, I heated my hot dog without burning it, without setting the stick on fire, and without dropping it. I put it into the soft bun and ate it. A hot dog has never tasted as good as that one did that night. I savored every morsel, even if I did eat the whole thing in three bites.

All of Glittering Trillium was abuzz about what would be coming soon... dessert! And everyone knows it's a tradition at Birch Bog's overnight to make s'mores! Now, if you've been living under a rock, you might not know that a s'more is when you roast a marshmallow and then make like a sandwich with it using two graham crackers, instead of bread, and a piece of chocolate candy bar! Oh, it sounds heavenly good! Okay, I haven't had them before, because I don't camp. But toasted marshmallows are good, and Mom did say I am supposed to have one for her. When Mom roasts marshmallows, she always picks a warm ember and holds the marshmallow patiently over it until it turns a perfect shade of tan. Not me, nope, I put it near enough to a flame where it catches on fire and then I wave it and blow it out. It turns out kinda black on the outside, but *OH*, it tastes so good!

Sandy stood up to speak to all of us, "Campers, it's time for bed for you, and the s'mores will be for the counselors only! Good night!"

"Say what?" the tall girl asked.

71

"That's not fair!" Ms. Diva complained, and miraculously, for once, she was right.

"But we brought in the ingredients," I reasoned, "Our parents want us to have the s'mores!"

"Well, thanks to your parents, *we* will be eating all the s'mores! None for you Brats! And no complaining, or *else!*" Traci threatened.

"That's right, shut your faces and go to sleep!" Sandy chimed in. The counselors laughed and started talking loudly on their side of the fire. I hoped they were joking, but they really weren't. They expected us to actually go to sleep. I could hear the other campers crying. This was *not* the overnight experience that any of us expected or that our parents wanted for us. Something needed to be done.

chapter six

Marshmallow Oozed and Bruised

I desperately tried to do the right thing. I attempted to just lie in my sleeping bag and relax and fall asleep. It was *almost* peaceful staring up at the night sky and watching for the shooting stars in the Perseid meteor shower. It would have been far more enjoyable if the counselors weren't being obnoxiously loud over on their side of the fire, using inappropriate language, and cackling as they ate *our* s'mores. I knew that Mom and Dad would buy the makings for s'mores anytime I asked, so I could seriously eat them anytime I desired. That was absolutely not the point. The problem was that these counselors were bad people, and they were taking advantage of us kids, mistreating us and saying really awful things to us. They needed to be stopped. We had a right to our s'mores, as we had supplied the ingredients! I had *promised* Mom that I'd eat a roasted marshmallow for her. These no-good counselors were going to make me break a *promise*?

"I don't think so," I mumbled aloud. I watched the stars another moment, a rage building within me unlike any I had felt before. Mind you, I'm a natural redhead, so I'm known to have a temper, but what was growing inside me wasn't one of my normal anger outbursts... it was coming up from my toes and encompassed my whole heart and soul. A shooting star glowed quickly by my frame of view as this voice boomed from me in a way I've never spoken before.

"I want roasted marshmallows!!!" I yelled from my sleeping bag.

"Did somebody dare to say something?" Sandy asked.

I stood up and glared at her through the bonfire. I noticed a look of panic swept across her face, but I didn't care. This time I spoke with a fury that was exponentially greater than my initial utterance of the words. "I said, 'I... want... *ROASTED MARSHMALLOWS!!!!*'"

At once, the bags of marshmallows went inexplicably flying through the air, landing in the bonfire. I immediately recognized the scene straight from my dream and knew exactly what would happen next. I panicked to find something to alter – something that could be changed so as to not allow my nightmare to come true! I remembered that in the dream, I had stood there watching the fire and watching the marshmallows pop like popcorn! Molten, gooey, sugary explosions would soon shower everyone around the fire in a scream-provoking, disgusting, white, sticky mess! There wasn't much I could do – the bags of marshmallows were *in* the fire already... my only hope was to escape! I grabbed my backpack and ducked into the bottom of my sleeping bag, taking cover from the white lava that would be erupting momentarily. I found the cell phone that Mom had packed away for me and called home. I knew I needed my parents there as soon as possible.

"We're on our way," Mom's voice answered, "or should I start with the traditional greeting of 'Hello, how are you tonight, my Little Dragon?'"

I giggled. "You're really on your way?" I was instantly relieved.

"Of course! We're in the car and heading out the driveway," she reassured.

"Please tell me you weren't sitting in the car waiting for me to call, Mom..."

"As much as I considered doing that, we actually just jumped out of our chairs when we heard the phone ring, as we knew who it would be, at this hour," she soothed. "Are you safe?"

"Apparently I caused my nightmare, Mom," I explained. "I'm currently in the bottom of my sleeping bag which is probably getting pelted with melted marshmallow ooze."

"Wow, you do know how to have a wild time, Persephone," she laughed. "If anyone tries to hurt you, you run for the woods near the camp's driveway, but not *in* the driveway, okay?"

"Okay, Mom." I felt the cell phone's warmth on my cheek and it almost felt like the warmth of the hugs and kisses I get from the 'Rental Units. I knew they would be there soon and that the counselors would be miserable to see them.

"We should be there in about fifteen minutes, but try to stay on the phone, okay?" Mom comforted. "If you can't say anything for your safety around there, just tap on the mic with your finger and I'll hear that."

"I love you, Mom," I trembled.

"I love you, too, Persephone, and you're going to be alright!"

I could hear screams and panicked feet running around outside my sleeping bag. I sincerely hoped nobody would step on me. I knew it was just melted marshmallow, so as messy and gross as it seemed, it wouldn't actually harm anyone. After a few moments, I didn't hear the counselors' voices anymore, so I calculated that they had likely made a break for the ironically named Mess Hall, to escape the actual mess in the Great Space.

"Are you still there?" Mom's voice was reassuring amid the confusion outside my sleeping bag.

"I don't hear the counselors anymore," I admitted, "I think they left us out here."

"Do you feel safe taking a peek?" Mom asked. "Our ETA is about ten minutes."

"It's getting quieter out there," I noted.

"It is up to you. Do whatever keeps you safe," Mom suggested.

"I just *have* to peek as the suspense is killing me," I acknowledged. I unzipped the sleeping bag slightly and saw nobody around. Gobs of remnants of marshmallows fused with pieces of melted plastic bags were everywhere. "They must've all gone inside," I guessed.

"Can you get somewhere safe but out of their view?" Mom begged.

"I'll make a run for the woods," I agreed, already running towards the forest. Sure, the trees were spooky, but those counselors were downright dangerous.

"Don't go far into the woods, just like behind the first tree, okay?" Mom pleaded.

"I'm in the woods near the driveway, Mom," I revealed. "I can see the driveway perfectly and all the buildings of camp, too."

"Okay, stay put and we'll be there in five minutes," Mom reassured. "Honey, can we please go faster?" she requested of my dad, who was driving. He let her know that they were going as fast as they could go safely.

"Mom, I am gonna have a humdinger of a story to tell you when I see you," I bragged, grinning.

"How on earth *did* you cause such a ruckus, young lady?" she demanded.

"Don't worry, I'll tell you the whole thing soon," I sighed. "Oh, and Mom, what would constitute an appropriate sacrifice for being the person responsible for several bags of roasted marshmallows?"

"You're coming home from camp early," she determined, without hesitation.

"That sounds more like a reward than a sacrifice, Mom," I admitted, smirking.

"Karma decides what Karma decides, Kiddo," she said with a gentle giggle. I just sat on the forest floor with the cell phone to my ear. I was traumatized enough that I was rather exhausted even if my blood was still pumping with adrenaline. I focused on my breathing to ensure that I wasn't making too much noise so as to give away my location.

Soon, I saw the group of counselors reemerge from the Mess Hall, covered in white globs and loudly saying inappropriate things

77

that I truly cannot repeat. Glittering Trillium followed them, with the same marshmallow accessories. They examined the sleeping bags and bonfire area, looking in my sleeping bag, but apparently didn't find what they were looking for. Then, I heard Sandy scream, *"FIND HER!!!!!"* at the top of her lungs and everyone scattered in pairs.

"Mom!!!!" I whispered loudly, "They're all looking for me now!!!" I trembled. I didn't know what they would do to me when they found me. I started to cry.

"Relax, my Little Dragon, we're almost there..." Mom sounded worried despite her attempts to sound soothing. "Can't you drive faster?" she said away from the phone.

I looked up and saw three pairs of feet with flashlights coming straight at the woods where I was hiding. My heart was pounding so hard in my chest that I thought its noise was what was attracting my hunters. I tapped the phone with my finger so Mom would know we needed to be silent, but I kept her on the line. If the counselors or campers were going to do something brutal and illegal to me, I wanted Mom to hear it so she'd make sure they would go to jail!

I held my breath and didn't dare move a muscle as the footsteps got uncomfortably close to me. Then I felt a hand clench my wrist, *"GOTCHA!"* Julie yelled. I was pulled forcefully up to my feet before being lifted to dangle by my wrist. "You are going to pay for what you have done, you good for nothing, rotten, witch!"

"LET GO OF ME!" I screamed, kicking. The black haired counselor, who was with Julie, grabbed my legs and covered my mouth to silence me. Julie grabbed my cell phone with her other

hand, dropping her flashlight to do so. At that same moment I saw headlights careening down the driveway towards us.

"You won't be needing *this!*" Julie sneered as she snapped the phone closed and tossed it into the woods. I struggled to free myself from them but they held firm, hurting my body with their tight grips. "Don't witches get burned at the stake, Mirabelle?" Julie asked the black haired counselor who was holding me.

"We've got that big bonfire over there," Mirabelle answered. "That oughta work." They carried me out of the woods a total distance of about five steps before the car that was approaching, spotted us and slammed on the brakes.

My father was out of that car in a shot so fast that I wasn't sure he had time to put the vehicle in park. The headlights shone right on us. "*UNHAND HER, NOW!*" he demanded in a terrifying voice. The counselors immediately dropped me, literally, and ran towards the Main Cabin. My father scooped me up gently in one motion and carried me to the car, setting me in the backseat. "You're safe now. Mom and I are here. Just relax, the police are on their way," he said in a soothing tone. Meanwhile, Mom bolted from the passenger's side and chased the counselors to the Main Cabin, cell phone virtually attached to her ear.

Dad returned to the driver's seat and drove right across the green to follow Mom. Our headlights illuminated the Main Cabin. "I need to get your mom back to the car before she does something," he worried aloud. "I'm locking you in the car, but you can unlock the door for anyone you trust!" He held up his car keys and continued, "I have the keys, so your mom and I are the only ones who can get in without you unlocking the doors, okay?" He tossed me his cell phone and closed the door, hitting the "Lock" button on the remote as he ran off to find Mom.

I felt completely safe sitting in the backseat of our family car. I knew my parents were there and that they wouldn't let anyone get to me now. The police were on their way and – oh, wait, the police? They would certainly have some questions about the marshmallows. Yet, something told me that they would have significantly more questions about the behaviors of the adults of Birch Bog Camp.

My eyes peered through the darkness towards the building, looking intently for any sign of the 'Rents returning to the car. Within two minutes I saw Dad with his arms wrapped around my mother, restraining her from letting those horrible women have a piece of her mind. He pressed the unlock button and walked her to the car. She climbed into the backseat with me.

"*MOM!*" I yelled, hugging her tight.

"Are you okay? I am so sorry that we didn't get here in time," she held me snugly.

"You most certainly *did* get here in time," I reassured her. "They were going to burn me at the stake in the bonfire."

"They *WHAT?*" Dad interrupted, hearing the conversation as he climbed into the driver's seat.

"They called me a witch and said witches are supposed to be burned at the stake, but since they didn't have a stake, they were going to put me into the bonfire," I remembered.

"Why are the police taking so long?" my father snarled. Just then we saw flashing blue lights coming up the driveway.

"Are you going to be okay to talk to the police, Persephone?" Mom asked. "I think they are going to have a lot of questions."

"No problem, Mom," I replied, smiling feebly. "I will tell them the truth. All of it."

"You won't get into trouble if you tell them the truth, just remember that," she pulled me tighter.

"I hope not," I confessed. "I don't know that they're going to like the part about the marshmallows, though."

"The marshmallows are the least of their worries right now," Mom reassured me.

My father went to speak with the officers. He must have told them what he had seen when he drove into the camp's driveway because Julie and Mirabelle were both immediately taken out of the Main Cabin in handcuffs and put into the back of police cruisers.

An older police officer knocked on our car window and my mother opened it. "Is this Persephone?" he inquired.

"Yes," I gulped nervously. I put on my brave face. "Is there some information I can give to help you this evening, officer?"

"Well, young lady, you are a mighty brave kid," he started. "I am Officer Springfield and I would like to find out what has happened here tonight."

I smiled. "It's nice to meet you, Officer Springfield," I said.

"Can I ask you, your mom, and your dad to come with me into one of the buildings here so you can answer some questions and give us a statement about what happened here tonight?"

"Definitely," I bounced out of the car but my body was sore from having struggled with Julie and Mirabelle. "Ouch," I couldn't help but complain.

"'Ouch' is not a word I like to hear coming from someone so young," he said with concern. "Young lady, I want to hear the *whole* story." He held the door to the Main Cabin open for me.

"I've never been in here before," I admitted, stepping nervously into the building, with Mom and Dad close behind. I started at the beginning of the evening, recounting every detail from when the bus pulled away at the end of day camp. I even told them about the phone call I heard in the Mess Hall, because as much as I don't like Sandy, if Mirabelle tried to do her harm, she and anyone else involved needs to be appropriately punished. When I told Officer Springfield about the marshmallows, I thought he would arrest me for sure, but instead he smirked, kept taking notes, and let the story continue.

When I was finished with everything I could think of, and I had answered all of his questions, he spoke with Mom and Dad separately and then sent for me again. "Are you going to arrest me for the marshmallow thing?" I asked nervously.

He chuckled, "I don't quite know what happened with the marshmallows, Persephone, but there's no way that you could have caused bags of marshmallows to fly into the fire from the other side of the fire." He paused. "Besides, even if you *did*, you were just taking away what didn't rightfully belong to the counselors, right?"

"Well, I suppose that's true," I pondered.

"My officers have been looking around the grounds, and they tell me that there *is* a sticky white mess by the bonfire, but that it looks more like people were having a marshmallow fight than anything malicious," he explained. "Also, they searched the woods in the area where you say the counselors grabbed you, and they did find your cell phone nearby."

"Oh good, I wouldn't want to lose that," I said, heaving a huge sigh of relief.

"We will be keeping some items for evidence and we're still investigating the scene, so as much as I'd love to say you can take your stuff and go home, unfortunately, I'm only able to advise you to go get checked at the hospital and then go home with your mom and dad," Officer Springfield said.

"Okay," I said hesitantly. It felt really strange to just leave my things laying where I had left them - my sleeping bag, my overnight stuff, my cell phone, my swim gear, and the rest of my junk. "Eventually, I will be able to get most of my stuff back, right?" I asked nervously.

"Absolutely," he agreed. "I really want you to be examined to make sure that you're alright after this ordeal, and I know we won't have sufficiently processed the scene in a timely manner to allow you to wait for your stuff and to receive appropriate medical attention."

"What's going to happen to the other campers and counselors? They're still out there looking for me!" I mentioned.

"Sooner or later, they'll come back here, and we'll be waiting to question them as to their involvement," he revealed. "In the meantime, the parents of the minors will be contacted, and it will be all sorted out by the morning."

My mind wandered to thoughts of Glittering Trillium drenched in marshmallow, returning from the woods, and how scary a sight it would be for them to approach Birch Bog Camp with the flashing blue lights illuminating in all directions. "As exciting as it would be to see everyone again, I think I'm ready to get out of here, if that's alright, Officer Springfield," I requested.

"We have statements from the three of you, and we know where to reach you if we require further information. You are free to go home, but I do hope you'll go get those bruises checked out before you do," he suggested.

"Bruises?" I asked. Then I looked at my wrist that had been grabbed. I could see discoloration where Julie's individual fingers wrapped around my tiny wrist. "Oh wow, bruises," I concurred.

"Thank you, Officer Springfield," Dad said, shaking the policeman's hand as Mom brought me to the car. As Dad climbed into the driver's seat, I could see four flashlights coming towards the Mess Hall. We were leaving at just the right time.

On the local news the next evening, I saw that most of the counselors who had been there that night were arrested for one reason or another. Charges had also been brought against the counselors who were involved in the attack on Sandy at the pool. The health department came in and discovered that the lagoon, latrine, and kitchen all had major health violations, but they didn't say if Boggy, the swamp monster, was among those violations. The campers from Glittering Trillium had been reunited, Friday morning,

84

with their families, but Birch Bog Camp had been hereby closed indefinitely.

As for me, well, I'm being pampered by the 'Rental Units while I am icing a bunch of hideous bruises. There won't be visible, physical, scars, and I'll be alright. Those counselors didn't realize just how tough the lil "Brat" who they picked on was. Maybe they should've picked on someone *their* own size.

That said, the next time I'm tempted to request that the universe gives me something, remind me to heed Mom's advice and not do so, because with unanticipated sacrifices, like severe thunderstorms, or unexpected consequences, like violence, willing the universe to grant me stuff is just not worth it.

chapter seven
The First Day of Fifth Grade

The final couple weeks of summer flew by faster than I could fathom, and before I knew it, the first day of school was nearly upon us. On the last day of summer vacation, Mom, Dad, and I went back-to-school shopping. Mom insisted I get this Flappy Folder thing cuz she had one when she was my age. There was one with a unicorn on it, so I agreed, because unicorns are the coolest animals ever! They also had a cheetah print Flappy Folder, so Mom got that one for herself.

"Mom, you're not going to need a Flappy Folder at school! You're the teacher!" I chuckled.

"You know me… if it's leopard or cheetah print…" she started.

"You have to have it," I finished.

"Just like you want everything teal or with unicorns, my Little Dragon," she said, giving me a kiss on my forehead.

The best thing about going to a parochial school is wearing uniforms because we already know what we'll wear everyday, and therefore, we don't have to stay hip to the latest fashion trends for the first day of school. Being a full-fledged girl though, I simply had to have an adorable teal t-shirt and a pair of denim overalls that I found! Predictably, Mom picked out a purple tee for me, too, cuz not only is purple her favorite color but also because she still enjoys selecting cute clothes for her only daughter to wear. Dad chose a green tee for me because he swears it is the best color on redheads.

Into the shopping cart, we threw pencils and ink cartridges and even a backpack that was a super cute patchwork of denim, floral, and paisley! It was the coolest backpack ever! Mom said it wasn't sensible for school though, so when we got home, she revealed she had already been online to order me a teal backpack and lunchbox set, that came with a lifetime warranty.

"They're gonna go broke replacing those for life for me!" I said, coming up behind her and wrapping my arms lovingly around her.

"That's pretty much the idea, my Little Dragon," she said hugging me back. "Are you all ready for the first day of school tomorrow?"

"You bet!" I exclaimed, delighted about the onset of the school year. I was entering fifth grade, the year that we ruled the school, as Saint Bart's School was kindergarten through fifth grade. I looked forward to being back in school, as I love school. Admittedly, I am one of those geeks who know everything, but I'm not obnoxious about it. I typically keep my knowledge to myself and am consequently a teacher's worst nightmare because it is hard for them to determine what I know and what I am thinking. I never got to be in Mom's class because I skipped first grade, going right from kindergarten to second grade, but Mom taught me all that a first grader should know when I was about two years old, so my presence in first grade would've been rather pointless. By the time I was six, I could read chapter books and knew my multiplication tables and long division. Now that I'm nine, well, I certainly hope my fifth grade teacher is prepared to adequately challenge me academically!

After a good night's sleep, attired in my plaid uniform skirt, short-sleeved uniform blouse, white ankle socks, black shoes, and with my hair in two ridiculously adorable braids, I thought I looked perfectly suited for a first day of fifth grade at a parochial school. My teal backpack and matching lunchbox were packed and ready, too. Mom and I left in the car before Dad was even showered for the day, because Mom had to put the finishing touches on her classroom to make it ready to welcome her little first graders.

Truth be told, Mom had been setting up her classroom for weeks, so there was positively nothing left to do. We went out to the playground to wait for the students to arrive.

Do you believe in love at first sight? I am still deciding my belief on that one. I most definitely believe in *crush* at first sight. Oh, come on! Are you saying you haven't ever met someone and instantly had the overwhelming urge to walk over and give that person a bigger hug than you give your parents, squeeze their cheeks, and plant a big smooch right on 'em? I won't say it happens to me all the time, but I'll confess that it has happened on a few occasions.

Little did I know that my first day of fifth grade was going to spawn another crush at first sight! Okay, it wasn't actually *first* sight because I've been in his class since second grade, and technically I had a crush on him last year, too, but wowzers he grew up cute over the summer.

But if you expect me to tell you his name, you had better breathe if you're holding your breath, as I am not telling. No way!

"Hi, Joey!" I blushed as I hurried over to him after he had gotten out of his car.

Oh, drat! Where's my eraser? I *so* did not just write his name, did I? Oh, I think I shall die of mortification! What if someone who read that knows Joey? Oh, wait! I know what I can do! *If* you know Joey Gardens, just *forget* you ever even read his name! There, that oughta work! Anyways...

"Hi, Joey!" I blushed as I hurried over to him.

"Hi, Persephone," Joey said with an ear to ear smile. "How was your summer?"

"It was great!" I replied with a smile. "How was yours?"

He told me all about his baseball season. His team was the Blistering Bats. He's not exactly their star player, but he loves to play ball. Then he told me about his month in Maine with his grandparents. "One of these summers you should come visit me in Maine so we can go clamming together."

"Clamming?" I asked. He went into explicit detail of being knee deep in mud, digging for clams. "Don't they snap off your toes?" I worried.

"Noooo!" he insisted, laughing at my naivety. He explained why they didn't, but I was too busy thinking, "Look at those dimples... he's gotten so cute!" to understand what the rationale was.

"Oh, okay, as long as they won't bite off my toes," I dreamily lamented when he stopped talking.

"Um, yeah," he mumbled, confused. The bell rang and the students started lining up to go into the building. He asked, "I'll see you at recess, right?"

"Of course! We have tons to catch up on!" I exclaimed. I ran over and gave Mom a hug and joined my class. Being the "big kids," we were the first class to enter the building, and we knew right where to go.

My classmates and I read the nametags on the desks that assigned us to seats. In my row, I had Jodie Edwards in front of me and Sam Anderson behind me. Apparently this teacher hadn't yet adopted the collaborative learning models where fifth graders worked best in cooperative groups at round tables. What can I say, when you have a progressive teacher as your mother, you learn a thing or two.

"I am Mr. Harper," the teacher introduced himself, breezing into the room. I couldn't believe my eyes! A boy teacher? Mom hadn't told me of this!

Alright, I'll level here... not just a boy teacher but an exceptionally handsome, wicked young, boy teacher! He had wavy dark brown hair and blazing blue eyes that reminded me of an electrified version of the color of robin's eggs. He wore these small wire framed glasses that made him look so sophisticated. And his smile! Wow. If they made more teachers that looked like him, kids would never skip school ever!

"Welcome to fifth grade!" he exclaimed. "You might think you get to rule the school this year, and well, that's true!" He laughed. "But with all the responsibility of being the role models of the school, you must remember to always behave appropriately and to learn something this year."

"What are we supposed to learn?" Tisha Boldrums asked without raising her hand.

"As much as you can," Mr. Harper replied with a smile. I noticed he had a cleft chin. Seriously? I couldn't figure out how I'd be able to focus enough on academics to learn anything this year. "This year, and every day of your life, you should always learn as much as you possibly can."

His first lesson for us was immediate. "Now that you've found your desks, let's modernize the classroom a bit. Move your desks so they're in groups of three, but be sure you sit with people who won't get you in trouble with note passing and talking."

"We're allowed to pass notes?" Tisha asked.

"No, that's the point," he firmly corrected. "Now, on your marks, get set, go!" He stepped back as desks slid around the freshly waxed floor.

I hadn't had time to think before Joey had abutted his desk to mine. "Hey, we can sit together!" he announced. We waved over our friend, Freddie, and we had our grouping of three.

"Very interesting," Mr. Harper commented as he inspected our group. "Looks like trouble," he said with a playful smirk. Then he read our nametags. "Let's see... Joseph Gardens, Fred Stewart, and

Persephone Smith. Aha! You're Mrs. Smith's daughter! I've heard a lot about you."

"And I've heard nothing about you other than that you just graduated from college last spring and are very excited to meet me!" I responded.

"Both of those accusations are true," he confessed. I laughed quietly. I had a feeling it was going to be a good school year.

At the end of the day, I went to Mom's classroom to wait until she was able to give me a ride home. "So, my big fifth grader, how was your day?" she asked when I arrived.

"Um, Mom... you didn't tell me my teacher was a *boy* teacher!" I grinned at her.

"He is?" she teased. "I hadn't noticed," she said with a joking smirk. I rolled my eyes. "I had a feeling you'd take to him though, because he's smart and he has a great sense of humor, just like you, my Little Dragon."

"Mom!" I giggled. "Yeah, okay, you're right. I daresay he's the second best teacher, ever."

"I wonder who the best teacher ever is..." Mom supposed, pretending to think.

"You, Mom!" I announced, giving her a big hug. "Not that I'm partial or anything."

"Eh, I don't mind if you *are*, in this situation," she admitted, as we hugged and laughed. Yep, it was most definitely going to be a good school year.

chapter eight
Choir Or Else

Although Mr. Harper is, by far, the coolest teacher I've ever had, I love our specials at school because two of them are two of my favorite activities on the planet: art and music! There's also physical education, but truthfully I can only be limited in my enthusiasm about playing kicker in a short, plaid skirt.

Alright, honestly on gym day, we wear a different school uniform that is more conducive to playing sports. But truthfully, playing outside with my friends provides sufficient daily physical activity for me! I'd much rather do art and music.

Our first day of music was the day after Labor Day. Oh, how I love to sing! Mom and Dad have always incorporated music and singing in everything we do, so I always look forward to music class so I can practice reading sheet music. As the "big kids" at Saint Bart's, it was our duty to lead the younger kids in singing at our weekly school church services by knowing all of the hymns and singing loudly. Ms. Peyton, our music teacher, told us she knew no sound as perfect and angelic as the sound of children's voices singing in harmony. Either Ms. Peyton was tone deaf or we weren't bringing her bliss because the voices of Saint Bart's fifth graders were anything but harmonious.

At the end of music, Ms. Peyton passed out an information sheet and permission slip to be in the choir. As much as I love to sing, the thought of singing in the children's choir at church on Sunday mornings is completely and utterly unappealing. "We need you in the choir," Ms. Peyton pleaded as she handed me the information. "If you come for choir auditions, you'll be a shoo-in."

"No, thank you, Ms. Peyton," I said as I handed the info sheet back to her.

"Persephone, this isn't your decision," Ms. Peyton pressured. "It is the decision of your parents."

"My parents don't support my presence in the choir because they know I don't want to be in the choir," I explained.

"I find *that* hard to believe," Ms. Peyton sneered. "Well, Persephone, let me put it this way... if you don't join choir, you won't be in the Christmas pageant," she threatened. I was in utter disbelief that she was using my potential participation in the Christmas pageant to bully me into doing choir. I paused, silently, and looked at her. The look she gave in return made her seriousness very clear.

"You do what you have to do and I'll do what I have to do," I replied, with my best effort to seem completely unaffected. But on the inside, my heart was breaking. The Christmas pageant was a Saint Bart's tradition! The fifth graders got the meaty roles, and everyone knew I was the strongest female vocalist in our class. I had been looking forward to a shot at starring in the Christmas pageant ever since I was a kid!

"She can't threaten you like that," Freddie whispered, having overheard the exchange.

"I know, Freddie," I fumed, "but what can I do about it?" Freddie and I shrugged at each other.

I was still so perturbed when I got back to Mr. Harper's classroom for math that I couldn't pay attention at all. It was churning in my brain so much that I was completely oblivious when I was called on to go to the board to solve an equation. I usually love to use the dry erase markers with the fantastic array of colors, including teal!

Joey lightly kicked at my foot to get my attention. I glared at him until I saw him deliberately look away. When I followed his look, I saw that Mr. Harper was standing two feet away with his arms crossed, watching me.

"Welcome back," he said without smiling.

"Sorry, Mr. Harper, I'm stewing," I explained, embarrassed by my behavior.

"I'll give you more than ample time to stew at recess," he suggested. "Now solve the problem on the board, please?"

"Yes, Mr. Harper," I sniffed, getting teary-eyed because I wanted to crawl under a rock. I don't ever get in trouble at school, and leave it to me to get in trouble with Mr. Harper. I slinked over to the dry erase board. The only marker in the tray was orange. I picked it up and effortlessly solved the problem. I pushed back the tears and bit my lip as I returned to my seat.

When the class was dismissed for recess, I stayed at my desk. As my last classmate left the room, I put my head down and burst into sobbing tears. I hadn't noticed that Mr. Harper had returned from bringing my class outside and was sitting at his desk, waiting for me to regain my composure. "Are you quite finished now?" he suggested, smirking, when I had finally looked up and spied him there.

"Yes, Mr. Harper," I said softly.

"So, can you explain what's going on?" he questioned. "It's not like you to daydream during math, almost missing out on an opportunity to write on the board." I told him all about the choir and Ms. Peyton's threat. "You *do* know she cannot force you to do choir," he agreed.

"But she won't let me be in the Christmas pageant!" I sniffled.

"She can't keep you out of it," he defended.

"Yes, she can," I argued, "because she's the director."

"It would be discrimination if she holds a different set of conditions for you than for the other kids," he explained. "She could get into a lot of trouble."

"You watch," I predicted, "and she'll get away with it, too."

"Are you going to talk to your mom and dad about it?" Mr. Harper inquired.

"Of course!" I agreed. "I tell them everything that happens in my life."

"Good," he approved, smiling, "as then I don't have to!"

"Thanks, Mr. Harper, I'll take care of it," I determined. "But I want to know, if you're not mad at me, why did you keep me in from recess?"

"Oh, well, I had thought my math lessons were boring you, and I wondered if you'd consider doing an independent study in math?"

"That'd be awesome!" I exclaimed.

"I have an old sixth grade textbook that you can use, and I can help out if anything is confusing," he offered.

"Thanks, Mr. Harper! That would be so great!"

"Okay, talk to your parents about the choir and the Christmas pageant," he insisted. I nodded. "Now, get outside and play!" he directed. I scooted out the door and was barely outside the building when Freddie and Joey ran up to me.

"Come on, we're playing on the monkey bars!" Freddie announced. He and Joey ran back over to the monkey bars, and I chased them. It continually amazes me how quickly life in fifth grade goes back to completely normal.

After school, I told Mom about the conversation with Ms. Peyton. She was visibly not amused. She marched immediately to Ms. Peyton's room and closed the door so I couldn't hear what was said. When she reemerged, she said nothing but marched back to her classroom, picked up her bags of homework, turned to me, and asked, "Ready to go home?" I nodded, eyes transfixed on Mom.

Once safely in the car, I was compelled to find out what had transpired in the closed-door meeting. "Mom? What happened with Ms. Peyton?" I softly inquired.

"Ohhh, you won't be in choir," Mom said with a tone I didn't often hear from her. "Nobody is going to strong-arm *MY* child into doing *any*thing she doesn't want to do!" Her words had a snap to them that made it perfectly clear that Mom was furious at Ms. Peyton. "How *dare* she think she can get away with pressuring you to blindly do what she wants you to do?" Mom rambled angrily.

"What happened?" I pressed, my curiosity simply overwhelming me.

"You don't need to hear the details, my Little Dragon," Mom placated, "just know that if anyone ever tries to bully you like that into doing something you don't want to do, don't fall for it, and get Dad or I to take care of things."

"I was already resolved to just not be in the Christmas pageant, Mom," I admitted, "I had fought my battle."

"She had no right to connect your participation in choir to your chances in the Christmas pageant!" Mom boomed. "I can't believe she had the audacity to do that!"

"Mom, it's okay, I'm still the best female vocalist in my class, whether or not I'm in the Christmas pageant." I tried to calm her with my self-assurance.

"That's not the point." Mom was sounding more rational. "You have every right to go out for the Christmas pageant, and she had *no* business threatening to take that from you."

"Did you fix things so I can audition for the Christmas pageant?" I asked.

"What do you think, my Little Dragon?" Mom glanced over at me with a smile, carefully not diverting her eyes from the road for but a millisecond. "Ms. Peyton has no power over you, me, Saint Bart's," she paused, "or the Christmas pageant." She smiled a rather evil, vengeful, smile. "Karma is a beautiful thing," she hinted.

"I'm not following," I admitted.

"All you need to know is that you have nothing to worry about, Kiddo," she spoke calmly, "and that you absolutely did the right thing by telling me what happened."

"Did I mention the part about getting in trouble in Mr. Harper's class?" I nervously asked.

"Oh?" she inquired with one syllable. "No, no, you did not."

So I did. I told her everything. And guess what? She was just as excited about the opportunity for me to do the sixth grade math as I was! She wasn't mad at me for staying in for part of recess at all! I so have the best mom on the planet!

But I *still* want to know what was said in Ms. Peyton's room... and I can't wait to see what happens as a result of that conversation. Sometimes adults have good reasons to keep information from their children, but I have no reason to ever keep a secret from my parents. They truly do love me, no matter what, and apparently as a fifth grader, I'm going to be testing that, albeit inadvertently, on a regular, if not daily, basis.

chapter nine

"It's Evil!"

Despite that most of my friends are boys, I do have a best friend who is a girl. Her name is Coral Jones. Her mom's name is Marina, and the crazy thing is that she is also Mom's best friend, other than Dad. Mom and Marina have been friends ever since they were little girls! Sometimes the four of us ladies go out for "girls' day out," but oftentimes Marina and Mom visit while Coral and I play, at either their house or ours.

Coral goes to one of my town's public schools, so we don't get to see each other as much as if she went to Saint Bart's, and the first time we hung out after the start of the school year was after the third week of school! It was a sunny Saturday afternoon and we were playing outside in my backyard when I saw my fairy house and realized I hadn't checked it since that first time, way back in August. I ran over to it and stooped down to peer in. "Coral, have you ever made a fairy house?" I called over to her.

"A what?" Coral asked, coming over to see what I was doing.

"A fairy house," I repeated. "At camp, this summer, we made fairy houses, but I didn't believe in fairies, so I made another one when I got home to see if the results would be duplicated," I explained.

"You don't believe in fairies?" Coral asked.

"I do now," I answered, smiling at her.

"Well, I have always believed in fairies, Persephone," Coral bragged. "I can't believe you didn't believe in them," she shunned.

"I mean, I always knew the Tooth Fairy was real," I defended.

"You believe in the Tooth Fairy?" she reiterated, laughing. "The Tooth Fairy isn't real, you dork!" She fell onto the ground in peals of laughter.

"How can you believe in fairies but not the Tooth Fairy?" I asked, completely dumbfounded.

"Fairies aren't out there taking teeth from under pillows – that's crazy!" She rationalized, "Fairies fly through the air sprinkling a rainbow of fairy dust that brings magic to everyone they sprinkle."

"They what?" I asked, hoping she wouldn't repeat such garbage but that she would level with me and reveal that she didn't believe such nonsense.

"Haven't you heard of fairy dust?" She looked at me like I had three heads. "They carry a pouch of sparkling, magical fairy dust with them and use a magic wand to scatter it onto living things that need a little fairy magic."

I looked at her with incredulous eyes. "Must be you and I don't know the same fairies, Coral, cuz I can't see Rosette acting so silly, and I don't understand why the Tooth Fairy wouldn't exist, based on your reasoning."

"Your precious Tooth Fairy is nothing but a myth," Coral deflected. "I'll bet this Rosette you mentioned is a myth, too!"

"No, they're not!" I protested.

"How do you know?" Coral asked. I explained to her about what had happened at camp and here in the backyard. "Fairies don't speak English, you fool!" she chastised.

"'Merci beaucoup' isn't English, *you* fool," I defended.

"Well, I mean, they don't write words," she rebutted.

"You're implying that fairies are illiterate?" I reasoned.

"Of course they draw pictures, Persephone! Duh!" she huffed, "They just don't read and write."

Okay, Coral might be a lot of things, but smart is obviously not one of them. I didn't feel like insulting her by explaining the difference between "illustrate" and "illiterate." And how on earth could she believe in these dusty fairies she describes but not the Tooth Fairy? I wondered why I had even told her about the fairies. It seemed like I was giving her a secret part of me that I was no longer sure I wanted to share, because sometimes I wondered if she was trustworthy enough to deserve my secrets.

"Well, do you want to make fairy houses here in the backyard and test your theory?" I asked, hoping to get her away from mine.

"Yeah!" she exclaimed, running off to find a special spot for her fairy abode.

Meanwhile, I leaned down to the overgrown remains of my pre-existing fairy house. I noticed something and reached in. My hand brushed a cobweb, and I realized the dwelling hadn't been used in a long time. I felt horribly that I hadn't kept the place nice for the fairies. My hand touched something smooth and hard and I wrapped my fingers around it and retrieved it from the darkness. In the sunlight I saw that I held a green and purple crystal in my hand, with an attached note that read, "Merci Beaucoup! – Violette."

"What do you have there?" Coral asked, running across the yard to me.

My hand holding the crystal was shaking inexplicably and uncontrollably. "It was in the fairy house I made last month," I explained, staring, without understanding, at my shaking hand.

"Drop it! It's evil!" she yelled.

"What?" I asked, confused, shocked, and with a disbelief that made me hold the stone tighter.

"*DROP IT!!!*" she screamed. "Look what it's making you do! You're shaking! It's evil!"

"Evil?? What are you talking about?" I looked at her, realizing my hand was trembling harder and more violently than before.

"When someone holds a stone that makes them shake like that, it means that the stone is evil!" she gasped. "It's going to hurt you!"

"Holding a stone can't hurt a person," I explained.

"It has negative energy," she revealed, "so that's why it makes your hand shake. It's only aimed at you. Whatever kind of crystal that is, it's evil against *you*! *DROP IT!*" Then she struck my hand with a blow so hard that it knocked the crystal out of my hand and sent it flying across the backyard.

"*OWWWWWW!*" I screamed.

"Promise me you will never hold that kind of crystal again," she stared me down, truly concerned.

"You know I don't make promises," I reminded her.

"Yeah, yeah, yeah," she pishawed my words. *"PROMISE!"*

"I'm not promising anything," I confessed. Sometimes I wish I weren't so honest, but I *knew* exactly what I would do the moment she wasn't paying attention. I had not lost sight of the spot where the stone landed, even though the grass disguised it well. Coral ran towards the house.

"I'm telling!" she yelled over her shoulder. Really? Are we five? Why are we tattling at this age? Ugh. I don't understand girls. I really don't.

I took her absence as my signal to go find that crystal. I wasn't going to let some foolish little girl get between me and my contacts with the fairies! Violette left *me* a crystal – no way, no how, was Coral going to ruin my gift. Despite having watched the flight of the stone, I had to look around for it among the blades of grass. Thank goodness it still had Violette's note on it, because that made it slightly easier to locate. When I spotted the rock, I grabbed it as firmly as I could and quickly plunged it into my pants pocket. I wondered if my whole leg would start shaking. I pondered if it truly could be evil, because I didn't have an explanation as to why my hand had shaken so much, but it didn't seem like the actual reason. I couldn't help but be completely drawn to this stone, and I couldn't wait to ask Mom a lot of questions about this one.

Crystal in my pocket, I ran to the kitchen door. Marina and Coral were "just leaving" as I opened the door. Coral was crying and saying I was evil, and shell-shocked Marina was explaining to my mother, "Someone is obviously overtired."

Mom followed them out onto the porch and waved goodbye. Then, she turned and re-entered the house. "What on earth is going on, Persephone?" she started.

"What kind of crystal is this?" I asked as I reached into my pocket and pulled out the green and purple stone, note still attached. My hand shook uncontrollably again as I held it out for my mother to view.

"That's fluorite," she answered, extending her hand to take the crystal from me. I instinctively handed it to her, and the shaking of my hand immediately ceased. Mom chuckled.

"That's weird," I said, "cuz isn't that in our drinking water?"

"You're thinking of fluoride," she corrected. "Fluorite is something quite different." She elaborated, "I'm laughing because I know exactly what Coral was screeching about, now."

"I'm not evil, Mom!" I defended.

"Of course you're not," Mom reassured and hugged me. "Did she tell you this stone is?"

"YES!" I exclaimed, jumping back, completely in shock that Mom would have the insight to deduce that without any hint or explanation.

"Relax, my Little Dragon," Mom comforted, "Marina did nearly the same thing to me when we were teenagers."

"Really?" I asked.

"Yes," she revealed, "and crazier still is that it was in reference to fluorite!"

"So what is the deal with fluorite?" I inquired, "Is it evil?"

"Not at all," Mom laughed. "I can't explain why, but it seems that it is very powerful in your hands, as it is very powerful in my hands."

"But you're not shaking," I noticed.

"This is not the first time I've held fluorite," she explained. "It took a lot of practice to be able to harness its power in a way that doesn't manifest in shakes. The shaking isn't a sign of evilness, but instead it's a sign of the power that the stone has."

"It's so beautiful, Mom," I observed, gawking at the crystal in her hands.

"Have you ever mixed green and purple, Persephone?" Mom asked.

"Well, yeah," I admitted.

"What color was created?" she pressed.

"It was... you know... teal?" I smirked at the idea of teal, my *favorite* color.

"And what colors do your father and I tend to suggest for clothing for you, if we're picking things out?" she continued.

"Green and purple," I instantaneously replied.

"And do you know why?" she led.

"Because they are your favorite colors and they happen to look good on me?" I assumed.

"That they do," she admitted, "but do you know another reason why?"

"Because mixing them together makes teal?" I guessed.

"Because purple and green are your power colors, Persephone!" she revealed.

"And since fluorite is purple and green it is my power stone?" I connected.

"Something like that, Kiddo," she agreed. "And when you have better abilities to not shake when you hold the stone, you will see that if you look at it in the right light, you can see hints of teal and you can see rainbows within the crystal."

"*Really?!*" I exclaimed, reaching to grab the crystal from her hands. Unfortunately, I couldn't see much detail in the stone because the moment I held it, my hands shook so violently that I was unable to focus at all. Mom grabbed the stone back, to stop my shaking. I looked in awe that she could hold fluorite without a trace of movement, particularly knowing that she used to tremble just like me.

"It will take awhile before you can hold it without shaking," Mom explained. "It's a bit of mind over matter, and a bit of practice, and a whole lot of stubbornness."

"I think I've got the stubbornness to do it," I whispered.

"Oh, I *know* you do," Mom agreed, ruffling my hair. "Let's go put this one with your other crystals," she suggested. "You're really getting quite a rock collection," she noted.

So, for now, the fluorite sits on my bookshelf next to the rose quartz and the clear quartz. I am completely determined that it will not just sit there collecting dust. No, it will be in my hand every day until I can hold it without shaking. At that time, maybe, just maybe, I'll actually want to hang out with Coral again, if for nothing else than to see her reaction when she realizes that I have harnessed the power of fluorite.

Cue playful, evil laughter.

chapter ten

Competitive Spirit

It goes without saying that I am rather proud of my intelligence. I love learning and crave knowledge. Some people call me affectionate names like "nerd," "geek," or "brain," and some choose to call me related names that are clearly tinged with meanness. However, their jealousy is not going to stop me from my academic pursuits and growth. If I have an opportunity to showcase my smarts, I will, by all means, take it!

When Mr. Harper announced that he was going to round up Saint Bart's first ever spelling bee team, to enter the Citywide Spelling Bee, I nearly jumped out of my seat! "The education we provide at Saint Bart's is comparable, if not superior to, the schooling that the other students receive in this town, and it's time we show the community that we are certainly academically competitive."

I raised my hand, and Mr. Harper called on me. "How do we join the team?" I asked.

"I'm looking for volunteers," Mr. Harper answered. "As far as I am concerned, if you *want* to be on the spelling bee team and you are committed to studying the words, coming to the practices, and doing your best, then any of you can be on the team."

"What if we're not good spellers?" Deena Green asked.

"Deena, you and everyone else in this class are plenty good enough to be on our team," Mr. Harper welcomed. "This is the first time Saint Bart's has *had* an entry in the Citywide Spelling Bee, so the expectations for us aren't very high. I think it'll be tremendously fun to surprise the other competitors with a team that surely surpasses their expectations!" I chuckled at the thought that it, in fact, would not be hard for our team to be better than the town was anticipating, because most residents don't care much for the city's private school.

"When is the spelling bee?" Freddie asked.

"Not until spring," Mr. Harper answered. "That means we have at least six solid months to study and practice! Who's with me?" he asked, albeit much too excitedly.

I raised my hand. "I'd like to be on the team," I admitted.

"Great!" Mr. Harper encouraged, "Who else?" Freddie, Joey, and Deena raised their hands. Skye Stanley, Danielle Gibbons, Arnold Whitmore, and Curt Lyons raised their hands, too. "Excellent!" Mr. Harper exclaimed, jotting down the names of the volunteers. "A team of eight would be a perfect entry into the spelling bee! Thank you for your enthusiasm!"

"Are the practices after school?" Danielle asked.

"We can work out what times are the best for the team to meet up," Mr. Harper skirted the question. "I wouldn't rule out before school, after school, recesses… whenever is good for the team!"

"Recesses?" Curt objected.

"We'll see," Mr. Harper hinted, "but you might like recess practices."

Jodie whispered to Tisha, "I'm so glad I didn't sign up, because there's no way I'd like recess practices."

"Me either!" Tisha mouthed.

"Our first meeting will be right after school this afternoon for a maximum of five minutes, just to hand out the spelling word lists, permission slips, and that sort of thing," Mr. Harper announced. "And if anyone else wants to join the team, hang out after school for a couple of minutes!"

At the end of the school day, only Joey, Freddie, Skye, Danielle, and I waited for the meeting. Curt looked at us waiting and told us he forgot all about it and walked out the door with the other members of our class. Deena informed me, when we were packing up, that she was counting on me to make an excuse for why she wasn't going to be there. Arnold's exact words were, "No way, José, do you think I'm gonna miss out on recess to be on your spelling bee team!" as he ran out the door. I guess we had gone from a team of eight to a team of five.

"Mr. Harper, Deena told me to make up an excuse for why she's not here," I announced when Mr. Harper returned from walking the class outside.

"Why do you always tell everyone's business?" Skye asked. "You *know* nobody likes a snitch, right?"

"I'm not going to lie for someone, Skye," I clarified. "If Deena can't make up her own excuse, it's not my job to make one for her."

"Snitch," Skye name-called.

"Girls!" Mr. Harper interrupted. "Skye, honesty is actually a good character trait. You might like to try it sometime."

"Ooh! He takes the side of the kid whose mom teaches here," Skye snidely retorted. "Big shocker there!"

"If there's anyone here who doesn't feel he or she can be a part of the team spirit we need, then feel free to not participate on our spelling bee team," Mr. Harper warned.

"I'll be on the team if I want to be on the team," Skye responded.

"What is her problem?" Joey asked me. I shrugged. I didn't have any idea why she was being so defiant and obnoxious.

"I never knew Skye was so jealous of you," Freddie whispered. I looked at him in complete disbelief. Skye was the second smartest student in my class. She had no reason to be jealous of me!

"Why would she be jealous of me?" I inquired.

"You're the teacher's pet," Freddie explained, with a grin.

"Am not!" I snapped back. Freddie smirked even more. I quickly reviewed Mr. Harper's actions and attitude towards me since the beginning of the school year. I regrettably drew a quick conclusion: it would certainly appear, from Skye's point of view, that Freddie was right! I did get preferential treatment. I did feel as though I could get away with almost anything. And well, in class, I always tended to get my way. I put my hand over my eyes as if I could hide from the truth.

"I *AM* the smartest person in this class, and I am tired of Little Miss Persephone Perfect getting all the accolades!" Skye erupted. I couldn't help but uncover my eyes so as to witness this verbal tantrum. Skye continued, "Mr. Harper, you will *NOT* keep me off the spelling bee team! I *will* show everyone, once and for all, who the true brain of Saint Bart's fifth grade class is!"

"Wow," I mouthed.

"Persephone? Are you game for that challenge?" Mr. Harper asked as he passed out the word lists and permission slips.

"You betcha," I said, without any hint of smile or joking. I glared at Skye and seethed, "Game on."

chapter eleven

Road Trip!

$\mathbf{A}$s an only child, I've always been accustomed to simply getting my way without ever needing to develop a competitive bone in my body. Being on the spelling bee team was certainly building my ability to strive for not merely excellence but also to be the very best. No way was I letting this little Skye girl take over my place as the best student at Saint Bart's. Luckily, her bark was far scarier than her bite, as her vocabulary and spelling ability was comparable to mine... back when I was in third grade, that is.

Mom decided I had been studying more than hard enough and that we needed a girls' Halloween weekend getaway with Marina and Coral, leaving right after school on the Friday before Halloween. I hadn't seen Coral since she called me "evil," so I wasn't quite enthralled with the idea.

"Forgive and move on, my Little Dragon," Mom coached.

"She called me *evil*," I pouted.

"Well, Persephone, you *are* studying doubly hard for the spelling bee *not* to impress the cute boys on your team but to trounce the jealous girl on your team!" She pointed out, "You might be a little bit evil." I glared at her. She laughed, "Yes, I do believe that ordinary mortals would drop dead if you gave them an evil death glare like that!"

I laughed, too. "Oh, come on, is it really a bad thing to be evil?" I asked, jokingly.

"I *so* came in on the wrong part of this conversation," Dad admitted, joining us around the kitchen counter. "Yes, Squirt, 'bad' is actually the watered down definition of 'evil.'"

"We were discussing if Persephone is evil," Mom explained.

"No, Squirt, you're not evil," Dad reassured me, "Coral is just a jealous punk."

"Mom! You told him?" I accused.

Mom shrugged. Of course Mom had told Dad. As romantic as it is that Mom and Dad harbor no secrets, at the moment, I was simply feeling ganged up on to go on this trip that was evidently a surprise only to me. My redheaded temper flared, and I stormed off to my room.

Fifteen minutes later, I found myself strapped into the back seat of Marina's car, sitting silently alongside Coral. Mom rode shotgun and yapped with Marina about I daresay everything under the sun. Unbeknownst to me, Mom had packed my suitcase in advance, so I didn't know where we were going or why, but it was a road trip with the Joneses and those were *always* an adventure. I pulled my mp3 player from my pocketbook and plugged in so as to avoid conversation with Coral, who herself was engrossed in some DVD on her personal DVD player. I put on my sunglasses and closed my eyes.

I opened my eyes when I felt a nudge. I immediately saw my mom standing outside the car, in the dusky dark, leaning in my door. "Did you have a nice nap?" she inquired.

"Where are we?" I asked, looking around but not seeing Marina or Coral.

"We're at the rest area," Mom announced. "We need to talk."

"Mom," I whined, "I've been nice." I bounced out of the car and walked slowly with Mom towards the visitor center.

"You've had your headphones on and have ignored Coral thus far," Mom pointed out. "You haven't been picking a fight, but *nice* is surely an overstatement."

"I'm just being evil," I smirked.

"Persephone??" Mom said in a tone that made it clear that cute wasn't cutting it at the moment. "Just let it go."

"She's been completely caught up in her DVD and hasn't said anything to me either!" I defended.

"Okay, I did notice that, too," Mom admitted, "but you're older than she is, and you need to be the bigger person here. The four of us are going to be together today, tomorrow, and Sunday with two nights overnight in between. We can either fight or get along, but it's going to be a miserable weekend if we're not getting along."

"Where are we going?" I asked.

"Salem, Massachusetts," Mom replied.

"Why?" I inquired.

116

"Have you ever been to Salem for Halloween?" Mom asked, knowing full-well I had not. I shook my head. "Well, it's an experience you just need to have," Mom predicted. "Salem is notorious for being the home of the Salem Witch Trials, and many witches make their homes in Salem."

"Witches are real?" I asked.

"Yes, some people are witches," Mom explained.

"You know so much about this stuff," I noticed. My mind jumped to when Mom gave me the advice to speak from my every pore and fiber to make things happen. That speaking certainly resembles casting a spell. And Mom is obsessed with leopard and cheetah print, and witches usually have black cats. And now she was bringing me to Salem, a place rich with witch culture and real witches? A brilliant idea dawned on me, so I inquired, "Are *you* a witch, Mom?"

"No, Persephone, I am not a witch," Mom answered. She held the door open so I could go into the building. I was relieved. I loved Mom just the way she was, and if I discovered that her deep dark secret was that she was a witch, I would be shocked. Then it hit me!

"Is Marina a witch?" I whispered, but Mom acted like she didn't hear me. I totally had my answer. Mom always answers my questions unless there's a reason she doesn't want to answer – like if she would *want* to lie to me. But Mom doesn't lie, so if she would feel a need to lie, she changes the topic or simply doesn't say anything. Yes, it's clear to me that the reason Mom knows so much about Salem is because her best friend is… a witch!

We had gotten about fifteen feet into the building before we ran into Marina and Coral, as they were exiting. "Coral, do you have something to say to Persephone?" Marina prompted.

"I'm sorry I called you 'evil,'" Coral apologized and pathetically held her arms out for a hug.

"I forgive you," I lied and walked past her to the Ladies' Room. Okay, I know I said I always tell the truth, but seriously, Coral wasn't really apologizing, she was simply placating her mother. She had said the words so begrudgingly that I knew, beyond a shadow of a doubt, that no genuine feeling or emotion was behind them. She was going through the motions to appease Marina, to pacify my mom, and to make me look truly evil if I didn't accept her "apology." By no means do I consider telling someone I forgive them, when they're not honestly seeking my forgiveness, an actual lie.

"She didn't mean it," I said to Mom when the Joneses had left the building.

"Neither did you," Mom detected. "Just let it go, Persephone, or it will eat away at you."

"I'll put on my happy face for the trip, Mom," I promised.

"I don't want your happy face," Mom admitted, crouching down to my height and forcing me to make eye contact. "I want my happy Little Dragon," she directed. "I want to have a good time with my daughter this weekend. I know you're not evil, and Marina knows you're not evil. Why can't you let a little twit's jealous words go?"

"Why would Coral be jealous of me?" I wondered aloud.

"You have everything going for you!" she stated, looking flabbergasted that I hadn't automatically understood Coral's jealousy. "You're ridiculously smart. You're breathtakingly beautiful. You drive every young man who meets you positively wild." I laughed. Mom clearly appreciated my genuine happy face.

"You think boys like me?" I chortled. "Oh Mom, if only that were true!"

"Do you need me to go on and tell you more reasons why Coral is so jealous of you?" Mom asked, brushing a strand of hair away from my face. "Or are you sensible enough to see that you should forgive her for committing the unfortunate crime of being so inferior to you that she can't help but to be jealous and thereby lash out to get a rise out of you?"

"You really think I'm that much better than she is?" I was taken aback by Mom's blatant favoritism.

"You're *my* daughter," she answered without missing a beat. "Put you up against anyone on the planet and I *know* you're better than they are, because you're the best!"

"Awww," I cooed. "That's awesome of you to say… even if you are showing clear-cut bias."

"Moms are supposed to favor their children," Mom revealed. "It's in the instruction manual that comes with each kid. Why else would Marina put up with Coral?" I quickly looked at Mom, in total disbelief that she said such a thing! Then, we shared a good laugh. When we caught our breath again, Mom asked, "So are you ready to put all of this behind you and have an incredibly good weekend?"

"I'm actually really anxious to experience this Salem place for Halloween!" I joyously announced.

"Good! I think we're in for a great time!" Mom gushed, "And I have a surprise for you that you will be SO excited about!"

"Ooh, what?" I inquired with intrigue. "And don't pull that, 'If I tell you it won't be a surprise' stuff with me this time!"

"I plan to allow you to get something you've wanted for a long time, if you find exactly the right one," she hinted as we walked to the vending machines.

"OOH! I'm getting a tattoo!?!?!" I exclaimed. The resulting expression of horror on Mom's face was priceless. I laughed and admitted, "You're the best Mom, ever!"

"What? No!" Mom exclaimed. "Absolutely not!"

"I was joking, Mom, I don't want a tattoo," I acknowledged. "I don't even want my ears pierced!"

"Okay, you totally had me going there for a minute," Mom confessed. We ran into Coral and Marina in front of the snack machine.

"Coral, I think we should see if our moms will let us get tattoos on this trip!" I persuasively encouraged.

"Ooh, yeah!" Coral nodded, "Mommy? Can we get tattoos in Salem?"

"Not this time, Coral," Marina replied, "but maybe when you're a teenager."

"Aww, you're so mean, Mom!" Coral pouted.

I looked at Mom. She smirked at me, shaking her head like she didn't know exactly what to do with me. Then the four of us climbed back into the car and continued to Salem, noisily chatting away the miles. Things felt perfectly back to normal.

Now, not having planned this Halloween weekend in Salem, I didn't really arrive with many preconceived expectations. As soon as we got to town, I knew this place was truly unique. In many ways it looked like an old fashioned New England village, but people were walking the streets in elaborate garb that looked Medieval or something. They were dressed in cloaks, capes, gowns, and all sorts of attire that I don't even know the names of, and they appeared to float through the dark, lamplit, streets, as though they were in a movie.

"Isn't this place the best?" Coral babbled at me.

"It's something," I agreed, words escaping me as I gawked out the window. I noticed three well dressed women together wearing pointed hats. "Are those witches?" I asked Coral.

"Not all witches wear pointy hats," Coral informed me.

"How do you know this stuff, Coral?" I asked.

"Mommy tells me," Coral revealed with a smile. "She knows everything about Salem, because her best friend, Erica, lives here." I saw Marina shoot Coral a glare via the rear view mirror, as if she hoped I wouldn't have noticed the faux pas of referring to "Erica" as Marina's "best friend," when that title was allegedly my mother's, but Coral didn't notice. She just prattled on, "We come down to visit Erica like all the time, but Salem is the best for Halloween!"

"Well, it seems like a cool place," I admitted, just looking out the window, taking it all in.

We stayed at Erica's house, not too far from the ocean. I love the ocean and I had no clue that Salem was located by the sea. Mom and I got to stay on the pull out couch in the basement. "Plunk down

121

your bags and get ready to take a walk into town for dinner," Mom announced as we reached our basement accommodations.

"We're going out at night here in Salem?" I excitedly inquired.

"Yep, and we are going to have an awesome weekend," Mom reassured me.

Marina, Coral, Erica, Mom, and I walked to a sorta fancy restaurant and ordered our dinner to go! The staff looked as though they don't often get take out orders, but they boxed it all up nicely for us. We carried our supper to the ocean and ate right on the beach.

"I've never had dinner after dark on the beach!" I exclaimed. "This is amazing!" There really isn't anything quite as primal and earthy as sitting at the beach, toes in the sand, eating food that probably should be eaten with proper silverware, inside a dining room. We didn't care if it was messy. It was just a nod of appreciation to the basic necessities of life: food, air, earth, water, and friends. My soul felt completely renewed and refreshed by that meal, and I felt one with my surroundings.

As a surprise treat, Erica had brought along plastic goblets and a cooler of several unusual flavors of soda: cotton candy, sour apple, vanilla cream, and raspberry lime. So, after dinner, as we sipped our tasty, carbonated beverages, she told us stories about Salem, focusing on tales about witches and ghosts! She promised that we'd get to go to some of the haunted buildings the next night – Halloween night! The idea was inconceivably exciting!

Late in the evening, we walked back to Erica's house, and my exhaustion propelled my feet right to bed. I could hear Erica, Marina, and Coral having a boisterous, grand time upstairs, but my eyelids were closed so quickly that I barely heard Mom tuck me in and whisper, "Sleep, my Little Dragon, as I have a surprise for you very early in the morning."

chapter twelve
Halloween Morning

In the pitch blackness of the middle of the night, Mom's voice jolted me awake. "Wake up, Persephone, it's time for your surprise!" she whispered loudly. I groggily rolled over and after several blinks could make out the silhouette of Mom standing with lots of layers of clothing on, smiling and seeming to be wide awake, with a packed bag next to her.

"Mom, it's the middle of the night!" I croaked.

"I know! It's the perfect time of night for your surprise!" she excitedly whispered, holding out my hoodie as a suggestion for me to put on. With Mom *so* anxious to get me up and out of there at that hour, I figured the surprise would be something I'd enjoy, if only I could roll out of bed and be awake enough for it. "Brush your teeth, splash cold water on your face, let's go!"

I followed her directions and was soon dressed to be outdoors and as ready to go as I could be at whatever ridiculous hour it was. "Mom, this had better be good…" I grumbled skeptically.

"This is going to be unforgettable, my Little Dragon," she reassured me, kissing me on the forehead, grabbing the packed bag, taking my hand, and leading me out the door.

"It's just us?" I asked when we got away from the house.

"Yep," Mom smiled. "Some true mom and daughter time." She swung our joined hands happily as we headed towards the ocean.

"Are you going to give me a hint about what on earth you're up to, Mom?" I questioned.

"Well, what have you wanted forever?" Mom asked.

"A boyfriend?" I replied truthfully, knowing it wasn't the answer she was searching for.

"You're nine! You don't need a boyfriend yet!" Mom laughed.

"Well, you *asked*," I defended with a giggle.

"Good heavens, you're like nine going on nineteen!" she said with a tone of exasperation. We laughed. "Okay, how about something *else* you've been wanting forever?"

I racked my brain. I want a puppy, but that's an illogical answer, given the circumstances. I want a house at the ocean, and we're at the ocean, but I don't think that's what's going on either. "I have no idea, Mom," I admitted.

"You've been asking me for years when I'll give you one," she teased. "Specifically *me* and not your father," she hinted, "and I always say you're too young, but you're honestly not, and there's nowhere better than Salem for one."

"Mom!" I exclaimed, "A tarot reading!?!" I couldn't help but to jump up and down, skipping, while we were walking. "I'm right, I know I am!"

"Can't say you aren't psychic, my Little Dragon," Mom praised.

"I learned from the best," I chuckled, stopping our walk for a moment to hug her. We then continued onward to the beach where Mom set down her large bag and pulled out a huge piece of fabric, laying it out on the sand. It was obviously to be used as a surface for the tarot reading, with room for the two of us to sit across from one another.

"Have a seat," she encouraged. I think she wanted me to both hold the fabric down and stay out of her way as she set up the area. She pulled a bunch of candles out of her bag and placed them around the perimeter of the fabric. She used a lighter to light them and I was amazed at just how bright the area became. I could see that the lightweight fabric was perhaps a wall tapestry, printed with cheetah print. The candles were a mishmash of sizes, colors, scents, but they gave such a magical feeling to that little spot on the beach. Mom wasn't done with setting up yet though. She pulled out some incense sticks and lit them at each of the corners. "That oughta keep the mosquitos away," she grinned.

"Mom, this is *too* cool!" I noted, gawking, turning my head quickly time and again, trying to capture every part of the scene, inhaling the smell of the salt air and the incense and the scented candles, but there was just too much to take in. I was having sensory overload with my eyes practically popping out of my head with excitement, hoping not to miss any details!

Mom slipped off her shoes and stepped onto the fabric, sitting facing me, with space between us. She had two velvet bags with her. She set them atop the fabric, untying the goldenrod satin cord that held the purple bag closed. She reached inside and when her hand emerged it held a clear crystal. I recognized that it was a large piece of quartz. She handed me the crystal and directed me to hold it and close my eyes and then to set it on the other velvet bag when I felt the time was right.

I didn't know how to know when the time was right, so I just held onto it for awhile. This sense of calm enveloped me and I felt so many of my extraneous thoughts fade away. Soon, my thoughts were focused on the serenity and magical feelings of that unique, temporary place in that special, fleeting moment... and of love. When those thoughts were the only ideas in my head, I knew the time had arrived to set the crystal onto the other velvet bag.

With my eyes open again, I realized that my mother had laid other crystals on the fabric around us, and that she was holding something in her hands. She had her eyes closed for a moment, then opened them and looked at me, smiling. "Close your eyes, hold out your hands, and don't open your eyes until I give you the okay," she directed. I did as she told me to do, and I felt a smooth heavy object placed gently into my hands. It certainly felt to me like a crystal. It was warm to the touch, due to having been in my mother's hands before mine.

It sounds positively crazy, but I felt this – for lack of a better word – *strength* come through my body. It started in my hands and I could feel it stream through my forearms and biceps and shoulders and it just kept moving along in a wave through my head, torso, legs, and all the way to my toes. Yet, it was a calming sensation that made me feel secure that I could do anything and that I was invincible. I felt my heart pound a bit stronger and I gasped to catch my breath, as I discovered I had been holding my breath ever since Mom handed the crystal to me. As I started to instinctually open my eyes, Mom said it was okay to do so.

As my eyes opened, I looked directly into Mom's eyes, without looking at what was in my hands. "It's fluorite," I said smugly.

"How do you know?" she asked with a smile.

"I can feel its power," I calmly replied. I was not certain that I believed rocks had power, but I knew what I was feeling. It was unlike anything I had ever experienced before, so I had no choice but to just admit to the energy that was pulsating through my body. Somehow this stone was having a profound impact on me, and I knew beyond a shadow of a doubt that it certainly wasn't evil. It was simply power.

"Look at your hands," Mom softly said, with an ear-to-ear grin.

They weren't shaking. Not even a hint of a tremor. Not at all.

"Congratulations, my Little Dragon," Mom began, "you've officially begun to fully harness the power of fluorite."

"My power stone…" I said knowingly, looking at the crystal in my steady hands.

Mom picked up the quartz crystal again and started saying all these words I didn't comprehend about a circle of protection around us. Then she untied the blue satin cord from the silver velvet bag and pulled a deck of cards from the bag. Mom hadn't let me touch her tarot cards before, so I set the fluorite in my lap and reached for the cards. "Not yet," she deterred me. She held the quartz together with the cards and closed her eyes for a moment. Then, she handed the

128

deck to me and set the quartz on her left side, nearer the ocean. "Think about your question and as you're thinking about it, shuffle the cards. When you're done shuffling, place the cards in front of you however they tell you to do so."

I know Mom's a smart lady, really I do, but cards don't talk! But I trust her implicitly and with all the strange, inexplicable, magical sorts of awesome and lovely things that were occurring, I couldn't rightfully argue with her – particularly not before she gave me my first ever tarot reading! So, I began to shuffle. The oversized cards felt peculiar in my small hands. I realized that my thoughts were turning to Joey and then I had a flash of me as a grown up in a wedding dress, but I didn't see Joey in that image, which is okay because I'm just a nine and a half year old with a crush. I daresay I had a glimpse of me as a mother, chasing a redheaded toddler around in a yard overlooking the ocean. As I continued to shuffle, the cards seemed to have their own ideas as to how they would shuffle, and I felt that maybe Mom wasn't crazy when she said they'd tell me when I was done shuffling. One card jumped out of the deck, mid-shuffle, three feet away from me! I paused and looked at it in disbelief. Mom reached for it and placed it between us. "This one clearly has something to say," she said, smirking.

The images of love and of my future love life kept flooding me. I continued shuffling. Suddenly my mind thought "L-O-V-E" and with each letter I shuffled the deck one time, realizing my shuffling was over with the final letter of the word. I placed the pile of cards in front of me.

"Are you finished?" Mom asked.

"Yes," I calmly stated.

"What is your question?" Mom inquired.

"Can you tell me about my love life?" I asked.

"Of all the things you could find out about in the world, you want to know about your love life?" Mom questioned. "You're nine! Really?"

"Yes, Mom, it's what I want to know," I replied. She laughed. "What's so funny?" I asked.

"I always ask about my love life whenever I get a tarot reading, too," she confessed.

"Really?" I was stunned. "But you're married to Dad! You don't have a love life!"

"Persephone!!" she exclaimed. "Being married to your dad IS my love life, you goose!" We laughed.

"Well, I mean, you don't need to know about your love life because you already know who the love of your life is, Mom!" I tried to explain.

"I knew you were coming into my life before I had even met your dad, because of a tarot reading," Mom reminded me. I recalled the story I had been told time and again. In 1998, Mom received her first tarot reading, and she asked about her love life. The tarot reader told her about this man she was going to meet and that she was going to birth a dragon. She thought the lady was slightly crazy but she met Dad within days, they got married on New Year's Eve, 1998, and I was born February 7, 2000, in the Chinese Year of the Dragon. So Mom met the man the tarot lady described and birthed a Dragon.

One can't help but start to believe these things when they actually come true.

"So... you want to know about your love life..." she began. She did the card formation known as a Celtic Cross and as she turned the cards over I could see that there were depictions of dragons and unicorns on the cards. I was impressed that she had stories for every card that she flipped. She didn't quite seem like Mom when she was reading; she was more this... like mystical, psychic, magical tarot lady or something. It was kind of bizarre and really exciting. She didn't have any stories about me birthing a dragon or anything, but she did tell me that I would meet and marry the love of my life at a very young age. I tried to pinpoint how young, but the cards wouldn't say. They did hint that I shouldn't be surprised if I get married when I'm a teenager!

"Mom! That's in four years!" I interrupted.

"They didn't say *thirteen*," she reassured me, "so let's hope more like eighteen or nineteen?"

The thought of being married in ten years was still a lot for me to digest. And that I'd meet the love of my life at a young age? My mind was racing. What if I already know him? Maybe it *is* Joey? Or what if it's one of the gross boys in school? Eeeww, some of them pick their noses and eat the boogers! I don't want to marry one of them! Why had I asked the cards about my love life? I should've asked something more relevant, like what's the rest of fifth grade going to be like. But no, I had to ask about *love*, and now I knew, and apparently, I could meet the love of my life *any day*!

As my first ever tarot reading concluded, I noticed a glow on the horizon to my right, over the ocean. It was nearly dawn, and with the morning light, Mom extinguished the candles and sat with me to watch the sunrise.

"Thanks for the tarot reading, Mom," I said. "I am too young to get married," I fretted.

"Persephone," Mom said, giving me a hug, "it's just a tarot reading. They're just cards. Anything can change at any time and alter the course of how things actually go."

"Great, so I'm *not* getting the love of my life after all?" I complained.

"No, you will," Mom pacified. "You will find the love of your life when the time is right."

And as the sun sizzled the Atlantic Ocean to start this Halloween day, I realized that apparently the cosmic universe believed that the right time for me to meet and marry Mr. Right was much, much sooner than any of us anticipated. I only hope I'm ready for true love and recognize that it's this guy whenever he comes along.

By the time we had finished watching the sun take its place in the sky, picked up all the items from our early morning tarot reading, and hiked back to Erica's house, Coral, Marina, and Erica were awake and eating breakfast in the kitchen.

"Where did you two disappear to so early this morning?" Marina inquired.

"We went to watch the sunrise," Mom answered. Marina and Erica exchanged aggravated looks.

"Well, you could have seen the sunrise from here," Marina whined.

"I wanted to see it from the beach," Mom responded, heading immediately downstairs to prepare for the day. I followed her.

"Get ready fast! We have a busy day ahead of us!" Erica shouted down the stairs. The look on Mom's face at the overinvestment in our whereabouts and the overbearing barking of commands was priceless.

"How about you three go on ahead and we'll catch up," Mom proposed through shouting back.

"Coral needs Persephone to keep her company," Erica retorted.

"Well, we'll catch up," Mom insisted. Mom then turned to me, saying, "I'm a grown woman and you are my daughter. Nobody tells us what we're doing."

"What are we doing?" I whispered.

"I don't know," Mom admitted, "but it will be a hundred times better if it's not with them!"

"Mom!" I was astonished. Mom usually never says anything negative about anyone.

"I know you heard Coral refer to Erica as Marina's 'best friend,' Persephone," Mom revealed. I nodded in disbelief that Mom had caught that. "Yeah, I knew that wouldn't go over *your* head. And well, don't you just have a feeling that something's... off... in the pit of your stomach?" she challenged me.

"They're way too insistent to not lose sight of us," I concurred.

"And is it me or does it seem like they want to separate you and I?" she pondered.

"I got that feeling, too," I admitted.

Mom decided to get ready for the day and suggested I get some breakfast in the meantime. "Promise you will *not* leave this house without me, at all," Mom insisted.

"No way, no how, are they getting me out of here of my own free will, Mom," I agreed. I went back upstairs and found the three of them sitting around the kitchen table. "So, is there anything for breakfast?" I nonchalantly asked.

"Cereal or toast," Coral answered with a mouthful of mush.

"Great!" I exclaimed with too much energy. I saw there was some granola and I grabbed the box and a bowl. I love granola. It reminds me of preschool because it was oftentimes my snack.

"Want some yogurt with your granola?" Erica asked.

"That'd be swell," I replied. She got me a single serve container of yogurt from the refrigerator. "Thanks," I said.

"What's going on with your mom?" Marina asked. "It's like she's got some other agenda going on," she prodded.

"Oh, you know Mom," I dodged the question by saying nothing of consequence whatsoever. Little did I know that I'd set off a firestorm of backstabbing.

"Your mother is such a loner," Marina started. "We come down here for a girls' weekend and she isolates herself and keeps you away from us."

"You should come with us," Erica joined in, "as we're going to all the fun places that are authentic here in Salem."

"Erica lives here, so she knows more than the tourist junk your mom will do," Coral chimed in.

"What is wrong with you?" I asked, looking at Erica and Marina. "Attacking my mom to me? Really?"

"We didn't say that," Marina defended.

"Sure ya didn't," I accused. I grabbed the yogurt and headed back downstairs. "Thanks for breakfast. We'll be ready soon."

"Uh-oh, you're eating breakfast down here? What happened up there?" Mom asked, emerging from the bathroom, drying her hair with a towel.

"Mom, how can you stay friends with someone who you know backstabs you?" I asked.

"I have forgiven her one too many times," Mom coldly replied.

Just then Marina came running downstairs. "Demi, I'm sorry, I shouldn't have talked about you to Persephone," she explained. "It's just that you don't need me as your friend as much as I need you as my friend, and it hurts my feelings when you are perfectly happy going off to do your own thing on a girls' weekend."

"I'll always be completely content making my own choices in life, Marina," Mom explained. "I always have been, and I always will be. This isn't news."

"I'm not as independent as you," Marina stated, "I *need* my friends."

"I don't," Mom snapped.

"I know you don't," Marina acknowledged, "and that's what hurts the most. But enough fighting. It's Halloween, and Erica has so many fun plans for all of us today!"

"Well, I do suppose Persephone deserves the full Salem experience," Mom allowed.

"Oh, you are my *BEST* friend ever!" Marina exclaimed, hugging my mother.

"I know," Mom replied. "We'll be ready soon." Marina ran back upstairs.

"So now you have forgiven her *two* too many times, Mom?" I asked.

"Sometimes it's safer and easier to just let someone's mistakes go," Mom answered.

"Ah, so you *didn't* forgive her this time?" I deduced.

"Not even a little bit," Mom admitted, "but I just want a nice weekend. I don't want to fight or have her and Erica angry at us."

"Is Erica a bad person?" I inquired.

"I don't know Erica very well," Mom hedged, shrugging dismissively. As we all know, there's only one reason why Mom avoids answering a question. So therefore, I do believe Erica is... not a good person.

"Keep your friends close and enemies closer, huh?"

"Good advice, my Little Dragon, good advice."

chapter thirteen

M'Lady?

Little did I know that walking around Salem on Halloween would require us to wear special clothing. "We're wearing costumes all day?" I asked Mom when she pulled out a cheetah print cloak for herself.

"Well, when in Rome..." she shrugged.

"But we're in Salem, not Rome," I joked.

"Have you looked in your garment bag?" she inquired, nudging me towards my bag. I had indeed *not* yet opened it. Inside, I found a teal velour cape and a purple and green velour gown.

"Um, this is just too cool not to wear today!" I exclaimed. Suddenly I didn't care if it was a little weird to dress up all day – these clothes were just awesome! I quickly got dressed to fit in with the Salem locals.

When I was all done up in my fancy garb, I noticed that my head needed something. "Mom, do I get to wear a pointy hat, because we're in Salem where the witches hang out?" I asked.

"No, I have something special for you to wear on your head," she announced, handing me a velvet pouch. I opened it up and inside was a tiara with fluorite in it. "I had that made especially for you," she noted.

"Mom, it's fluorite!" I exclaimed excitedly.

"Why yes, yes it is," she laughed. "Gosh, you get so excited about fluorite."

"It's my power stone!" I reminded.

"Well then, they can't hurt you anymore today," she stated.

"They can't hurt either of us anymore today," I decided. Donning the fluorite tiara, I felt a surge of power swirl and plunge from my hair to my toes. Mom had added cheetah pants to her ensemble. "Mom, is cheetah your power print?"

"Well, remember my spirit animal is apparently the cat," she reminded.

"But you're allergic to cats, Mom," I pointed out. I was still unfamiliar with the concept behind one's "spirit animal," as although Mom has referred to the cat as hers, she hasn't ever explained what she meant by that.

"It's a long story," Mom delayed, "I'll tell you about it some other time." I sighed an annoyed sigh due to not hearing the story behind spirit animals yet again, but I agreed to the raincheck so as to allow us to go upstairs to join the others. Coral was dressed like a ballet princess or something with a lot of pink tulle as part of her outfit. Marina was wearing a black dress with an orange cape, and Erica was attired in a silver sequin dress with a red sequin cape and sparkly red shoes. Each of the three of them wore a pointy witch hat.

"Hi, witches," I joyously exclaimed.

"What are you wearing on your head?" Coral asked.

"It's called a tiara," I mocked, "not to be confused with a witches' hat."

"You have that evil stone in your tiara!" Coral recognized.

"Fluorite isn't evil," I explained.

"You are wearing fluorite?" Marina asked, shooting a look of curiosity at Erica.

"Yep," I answered, "and I like it."

"Why isn't she shaking?" Coral asked her mother.

"She's learned to control the power that fluorite has over her," Marina rationalized.

"So she IS evil!" Coral announced.

"So much for you being sorry," I snapped.

"Apologize, Coral," Marina directed.

"I'm sorry," Coral said.

"It means nothing when you don't actually mean it," I pointed out.

"I mean it," Coral defended.

"If you meant it, you wouldn't keep insisting that I'm evil," I explained.

"Why do *you* keep on insisting to have that evil stone?" Coral complained.

"Fluorite isn't evil, Coral," Erica jumped in. "Your little friend is just able to derive power from fluorite, so it makes her appear evil, but truthfully, it's just power. Whether she uses that power for evil or good is completely up to her."

"So what is it, Persephone, evil or good?" Coral pressed.

"That's for me to know and for you to find out," I teased. Coral screamed and ran to hide behind Marina. I guess she didn't get my humor. Oh well. Marina glared at me like I owed her bratty daughter an apology, but I didn't apologize, because frankly, I wasn't sorry.

We walked into town and went shopping and sightseeing. We hit all of Salem's historical sites and had lunch at a neat little restaurant. Everywhere we went, people were whispering and pointing at us. I found it odd that in several shops, the clerks stopped what they were doing to gawk at seemingly me and Mom, even though we weren't the ones wearing the pointy hats.

Mid-afternoon, Marina, Coral, and Erica wanted to go into yet another store that specialized in witchy stuff. Mom and I had seen enough cauldrons to last a fortnight, so we went to a little shop next door. They had shelves and shelves of tarot cards! "Aha, it's right where I remember it being," Mom said aloud when we walked in. "Check out the cards, and if any of the decks speaks to you, it's yours."

"Cards don't talk, Mom," I said, not quite getting her point.

"Did the cards talk this morning, Persephone?" she pressed.

"Ohhhh, right, okay, like *that*," I understood. I went to the first shelf and started looking at the titles of the decks.

"You have to actually look at the cards, not just the names of the decks, my Little Dragon," Mom advised. "Sometimes the box is deceptively cool or boring for how the deck truly is."

With that advice, I started pulling the boxes with sample decks off the shelves and flipping through the cards. Some of the pictures were not suitable for a nine year old's eyes. I daresay I'm not so sure some were suitable for *any* eyes, but apparently someone out there liked them, because they were for sale. Then I found them… a deck like no other… with actual *photographs* of unicorns! "Mom, how do they have photographs of unicorns?" I asked.

"Those are beautiful," she agreed. "I don't know how they have taken pictures of unicorns," she admitted.

"You don't believe in unicorns?" a boy, maybe thirteen or fourteen years old, approached us.

"Unicorns are mythical creatures," I explained.

"See, that's where you're wrong," he continued, "just because you haven't seen one doesn't mean they don't exist."

"Where have I heard that logic before?" I wondered aloud.

"Unicorns are very rare creatures who are intensely shy and wish to remain completely elusive to the majority of humans on the planet," he shared. "The photographer, Charlotte Kraft, has spent years of devotion to befriending the unicorns so as to allow her to photograph them."

"So that she can turn around and exploit them by selling those pictures to the tarot card companies?" I interrupted.

"It's not like that," the boy defended. "They are just too beautiful not to share with the world, and most people simply look at the cards and figure they're computer generated or created with Hollywood special effects. You two are the first customers who pondered that they were real photographs. Such thinking is clearly

141

indicative of membership in the elite inner circle of leadership among common witches." The teenage boy then bowed to my mother and dropped to one knee in front of me. "Forgive me, M'lady," he solemnly spoke, taking my hand and kissing it.

"For what?" I asked, completely baffled.

"For not assuming this position upon the onset of our conversation," he revealed. He looked like he was waiting for me to promote him to knighthood or something. "I meant no disrespect, M'lady, I simply was overcome with excitement in the moment of someone having inquired of the photographs. It is so rarely that I meet a truly powerful witch in this town."

"We're in Salem," I said incredulously. "Witches are everywhere, if you haven't noticed."

He looked up into my eyes, still holding my hand. He was searching for something within my eyes, within my face. "Forgive me, M'lady, for staring, but I realize now my previous error," he spoke softly. "You have no idea how powerful a witch you truly are!"

"That's rather obvious," I snidely replied, "because I'm not *even* a witch!" I giggled. "Now stand up, you're causing people to stare!"

He followed my command, adding, "From your lips to my ears I will follow you and your words until I no longer draw breath." As he rose from his knee, he kissed my hand again. I retracted my hand from his and looked at Mom with a "What on earth is going on here?" look. She shrugged. "M'lady, 'tis not because I kneel before you that others in this town stare, it is the recognition of the sheer power that you hold within you."

142

"Everyone has power," I explained. "Maybe I'm more in tune with mine, but everyone can do what I can do. Most people just don't bother to use those parts of their brains. I'm actually wicked normal."

"And so humble," he said under his breath. "Please accept the deck of tarot cards with the unicorn photographs as a gift from me."

"Don't be ridiculous," I chided, "we'll pay for them."

"It's no trouble at all, as this is my mom's shop. It would be our honor to give this deck to you. By the way, is there a deck that your sister would like today?" he asked.

"My sister? I don't have a sister!" I explained. Then I followed his eyes to my mother! "Oh, that's my mom!" I laughed.

"There's no way that she's old enough to be your mother," he grinned nervously in disbelief. "She's what, nineteen years old? And you're probably... thirteen?" I couldn't control the peals of laughter that erupted at his gross misjudgment of age.

"Well, I'm *nine* and Mom is ... well, she'd kill me to tell exactly, but let's just say you've got the decade wrong in her birthdate."

"Ohhhh," he said with a tone of understanding, "So, your mother is a vampire!"

"No!" I stopped him.

"Don't worry, M'lady, I remain your faithful servant and readily offer myself as protection to you if ever you need a shield of protection. Whether your family be vampire, witch, wizard, sprite, werewolf, merma-"

"How about mere mortals?" I interrupted.

"I meet mere mortals every day and the two of you are not mere mortals," he corrected.

"Actually, we are," Mom announced, stepping into the conversation. He stopped staring at me and stared at my mother's face, seemingly getting lost in studying it. "Do you have a staring problem, shield of my nine year old human daughter?"

"No, Matriarch of M'lady," he stammered. "You don't have a single wrinkle or gray hair," he pointed out. "You couldn't be of an age known as at least twenty-nine!"

"It's good genes, shield of my nine year old human daughter."

"Oh, forgive me, my name is Charles. Charles Hammock, also at your command, Matriarch of M'lady," the boy announced, bowing to my mother again.

"Charles, you're becoming much too over the top now," Mom explained. "It's getting bizarre and rather scary. Now, we'd like to purchase the deck of cards that spoke to my daughter, and I'd like this deck of leopard spot cards for myself. Do you run the register or should we take our business to an official employee?"

"You believe in tarot cards speaking to your daughter but you don't call yourselves witches?" Charles asked in confusion, walking towards the counter.

"Because we're not witches," Mom explained.

"What are you then?" Charles inquired as he reached the cash register.

"Vermonters," Mom answered.

144

As soon as Charles had completed our transaction and Mom and I had taken our bags, Coral, Marina, and Erica entered the store. "See the pointy hats, Charles? Those are witches," I pointed out.

"Those are but costumes, M'lady," Charles insisted.

"We got a silver cauldron!" Coral announced, running up to me. "What are you guys doing in here?"

"Shopping," I replied, unimpressed.

"What did you get?" Coral pressed, trying to look into my bag.

"Tarot cards," I answered with intentional annoyance in my tone, despite feeling such an excitement inside me, about my purchase, that it seemed as though it would cause me to burst.

"Really?" Coral asked jealously. "Mommy, Persephone got tarot cards and I want tarot cards too!" Coral rushed to Marina and began to pitch a fit, tugging at her dress like a toddler.

"Are you going to argue that those are witches *now*?" Charles whispered in my ear. I turned to reply to him only to realize that his face was much too close to me. We were nearly nose to nose when I faced him and feeling his breath on my face, I saw his eyes dart from my eyes to my lips and then he began to lean closer to me. I jumped back, completely freaked out. I hurried to Mom's side and grabbed her hand.

"Are you okay?" Mom asked.

"I think Charles was going to kiss me," I revealed. "It creeped me out."

"There's something unusual about that kid," Mom agreed and led me to the door to leave.

"Please don't leave M'lady," Charles shouted, hustling to the door in an effort to stop us.

"M'lady?" Erica snarled. Marina shot her a look that I can't quite describe, but the corners of her lips were straight, so I knew it wasn't exactly a happy look.

Mom opened the door and we exited the shop. I spotted a bench outside and sat on it, with Mom joining me. Apparently Charles saw that as his invitation to join us as well, as he followed us.

"Okay, Charles," I started, "I don't know why you're following us, but you're not being even a little secretive about it."

"I am your shield. I am your protector. I know you need me to save you from the evil forces I can feel in your environment," he announced.

"If you're referring to the three witches in your mom's store, they're longtime friends," I cautioned.

"You are friends with those demons?" he questioned.

"They're not demons, Charles," I laughed.

"M'lady, I fear you do not know those three as well as you believe you do," he insisted.

"The one with the orange cape has been my best friend since we were kids, Chuckster," Mom stated. "We don't know *you*, but we certainly know them, so if my daughter is telling you to get lost, skedaddle already, got it?"

"From your lips to my ears, Matriarch of M'lady," Charles announced, "but be reassured I shan't be far away, as I shall protect her from the demons at any cost and for all of time."

"Um, Stalker Boy, if you follow us around, I will call the cops on you, be assured of that," Mom threatened.

"I needn't follow her to keep her safe from harm, and I shall do just that," Charles vowed. He bowed to my mother and then to me, taking my hand and kissing it before retreating to the tarot shop.

"What a freak!" I exclaimed once he was out of earshot.

"You can say that again," Mom agreed.

"Don't tempt me too much, because I *might* say it again," I replied. Then we looked at each other with "get us out of here" looks and laughed heartily. We were trying to catch our breaths when Coral burst from the store, followed by Marina and Erica.

"Not only did Mommy buy me the coolest tarot cards ever, but I got a new boyfriend!" Coral exclaimed, running to us. "And his name is Char-les..." she said taunting.

I was speechless. Just speechless. Methinks someone is taking his vow to protect me just a teensy bit too seriously... unless, of course, he was absolutely correct about the level of danger that certain people brought into my life.

For the rest of our day walking around in Salem, Coral's giddiness was nauseating. She could not stop going on and on about Charles. "I'm joining Charles for dinner tonight!" she gloated. "He's my boyyyfriend!" she continued, "Oh, I think I'm in love!"

I rolled my eyes.

"Oh Coral, I'm so happy for you," Marina encouraged. She turned to my mother and said, "Demi, I really think Charles might be the one!"

I looked at my mother, who looked at me, and I rolled my eyes even harder.

"Persephone, don't be jealous!" Coral cautioned. "Be happy for me! I know how you feel about Charles, but Charles doesn't love youuu, Charles loves *ME*!"

Coral obviously had no concept whatsoever about how I felt about Charles. I wasn't jealous. I was merely annoyed. I realized, yet again, that my best friend is a buffoon. Seriously? She's claiming love and is hoping for marriage with a guy she *just* met, who almost kissed *me* earlier this afternoon, and who is a total yuck? I wanted to tell her everything, but I knew she wouldn't listen.

"I think Charles is going to kiss me tonight after dinner," she went on.

"That wouldn't surprise me," I mumbled, remembering his attempt to touch my lips with his, in his mother's shop earlier that afternoon.

"What was that?" Coral overheard me.

"I said I wouldn't be surprised if he kissed you," I began, "because he tried to kiss me when I was in the tarot card store earlier."

"Liar!" Coral defended, "You're so jealous of me and Charles that you're making things up to break us up! It won't work! He loves *ME*! He doesn't love *YOU*!"

"I don't want him," I admitted.

"That's not true and you *know* it!" Coral was unrelenting, "You think every guy loves you, but face it, this one didn't pick you! He picked *me*! He loves *me*! He's going to marry *me*! *You* don't get him! He didn't want to kiss *you*, he wants to kiss *ME*!"

"Wow, delusional much?" I muttered under my breath.

"Oh, you can have your 'I'm better than Coral' attitude all that you want, but you're *not* better than me, Miss Thang!" Coral tiraded. "I can't believe you're even claiming that he tried to kiss you! Really? He's *my* boyfriend, Persephone, you lose, game over, he's *MINE*!"

"Wow," I mumbled in disbelief that Coral would actually cop this much attitude towards me without any parental involvement to stop her. I looked up to find Marina or Mom and realized that they had stopped to look at something a few hundred feet back. I retreated to stand near them, hoping to escape the nutty lovebird. The maneuver didn't exactly work.

"Mom, tell Persephone that she is crazy," Coral begged Marina.

"Why is she crazy?" Marina asked.

"She says Charles tried to kiss her today," Coral tattled.

"Don't be ridiculous, Persephone," Marina scolded, "Charles is Coral's boyfriend, not yours."

"What? You don't even know what happened!" I snapped back.

"You have always been ridiculously competitive with my daughter," Marina accused, "and I don't like it."

"Wait, you think *I* am the competitive one?" I asked in disbelief.

"I'm sick of you constantly trying to best Coral," she continued, "and well, let's face it, she's got Charles and you don't."

"I don't want that jerk!" I announced.

"You were doing anything you could to capture his attention earlier," Marina suggested. "You're only calling him names now

149

because he isn't interested in you, he loves my daughter! And you're jealous!"

"Mom?" I turned to my mother. "Can you please do something to control your best friend?"

"Marina, you flinging unfounded accusations at my daughter is completely unacceptable," Mom said to her in a monotone, yet somehow rather scary, calm voice. "It is one thing for your flakey daughter to pick a fight with Persephone, but if Coral is unable to fight her own battle, you will NOT jump in to tag team attack my *nine* year old. She's a child, you're the adult. Leave my daughter alone."

"And what are you doing right now?" Marina asked snottily.

"I'm defending my child," Mom began.

"As I defended *my* child," Marina interrupted.

"You didn't let me finish," Mom snapped. "If you had *let* me finish, you would've heard me say, 'I'm defending my child *by* speaking directly to that menacing, spineless, inappropriate adult who was verbally attacking her.' You see, Marina, I'm not speaking to your foolish, giddy, nuisance of a child, I'm addressing *you*. How dare *you* speak *to* my daughter in anything less than a mature, role model way! Persephone is a child. Behave like the adult you allegedly are!"

"You're just jealous because that boy picked *my* daughter and not yours!" Marina defended.

"Thank you for actually addressing *me*, Marina, as now I can clear things up for you," Mom smugly replied. "Chuckster is a very creepy young man. I wouldn't want him anywhere near my daughter. If you think he's a catch, then you do not know him as

150

well as Persephone and I do. I can completely understand why your daughter is excited about having a boyfriend, but your job as a mother is to be the sensibility to her, and you're failing her miserably right now."

"Jealous! Just like your daughter!" Marina huffed and walked off. Coral trailed her.

"Charles isn't a bad kid," Erica, who had witnessed the whole fight, explained, trying to calm my mom and I down. "He's a bit different, but he's got a good heart. He's an honor student and comes from a good family."

"He tried to *kiss* me, Erica," I reiterated. "I don't think a guy is a good guy if he tries to kiss one friend and then asks her best friend to be his girlfriend."

"He has a little brother, if you want me to set you two up," Erica joked. I raised my eyebrow at her to suggest that I wasn't condoning that idea. "It's a good family," she insisted. "They're a well-known, respected, powerful Salem family."

"When you say 'powerful,' Erica, are you implying that they're witches?" Mom concluded.

"Of course," Erica shrugged, "as witches do hold the power here in Salem."

"I'm still not interested," I repeated, "and I have no use for the power of witches."

"Maybe not, but witches certainly have use for *your* power," Erica whispered under her breath and walked off towards Marina and Coral. I turned to Mom and shuddered.

151

"Are you as ready to go home as I am?" Mom asked. I hugged her. "They can't hurt you, my Little Dragon. Don't ever forget that, and don't ever let them."

"Why were Marina and Coral so mean to me?" I asked. "I only told the truth."

"You did nothing wrong," Mom reassured me. "Let go and let Karma take care of them."

"It's not okay for a grown-up to act like Marina did," I stated.

"No, it's not," Mom agreed, "so, maybe we should go to dinner with them tonight and see Karma in action?" Mom grinned one of her evil grins.

"I love you, Mom!" I laughed.

"I love you, too, my Little Dragon!" Mom whispered as she hugged me. We followed after Erica. "Is it almost suppertime?" Mom called to them. They acknowledged that it was, and we headed back to Erica's.

Suddenly, I had a lion-sized appetite for tonight's dinner.

chapter fourteen

Dinner and a Show

Back at Erica's house, Erica announced we would be dining at an upscale, popular, local spot that overlooked the ocean. As much as Mom and I wanted to freshen up, Erica insisted that our costumes would be the perfect addition to our Halloween dinner. So after deciding what layers of clothing would be most sensible for the nighttime versions of our outfits, we simply primped and preened and refreshed our hairstyles and Halloween makeup.

When Mom and I emerged to Erica's kitchen to await our departure for dinner, we looked like sensible, warm forms of our previous selves. A turtleneck under a dress and a fuzzy cloak are smart additions for New England Halloween nights. My fluorite tiara was again atop my red tresses, albeit with a set of cheetah print earmuffs, courtesy of Mom's innate ability to be ready for anything.

Erica came to the kitchen in a black evening dress with a black shawl and knee-hi black boots that had heels so high on them that I wasn't sure how she would ever walk in them. She had brilliant red lipstick and smoky eyes, and her hair was now perfectly curled into a flip, with a different black witch hat as the finishing touch.

"Wow, Erica, you look fantastic!" I complimented.

"Thanks," Erica smiled, "I had better, as Halloween *is* my favorite night of the year!"

Marina appeared next, wearing a sleeveless royal blue gown, long royal blue gloves, black cloak, and a royal blue witch's hat. She looked a lot like the evil queen from one of those childhood fairy tales, but maybe I'm judging more on the personality she exhibited this afternoon than on her ensemble this evening. She smiled a phony smile. "Oh, Persephone, are you still wearing that same getup you've worn all day?"

"Of course, Marina," I contemptuously answered. "Unlike yourself, I am merely wearing my Halloween *costume.*"

"Are you saying I'm a witch?" Marina questioned. I didn't answer. I didn't feel like being dragged into another fight. Besides, I didn't *say* she was a witch. I merely implied it.

"Of course you're a witch, Marina," Erica interjected, "I mean, look at your hat!" She cackled. Marina cackled, too. I was relieved that Erica had broken up the tension. They exchanged air kisses and waved their fingers at one another in a way that clicked their long, fake, fingernails together. Then they threw their heads back and cackled again. It certainly seemed to me that they took this storybook witch concept way too seriously.

154

Coral took the longest to get ready for dinner. I assume her preparation time was in response to her inner need to look perfect for Charles. If I ever take too long getting ready for some guy who isn't worth my time, please do say something to me, because I now know from experience that it's highly annoying to wait for someone to get dolled up over some freakazoid we met at a witchy shop earlier in the day.

When I saw Coral, I was taken aback by how much she was apparently trying to resemble me. She was now wearing an aqua colored gown with crinoline and a purple cloak. Her shoes looked like aqua sequined ballet slippers, and they were completely impractical in the autumn streets of Salem. But the crowning jewel of her evening attire… atop her straightened hair, a tiara!

"Oh, Coral, you look like a princess!" Marina cooed. She whipped out a camera and snapped more pictures than I could count, even if I had *tried* to tally them. "My big girl is going on her first date!" She clicked more photos. "Demi, don't you remember when the girls were just babies, and look, now they're going on dates! Well, at least my *Coral* is going on dates."

"Oh, Marina, you must be so proud to have raised a nine year old who needs to have a boyfriend to feel good about herself!" Mom said snidely.

My jaw dropped at Mom's rebuttal and I mouthed the word "Wow!" to her. I didn't expect Mom to be so catty back at Marina. Mom glanced at me a purposely innocent look and shrugged as if to suggest she didn't know what I was talking about.

"My tiara is better than yours," Coral bragged, "because it doesn't have that evil fluorite in it!"

"Wow," I said out loud this time.

"Yeah, I know I look so good that 'Wow' is all you can say," Coral boasted. "Charles will never forget tonight and how amazing I look. This will be the best Halloween ever!"

"Coral, you might try a little humility towards your best friend," Erica suggested.

"A best friend doesn't try to steal her best friend's boyfriend," Coral replied.

"Coral, I don't like Charles," I interjected. "In fact, I'm glad *you* are his girlfriend. You two seem well matched." I smirked. They did seem right for each other.

"I don't believe you," Coral snapped.

"I'm hungry, can we get to dinner already?" Mom requested, changing the topic.

"Oh, yes, my baby is off to her first date," Marina noted, straightening out Coral's tiara. "You look beautiful tonight, Coral. You will have Charles mesmerized." I giggled. My brain was thinking about how Coral wouldn't be capable of mesmerizing anyone with her argumentative conversational skills, so we can all only hope that her looks will get her far in life.

We walked to the restaurant, Marina snapping pictures nonstop. She should've taken the camcorder, as it would've been less work for her to capture the evening. I can't imagine being that caught up in such a trivial moment. We're *nine*! It's not true love at nine. It's not an actual boyfriend at nine. Am I missing something here? Am I jealous that Coral is getting all the attention tonight? *Am* I jealous that Charles chose Coral? Charles made it clear that he was devoted to *me* and *my* protection and safety. Am I doubting his word? Maybe I'm just jealous because I don't have a boyfriend? Or maybe, just maybe, Mom and I are currently surrounded by some very weird people. I wondered what Dad was doing right about now. I wished I was home, too, instead of dealing with The Coral Show.

We arrived at the restaurant and Charles was waiting at the door. He had a peach colored rose in his hand. "Coral, you're enchanting tonight!" he exclaimed when she reached him. "I brought a coral rose for my Coral Reef, but it pales when you're near!" He threw the rose over his shoulder and took both of her hands in his.

"Why'd you throw away my rose?" Coral asked, confused by his gesture. I laughed. "It isn't funny, Persephone!" Coral insisted, stomping her foot.

"Actually, it *is* funny, because he's saying that you're more beautiful than the rose so you wouldn't want something ugly like that, Coral," I explained. I pushed by them and opened the door to go in the restaurant.

"No, M'lady, allow me." Charles dropped Coral's hands and grabbed the door from me, holding it open so I could go in.

"She's not your lady, I am!" Coral shouted, shoving me aside so she would enter before me. She grabbed Charles's jacket and pulled him right behind her, so that he would be unable to hold the door for the rest of us. Marina laughed at her mannerless daughter, and then picked up the rose from the ground.

"She'll want this as a souvenir of the evening," Marina explained, entering the restaurant and holding the door open for Erica to follow her. The door closed behind Erica, and Mom and I were still outside.

"Are you sure we can't just make a run for it, Mom?" I asked.

"We'll miss all the fun if we do!" Mom hinted.

"You do realize I'm willing to take that chance," I warned.

"I'm not missing out on *this* Karmic retribution," Mom laughed. "Now let's get in there!"

For whatever reason, when we entered the restaurant, the table had already been seated and the open seat for me was next to Charles, with Coral on his other side. A boy approximately appearing around my age sat on the other side of the empty chair. Mom's seat was between a woman who introduced herself as Charles's mother and Erica. Next to Charles's mother, a boisterous, jovial, burly man introduced himself as Charles's father, and he named the boy next to me as Charles's brother, Drew.

"So you're the chick known as M'lady, right?" Drew whispered to me.

"Um, yeah, I guess?" I whispered back.

"My big brother is such a freak," Drew whispered, shaking his head. "Why can't siblings be cool?"

"I don't have any siblings," I admitted.

"I envy you," Drew confessed, narrowing his eyes. "I would give anything to be an only child, albeit with different parents."

"I love my parents," I declared.

"Can your parents adopt me then?" Drew asked. "Mine are freaks like my brother."

"If my parents adopted you, you wouldn't be an only child," I explained.

"I think I can live with one sister who isn't a witch, as opposed to a whole family who is," Drew revealed.

"Your parents are actually witches?" I asked.

"Yep," Drew replied, "and Charles, too."

"I didn't know boys could be witches," I admitted.

"Yep," Drew replied, "not all witches wear pointy hats."

"Apparently some people didn't get that message," I whispered, glancing purposely at certain dinner guests. We laughed.

"Behave yourself, Drew," Drew's father sneered at him.

"Yes, sir," Drew answered, dryly.

I appreciated sitting next to Drew because conversing with him distracted me enough so I didn't have to stomach watching The Coral and Charles Show. They held hands and looked into each other's eyes and whispered into one another's ears, smiling and giggling, as if on cue. When Coral excused herself to "powder her nose," Charles turned to me the moment she was out of the room.

"M'lady, you know I'm doing this all for you," he quickly spoke. "I do not want you to ever feel as though I am choosing the lovely Coral over you," he explained.

"Really, Charles, I don't mind if you do," I replied.

"I gave you my word that I will be your shield, and I will protect you from evil," Charles continued. Drew, overhearing the conversation, started snickering uncontrollably.

159

"Coral's not evil, Charles," I assessed.

"No, she's not," he agreed, "but with her in my life, I keep you in my life, despite M'lady wanting a restraining order against me."

"Oops, did I make it that obvious?" I asked, flippantly.

"Someone with no intelligence whatsoever would figure out your inherent distrust and dislike of me, M'lady," Charles admitted.

"Oh, so you *did* figure it out," I smirked.

"Good one," Drew piped in.

"M'lady, you protest too much," Charles started. "I daresay you care far more deeply for me than you're willing to admit, and I respect that and remain faithfully your servant and protector."

"Not very faithful to be dating her best friend, Charles," Drew added.

"Stay out of this, menace to Salem," Charles snapped.

"Boys, settle down," I attempted to quell their verbal combat, as I was seated betwixt them.

"M'lady, do not allow my brother to influence you in life whatsoever, for he shuns his roots, ancestry, and predetermined path," Charles cautioned.

"Oh, in much the same way as I will continue to insist that I am *not* a witch, Charles?" I asked.

"Very much the same way, M'lady, except you would never turn your back on your powers."

"Drew, you have powers?" I asked with curiosity.

"So they tell me," Drew reluctantly admitted.

"Can I get a demonstration sometime?" I inquired, heart inexplicably aflutter with intrigue.

160

"Whatever," Drew agreed.

"So, before fair Coral returns and I am forced to resume my cold shoulder to you, know, M'lady, that I am devoted to you out of honor, and I will remain your shield and protector as long as need be," Charles promised.

"So 'need be' is still occurring now?" I asked.

"'Need be' is about to become most evident, M'lady," Charles cautioned, grabbing my hand and kissing it. "Be well, M'lady!"

"You're not going to argue that my brother isn't a freak, right?" Drew asked, redirecting my attention, as Coral returned to the table.

"Glad you're back, Coral! Your best friend was flirting with your boyfriend," Marina tattled.

"Seriously, Marina?" I chastised her, "You're making up stories just to hurt your daughter? That is rotten!" Marina looked floored that I had spoken the truth in front of everyone.

"Mom, you're trying to hurt me?" Coral inquired.

"I would never flirt with your best friend," Charles defended, "and although she and I do speak, we're merely friends."

"Just friends, Persephone?" Coral asked.

"Yes, Coral, just friends," I reassured her. "I have already told you that I am happy that he's *your* boyfriend!" Charles shot me a glare, that Coral didn't detect, that hinted strongly of his being offended that I would imply that I would not like to be his girlfriend.

"Mom, why did you lie to me?" Coral demanded.

"I didn't lie, Coral, it looked like she was flirting with him," Marina explained.

"Liar!" Coral exclaimed.

"Marina, why *do* you constantly feel the need to get involved in the girls' business?" Mom inquired. "They can sort out their love dramas without the intrusion of us old people."

"Oh, I see, it's gang up on Marina time," Marina complained.

"Get a life, you melodramatic bully," Mom retorted. "Stop trying to cause trouble at my daughter's expense!"

"Persephone, you're so fortunate to have someone to fight your battles," Marina gloated.

"Seriously, Marina! Put a sock in it!" Mom rolled on, "I will not tolerate you antagonizing my *child*! If you're gonna pick a fight, at least pick it with an adult, you stupid cow!"

"What did you call me?" Marina seethed.

"You heard me," Mom spoke without a hint of remorse in her voice.

"Take it back," Marina challenged.

"Or what?" Mom escalated. "You know you'll never win against me, so you try to ruin life for my daughter? I will not let you hurt her for a millisecond."

Marina jumped up from her seat and quickly said a bunch of words I didn't understand. She moved her arms, flailing her hands while she chanted, and when she reached the last word, she lunged her arms in front of her as though she were passing an invisible basketball, straight at my mother. From her hands sprang a vibrant jagged blue beam of light that almost resembled sideways lightning. Mom calmly held up her hand and the blue lightning stopped about one inch from her hand and bounced straight back at Marina, rocketing her off of her feet and backwards across the restaurant until she smashed back first into a wall, landing with a tremendous thud.

"Wowzers," Charles's father said, in complete awe.

"That was awesome!" Coral exclaimed before rushing over to her mother's side.

"Threefold," Erica whispered, her eyes as big as saucers.

"So, is it time for dessert yet?" Mom asked, seemingly unscathed. All eyes were on Marina, who simply sat against the wall that had stopped her backward flight.

"Coral, say goodbye to Charles," Marina whimpered. "We're leaving." She agonized to her feet and limped out of the restaurant. Coral ran to Charles who gave her a big hug goodnight. Then, in hysterical tears, she ran after Marina. Erica also rose, to accompany them presumably back to her home.

"I'll pack up your bags and leave them on the back porch," Erica whispered to my mother. "I don't mean to kick you out, but I can't welcome you back into my home while Marina is there. I hope you understand. My loyalty is to Marina."

"You do what you need to do, Erica," Mom replied. Erica hurried out of the restaurant.

"Mom, where are we going to stay now?" I asked.

"You'll stay with us, of course!" Charles's mother invited.

"Thank you for your generous offer, but we'll make other arrangements," Mom graciously declined. She whipped out her cell phone. "If you'll excuse me, I have a phone call to make." She smiled and went to the other side of the room where she could still see me, but where she could not be heard. After her phone call, she returned. "Your dad will be here in about four hours," she told me.

"What are we going to do until then?" I inquired.

"We'll show you haunted Salem!" Charles's mother announced.

"You'll enjoy the haunted stuff," Drew reassured me.

"Really?" I asked. "I can't think of enjoying anything after what's gone on tonight."

"Trust me," Drew continued, "it's fun times. You'll like it."

"Yes, M'lady, you shall be accompanied by myself and Drewius this evening," Charles added.

"Drewius?" I asked.

"Told you my brother is a weirdo," Drew concluded.

After dinner, we, indeed, got the tour of the haunted houses and haunted ghost walks and all things spooky and eerie and creepy in Salem that became even more magnified with the knowledge that it was Halloween night. All things considered, it *was* fun, and the four hours passed quickly. Before we had finished all the hoopla, Mom's cell phone rang. Dad was in Salem, ready to pick us up. Anticipating our departure, Charles and Drew both gave me their email addresses so that we could keep in touch.

Then, we bid adieu to the Hammock family, thanking them for their tremendous hospitality, and we headed off to the appointed place to meet up with Dad. The eventual conversation with Mom and Dad about my newfound need for an email account would need to wait for another time, as I anticipated that concept would go over like a lead balloon, and we had all already endured enough altercations for one night.

164

chapter fifteen
Family First

I don't know if Dad was happier to see Mom and me or if we were more relieved to see him, but being together brought each of us a sense of peace and safety. Reunited in the family car, we directed him to Erica's house where he went to the back porch to get our bags. After depositing them in the trunk of the car, he climbed into the driver's seat and asked, "Are we ready to go back to Vermont?"

"Aren't you too tired to drive, Dad?" I inquired.

"Naah, I'll be fine," Dad reassured me. "You sleep and your mom will keep me awake with stories from the weekend."

As much as I wanted to hear Mom retell the stories, my eyes would not allow me to stay awake to hear them. I dozed off and dreamt of Coral and Charles getting married. Drew was the Best Man and I was the Maid of Honor. When the celebrant got to the part about objections, Charles actually objected saying that he wanted to marry ME! Coral threw her bouquet of flowers at him and stormed down the aisle, calling the whole thing off! Oh, what a horrible, dreadful, terrible, disgusting, dream! I woke up from the nightmare and found I was at home, in my own bed. A sense of relief and calm overtook me. I closed my eyes so I could fall back asleep.

Suddenly, my eyes popped open with an awful thought! Marina and Mom were no longer friends. Therefore, Coral and I were no longer friends. I would never be her Maid of Honor. I would probably never see or speak to her again! As soon as the thought had fully crossed my mind, a slightly more disturbing realization came over me. Frankly, maybe the end of that "friendship" was not such an awful thing after all. With that in mind, my eyes closed peacefully, and I resumed my restful slumber for the remainder of the night.

The next morning, Dad greeted me as I entered the living room, where he was sitting, drinking coffee, and watching TV. "So Squirt, you had a rather exciting Halloween!" he teased.

"You could say that again, but please don't," I responded, still groggy from the events of the last twenty-four hours. "Is Mom okay?"

"She's still sleeping," Dad replied.

"How did she know how to do... um," I paused, not knowing what to call it. Then I put my hand up the way Mom had done. "You know, THAT!" I pointed to the gesture with my other hand.

"Your mom doesn't believe in witchcraft and therefore it cannot hurt her," Dad stated calmly.

"Seriously?" I asked, astounded. "That's all that it takes to battle evil?"

"Pretty much, Squirt," Dad smiled.

"So, if I don't believe in witchcraft, then witchcraft can't hurt me?" I summarized.

"More or less," Dad reassured.

"But I believe I can make things happen by saying them, and I believe I sometimes dream about things that actually happen," I said, slightly confused.

"Are you a witch?" Dad calmly asked, clearly in an effort to aid my understanding.

"No," I said hesitantly.

"Then it's not witchcraft, and you can believe in all the powers you naturally have," Dad concluded. "Your mother has this almost cat-like, natural ability to always land on her feet, in any and all circumstances, and she has an uncanny aptitude to protect each member of this family from harm, so Marina's little light show would never *ever* be powerful enough to hurt her."

"Methinks m'lord and m'lady are talking about me behind my back," Mom joked as she came into the living room.

"Oh, Mom! I'm so glad you're okay!" I ran over to hug her. "Even if you do now talk like Charles!"

"Chuckster is so ghastly," Mom recalled. "His age-appropriate, funny, cuter little brother seemed much more your type," she teased.

"Drew is startlingly easy-going and normal," I admitted. "He's adamantly opposed to the witch lifestyle of his family."

"The Hammock family was very kind to give us the tour of Salem's ghostly stuff last night," Mom reminded.

"That was nice of them," I agreed. There was an awkward pause. Clearly someone needed to address the elephant in the room. Mom managed to find a way to proceed with dignity and grace.

"Marina has been texting me all morning," she simply stated.

"I hope you haven't been responding," Dad admitted.

"I haven't answered yet, but I can't ignore her forever," Mom muttered, shifting uncomfortably.

"Um, yeah, actually, you can," Dad said with evident irritation in his tone.

"She's just going to keep calling," Mom countered.

"We'll go get you a new cell phone with a brand new number today," Dad levied.

"You want her out of my life that badly?" Mom asked.

"Yes," Dad confessed. Then, there was an awkward silence. I sensed that it was my cue to disappear so that they could have a grown-up conversation.

"I'm going to go unpack my stuff from the trip," I explained. "You two talk." I hurried to the kitchen where I found my bags that had evidently been barely brought into the house way-too-late last night, or early this morning, depending on how one looks at it. I carried my stuff to my room and began to put my items where they belong. I hung up the clean clothes, threw the dirty laundry into the hamper, and placed my toiletries back onto the bathroom shelf.

It wasn't until I had put everything away that I realized I was missing something. "Mom!" I called, "Mom!!" Mom and Dad appeared quickly in my doorway.

"What's up, Persephone?" Mom asked.

168

"Have you seen my tarot cards?" I inquired.

"Marina has them," Mom answered.

"Marina?" I repeated. "How do you know that?"

"She told me in one of her text messages," Mom explained. "She's holding them hostage so that we'll talk to her and Coral ever again. I'm sorry, Kiddo."

"Guess I'll have to find another deck of tarot cards that speak to me," I relented, dejected. The memory of Charlotte Kraft's beautiful unicorn photographs bombarded my mind and despite my efforts to be strong, my lip stuck out in a pout.

"Sometimes things aren't meant to be," Mom hinted, in an attempt to pacify my sadness.

"So, are we going cell phone shopping?" I inquired, curious as to the outcome of the adult conversation I had missed downstairs.

"Yep," Dad replied.

"Wow, I can't believe you're really done with Marina," I revealed, shaking my head in disbelief.

"I have no use for an alleged *best friend* who would verbally attack my child the way she targeted you this weekend," Mom replied. "She can apologize until she's blue in the face, but I cannot allow her to be anywhere in your environment."

"What about your environment, Mom?"

"No," she stated, "your environment *is* my environment, and I'll always pick you and your dad over anyone else, no question. My family is first and foremost to me and I will always do anything to keep you and your dad safe and happy. I like to think that our family is an all or nothing commodity; give all of us love and respect or get nothing from any of us, whatsoever. Our lives are way too fleeting and precious to waste time on people who don't enhance them."

"And I feel the same way as your mom does, but she puts it much more eloquently than I could," Dad suggested, wrapping his arms around Mom.

At that moment, I realized exactly why Drew wanted to be part of *my* family. I giggled as I hurried over to join the 'Rents in a group hug, and I proudly announced, "I've got the best family *ever!*"

chapter sixteen

Thanksgiving Recipes

Autumn in Vermont goes by very quickly. Maybe it only seems to speed along because it is only ever a matter of time before snowflakes fall and winter blankets the state for about six months. The first half of November was such a blur of activity that it passed before I even realized that we were almost entering that most wonderful time of the year - the holiday season.

In my opinion, Thanksgiving is *the* kickoff for the holiday season. By then, retail stores are definitely decked out to attract shoppers. Oftentimes, there's been at least one snowfall that makes the ground white, even if it is completely melted on Thanksgiving Day. And the surest telltale sign of the onset of the holiday season... for every Thanksgiving Day that I can recall, Santa Claus comes down from the North Pole to provide the final hurrah of the parade! Mom and I always stop whatever meal preparations we're doing and run to the television to watch him make his annual appearance.

So, when Mr. Harper announced that our class had been invited by our town's newspaper, the *City Times*, to submit our responses when asked, "How do you make a Thanksgiving meal?" I nearly jumped out of my seat! First, the CITY TIMES wanted us to write something for them? Second, I totally know how to make a Thanksgiving meal, because we always go to Grampy's house for Turkey Day and he's the best cook ever and I'm always his assistant! And third, this announcement made me suddenly realize that Thanksgiving was only a week away!

Joey looked at me like I was making a scene. "Are you okay?" he mouthed at me. I nodded, albeit overzealously. My mind was racing with thoughts of all the delicious dishes that Grampy and Grammy served every Thanksgiving. As soon as Mr. Harper passed out the lined paper, my hand was off like lightning, writing what would surely be a how-to manual on doing Thanksgiving right.

Whereas my classmates had completed their first drafts in about a half hour, I was still embellishing the appetizers in my story. "A last minute dollop of orange sherbet adorns the top of the citrus fruit salad that should be made up several days before." The other students met with one another for their conferences, but I just kept on writing.

"Persephone, keep in mind this is a newspaper article, not a novel!" Mr. Harper encouraged.

"Maybe you should have reminded me of that before I reached the side dishes, Mr. Harper," I said with a laugh. He let me stay in at recess to keep writing. Truth be told, I didn't want to go outside in the gray November weather. Brr. No, thank you, I'd rather write the recipe for turkey, and that's just what I did. I put every detail I could recall. I sincerely hoped that anyone reading our recipes didn't mistake them as actual recipes, because my classmates finished their responses way too quickly to have the accurate level of details necessary to duplicate a recipe, and even I couldn't remember if the oven temperature was supposed to be set at 350. Hey, I'm nine, don't blame it on me if your turkey comes out raw! Just keep it in the oven until it's fully cooked!

Mr. Harper wasn't on recess duty, so he returned to the classroom to check in on me after the rest of the kids were out on the playground. "May I read what you have written so far?" he requested. He read carefully, a smile crossing his face every now and again. When he finished, he addressed me, "May I request that you stop writing this now?"

"Aren't you supposed to encourage your students to write until they can write no more?" I asked, puzzled.

"Of course! However, the *City Times* is publishing a total of one article from all of the responses from your class," he explained. "They can't print all that you have already written."

"So nothing else I write matters?" I was hurt.

"I don't mean it like that," Mr. Harper began, "just when the class gets back from recess, I'm going to ask each student to pick out the recipe that they think that they described best. I want you to be our turkey!" I couldn't help but burst into laughter. "What's so funny?" he inquired.

"You just said you want me to be a turkey," I chuckled, "I don't think you're supposed to call students turkeys, Mr. Harper!"

"Ohhh, yeah, okay, bad choice of wording," Mr. Harper admitted. "How about I want your description of how to make a turkey to be printed in the *City Times*?"

"Really?" I asked, "Is it that good?"

"I'm shocked that you wrote it from memory," Mr. Harper praised. "Are you sure you don't have a cookbook or two stowed away in your desk, Persephone?"

"Mr. Harper," I scoffed, "of course I don't!"

"I know, I was just joking," he confessed. "So although I think your recipe is perfect the way it is, you're *you* and you'll want to edit it for whatever reason, so while the other students are working on their appetizers, side dishes, and desserts, you can tinker your turkey description as you see fit."

"I actually was quite pleased with how it turned out," I gleamed.

"Good!" Mr. Harper agreed, "I'll hang onto it then, and you can play a game on the computer while your classmates finish up." I loved playing the school's computer games, but I rarely had time to play because I was always rewriting or doing extra credit or reading a book. "At the end of the day, each student will read her or his recipe in front of the rest of the class, and I'll bring the recipes to the *City Times* office after school this afternoon."

"That's cool, Mr. Harper!" I said, without really listening, as I was still simply excited for my computer time.

In between blasting math facts, I noticed the class returned from recess and sort of overheard Mr. Harper explain that he wanted each student to choose only one part of the meal – the best recipe of their Thanksgiving – and to focus their writing on that part. I didn't wind up getting too much computer time, as my classmates don't revise their writing to the same perfectionist degree that I do. I was actually quite anxious to hear their recipes, though I was nervous that my piece wasn't good enough, as I had not taken my typical amount of rewriting time. "Who wants to read their recipe first?" Mr. Harper requested.

Skye's hand shot up first. She wrote about green bean casserole. Yuck. I don't like green beans. But that's okay, cuz I'm not too fond of Skye, either. I made a mental note that I never want to go to Skye's house for Thanksgiving, if that is the best recipe of the meal.

Joey wrote about his grandma's pies – mincemeat, pumpkin, and apple. We always have pie at our Thanksgiving, too, but since I'm spoiled rotten, there's always chocolate pie for me, as it's my favorite! Freddie told how to make mashed potatoes. Oh, I love mashed potatoes with lots of butter – yum! Jodie went on and on about yams. Ew, I can't even say "yams" without wrinkling my nose! Deena told about lasagna being one of her family's traditional Thanksgiving dishes. I love lasagna, but I would never think of it for Thanksgiving! Sam loves stuffing. He didn't give much information on the recipe aspect of it, but he definitely praised it as the best part of holiday meals!

Danielle's recipe made me laugh out loud. Mr. Harper shot me a look like I shouldn't laugh, but I couldn't help myself! She was writing about cranberry jelly. So as not to get in trouble for plagiarism, I'll give her full credit for this recipe. "First, open the can of cranberry jelly. Mom says use a can opener. Next, dump the can of cranberry jelly onto the fancy yellow glass dish. Mom says be careful not to break it. Last, eat it. Mom says leave some for the rest of the family." How could someone hear that and not be falling over in stitches? Seriously? Dump it out of the can is a recipe? I'm laughing just thinking about it! Again, full credit for that exemplary written piece goes to Danielle – I did *not* write it and take absolutely *no* credit for that vivid and detailed description.

Tisha apparently has whoopie pies for Thanksgiving. I don't like whoopie pies. Arnold wrote about corn three ways. His dad is a chef, so their meal is gourmet. The corn three ways featured a corn salad, cornbread, grilled corn on the cob with garlic butter, and kettle corn. Apparently chefs can't count because that's actually four takes on the featured ingredient, corn. Curt's essay admitted that his favorite part of the Thanksgiving feast is having leftovers for sandwiches. And the new girl, Katie, raved on and on about making dumplings and egg rolls with her family.

"It's your turn, Persephone," Mr. Harper reminded.

Having heard all of the other recipes, I knew that mine contained a much deeper level of detail than my classmates' recipes. I was no longer nervous to present my recipe in front of the class, and I bounded to the front of the room with tremendous enthusiasm. "This is how to make turkey," I began. The first part of my recipe explained how it's essential to make sure the turkey is completely defrosted prior to the morning of Thanksgiving. I admitted, "I am not sure exactly what transpires if you do *not* do this critical step, because Grampy has never messed up. I think it burns to a crisp on the outside and is raw on the inside, but I don't want to find out the hard way, so I just do like Grampy says. Then you preheat the oven

176

to 350 degrees. As you're waiting for the temperature to warm up, you begin preparing the turkey by washing it really well." I then did mention that soap is not used to wash turkeys, even though we fifth graders need to be using it when *we* bathe. "When you're washing the turkey, you have to reach inside the carcass to remove the sack that contains the heart and gizzards." Some of the girls made squeamish faces when I talked about pulling the gooey guts out, and the boys made faces, too, but they were certainly different than the grossed-out faces, being more of the fascinated kind. I grinned and continued, "After the turkey is washed thoroughly, you place the large bird into an even larger roasting pan." I described the procedure for stuffing the turkey, putting pats of butter on the turkey, seasoning the turkey, and tying the legs together with the special cooking string so that the stuffing doesn't fall out while it's cooking.

"Once the turkey is fully prepared and the oven has reached the temperature of 350 degrees, the turkey is placed in the oven for about four to six hours to cook, depending on the size of the turkey you have selected." I cautioned not to just put the turkey in the oven and walk away, as you need to baste it every few minutes. Turkey basters are so cool! They suck up the juices from the pan when you squeeze the bulb once and then squirt them out when you squeeze the bulb again! Such a simple but marvelous invention!

"When the turkey's little thermometer has popped out to indicate it's done, and the skin is golden brown, as long as an appropriate amount of time has passed, then the turkey can be removed from the oven." I encouraged being very careful when removing the pan with the drippings and the heavy, large bird, from the oven and to always use potholders when touching hot items. "You can check the doneness of the turkey by cutting into it and ensuring it is not pink inside." All that was left to do is to remove the stuffing, carve the turkey, and turn the juices into succulent turkey gravy. "Then serve and enjoy!"

I hadn't realized how long it took me to read my recipe, and the schoolbell rang just as I finished, dismissing us for the day. My classmates all hustled to get out of there as quickly as possible, but I didn't have a reason to rush, as I'd just go to Mom's classroom, like always. After everyone had piled out, I helped Mr. Harper straighten up the classroom a bit. "I'm sorry I laughed at some of the recipes," I mentioned with a smirk.

"I'm very proud of my class," Mr. Harper beamed. "It's outstanding that no two students wrote about the same Thanksgiving item, and each clearly brought his or her own voice to the assignment."

"Oh, come on, Mr. Harper, you *know* you were laughing on the inside, too!" I interjected.

"Some of the pieces were so forthright and honest that they could be duplicated in the kitchen by most anyone who reads them," he defended, "and their simplicity will be endearing to readers."

"In other words, you have great self-control of your need to burst into laughter at ridiculous writing," I deduced.

"And you would do well to learn that power as well, Persephone, if you don't want to go through life hurting other people's feelings," he argued.

"I didn't hurt her feelings," I defended. "She doesn't care what I think."

"Well, it hurt my feelings that you would laugh at someone else's best effort," he explained.

"I thought she was joking! I didn't know *that* was her best effort!" I blurted out.

"It was, and it was actually a well-constructed piece. And you're right, you didn't hurt her feelings, but not because she doesn't care what you think, but because she didn't hear you," Mr. Harper stated, shooting me another one of his glares.

"You're making me feel like pondscum, Mr. Harper," I admitted.

"I have high expectations for you, Persephone," he encouraged.

"I'm only nine, Mr. Harper," I pouted, "I mess up sometimes." I paused. I'm not so good about arguments, because I always believe I'm right, and in this case, I knew I had needed to laugh when Danielle read her recipe because it was funny! "But readers *will* laugh at that recipe! You do know that, right?"

"Of course they will," Mr. Harper admitted, "but they won't be laughing *at* her, they'll be laughing because they find children so innocent and endearing and they love to hear kids say funny stuff that's from their hearts. They'll laugh at your recipe, too."

"I put jokes in mine, Mr. Harper," I pointed out, "I would *hope* they laugh at mine."

"I just want you to be sensitive to the other students, Persephone, because I know you wouldn't go up to someone and pick on them or be mean to one of your classmates because of something about them physically, but you have to always remember

179

that you do have a gift for writing and schoolwork that many kids your age just don't have. And laughing at someone's best work is one way to make fun of somebody, which simply is not acceptable behavior."

"So you don't think grown-ups are going to laugh at her recipe because it's ridiculous?" I questioned.

"Honestly, grown-ups who read the *City Times* are going to react to the recipes however they're going to react to the recipes. I cannot possibly know if they are laughing because they think it's so sweet that someone who is in fifth grade would write a recipe about cranberry jelly in a can or if it's because they think it's ridiculous that she doesn't make it from scratch. Just like I wouldn't know if they think it's funny that you put in a joke about soap and fifth graders or if they are laughing because they think it's preposterous that you'd rely on a pop-up thermometer to tell you when your turkey is done."

"But that's what the pop-up thermometer is for," I said, confused.

"And that's what the can of cranberry jelly is for," he countered.

"Mr. Harper, now I feel like pondscum *and* I'm confused," I admitted.

"Your piece is excellent, and I know you know that, but Danielle's is excellent, too," he tried to explain. "Each student did his or her best work today, but there are certainly holes in everyone's recipes that grown-ups, who have personally made many Thanksgiving dinners, could find. In your recipe, most people don't rely on the pop-up thermometer, because sometimes it doesn't work right. In Danielle's recipe, not everyone has the exact serving dish she mentions. It doesn't make either recipe wrong or less wonderful – they are each superb because my awesome fifth graders wrote them from the heart. *City Times* readers will find them perfect because they capture what it is like to be nine or ten or eleven years old and writing about Thanksgiving dinner. It will bring back memories of when they were young and of their families and loved ones."

"Okay, but I thought it was funny," I continued defending. "How was I to know she didn't mean to be funny?"

"Usually if someone makes a joke, they pause for laughs," Mr. Harper conceded. "If something strikes you as funny, maybe if you slightly smirk until you see if they pause for laughter or not, you can show enjoyment and appreciation without crossing the line into potentially hurting their feelings?"

"I did *not* mean to hurt her feelings," I confirmed, "I only thought it was funny."

"I hope you don't think I'm accusing you of *trying* to hurt anyone's feelings," Mr. Harper said. "I know you are too nice to want to hurt someone's feelings, but I know you'd feel badly if you ever did, accidentally, so I wanted to show you how you need to watch your actions before you actually hurt someone else's feelings or self-esteem."

"I still feel like pondscum," I confessed.

"Stop feeling like pondscum!" Mr. Harper rolled his eyes. "I forgot how oversensitive fifth graders can be. Remember, I said you didn't hurt anyone's feelings?"

"You said I hurt *your* feelings, Mr. Harper," I reminded.

"And it did hurt my feelings that you would mock one of your classmates' work," he maintained.

"So, if I apologize to you and promise to try harder not to laugh at other students' answers and schoolwork, unless they truly invite laughter, then all is well and I can continue on in my day?" I asked.

"That works," Mr. Harper agreed. "Besides, I need to get to the *City Times* with these hot off the presses recipes!"

"I'm sorry that I hurt your feelings by laughing at the writing of one of your students, Mr. Harper," I apologized. "I will do my best to not laugh at students in the future."

"Apology accepted, Persephone. Now, skedaddle!" I grabbed my stuff and went out to the hallway, heading towards Mom's classroom. As I plodded down the hall I felt my eyes getting very painful and stinging and wet. I turned the corner into the hallway where Mom's classroom is and leaned my back against the wall, sliding down to sit on the floor, in tears.

I still felt like pondscum.

chapter seventeen

Anyone Can Be Wrong

The next day, at school, I was still feeling upset that I had disappointed Mr. Harper and that I had inadvertently mocked one of my classmates. It wasn't hard for me to avoid Danielle, because we weren't exactly tight friends, but all morning, I felt like Mr. Harper was looking right through my outer shell to the pondscum that lurked inside of me.

"What's with you today?" Joey asked me at lunch. I shrugged and poked at my mashed potatoes with my spork. "Okay, spill it, Persephone, what on earth is going on?" he pressed.

Now, come on, you don't honestly expect me to confess my deep dark secrets to my crush, do you? No way! Get real! It is so *not* going to happen! I thought fast of any excuse I could possibly muster that would explain whatever it was that was tipping Joey off that something wasn't typical.

"I liked your pie recipes," I mumbled nervously.

"Thanks," he looked at me with eyes that seemed to search my soul. I realized it was foolish of me to mention the recipes. Ugh, I'm so lousy at this changing the topic stuff. "Have you really made turkey before?" he asked.

"I was telling the truth when I said I was Grampy's special helper!" I smirked. It felt good to smile again.

"My dad said your turkey recipe is wrong," Danielle interjected, from the next table. "I told him all about it, and he said that it wouldn't be cooked right at all!"

"That's okay, Danielle, the readers know we're only kids," I reassured.

"My cranberry jelly recipe didn't have any mistakes in it," Danielle boasted.

"You did a really good job at writing that recipe, Danielle," I told her.

"Oh, I know," Danielle bragged, "I know my recipe was perfectly right. It was *your* recipe that was wrong though."

"I would hope that nobody's going to use our class's newspaper article as a cookbook," I defended.

"Nobody's going to use *your* recipe," Danielle persisted.

"Leave her alone, Danielle," Joey interrupted.

"Mr. Harper thought that each of us did a great job," I said.

"Just ignore her," Joey whispered.

"Less talking, more eating," Mrs. Shasta, the teacher on lunch duty, reminded. Danielle stuck her tongue out at me, behind Mrs. Shasta's back. Joey stuck his tongue out at Danielle, in defense, but

Mrs. Shasta caught him. "Joseph, you are finished with your lunch," she scolded.

"Yes, Mrs. Shasta," Joey agreed, packing up what was left of his lunch, even though he was far from finished. Danielle laughed. I scoffed and raised my hand.

"What is it, Miss Smith?" Mrs. Shasta called on me.

"Danielle stuck her tongue out at Joey and me first," I revealed. "He hasn't had enough time to eat his lunch."

"Tattletale," Danielle whispered. I glared at her.

"Miss Smith, you are finished with your lunch, too," Mrs. Shasta announced.

"No, I am not," I responded. I began to pack up my lunch anyways, as I knew where this conversation would ultimately resolve itself.

The principal's office is definitely the scariest place in a school. It was unusual for me to be there, and I only had ever previously gone there to eat lunch as the Student of the Week or when running errands for the teachers. I sighed and fidgeted in the uncomfortable chair in the office as I waited my turn. I knew I was doomed to a lecture when I saw Mr. Harper enter the room.

"Seriously, Persephone?" he asked, incredulously.

"Apparently so," I muttered, looking down. I couldn't face him. Luckily for me, we went right into the principal's office as soon as Mr. Harper arrived.

"Persephone Smith," Mr. Jacobs, the principal, began. "In all of your years at Saint Bart's, I've never had the misfortune of hosting you in my office for solemn behavioral consequences." He then

185

paused so long that I felt compelled to look up at him, because he had been silent for such an outlandish length of time that I sensed perhaps he had left the room. Much to my regret, he was still there, eyebrows furrowed together and staring at me with what felt to be a death glare. I shivered. "Would you be so kind as to inform Mr. Harper and me of what happened in the cafeteria just now?"

"Yes, Mr. Jacobs," I stammered. I could feel the tears forming in my eyes already, and I hadn't even told my story yet! "I was talking to Joey about the recipes we wrote in class yesterday, and Danielle told me my recipe was wrong," I recounted as my voice cracked. I gulped and continued. "I told her that her recipe was good, because I felt bad that I had laughed when she read it in class, and after school yesterday, Mr. Harper explained to me why it was actually good," I squeaked as I looked over at Mr. Harper who seemed to have exceptionally moist eyes. I paused when I noticed how upset he looked, and I needed to look away from him to continue. "Mrs. Shasta reminded us to talk less and eat more, so Joey and I went back to eating lunch, but Danielle stuck her tongue out at me, so Joey stuck his tongue out at her. Mrs. Shasta didn't see Danielle, only Joey, and she told him he was done with lunch, but he hadn't had time to eat enough lunch." I felt my eyes overfilling with wetness and the drops began flowing onto my cheeks. "So, Joey put his lunch away, but I told Mrs. Shasta what had happened, and she made me put my lunch away, too." My voice was very shaky, and I knew the full-on crying waterworks would be coming soon. "It's just not fair!" I blurted, before the sobbing made speech impossible.

After a few minutes I was feeling cried out, and I tried to regain my composure. Mr. Jacobs and Mr. Harper hadn't said anything during the seeming eternity that was my crying fit. I sniffled and wiped my eyes on my sleeve. Mr. Harper handed a box of tissues to me, but I never know what I'm supposed to do with tissues when I've been crying, so I just held the box.

Mr. Harper stated, "It sounds like there was a misunderstanding." He hypothesized, "Mrs. Shasta didn't see the catalyst of Joey's misbehavior, and so, since he was inappropriate, he had the consequence of forgoing the rest of his lunch."

"Why am I in the principal's office, then?" I sighed with a squeak. "I simply pointed out the unjustness of his not being able to finish eating because he wasn't the only person sticking his tongue out, and he didn't even start it."

"You spoke back to the teacher," Mr. Jacobs accused.

"Mrs. Shasta was wrong," I defended.

"Teachers are never wrong," Mr. Jacobs insisted. My jaw dropped, but I was too scared to speak. Apparently principals can be wrong, too! Teachers are just people, and any person *can* be wrong sometimes! I couldn't believe he was siding with Mrs. Shasta when she had been clearly mistaken!

"I want my mother in here to witness this, Mr. Jacobs," I demanded.

"That is unnecessary, Miss Smith," Mr. Jacobs firmly stated. "I am your mother's boss, and as such, she'll simply support my decisions in your consequences."

"No, she won't," Mr. Harper interrupted.

"Excuse me, John, but this is not your place to speak," Mr. Jacobs insisted with his nostrils flared. Mr. Harper pulled out his cell phone and apparently sent a text message. "I hope you didn't just-"

"Oh, I did, Jason, make no mistake of it," Mr. Harper smugly retorted. "And Jason, I think it's about time for Persephone and me to take a little walk and get some fresh air, as she shouldn't witness authority figures in confrontations." Mr. Harper turned to me, "Persephone? It sounds to me as though the whole story has come out, and that no further consequences should be garnished onto you, right Mr. Jacobs?"

Mr. Jacobs's face was beet red. I think he would have agreed to anything to keep me from going to get my mother and to guarantee that Mr. Harper and I left his office at once. I wasn't sure what had been meant by "authority figures in confrontations," but I was perfectly fine with not finding out. "Good day, Miss Smith," Mr. Jacobs choked out from behind gritted teeth.

"I'm sorry for causing a ruckus, Mr. Jacobs," I apologized.

"Let's go," Mr. Harper encouraged, opening the door and holding it for me. As we exited into the office, Mom came in at the same time!

"Persephone! What are you doing in the principal's office?" she asked sternly.

"I got in trouble for defending Joey and telling Mrs. Shasta that I hadn't finished my lunch," I admitted.

"You what?" Mom asked with a shocked, yet puzzled, expression across her face.

"Persephone, would you be okay sitting here in the waiting area while your mom and I go back in to talk to Mr. Jacobs?" Mr. Harper inquired. Suddenly I understood what "authority figures in confrontations" meant. My eyes became very large and I nodded, gladly taking a seat in the waiting chair.

Oh boy, would I have loved to have been a fly on the wall during *that* meeting! I didn't hear any yelling or objects being thrown, but I do know that when the door opened, Mom emerged first, smiling when she saw me.

"I think Mr. Jacobs has something to tell you," she said, crouching down to look me in the eyes when she spoke. "I'm going to go back to my classroom now, so don't be causing any more trouble," she requested gently with the corner of her mouth curving up mischievously at the end of her sentence. She kissed me on the forehead and rushed out of the office.

Mr. Harper ushered me back into the principal's office. This time he sat in the third chair that was in there. I could see Mr. Jacobs's eye twitching and a vein was pulsating on his head.

"Persephone, your mother has convinced me that you are well aware that teachers are capable of making mistakes," he began. "I apologize for not taking your concerns of unfair treatment in the lunchroom seriously. Although I have complete confidence in the teachers at Saint Bart's, under the circumstances, it seems that there was blatant miscommunication today."

I opened my mouth to say, "Apology accepted," but Mr. Harper gestured to me to not say anything yet.

Mr. Jacobs continued, "Mr. Harper informed your mother and I of the circumstances from yesterday that led up to the tension between you and Danielle Wright, and at this time I would like to commend you for having taken the high road in the lunchroom conversation that led up to the inappropriate behavior. It must have been difficult to give her recipe praise as she was blasting yours."

"It wasn't easy, but I had felt so badly about my unintended rude behavior yesterday," I started to explain.

"There's something else that we want to tell you," Mr. Harper interrupted.

"Oh?" I questioned, sinking as low in my chair as I could sit.

"Sit up, Persephone, this is a good thing," Mr. Jacobs demanded of me. I obliged.

"When I went to the *City Times* yesterday, they read through the recipes and loved them," Mr. Harper stated.

"Just like you said they would," I acknowledged.

"But they liked your recipe for turkey best," he continued.

"I didn't know it was a contest," I admitted.

"It wasn't, but they really appreciated your details," he clarified, "and so they are hoping that you will become a weekly columnist for the *City Times*."

"You mean they want me to write a story for the *City Times* every week?" I clarified.

"Precisely," Mr. Harper agreed.

"It would be a tremendous honor to our school if you would put Saint Bart's on the map by fulfilling this request the *City Times* has made for you to write a weekly column for them," Mr. Jacobs encouraged. "It's a huge opportunity to get a student's perspective of the world publicized for the whole town to read."

I mulled it over, albeit not for very long. Imagine me writing for the *City Times* every week... at only nine years of age. "I'd love to do it," I confessed. Mr. Jacobs and Mr. Harper looked pleased at my decision.

"They are hoping for a young and fresh perspective on current events and important topics in the lives of Vermont kids," Mr. Harper further explained.

"Well, I'm a Vermont kid," I admitted, "so I think it should be no problem at all!" I was filled with confidence. The people at the *City Times* had liked my writing. I was going to be a published journalist while I was still in elementary school! Hopefully this opportunity would look good when I applied for colleges and cancel out this trip to the principal's office on my permanent record.

"Great, your first article is due to the *City Times* by a week from Tuesday, and it will appear in the Thursday edition of the newspaper each week. Next Thursday, for Thanksgiving, your column will be replaced by our class's recipes, but the column becomes completely yours beginning the next Thursday."

"I'm glad I have a little extra time before my first article is due," I confessed. "I don't even know what I'll write about yet."

"Well, congratulations on having the opportunity to represent Saint Bart's each week in the *City Times*," Mr. Jacobs concluded, extending his hand for a handshake.

"You betcha," I agreed, shaking his hand firmly. Then Mr. Harper and I left the office. Once we were safely down the hall and

191

nearing our classroom I couldn't help but ask, "Are you sure I can do this writing thing?"

"Absolutely certain," he maintained. From his expression I knew he believed in me, and it felt really good to have the support and reassurance of my teacher. "Now, can you promise me you won't get sent to the principal's office anymore?"

I looked up at Mr. Harper and smiled, but I did not say a word. I never make promises that I cannot guarantee, and when it comes to standing up for what is right, I always will. If that means I'll be sent to the principal's office again, so be it, but I feel a need to be the voice of fifth graders. Apparently the *City Times* feels the same way. I smiled even more and filed into the classroom, rejoining my class.

"Like mother, like daughter," Mr. Harper huffed quietly as he followed me in. He picked up a dry erase marker and led us in a vocabulary activity. I was grateful to already know all of the words he was teaching, as my mind completely wandered away from the task at hand to contemplate topics for my first article.

Apparently brainstorming a topic is a task easier said than done. I racked and racked my brain for a juicy idea for my column, but continued to come up blank. I almost wished I had astutely written a simple recipe for canned cranberry jelly myself. Almost.

chapter eighteen

How to Create a Scene

All weekend I was completely stumped as to what to write about for my first *City Times* article, until Monday when I finally conceived the perfect idea - the Christmas pageant! With all the excitement about my newspaper column, I had somehow completely spaced on the auditions being the Monday before Thanksgiving! Tryouts were after school in the gymnasium, with rehearsals every weekday beginning Tuesday, except for Thanksgiving Day.

Ms. Peyton stopped me as soon as I entered the gym. "Persephone Smith, there's no need for you to come to auditions," she snapped. "You won't be cast in my show."

"It's not your show," I argued, "It's Saint Bart's show."

"You won't be cast in *MY* show," she repeated.

"I'm auditioning," I announced.

"Actually, you're not," Ms. Peyton reminded, "You didn't join my choir so you're not going to be in my Christmas pageant."

"Erin, are you still holding that over Persephone's head?" Mr. Harper stood just inside the gym's door. "If you would like me to get her mother, I surely can do that."

"John, you will not threaten me in front of students," Ms. Peyton replied.

"I would hardly constitute allowing a student's mother to have a word with you as a threat," Mr. Harper declared, holding his ground.

"Fine," Ms. Peyton consented, "audition if you must, but you will not be cast."

"Maybe I should summon the school board to watch the auditions, Erin?" Mr. Harper egged on.

"It's not the school board's decision, John," Ms. Peyton insisted.

"But your job is," Mr. Harper threatened.

"Fine," Ms. Peyton snapped, "Persephone can audition, and good luck to her at getting a part!" She stormed off, sitting down in a seat in the front row of chairs.

"You know she won't cast me," I said to Mr. Harper.

"And you'll expose her in the *City Times* for the fraud she is," Mr. Harper projected. "You're Saint Bart's best singer, and you know it. If she doesn't give you the lead, reflect on the experience in your article."

"I could get in big trouble," I hinted.

"You already will have not gotten the lead," Mr. Harper encouraged. "What other trouble is there to get into?"

I decided right then and there that apparently Mr. Harper doesn't know me very well. Where there was a grown-up in the wrong, and Ms. Peyton was definitely in the wrong, there was

194

notoriously big trouble brewing for me. I am not someone who will risk my physical well-being to prove a point, but I definitely will verbally defend myself or my beliefs.

So did Ms. Peyton cast me in the play? Or did I have to assert myself through my newspaper article? I guess you'll have to buy a copy of next Thursday's *City Times* and read my article about Saint Bart's Christmas pageant and find out for yourself.

*　*　*　*　*　*　*　*　*　*

The ringing phone awakened my slumber, early in the morning of the first Thursday of December. It was Grampy and Grammy with congratulations to me for my first article in the *City Times*! I threw our front door open, dashed so quickly out I almost slipped on the icy stoop, and looked for the paper on the steps! It wasn't there! I realized I was very cold, and then I noticed I only had my PJs on! Dad called to me from inside.

"Persephone? Are you looking for this?" he asked, appearing at the door with the newspaper already opened to my article.

"Yes!" I exclaimed as he pretended to close the door and leave me on the porch. "No, Dad, let me in! It's cold out here!"

Dad reopened the door and handed me the newspaper, closing the cold air out behind him. There it was, in black and white... my article! I felt foolish and a little crazy to want to read it, as I already knew what it said because I had read it so many times while writing it, yet I felt compelled to make sure it was exactly the way I wanted it. I sat down at the dining room table to read my exposé of Saint Bart's Christmas pageant.

The telephone rang again when I was about three paragraphs into the article. I looked up, puzzled, because I couldn't think of anyone else who would be calling besides Grampy and Grammy. I suppose Grandma and Grandpa might call at this hour, but they didn't live locally and didn't typically call in the early morning. I looked up and saw Dad read the caller ID. "It's for you, hun," he determined to my mother.

Mom went to the phone and read the caller ID. She got an uneasy expression on her face as she answered with a tentative, "Hello?" She then listened with "Mmmhmm" and "Okay" interjected a few times at random, presumed points of agreement. When she hung up the phone she turned to me and said, "Get ready for school, Kiddo, we're going in early."

I couldn't figure out what was going on, but her tone and expression made me think I had better just do what she requested. I was ready faster than ever, standing by the door with my coat and boots on and backpack packed within ten minutes.

"It's going to be okay, Squirt," Dad said as he joined me to keep me company as I waited for Mom.

"What's going on, Dad?" I asked.

"They're going to talk to you about your article, Squirt," Dad informed. "Just stay calm, stay strong, and stay honest. They're not mad at you, and you're not in any trouble."

"Dad, I didn't do anything wrong! Why would I think they're mad or that I'm in trouble?" I asked.

"Sometimes adults are loud and talk scary when they're upset about something," he hedged.

"My article upset someone?" I asked.

"Your article upset a lot of someones, Squirt," Dad grinned, "I'm so proud of you!"

"Yes, my Little Dragon, you're a chip off the ol' block!" Mom beamed, hurrying to put her shoes on as a final preparation for the day.

"All I did was tell the truth of my experience with the Christmas pageant," I defended.

"And that's all you should have done and should continue to do," Mom encouraged, heading towards the door.

"Good luck, Squirt." Dad gave me a farewell hug and a kiss. "You will be fine!"

"I love you, Dad," I said with a wave as I headed towards the car. I was still unsure of what was happening, but I had a lot of uneasiness that I would soon be feeling as though I was in trouble. I kept repeating what Dad had told me, in my head. I didn't do anything wrong. I wasn't in trouble. Nobody was mad at me.

But someone *was* upset because of my article. And suddenly I realized who that would be... Ms. Peyton! Apparently some adults just can't handle truth.

Mom and I immediately reported to the office and sat in the waiting chairs to go into Mr. Jacobs's office. "Mom, Mr. Harper is going to be mad at me because he told me not to wind up in the principal's office again!" I worried.

197

"Mr. Harper will completely understand *and* take your side on this one, my Little Dragon," Mom reassured. "You have done nothing wrong. Just answer the questions honestly and know that I'm right out here if you need me."

"You're not coming in?" I panicked.

"I don't want to give the impression that I'm influencing your answers," Mom admitted, with a very sad look. "I know you're strong and can do it on your own."

"Mom, I'm scared," I confessed.

"They just want to hear the truth. You don't have a reason to be scared," Mom comforted. Just then Mr. Jacobs's door opened and he stood in the doorway.

"Persephone, we're ready for you," Mr. Jacobs said with a smile. Mom gave me a hug and I walked over to his door.

Maybe I should've expected it, but I didn't, and the roomful of people really took me aback! There were two chairs that were unoccupied, but there were many extras that had been brought in for the crowd that was assembled in that tiny office. I looked skeptically at Mr. Jacobs who went to sit at his desk and urged me to take the only other empty chair in the room.

"Persephone, this is most of the school board and many of the trustees," Mr. Jacobs introduced.

"Hi, everybody?" I greeted, nervously.

"We've gathered today and have invited you here to tell us, in person, about your experience with this year's Christmas pageant at Saint Bart's," Mr. Jacobs continued. "Could you tell us about the audition process?"

198

I started by telling them the conditions that Ms. Peyton had laid out for me at the beginning of the school year – that I would only be cast in the Christmas pageant if I joined the choir. I told them that I hadn't wanted to be in the choir, that Ms. Peyton knew that, and that I was feeling undue pressure to do choir only to maintain a chance of being cast in the Christmas pageant. I shared with them that I had told Mr. Harper and Mom about the threat, and that Mom had talked to Ms. Peyton to ensure that I wouldn't be in choir, but that I'd keep my opportunity to audition for the Christmas pageant.

I was surprised that nobody interrupted my story. I figured they'd inundate me with questions and accusations, but the room was silent. Everyone just listened to what I had to say.

Then, I told them about the day of auditions. I talked about how unwelcome Ms. Peyton had made me feel when I arrived, and how Mr. Harper had stepped in to fight for me to be able to audition. I noticed jaws dropping as I described the actual audition. I recalled how hurt my feelings were when Ms. Peyton did not allow me to sing, unlike every other student who auditioned. I admitted that she only allowed me to read three sentences before cutting me off and saying she had heard enough.

I told them about the posting of the cast list the next day, in the locked, glass case in the hallway. I recounted how I had said, "Just let my name be on that list," as I walked up to the case.

"And were you cast in the Christmas pageant, Persephone?" Mr. Jacobs asked.

"My name *was* on the list, at the very bottom, as the only person on set crew," I replied. I divulged that when I went to the first rehearsal, Ms. Peyton told me I wasn't supposed to be there because I wasn't cast in the show. I had argued with her that my name was on the list, as set crew, and the rest of the cast confirmed this information to her. She then accused me of writing my name on her list! Joey had told her it was typed just like the rest of the cast list, so she stomped off to the glass case to see for herself. She was livid when she realized we had told the truth. She had thrown her hands in the air and exclaimed that *she* did not put my name on that cast list and that I was not welcome to be on *her* set crew.

"So Ms. Peyton had told you that you wouldn't be in the Christmas pageant, unless you were in choir, knowing you didn't want to do choir, and then you weren't given a fair audition for the Christmas pageant and were consequently not cast in a role?" Mr. Jacobs summarized.

"Yes, sir," I replied.

"Persephone," an older lady with gray curly hair and glasses suddenly blurted out, craning her body to lean around the man who was sitting next to me. "I'm Ivy Bailey," she introduced. Then she smiled and asked, "What is your favorite Christmas song?"

"I really like 'Silent Night,'" I said.

"Would you mind singing a little of that for us?" Mrs. Bailey requested, with her face alighted in a manner that suggested it was her favorite, too.

"I would love to sing it for you," I blushed. I felt a little strange and self-conscious singing in front of my captive audience, but I do love that song, and I do love to sing. I noticed most of the faces watching me were smiling, and I got through the entire first verse without interruption.

"Like an angel," she whispered to the man sitting between us. He nodded. A few of the people clapped a couple of times, but they looked even more self-conscious of what others would think of them than I had felt when singing in front of them.

"You sing beautifully," Mr. Jacobs praised.

"Thank you," I smiled. "I love to sing!"

"I don't understand why she would not have received a role in the pageant, if the audition process was fair," Mrs. Bailey said to Mr. Jacobs. "Her voice is simply lovely." I noticed many of the adults in the room nodded in agreement.

"Persephone, why didn't you provide all of *these* details in your newspaper article?" Mr. Jacobs asked.

"I didn't think most *City Times* readers want to hear some sob story of a whiney kid who didn't get her way," I shrugged. "I did mention that the director told me I wouldn't be cast unless I joined her choir, last fall, but that I didn't *really* believe it until I wasn't given a fair audition and was the only student who didn't get a role."

"You are not a 'whiney kid' to point out this teacher's inappropriate behavior towards you," the man next to me said in a deep voice.

"Also, my friends are *in* the show, so I felt it was far more important to Saint Bart's and to my friends to focus on how excited the cast is for the show, that it'll be a great show, and that everyone should go to the show!" I remembered my article and smiled. "I thought it was pretty lucky of me to have the chance to really advertise it in the *City Times* to people in town who might not otherwise even know about our Christmas pageant!"

"I would like to make the motion to dismiss Ms. Peyton from the position of director of the Christmas pageant, effective immediately," the deep-voiced man said, suddenly.

"I second the motion," Mrs. Bailey quickly added.

"All in favor?" someone said. All the adults said, "I," and then a voice said, "Motion carried."

"Congratulations, young lady," the lady on the other side of me said, nudging me. "It looks like you're going to be in the Christmas pageant after all!"

"Ms. Peyton has made it clear that she won't allow it," I stammered, confused.

"Ms. Peyton is no longer the director of the Christmas pageant," the deep-voiced man stated. "She has *no* say in the matter."

"But who's going to direct the Christmas pageant?" I asked. "And I can't be in the pageant, as it's already been cast," I reminded.

"It was cast unfairly," Mr. Jacobs announced. "Therefore, someone will lose their part and you will have their part."

"I can't do that to someone in the show," I disagreed. "They've been working hard on the songs, dances, and lines. I won't be the bad guy who takes a part away from one of my friends."

"We will let the new director figure out how to resolve the issue of casting you in the show," Mrs. Bailey interjected. "I think we have some grown-up matters to discuss now that we have the full story. Thank you, Persephone, for sharing your experience with us, and I will speak for everyone when I say we can't wait to read your article each week in the *City Times*."

"Yes, thank you, Persephone, for coming in early today and being so mature about this horrible experience," Mr. Jacobs agreed. "Please accept our collective apology for Ms. Peyton's behavior towards you, and know that it won't happen again."

"Thank you for listening to me," I said, standing up in anticipation of leaving, "and it was nice to meet all of you." I smiled and backed towards the door. The adults smiled and waved, so I took that as my cue to leave.

"How'd that go?" Mom asked, as soon as I had escaped from the principal's office. I hugged her for a few moments before replying. I told her as many details of the meeting as I could remember. "Wow, I'm shocked that they discussed so much right in front of you," she admitted.

"I didn't understand what they were talking about, Mom," I told her. Mom explained that they had voted to not let Ms. Peyton be the director of the Christmas pageant anymore. She assured me that I shouldn't feel badly even if Ms. Peyton loses her job, because it isn't my fault. "Who do you think will be the new director of the Christmas pageant?" I asked.

"We'll just have to wait and see," she shrugged. "Now, let's get to our classrooms before we get marked tardy for the day!" she suggested.

"Deal," I said, relieved to have survived that nerve-racking meeting. "Are you sure Mr. Harper will understand that I wasn't in trouble by being in the principal's office this morning?" I asked sliding my hand in Mom's as we walked down the hallway.

"I have a sneaking suspicion that he'll forgive you for being at the principal's office, my Little Dragon," she said, seeming to stifle a laugh. I didn't understand what would be funny, but then again, it seems there's a lot of things grown-ups say and do that I just don't comprehend.

I reached my classroom before the other students arrived. Mr. Harper was already there. He immediately picked on me for having broken my non-promise about not being in the principal's office. "Hey, you're the one who said if I didn't get cast in the Christmas pageant, I couldn't get into any *more* trouble, Mr. Harper," I pointed out. "Besides, how do you know already?" I asked.

"Word travels fast?" he grinned. "*And* I happened to run into your mom when I was getting my mail in the main office," he admitted. "So, can you share what the outcome of your meeting with the School Board and Board of Trustees was, young journalist?"

"They're not letting Ms. Peyton direct the Christmas pageant," I revealed. Upon that news, Mr. Harper told me he needed to go do something and rushed out of the classroom. I had about one moment of quiet peace before the rest of my class clomped and stomped into the room.

Joey ran right over to me. "Persephone, I read your article in the *City Times*!" he exclaimed. "That is *so* cool that you're going to be writing in the *City Times* every week!"

Skye called over from the coat hooks, "Yeah, but hopefully she won't ruin the Christmas pageant every week, the sore loser."

"Skye, I'm going to write about different topics each week, so I only ruined the Christmas pageant *this* week," I jested, rolling my eyes.

"Speaking of the Christmas pageant," Mr. Harper announced, re-entering the classroom, "There's been a major change at the helm, and I want you all to be the first to hear the news!"

"What's a 'helm'?" Katie asked.

"There's a new director," Mr. Harper explained, "Actually there's two new directors."

"What about Ms. Peyton?" Skye asked in a panic.

"Skye, if you *read* Persephone's article today, you'd know that Ms. Peyton didn't give her a fair audition," Joey defended.

"It's not okay for a teacher to be mean like that," Freddie concurred.

"Persephone is just jealous because *she* didn't get the lead," Skye countered.

"Persephone sings better than *you* do, Skye," Curt added.

"Oh yeah?" Skye argued.

"Class, stop it," Mr. Harper boomed.

"Who are the new directors?" I asked.

"I'm so glad someone actually asked *that* rather than fight about silly stuff," Mr. Harper glowed. "The new directors are Mrs. Smith and myself!" I applauded. The rest of the class, except Skye, joined me in clapping.

"So, now, Persephone will be Mary because her mom's directing the Christmas pageant?" Skye accused. "It's not fair!"

"Persephone deserves the lead, Skye, because she would have had the best audition, if she had been allowed the same audition privileges as you," Mr. Harper explained. "So, Persephone, are you ready to take your rightful spot in the cast?"

"I am ready to take on the part I was meant to be cast in," I beamed.

And on Opening Night, when I first walked out on that stage and immediately got a standing ovation from a sold out, standing room only crowd of not only Saint Bart's School's family & friends, but of townspeople who came to the Christmas pageant solely because of my *City Times* article, I blushed, opened the folding metal chair and carefully set the legs on the glow tape spikes. Then I smiled at my admirers, knowing I had definitely fulfilled my destiny as the best set crew in the entire history of Saint Bart's School.

chapter nineteen

Turning Ten

One of the biggest challenges of having skipped a grade at school when I was younger is that I am, by far, the youngest student in my class. Whereas many of my classmates are now turning eleven, I am still nine. They are physically turning into preteens, and I'm still looking very much like a kid. The girls are wearing makeup, and Mom says lip balm is appropriate for me. I remain dominant as an academic presence in the classroom, but when I see everyone else passing love notes to their boyfriends and girlfriends, I often feel just so young. Obviously, I am absolutely boy crazy, but nine is just too young to have a boyfriend!

I totally have friends who are boys. I got a Christmas card from Charles and Drew. I play at recess with Joey and Freddie every day! Yet, none of the boys are my boyfriend. Mom and Dad tell me I can have a boyfriend when I'm thirty-four. *Thirty-four*? I don't think there will be *any* boys left by the time I'm thirty-four! Maybe *that* is

Mom and Dad's ploy… if they don't let me date until I'm old, there won't be any boys left for me to date!

Grr, why do I have to have parents who are smart and can outsmart me like that?

So, on the last day of January, Mom surprised me with a question about my upcoming birthday. "Do you want to have a small party with your friends from school?" she asked.

"My closest friends at school are boys, Mom," I groaned, knowing that would be the end of the conversation about a birthday party.

"So?" Mom pressed.

"So you and Dad have said I can't date until I'm thirty-four," I reminded.

"I don't see what dating has to do with having a tenth birthday party, Persephone," Mom stated.

"You'd let me invite boys?" I asked. I hadn't had any boys at my birthday party since I was in third grade and invited my then "boyfriend," Seth, who wasn't really a boyfriend boyfriend, cuz well we were like little kids, and you know, it's not like mushy-gushy, icky, lovey-dovey stuff when you're eight.

"It's up to you, my Little Dragon," Mom agreed, "but I think you'd be silly to not invite your best friends from school."

Being Sunday, I called Joey and Freddie and invited them both to my birthday party. I also invited my friend, Jade, who was in fourth grade but who was my friend from way back when I was in kindergarten with her. I didn't get to see Jade very often, because we weren't in the same class anymore, but we traditionally invited each other to our birthday parties every year.

"I can't believe you're going to be ten!" Jade exclaimed. "Double digits, Girl!"

"I know! It seems like we were just five!" I agreed. It was good to catch up with Jade. Maybe I would ask Mom to arrange more visits with her, now that the holidays were done for the season. We yapped on the phone for a whole hour! She was very excited to tell me all about her boyfriend! "Your mom and dad let you have a boyfriend?" I asked.

"They don't know he's my boyfriend," she confessed. "They think he's just my friend."

"Isn't that lying, Jade?" I grilled.

"Well, he is my friend, but we kiss when nobody's watching!" she revealed.

"Kissing, Jade? You're *nine*, like me!" I was shocked. "Aren't you too young for a serious, like kissy-kissy boyfriend boyfriend?"

"Persephone, haven't you kissed a boy?" Jade asked.

"No, Jade," I admitted. "I'm only nine."

"Wow," she said slowly.

"Not everyone kisses boys when they're nine, Jade," I defended.

"Well, no worries, Persephone, you're almost ten," she encouraged. "Maybe you'll get a boyfriend when you're ten."

I covered the mouthpiece of the phone with my hand and whispered to my mom begging that she should call me for dinner. "Persephone, you need to get ready for dinner," Mom called loudly enough so Jade would hear her through the phone.

"I gotta go, Mom's calling me for supper," I said, "but I can't wait to see you at my birthday party!" Jade said her farewells and that she would definitely be there.

"Why did you want to get off the phone?" Mom asked, after I had hung up the receiver.

"Jade was telling me all about her boyfriend," I stated.

"Ohh?" Mom shifted uncomfortably. "You're too young for a boyfriend, my Little Dragon."

"I know," I agreed.

"So Jade, Joey, and Freddie are all coming to your birthday party?" Mom segued.

"Yeah, it oughta be fun."

"Joey is the one you like, right?"

"Mom!" I blushed. "Do *not* embarrass me like that in front of him!"

"Oh, you know I won't," Mom reassured. Mom was really good about keeping my secrets from everyone on the planet, except for Dad. But since Mom knew that I liked Joey, Dad did too. I just hoped Dad wouldn't consequently break Joey's neck in order to ensure that his precious daughter didn't date boys until she was thirty-four!

The week passed quickly, and that was fine with me because I was definitely ready to be ten! I wondered what plans my parents had for my big day, and the night before my birthday I went to bed with a smile from thinking about all the possibilities.

"Good morning, sunshine," Mom urged me from my sleep. I grumbled and mumbled groggily, unable to connect how it was remotely possible that I could ever be referred to as "sunshine." "Okay, I know it's February, but you don't have to do your last rose of summer impression," Mom mocked, smoothing my hair and kissing my nose.

"Let me sleeeep, Mom!" I grabbed a pillow and put it over my eyes to block the light.

Dad rat-a-tatted the door before bursting into song, "Happy birthday to you, happy birthday to you, happy birthday, dear Persephone, happy birthday to you!" I removed the pillow from my eyes and saw Dad standing there, beaming, and holding a tray with a cupcake with a lit candle in it. "Make a wish, Squirt!" he encouraged, Mom standing aside of him.

I sat up, closed my eyes, made my wish, and blew out the candle. I'm not going to admit what I wished for, but I'm sure everyone who knows me knows what I wish for when I make wishes. I'll even confess that when I saw the shooting star at camp, I quickly made the *same* wish in my head before audibly requesting the roasted marshmallows.

"May all your wishes come true," Mom said softly, smiling.

"They will, Mom," I beamed confidently.

"Isn't it nice to have a self-assured ten year old daughter?" Dad proudly stated.

"Hey, you're double digits now, Persephone!" Mom thought aloud.

"That means you're going to give my room a makeover!" I exclaimed, remembering the promise they made when I was much younger. "Remember? You promised!"

211

"How do you remember these things?" Dad asked.

"I think the deal was we would paint or wallpaper your walls when you turned ten, dear," Mom recalled, with a raised eyebrow.

"That's a makeover, Mom!" I was sitting up in bed now.

"What color are you thinking?" Dad asked.

"Maybe a pastel teal?" I proposed.

"Well, that's a better idea than straight up, regular dark teal," he consented.

"I don't want it to be too dark," I rationalized, "so maybe I'd be better off with a brighter color."

"We're not painting your room today, Persephone," Mom alerted me. "We have a lot of things to do, but painting is not on the agenda."

"Since I'm ten now, can I have an email address?" I inquired.

"Gee, you waste no time in adjusting to double digits, Squirt!" Dad chuckled.

"We might be able to look into that," Mom suggested, "but not today."

"Well, can I have a birthday tarot reading, Mom?"

"You just had a tarot reading in October. What has changed since then?"

"But I'm *ten* now, I'm not a little child anymore," I argued, "pleeeeease??"

"We'll see," Mom smirked. "We already have a busy day planned for you, Persephone!"

"What is it with you girls and tarot readings anyways?" Dad asked, placing the tray on the bed and walking out of the room.

"I have an idea for a present for you," Mom started, "but you have to come with me to pick it out."

"Are you going to get me another tarot deck, Mom?" I jumped up so much I knocked my cupcake over on its plate.

"Maybe..." she hinted. "I'm planning to bring you to a store today and if you find a deck that you can't resist, then we'll get it! But if nothing's jumping out at you, I'll get you a deck another day, when you find the right cards for you."

"And will you please give me a reading?" I asked again.

"All things in time, my Little Dragon," she pacified, hugging me. "Now are you going to eat your cupcake in bed or are we bringing it down to the dining room?"

"Are there more cupcakes downstairs for you and Dad?" I asked.

"There very well might be," Mom hinted.

"Then I'm bringing this downstairs so we can have breakfast together," I announced, picking up the tray and heading for the door.

At breakfast, Dad told me he had things to do around the house so he'd be staying home while Mom and I went shopping in Burlington. I ran off to my room to get dolled up for my big day, and when I happened to look out the window, I noticed a stretch limo pulled up to the house to presumably take us away on our shopping adventure. "Are you for real?" I asked loudly. I ran downstairs laughing and hugged my mom and dad. "You guys are the best! I love you!"

213

"We love you, too, Squirt!" Dad exclaimed, hugging my mom and I. "Now, get shopping already, you two! There's money to be spent!"

I ran to the limo to find that Jade's mom and Jade were already inside! "Hey, birthday girl!" Jade exclaimed. She handed me a metallic teal gift bag with hot pink tissue paper poking from the top of it and a teal helium filled balloon tied to it. Mom was saying something to Dad and taking her time getting to the limousine.

"Come on, Mom!" I encouraged.

"Open your present!" Jade insisted.

Inside the bag there was a birthday card with a note inside. I read the note aloud, "This certificate is good for a mother/daughter manicure on February 7, 2010, in celebration of the tenth birthday of Persephone!" I smiled, "Thank you, I've never had a manicure before!"

"Keep looking, there's more in there!" Jade encouraged.

I looked again and there was also a thick book. I pulled out the book and read the title, "*The Ultimate Guide to Love, Love Spells, and Love Potions*." I caught my mom's eyes go extremely wide when she climbed into the limo and found *that* book in my hands. "What'd you get for your birthday, Kiddo?" Mom asked.

"A mother/daughter manicure and a book about love and spells and potions," I embarrassedly faked enthusiasm. "Thank you, so much, Jade, these gifts are great!"

"Well, everyone knows how you feel about finding true love," Jade explained.

"And a great girl like you shouldn't ever be single!" Jade's mom chimed in.

"She *is* only ten, you two matchmakers," Mom joked uneasily.

We waved out the window to my father and the limo pulled away to head to Burlington. Jade and I looked through the book, giggling about the spells and what effect each caused and looking at one another grossed out when reading the ingredient lists for the potions. Jade's mom and my mom caught up on gossip, happenings, current events, and anything else that grown-ups chat about when they're around one another and not having to entertain the kids.

I knew we had to be back for the party by 5:00 because we were having a pizza and movie night with Joey and Freddie from 5:00 – 8:00. I was amazed that I was allowed to have an evening party on a school night, but I guess that's what happens when one is *ten*!

"I'm just dying to tell you about my boyfriend!" Jade whispered in my ear, smiling.

"I can't believe you have a boyfriend!" I whispered into Jade's ear.

"Shhhhhh!" she said in reply. I just giggled.

"What are you two whispering about over there?" Jade's mom asked.

"Nothing," we replied in unison. Okay, so that's a little bit of a sorta lie, but we're girls, and we're supposed to whisper about girl things that moms don't know about. It's in the rule book of being girls... or it would be, if such a book existed! Besides, my head was still reeling from the news that my friend Jade has a real live boyfriend! And she's only a fourth grader!

"So my boyfriend is ten and he's in my class and his name is Seth Totter," Jade whispered in my ear. My blood froze! Seth Totter is the boy who was *my* boyfriend in kindergarten, second, and third grades!

"I know Seth," I said softly.

"I know!" Jade giggled.

My mind went through the blur that was my three year relationship with Seth. I remembered the many times we rode our bikes around the neighborhood. I recalled when we went exploring the abandoned building and decided it didn't seem safe enough to be a good clubhouse. Then I remembered the day he gave me a ring and asked me to be his wife when we got older. "But Seth was my boyfriend," I choked out.

"Well, you broke up with him two years ago, Persephone. You can't expect to keep him off-limits forever."

I remembered when our relationship ended. It was Easter Sunday, near the end of third grade. Seth had been riding up and down our street on his bike, doing that typical, silly, showing off thing that boys do, and well, he intentionally rode through a mud puddle, splashing me in my Easter dress! I was covered in mud! I can't remember ever being that angry before, because, well, I was only eight at the time, so I hadn't had too many reasons to be *so* mad yet in life! He tried to apologize, to explain, to make it up to me, but I didn't accept his apology, gave him no chance for an explanation, and simply ended it, coldly, then and there.

"But we were going to get married," I said, gazing out the window at the passing, snowy scenery. "He gave me a ring, and we planned to always be together!"

"Hate to break it to you, Girl," Jade said in a quiet voice, "but he loves me now." My face felt extremely drooped. Jade noticed and added, "Besides, who's that boy you play with every recess?"

"You mean Joey?" I giggled.

"Ah, Joooo-eeeeey!" Jade teased. "You love Joey now!"

The mere mention of his name made me whip around to look at her. I felt wild. I didn't know if I wanted to stick my tongue out or giggle, blush, and deny it. My face settled into a silly smile. "Shhhhhh!" I shushed her. "He's going to be at the party tonight, and you *have* to behave yourself!"

"Your boyfriend is going to be at the birthday party?" Jade's mom interrupted, clearly having heard only bits and pieces at the conversation.

"I don't have a boyfriend!" I defended.

"Persephone loves Joey!" Jade announced. "You're in love!"

"Am not!" I tried to defend. To be in love requires both people to love each other. I don't love Joey. He's just my crush! And Joey certainly doesn't love me. I'm just his friend! I've never been in love. I haven't found my true love yet... or at least I sure hoped I hadn't callously dumped him two years ago over a ruined Easter dress that doesn't even fit me anymore.

I mean, after all, I *do* still have Seth's ring.

"You should see if Joey will be your boyfriend," Jade whispered in my ear. "It would be perfect! We could double date!"

My eyes went big like saucers. Of course I had fantasized about what it would be like to be Joey's girlfriend and go to the movies with him and hold hands in the hallway after school and dedicate love songs on the radio to him... but it was only a mere fantasy! "Joey is just my friend," I whispered back to Jade.

"Well, when he is your boyfriend, we can double date," Jade planned.

"Jade, I'm ten, I won't have a boyfriend until I'm thirty-four!" I whispered.

"Okay, then when we're all in our thirties, we'll double date," Jade giggled.

"Alright you two, stop your scheming," Jade's mom interrupted again. "What are you two talking about?"

"Boys," Mom guessed. Jade and I giggled and blushed.

"Mom!!" I blurted out.

"Yup, definitely boys," Jade's mom agreed. Jade and I were too busy giggling to fight off the true accusations. Luckily, just then we arrived at our destination, and the moment the driver opened the door, we hopped out of the limo, ready to shop.

We first went to this cool shop that had like a magical, mystical feel to it. It reminded me of the shops in Salem, Massachusetts, because it had incense burning and crystals and tarot cards. None of the decks spoke to me like Charlotte Kraft's unicorns had. Mom encouraged me to not buy any, if none were jumping out at me.

"You know how to do tarot readings?" Jade asked.

"Not yet," I admitted. As we walked to the next store, I told her all about last fall's trip to Salem.

"I can't believe you and Coral aren't friends anymore," Jade shook her head. "She was at your birthday parties, every year!"

"Not this year," I scowled. I hadn't thought about Coral in a long time. Charles had mentioned that they were still boyfriend and girlfriend, in the Christmas card. He admitted that *she* had given him and his brother my address so she could say "Hi" to me, in secret, through him, but that was all I knew about her.

All of a sudden Jade stopped walking and said, "Wait! Sparks flew out of Marina's hands?" I had wondered why she hadn't been asking more about *that* part of the story. I reassured her that indeed there was like a spark of lightning that went from Marina towards Mom!

"What *are* you two going on about?" Jade's mom inquired.

"Marina's a witch!" Jade exclaimed.

"Who's Marina?" Jade's mom asked.

"Coral's mom," Jade explained.

"Oh," Jade's mom shrugged towards Mom clearly not knowing or caring who Coral was.

"Do you know how to shoot lightning bolts?" Jade jumped in front of me, grabbing my arm.

"No," I pulled my arm away from her clutches.

"But I thought you were a witch," Jade revealed.

"No, I'm not," I answered. We reached the manicure store and picked out the colors we wanted for our nail polish. I selected an iridescent teal. Mom chose an amethyst purple. Jade's mom wanted candy apple red. Jade decided on glow-in-the-dark orange.

"You could study to be a witch," Jade hypothesized.

"No, I couldn't study to be a witch," I snapped. "Someone either is a witch or isn't a witch, and I'm not a witch and I don't want to be a witch, okay?"

"Whoa, Girl, chill," Jade replied.

"I'm sorry, Jade," I apologized, "I am just really sick of everyone trying to force this witch thing on me, when I'm not some kind of monster!" I then told her about the incident at camp last summer, as we got our manicures.

"That's really scary what went on at that camp," Jade agreed.

"I don't like to think about it very much," I confessed.

I loved the warm, gooey feeling of the paraffin wax. And then it was super neat how it peels off! It reminded me how badly I want to get one of those peeling facial masks again sometime. Oh, my hands were so soft when the wax was removed.

"Your hands will be perfect to hold hands with Joey tonight," Jade teased.

"Well, that ain't happening," I replied.

"Aww, you two would be so cute," Jade responded.

"Let it go, Jade," I answered, watching the woman paint my fingernails. The iridescent teal was just the right color for me. Though Jade had a valid point... my hand would look really nice holding Joey's. I looked at her hands with the bright orange fingernails, and it suddenly hit me that those hands would be holding Seth's hands.

Apparently, I would soon need to visit an ol' blast from the past friend, as I still had something that belonged to him, though evidently, it was no longer his heart. I couldn't understand why I felt

220

so upset. I ought to be happy for my two friends, but I just wanted to cry. I closed my eyes really tightly and used all my energy to make sure I did *not* actually cry. After all, it was my tenth birthday and I didn't want to cry on my special day. Surprisingly, I did manage *not* to cry.

After our day of shopping, pampering, and sipping berry smoothies casually on the limo ride home, we returned to my house as true spoiled divas. I noticed that balloons were tied to the posts on the porch! My house looked like a party waiting to happen!

"Is it party time?" I asked Mom.

"Looks like Dad has been busy!" Mom laughed, "I don't know who is the bigger kid in our family!" Our limo driver opened the door for us to exit, and Jade and I ran inside with our purchases, to see what other transformations had occurred for the party.

As soon as we got in the door, Joey, Freddie, and Dad jumped out yelling, "Surprise!!" I jumped and laughed and got a big hug and a kiss from Dad.

"Oh, wow!" I said, "Thanks!" There were streamers and balloons in the dining room and living room. It definitely looked like the party of the year! Mom and Jade's mom came inside loaded down with the rest of our shopping bags.

"Honey, you really outdid yourself," Mom said to Dad, shaking her head with a smile.

"Is everyone ready for some pizza?" Dad asked, with enthusiasm that sounded as though *he* was more excited for pizza than any of us kids!

"Yeah!!!" we exclaimed. I kicked off my boots and dropped my coat on the floor and ran in my sock feet to get in line behind Joey and Freddie for pizza.

"Persephone, is this what we do with our boots and coats?" Mom nagged.

"No, Mom," I agreed. I straightened my boots on the shoe mat and successfully tossed my coat onto the coat rack. I was back lickity split quick.

"Manners, Persephone," Mom reminded, "could you take Jade's coat to the back bedroom?" I noticed that Jade *did* still have her coat and knew it wasn't really fair to join the boys in eating when my guest was still holding her coat. So, I did as Mom asked, running so fast that I skipped stairs on the way up and jumped down the last three on the way back.

"Is it pizza time *now*?" I asked Mom.

"Of course, my Little Dragon, but I think mushroom with anchovies is the only kind left now."

"*WHAT?*" I asked, revolted and horrified. I would never ever eat mushrooms or anchovies. Blech! Makes me make a wretched face just thinking about it!

"Psyche," Dad reassured. "Is pepperoni, pineapple, and extra cheese okay?"

"Oh, Dad, that's my favorite!" I exclaimed.

"Gee, I would have never guessed that," Dad said sarcastically. I took my paper birthday plate with the piece of pizza to my seat at the dining room table.

"Would you like root beer?" Mom asked.

"Gee, let me think... uh, yes!" I exclaimed.

"Yes, what?" Mom asked.

"Yes, Mom," I answered.

"Yes, what, Mom?" Mom hinted.

Joey leaned over and whispered, "Please!" I was embarrassed that I had forgotten my manners yet again.

"Yes, please Mom," I giggled nervously, "and thank you."

We ate our pizza and drank our soft drinks, and Mom drove Jade's mom home so there wouldn't be too many grown-ups at the party. Mom and Dad don't count as grown-ups because they're very cool and fun. I love them with all my heart. As two of my best friends, I obviously wanted *them* at my party!

Mom returned just in time for cake and ice cream. Every year I look forward to seeing my cake. Mom makes the best cakes in the whole world! Well, okay, her dad, Grampy, makes deliciously awesome cakes, too! Mom's cakes are fandancy though, often molded into creative shapes and decorated with so many colors of frosting. She tells me that it's important to her to spoil me rotten with fandancy birthday cakes because her mom always made the most triumphant cakes for her when she was a kid, too, and she wants to uphold the tradition.

So, when Dad led the party in singing "Happy Birthday," while carrying a normal looking birthday cake to the table, I was a bit taken aback and confused. In teal gel writing were the words "Happy 10th Birthday Persephone!" so I did know it was for me. Upon closer inspection, it didn't look like a typical cake. The frosting didn't look like frosting, it looked more like ice cream!

"You bought me an ice cream cake?" I asked, as the candles burned closer to the cake.

"Your mom and I thought you'd like something different," he admitted, with a panicked look that suggested they hoped I'd be happily surprised with the sudden change of tradition.

"Like it? It's awesome!" I exclaimed, making a wish and blowing out the candles with one big breath. "I've never had an ice cream cake before!"

"Dear, you don't have to do the second part," Dad called into the kitchen, "She's happy with the ice cream cake!" He turned back to me so he could take the ice cream cake back to the kitchen for cutting. "I told her you'd like the ice cream cake! I just knew you would!"

"Wait, what second part?" I inquired. Sure, it's greedy, but if they already planned a second part, why not find out what it is?

"Well, I didn't know if you'd be sad not to have a fancy birthday cake this year," Mom yelled from the kitchen.

"That ice cream cake is a fancy cake, Mom," I reminded.

"Right, but it's not one of *my* cakes," Mom called. "So I made something to uphold the tradition!" She carried out a tiered cupcake holder with the fanciest decorated cupcakes I've ever seen! They looked just like if one of those famous cake makers or magazines had made them. We all oohed and ahhed at them.

"Wow, Mom! You could sell these!" I was amazed by what Mom had done with frosting atop the cupcakes! I selected the unicorn. Jade picked the big sunflower. Joey chose one with bumblebees. Freddie decided on one that looked like a snowy hill with people sledding on it. Dad's had a frog on it, and Mom's was decorated with a rose.

"Mrs. Smith! These are outrageous!" Freddie admitted with frosting on his nose.

Dad carried in the slices of ice cream cake. The ice cream flavors were black raspberry and chocolate chip! Yum! I truly hadn't had ice cream cake before. It was SO good! Between the fancy cupcake and the ice cream cake though, I was very full and feeling rather hyper when I finished my birthday desserts.

"Ready for a movie now?" Dad announced.

"Yeah!" we all shouted simultaneously. Oh, my poor parents with four kids, hyper from sugar, on their hands!

"Is it okay if I invite Seth to come over to watch the movie with us?" Jade whispered as the boys piled into the living room to claim their seats for the film.

"I don't know about that, Jade," I answered. "Won't his feelings be hurt that I didn't invite him to the party?"

"You two don't really talk anymore," Jade reminded. "Besides, he already knows I'm over here for your birthday party anyways." Seth lived two doors down from my house. It was one of the perks of being such a young boyfriend and girlfriend, because we could just walk to one another's house to play.

"Well then, whatever," I answered.

"Oh, you're my best friend ever!" Jade exclaimed, hugging me while pulling out her cell phone. Apparently Seth is on her speed dial. "He'll be right over," she reassured as she closed her phone.

Now it's one thing to know that Jade is Seth's girlfriend now, but it's a whole 'nother story to have to see them together now that I know that. I didn't know if I was ready for that reality. I had always thought Seth liked me more than other girls. I mean, did he really go around giving rings to every girl in the neighborhood? No! He was my boy-

"Are you coming, Persephone?" Joey called from the living room. "I dunno about you *girls*, but Freddie and I wanna see the movie!" Joey's voice totally snapped me back into present day reality. I sighed with a smile. Joey. I ran into the living room and jumped in my teal bean bag chair.

"Yay! Movie time!" I exclaimed. Jade strolled in, looking out the window rather than taking a seat.

"What's with her?" Freddie whispered to me.

"She's keeping lookout because Seth Totter is joining us for the movie," I explained.

"Seth Totter?" Freddie repeated. "Ooh, your boyfriend is coming?" he teased. I noticed that Joey's face was getting red, but he was staring in silence at the DVD previews that were playing on the TV screen.

"Seth is *not* my boyfriend," I defended.

"Well he's a boy and he's your friend..." Freddie smirked.

"With that logic, you're my boyfriend, too, Freddie!" I laughed.

"Is that a bad idea, Persephone?" Freddie grinned widely.

"You're my *friend*," I blushed. "Girls and boys can be friends without being girlfriends and boyfriends!"

"Ahhh, so, you *do* like my good ol' pal, Joey, here then?" Freddie pressed.

I panicked. Freddie laughed. I looked at Joey who was still staring at the TV screen though his face was scarlet. I was positive sure that my face matched his because I have never felt that much burning in my face. I wanted to disappear *now*. Not just hide-a-little but POOF! Disappear! I knew that it wasn't possible to just disappear into thin air... or wait... was it? My brain got a longshot idea. If saying things made them happen, maybe I could *say* the words and disappear! I knew, for sure, I wanted to disappear right now more than anything on the planet!

"I will give up my birthday wish in exchange to just disappear right now!" I said, closing my eyes and making my hands into fists and curling into a ball in my bean bag chair. That was when the most remarkable thing happened!

Seth Totter walked in, cuter than ever.

Jade rushed up to Seth and gave him a hug. "Everybody, this is Seth," she introduced, "Seth, this is Joey, Freddie, and you know Persephone already." The guys waved their hellos, instantly becoming more interested in the previews on the TV.

"Hi, Seth," I greeted, knowing that despite offering a sacrifice and wanting it with all of my heart, my effort to disappear had indeed not worked.

"Happy birthday, Persephone," Seth blushed. "Thanks for inviting me over for the movie."

"No problem, Seth."

Jade decided that she and Seth should sit together on the loveseat, rather than share the remaining bean bag chair on the floor. Mom and Dad joined us as the movie started. I liked that the lights were dimmed because it wouldn't be so easy for anyone to see the expression on my face nor how much I was still blushing.

I racked my brain to figure out why I hadn't disappeared. I had made a sacrifice – what bigger sacrifice is there than giving up a birthday wish? I had spoken from my heart. Why hadn't it worked? Maybe I'd have to pick Mom's brain about it sometime, because it wasn't adding up in my opinion.

The movie was a goofball, age-appropriate comedy. I hadn't seen it before, so I got very involved in watching and all but forgot that my crush and my ex-boyfriend were both in my living room with me. I happened to look over at the loveseat at one point and saw Jade and Seth were holding hands. My nostrils flared slightly and my stomach flew into a big knot. I turned my attention back to the movie. It was an action packed scene which provided a nice distraction from my situation.

After the movie, Joey asked me if I was actually going to open my presents. I couldn't believe I had forgotten all about my gifts! Joey gave me a 1000 piece jigsaw puzzle of a scene in Maine. He told me that the picture was taken in the same town as where he spends his summer vacation with his grandparents. Freddie gave me a pack of colorful blank CDs and cases because he knows how much I like to make and listen to mix CDs. I thanked them both profusely.

"There's another gift that came in the mail, Persephone," Dad informed me. "Would you like to open it now?"

"Who's it from?" I asked, weighing if it would be more appropriate to just wait until my friends had left.

"It's from Salem," Dad revealed, reading the package.

"Salem? Who in Salem would get me a birthday gift?" I asked aloud.

"Open it!" Freddie encouraged. Everyone else agreed.

So I opened the outer wrap and found a wrapped gift inside. The paper was a maroon paisley embossed in gold. My friends whispered speculatively among themselves about the mysterious gift. I found the gift tag and read it. It was from Charles and Drew.

"Gee, how many boyfriends do you have?" Freddie asked. I glared at him.

"I don't have a boyfriend, Freddie," I clarified. I did not need anyone thinking I was not a single, eligible, awesome catch, and misunderstandings like that would be how rumors to the contrary get started.

"So, who are Charles and Drew?" Freddie pressed.

"Charles is my friend Cora- I mean, my former friend Coral's boyfriend, and Drew is his little brother," I answered.

"You and Coral aren't friends anymore?" Seth piped in.

"Long story, Seth," I brushed him off, returning my attention to the wrapped present in my hands. I opened the gift wrap and saw the same kind of tarot cards that had spoken to me in Salem! "Mom! It's the tarot cards with photographs of unicorns!" I exclaimed.

"Awww, Coral must have told them that you didn't still have your deck of unicorns!" Mom smiled.

I was bombarded with questions about tarot cards and what were they and all the questions you might imagine a bunch of kids my age would have about tarot. "They're cool cards that tell the future," I simplified.

"Can you tell us our futures?" Jade asked.

"Not tonight," I admitted. "I have to study the deck first."

"You do like studying," Joey teased, "so you'll know that deck in no time!" Then Mom called Joey to the door, to put on his boots and coat, because his dad had arrived to get him.

"Thanks for the puzzle, Joey," I called to him, "and thanks for coming tonight!"

"Happy birthday, Persephone!" Joey shouted on his way out the door. I ran over to the window to wave goodbye to him as his car pulled away. While I was looking out the window, Freddie's mom pulled into our driveway.

"Freddie, your mom's here!" I informed him. Jade's car came into view, too. "Looks like your mom's here, too, Jade," I said.

"That was a great party, Persephone," Freddie added, putting his boots and coat on.

"Thanks for coming, Freddie, I had fun, too!" I replied.

"That was a fantastic day, Persephone," Jade chimed in. "We really need to get together more often."

"We sure do," I agreed. "Thanks for the CDs, Freddie," I shouted as he headed out into the snowy evening. Freddie waved back at me in the window. I noticed Jade was saying goodnight to Seth before hurrying to her ride. "Thanks for today, Jade," I called after her. I waved to their cars as they drove away.

Then I realized I still had a guest. Seth. He may not have been invited to the party, but he was certainly still in my house. He didn't look like he was ready to leave yet, as he went and flopped onto a beanbag chair.

"So, how's it been going, Seth?" I asked, trying to make casual conversation.

"Oh, you know," he replied. "How's it going for you?"

"Well, I'm getting ready for the Citywide Spelling Bee soon," I informed him.

"You always have been Miss Smarty Pants," Seth chuckled. I stuck my tongue out at him for calling me a name. That immature action made him laugh harder. I daresay it certainly didn't feel like it had been two years since we had hung out.

"Wait here, I'll be right back." I jumped up to recover the ring from my bedroom. I was feeling a nagging sensation that I needed to give it back to him. He wasn't my boyfriend. I wasn't his girlfriend. I shouldn't still have the engagement ring from when we were kids. I knew I needed to actually return it to him. I hurried to my bedroom, went to my jewelry case, and pulled out the ring. I couldn't help but smile when I looked at it. Reminiscing of the old days with Seth always made me smile. We had had such fun together, playing in the woods, riding bikes up to the pond, sledding… good times.

With ring in hand, I ran back downstairs to the living room, jumping onto a beanbag chair. "Here," I said, handing the ring to him.

"You actually kept this?" he asked with a chuckle. "All this time?" he added.

231

"Yeah, I did," I confessed.

"Why?" Seth asked.

"What was I supposed to do, throw it away?" I asked.

"Well, I don't want it," he admitted, still holding the ring just like how I had given it to him.

"Come on Seth, don't be a stinker, just take the ring."

"You're the stinker, Persephone," Seth responded. He tried to force the ring into my hand. "Take it," he demanded.

"It's yours," I closed my hands tightly, unwilling to take the ring. Seth reached for my hands to try to force the ring into one of them, but seeing that was pointless, he tried tickling me. "You've forgotten how stubborn I am," I blurted out between squirms from the tickle torture. After wrestling for maybe a minute, he stopped suddenly and looked at my foot. "No, don't tickle my feet, Seth!" I protested. It was too late, he pulled my sock off. "Noooooo!" I exclaimed. But Seth didn't tickle my foot. Instead, he slid the ring onto my toe.

"You're not the only stubborn one, Princess," he announced, while I stared at him, mouth agape. "The ring is yours. It always has been." He stood up, bent over, and kissed me on top of my head before grabbing his jacket and heading towards the door. I felt frozen in shock and could do nothing but gawk at my foot, wiggling the toe with the ring on it. "Happy birthday," he said, as he left through the kitchen door. In what felt like an eternity of a few seconds later, I pulled the ring off of my toe and put it on my right hand's ring finger, chasing him, too late, to the door. I saw him turn at the end of our sidewalk and catch view of me at the window. He waved and then scooped up a handful of snow and gently lobbed a snowball at the door where I was standing. Then, he turned the corner towards his house.

I hadn't noticed that Mom had come into the kitchen behind me and had taken the ice cream cake out of the freezer. I turned around when I heard her set two dishes on the counter. "So, my Little Dragon," she began as she cut two small slices of the ice cream cake, "I think that was a highly successful tenth birthday, don't you?" She grinned, watching in apparent delight as I stood, reeling, in silence. She got two small forks from the drawer and presented one of the pieces of ice cream cake to me.

"Okay, spill it," she encouraged. We sat down on the stools at the counter in the kitchen, and I did exactly that. I told her everything. When I was finished, I felt like a huge burden of weight had been lifted off my shoulders. And the best part about it, Mom didn't tell me what to do, or even offer boy advice. She simply listened and ate her ice cream cake, and that was exactly what I needed to cap off my tenth birthday.

chapter twenty

Nightmare

Seth nearly looked ethereal in the moonlight. He waded through the knee-deep snow. His warm breath against the cold night marked the air as he exhaled it. The glittering, untouched snow was in pristine piles surrounding the flat area, under which the pond surely lay frozen.

I momentarily pondered if pond creatures really hibernated the way teachers had suggested in school. Seth edged towards the pond. I wanted to tell him to steer clear – that we didn't know how thick the ice truly was – that we couldn't be sure it was safe! But my voice did not eek a sound. In that perfectly beautiful moment, the world was completely silent.

Within moments, Seth reached the middle of the pond and turned around on the snow-covered ice. He looked up at the moon and smiled. I couldn't stop thinking that it was so quiet that I ought to be able to hear a snowflake fall.

But I didn't hear a snowflake. Nor did I hear a bird, a forest creature, nor any other life form. I didn't hear a tree or the wind. And all of a sudden, I didn't hear silence anymore.

The crack of the ice felt as loud as a train or a plane or the rumble of thunder when there's no time between the lightning and the boom. It was so loud that I didn't just hear it, I truly felt it through every fiber of my being. I tried to scream a warning, but my voice still wouldn't sound. I tried to run to help, but my body wouldn't move. There was nothing I could do but watch helplessly as Seth disappeared into the frozen pond... and being immobilized and muted, I watched for what seemed to be hours but saw absolutely no sign of him at the surface ever again.

And then I woke up.

The tears gushed down my face. I have never felt any dream or nightmare that was so realistic and terrifying. I threw back my blankets to get out of bed and run to the safety of my parents' room, but as I did, I noticed I wasn't alone in my room and I stopped in my tracks.

"Seth!" I whisper-exclaimed. "Thank goodness that you're here! I just had a horrific nightmare about you!" I realized I was struggling with breathing. The tears continued streaming with ferocity, but I couldn't tell if I was upset that I had just watched Seth die in my nightmare or just so happy that he was safe and sound and right here in my room! I blurted out, "You were at the pond where we used to go when we were kids, and you fell in and you died!" Seth nodded. I noticed he looked rather waterlogged and even in the darkness, he looked much paler than usual. I realized my emotions were making

235

speaking impossible at that point, so I rushed to give him a hug. I ran towards him, only I didn't run into Seth...

I ran through him!

As my arms flailed in the air and hit my own body with awkward thuds, I turned back to see Seth, only there was nothing there but my bed and the light of the digital alarm clock reading "12:00." I was overcome with nausea, and exactly then, I heard our phone ring. Someone answered it. I couldn't hear even a mumbling of what was being said because my own cell phone rang within seconds. Nobody has ever called me at this hour. I picked up my phone and saw it was Jade. Despite not being capable of speaking, I answered the phone anyways.

Jade didn't wait for a greeting. "Persephone, *please* tell me that Seth's sleeping over at your house, *please!*" Jade hysterically wailed into the phone. I was unable to answer her, but she didn't even give me time to respond, as she continued, "He didn't go home tonight, we don't know where he is, I last saw him at your house, please let him still be there!" I couldn't decipher half of what she said, but I certainly understood the point. Seth was apparently missing!

I flipped the light switch on with my free hand and frantically searched around my room to check if he was mischievously hiding somewhere, since I had just seen him with my own eyes only moments before! I quickly realized my eyes were playing tricks on me, as he was definitely not there! I closed my cell phone with Jade still hysterical on the other end, and instantly, my legs gave out under me, sending me to the floor in a heap of confusion and pain. I curled into a ball, shaking and sobbing.

About a minute later, my parents found me, still clutching my cell phone. Mom immediately rushed to me and sat on the floor, pulling me into her lap and holding me up with her arms. My shaking was completely uncontrollable. "It's going to be okay, Persephone," she reassured with a hug that was not going to end anytime soon.

My father was still on our phone. "Persephone, dear, Mrs. Totter's on the phone. Do you have any idea where Seth would have gone after he left here tonight?" he asked with calm urgency.

I wanted to tell them everything, but I remained incapable of speech or movement. I mustered all of my energy to form the most telling word I could think... "Pond..." I sputtered, and then began shaking even more vigorously and bawling whenever my breath would allow it.

"She said something about the pond," Dad reiterated. He immediately left my room, presumably so I couldn't hear anything more.

Mom simply held me, rocking me slightly from side to side. A few minutes later, Dad returned, without the phone, to find us in exactly the same placement as we had been when he stepped away.

"Has she said anything else?" he asked.

"No," Mom answered, "she's ice cold to the touch though." Dad grabbed the blankets from my bed and wrapped me in them. He sat with Mom and me on the floor, holding both of us. "Oh, my Little Dragon," Mom whispered, "I wish you weren't going through any of this."

Dad scooped me up and tucked me into my bed, safe and snug with all of my blankets. Mom climbed in on my right side, and Dad climbed in on the other side. I had absolutely no doubt that something was terribly wrong in the world, as they had never acted like this in my whole life. I soon felt as though I had no tears left to shed, and I found that my shaking had subsided and my breathing had resumed a deliberate, but controlled, pattern.

"So Squirt, what do you know?" my father dared to inquire.

"I was having a nightmare," I began, calmly and detached. "I saw Seth at Elk Pond, but he looked like he did tonight, not back when were kids. It was so very real that I thought I was there, too. He walked out to the middle of the pond, then he turned and smiled, and then he crashed through the ice when it broke under his feet."

"And you woke up when Mrs. Totter called?" Mom speculated.

"No, I woke up because the nightmare had upset me so," I explained. "I was going to come down the hall and tell you, but I saw Seth here in my room."

"Seth was here?" Dad asked.

"I don't know," I continued, "I saw him, and I told him about the nightmare. He didn't say anything, he just nodded, but I was so happy to see him that I ran to him to give him a hug, only he wasn't there."

Mom sat up slightly. "What do you mean by... that?" she asked.

"I tried to hug him, but my arms just went like..." I pulled my arms from the covers and flailed them in the air. "Like that," I demonstrated. "And I turned around to see if he had scooted aside, but he wasn't in my room anymore, and I couldn't help but think he never actually was here."

"Like your eyes played tricks on you?" Dad pressed.

"Yeah, like that," I agreed. All three of us were silent for a few moments. I decided to continue the story. "And then your phone rang, and then my cell phone rang."

"Who called you, Squirt?" Dad asked.

"Jade," I revealed. "She filled me in on Seth disappearing. She's a mess."

"She's not the only one," Mom hinted.

"I'm sure his family is also wreckage with so much uncertainty," I sympathized.

"I don't know what we would do if we lost you," Dad agreed.

"How are you doing, Persephone?" Mom asked.

"I'm scared," I confessed. "I'm terrified that my nightmare wasn't a dream but a vision, and that when Seth was in here tonight, it wasn't exactly my eyes playing tricks on me."

"You know you couldn't have stopped whatever happened, right?" Dad suggested.

"I suppose," I lied.

"So, how long have you been seeing ghosts, my Little Dragon?" Mom asked.

"I didn't say I see ghosts, Mom," I defended. It was in the silence that followed that I realized exactly what was being suggested. If my nightmare was a vision, then Seth came to me as a ghost to tell me where his family could find him! I racked my brain to think of any other possible ghosts that I've seen in life. "Does Grampy have a black cat?" I asked, randomly.

"The one you see walking around his house?" Mom asked, cautiously.

"Yes, that one!" I exclaimed, relieved that Mom knew about the cat. If other people knew about the cat, it wasn't a ghost, and therefore, I don't see ghosts. "I always kinda thought it was a ghost, cuz you're allergic to cats and Grampy has never mentioned the cat and has never left food or water or a litter box for it."

"Have you noticed that it always walks in the same circle?" Mom asked.

"Yes, like clockwork," I replied, puzzled. "Yeah, that's weird! Cats are anything but predictable!"

"You know how I've told you that apparently the cat is my spirit animal?" Mom reminded. I nodded slowly, recalling that Mom told me she'd tell me about it some other time. "Well, that's in part because I can see the cat, too," Mom admitted. "I've been able to see it ever since I was a little kid."

"That's an awfully old cat, Mom," I chuckled.

"It's a ghost, Squirt," Dad interrupted. "Your Grampy has never owned a black cat."

"So, when I saw Seth in here tonight, he was just a ghost, too?" I suddenly realized.

"Let's hope not, Kiddo," Mom comforted. Despite Mom's best efforts, she wasn't being very convincing.

"I didn't wish for any of this to happen," I admitted. "I wish for Seth to be perfectly fine," I spoke aloud. "I sacrifice... I give up chocolate for the next month, to make Seth alive and well."

"You can't just shape the world the way you want it, Squirt," Dad explained. "Sometimes things have to happen the way they happen, and sometimes we can't control them."

"There's no reason for Seth to be dead, Dad!" I raised my voice.

"You don't know that he is," Dad replied, "and even if he is, you are *not* responsible for it!"

I wondered if things would have been different if I had not ended our relationship when he splashed mud on me that Easter. I wished I had run out to him at the end of the sidewalk when he threw the snowball at me tonight and insisted on walking him home. Mostly, I couldn't stop kicking myself with guilt for having had that nightmare – what kind of friend dreams of her friend's death? That's ghastly! I felt as though it was totally my fault because I had dreamed such an abhorrent dream. "Why did I have to have that nightmare?" I asked aloud.

"His parents wouldn't have known to look at the pond unless you had that vision," Dad said. "If they find him there, your gift will have given them peace."

"I don't want them to find him there, Dad," I confessed. "If they find him there, he'll be dead. I want them to find him hiding under his bed."

"Persephone," Mom added, "we *all* hope for Seth to be alive and well. And we'll *all* gladly give up chocolate for a month to make that happen."

And as I fell back asleep, framed by my loving parents who truly would do anything within their powers to keep my life simple, innocent, and perfect, I knew the three of us would enjoy every bite of non-chocolate desserts for the coming month. Seth had to be alive... he just had to be alive... he... had... to be... alive... and...

I was out like a light.

chapter twenty-one

Never Again

I never thought I would be going to my first funeral at the age of ten. Funerals are terrible. Mourning is horrendous. Everyone wore black and was completely broken, crying an unimaginable number of tears. Providing comfort to family members who logically had even more of a right to be shattered than myself was emotionally exhausting. The whole day felt like a dizzying blur.

I never want to go to a funeral again. I never want to think about a funeral again.

And don't expect me to *ever* speak of this funeral again.

chapter twenty-two
The Citywide Spelling Bee

I had focused so hard on just putting one foot in front of the other for the remainder of February that I was completely caught off-guard when it was suddenly the first week of March and somehow the morning of the Citywide Spelling Bee!

"I think I'm going to be sick," I announced aloud as I ran downstairs with all of the stuff I could possibly need for the day packed in my teal backpack.

"You're fine," Dad reassured me, not even looking up from the newspaper.

"Really, Dad?" I sighed an annoyed huff. "Cuz I feel like I'm going to barf!"

"Calm down, you're fine," Dad replied, sipping his coffee. Obviously Dad didn't understand nerves, so I skedaddled to find Mom.

"Mom, I think I'm going to be sick," I announced, hustling into their bedroom and flopping myself onto their king-sized bed.

"Do you need me to call the school?" Mom inquired, still readying herself for the day.

"I can't miss today!" I scoffed. Seriously, did my parents completely space out that today was *the* day of *the* Citywide Spelling Bee that I had been preparing for *all* school year?

"Why not?" Mom asked.

"Mom!" I propped myself up on one elbow and stared at Mom, putting on her makeup. "Today is the Citywide Spelling Bee!"

"Oh, so it's just nerves," Mom pishawed. "You're just nervous, my Little Dragon, but you'll be fine."

I groaned and lay back onto the bed. I grabbed a pillow and held it on my mouth as I screamed, frustrated, into it.

"Persephone, you can spell every word any of us can think of," Mom declared, turning to me. "You're ready for this, just enjoy the day!"

Dad joined us in their bedroom. "Here, Squirt, have a peppermint, it'll calm your stomach," he encouraged as he handed me a mint.

"Thanks, Dad," I said begrudgingly and went to finish readying for the day. The peppermint did seem to alleviate some of the nervous nausea, and I knew in my heart that Mom was right. I did know just about any word anyone could think of. I had studied word lists for over five months, and I knew them all. My team wasn't quite as proficient at practices as I was, but as long as I did my part, we would fare just fine.

The spelling bee team was meeting at the school half an hour early so we could travel to the high school for the Citywide Spelling Bee. I told Mr. Harper about my nausea.

"You have *no* reason to be nervous," Mr. Harper reassured me. "You know every word in the dictionary, don't you?" I laughed and nodded at his slight exaggeration, as indeed, I *had* studied the dictionary fairly thoroughly.

We climbed into the thirteen passenger van, and Mr. Harper drove us across town. The Citywide Spelling Bee was in the high school's auditorium. There were chairs set up on the stage dividing us into our school teams. Saint Bart's was in the back, off to the side, in a position that suggested that whoever put together the Citywide Spelling Bee didn't think we'd fare very well. Ha. They hadn't seen us in action yet.

Mr. Harper pulled us together for a huddle and pep talk as the other schools found their seats on the stage. "Enjoy today, everyone - you've worked hard for this! Do your best and remember, this is supposed to be fun! So have fun!"

Then we all put our hands in the middle of the circle and cheered, "Go Saint Bart's!"

It was decided that I would spell first for our team, and Saint Bart's was chosen, via lottery, to go first. That made me the first speller of the competition. The rules were that points were given for each correctly spelled word, with different point values given for different rounds. I approached the microphone, sweating profusely, trying to recall not only all of the nice, uplifting things that had been said to me thus far today, but also to remember every spelling of every word I had ever seen in life.

"From Saint Bartholomew's School, fifth grader, Persephone Smith," the announcer said. I heard a clapping sound in the back of the auditorium and looked to find the source. My eyes went big as saucers and my jaw dropped when I saw who it was. Seth! He was standing up on a chair in the last row, wearing a t-shirt that said "I <3 Miss Smarty Pants." I felt dizzy and couldn't hear anything and then my vision looked kinda funny, like long tunnels, and then everything got dark fast.

The next thing I knew, my whole spelling team was gathered around me, and I was lying on the floor looking up at all of them. Mr. Harper said, comfortingly, "It's okay Persephone, you're okay."

Joey inadvertently reminded me exactly what had happened. "Persephone, it looked like you saw a ghost!" Freddie smacked him. "Oww," Joey complained, shooting Freddie a questioning look and then appearing to realize his faux pas. In general, people didn't mention anything to do with death around me anymore. "Oops, I mean, are you okay?" he corrected.

"If I may sit in a chair, I'm ready for my word," I said, sitting up too fast and realizing the room was still spinning. The judges approved the use of a chair, bringing me a chocolate chip cookie and a bottle of water as well. I politely refused the cookie. "Thanks, but I can't have chocolate." I took a few sips of water and then Mr. Harper helped me into the chair, cautioning that I didn't have to compete today. "I practiced too long to give up now," I muttered, eyes closed, holding my head with both hands.

"Ms. Smith? Are you ready for your word?" the announcer asked.

"Yes, sir," I replied, keeping my eyes closed.

"Your word is onomatopoeia," the judge said.

"Onomatopoeia," I repeated. "O-n-o-m-a-t-o-p-o-e-i-a, onomatopoeia." The judges announced that I was correct. And with that, Saint Bart's was on the board. I heard clapping from one set of hands in the far back of the auditorium. I couldn't help but open my eyes. Seth was standing on his chair again, pumping his fist into the air. I smiled at the sight, but as I saw that everyone else was looking directly at the judges, I realized nobody else could see what I could see. That realization wiped the smile off my face. It wasn't fair that everyone wasn't an audience to Seth's enthusiasm. I looked at Seth again and he got down off his chair and waved at me. I winked in subtle acknowledgement. Then I stood on my shaky feet and managed to stagger back to my seat with the rest of Saint Bart's team.

We each spelled four words before lunch. It was announced that the best three spellers from each school in the first four rounds would represent their teams in an additional four rounds after lunch. The school with the highest total at the end of the day would move on to the Statewide Spelling Bee. My other words that morning were "strenuous," "intergalactic," and "orangutan." As would be expected, I nailed each of my words. Skye and Joey were the other two Saint Bart's students to make it through to the final rounds.

"You three go make Saint Bart's School proud this afternoon," Mr. Harper encouraged, as we all grabbed our lunches and spread around the auditorium to eat. The Saint Bart's team congregated in

248

the front row of seats to the right of the stage, sitting down quickly to nosh their brown bags of deliciousness.

Crazy though it may seem, I walked right past them up to the row where I had seen Seth during the morning spelling session. I sat in the seat next to where I had seen him. I spoke aloud in a barely audible voice, "I saw you cheering for me today. Thanks." I didn't know if he could hear me. I didn't know if he was still there. I didn't know how these ghost things worked. I didn't even know if I believed in ghosts. All I know is last month, on the night of my tenth birthday, I had seen Seth in my bedroom, and then today I had seen him here in the high school's auditorium.

I opened my teal lunch bag to find a turkey, salami, and cheese sandwich on a fluffy, white roll, a grape soda, and cheesy corn crunchies. Healthy? Not exactly, but it wasn't every day that my parents packed me a spelling bee lunch. I looked a little deeper in the bag and found a small piece of key lime pie with whipped cream. As predicted, the chocolate-free life wasn't really so bad at all.

A finger pointed at the pie. I looked up the arm and found it was Seth's hand doing the pointing. He gave me a confused look. "I gave up chocolate as a sacrifice so that you would be found alive," I admitted. He looked himself over and then looked back at me with the same confused look. "Yeah, I know," I agreed, "but a sacrifice is a sacrifice, regardless of the outcome."

He grinned and looked as though he was going to ruffle my hair, but I just felt suddenly nauseated at the moment when his hand should've touched my head. His face looked disappointed that he couldn't ruffle it. "Hey, I'm new to this whole ghost thing, too," I admitted. "It's not like I've ever had a friend who is a ghost before." He smiled and did a fist pump in the air. I dove into my sandwich, chips, and drink. Soon, the judges announced the competition would resume in ten minutes, so I wolfed down my pie and prepared for the second half. "Thanks for having lunch with me," I said aloud.

"Yeah, you had lunch with all your *real* friends," Skye sniped with a laugh as she walked by.

"Not *all* of my friends, but one better than you'll ever have," I muttered under my breath. "I hope I see you soon," I said to Seth before heading back up to the stage. Onstage, they had reduced each school's chairs to just the three for the team members who were still competing. The remainder of each team sat with their coaches in the audience.

It was decided that Skye would be first, Joey second, and myself third for the afternoon's competition. I was pleased that Joey was sitting next to me, as I worried I'd have to hurt Skye if she were a foot away from me for an entire afternoon. The next three rounds remained easy for me, "philanthropy," "dilemma," and "hypothetically," but I knew that I'd be getting the final word of the final round, and the words of the final round are historically, of mind-blowing difficulty.

"Ms. Smith, as the first competitor this morning," the announcer remarked, "it seems only suitable that you are the final competitor this afternoon."

"Thanks, I won't pass out this time," I replied, reassuringly. A rumble of laughter passed through the audience and even the competitors on the stage snickered.

"The final word of the 2010 Citywide Spelling Bee is ophthalmologist," the man said.

"Ophthalmologist," I repeated. I smiled. Mom had made me memorize this one on the day I joined the spelling bee team, because legend had it, back when she was doing spelling bees as a kid, it was the final word of the competition the year before she competed. I took a breath, "O-p-h-t-h-a-l-m-o-l-o-g-i-s-t, ophthalmologist."

"Correct, and ladies and gentlemen, she didn't even ask for a sentence," the announcer grinned. "We invite all of the teams to rejoin on the stage as we tally the final results."

Mr. Harper ran up and gave me a hug that lifted me off the floor. "How on earth did you know 'ophthalmologist' when it wasn't on *any* spelling list we distributed?"

"It was a word Mom learned when she was on *her* school's spelling team back in the '80s."

"Ahh," Mr. Harper understood. We all stood in a nervous huddle awaiting the results. I knew we had done well, as we had gotten just about every word right all day. I got all eight of mine, and that's all I could do. I knew a perfect score was 223 points, and no team would be receiving a perfect score.

"Ladies and gentlemen, your attention please," the announcer spoke. "Today's competition was extremely close. Congratulations to all of the participants on a fantastic spelling bee. You all should be proud of yourselves. In third place, with 181 points, River Street Elementary School. In second place, with 196 points, Castle School. And in first place, with 201 points, moving onward to represent our city at the Statewide Spelling Bee in two weeks, Saint Bart's!"

Maybe we weren't the most gracious winners, as we screamed, hooted, hollered, piled onto one another with hugs and high fives, and jumped altogether in excitement, but for Saint Bart's to pull off the upset and *win*? That was completely unfathomable! They gave us a team trophy, and the judges presented each of us with a gold medal. Once we had accepted our accolades, we piled back into the thirteen passenger van, and Mr. Harper brought us out for ice cream, to celebrate!

"I am *SO* proud of my team," he announced. "I can't believe you did it!"

"Have a little faith in us, Mr. Harper, okay?" Freddie reminded with a smile.

"A little faith?" Mr. Harper repeated. "Team, I think we might win Vermont if you compete in two weeks at states like you did today! Those other teams didn't stand a chance!"

"The winning score at the Statewide Spelling Bee hasn't been below 220 in eighteen years, Mr. Harper," Skye pointed out. "We wouldn't have won there today."

"We have two weeks to study, Skye," Mr. Harper said enthusiastically. "Apparently on our team though, Skye's the limit!" he said, pointing at Skye on the appropriate cue. We laughed, albeit at Skye's expense.

"Glad you're amusing the troops with your juvenile humor, Mr. Harper," Skye pouted.

Even Skye couldn't ruin our mood though. We returned to Saint Bart's after school had been dismissed, and I ran to Mom's classroom to tell her the news.

"We won!"

"You did?"

"Why does everyone react with such shock? Doesn't anyone believe in us?"

"Saint Bart's never wins anything, my Little Dragon, that's all."

"We did today! Our score was 201! We're going to the Statewide Spelling Bee!"

"*YAY!!!*" Mom exclaimed, hugging me and swinging me in a circle, "Congratulations!"

"Thanks!" I answered. "And Mom, guess what the last word of the competition was?"

"I don't know, what?"

"Ophthalmologist."

"And did the person spell it right?"

"The person was me, and yes, of course I did!"

Mom laughed. "I can't believe they actually used that word in a final round. After all the years of hype and rumor and urban legend about it... and best yet, my daughter got to spell it, correctly."

"I would've never heard the end of it had I *not* spelled it correctly, Mom."

"That's true, my Little Dragon, that's true," Mom agreed, smoothing my hair. "So, are you ready for states?" I looked at her *incredulously*. Then I nodded *exuberantly*, realizing I knew exactly how to spell "incredulously" and "exuberantly" without any hesitation or worry whatsoever.

"Piece o' cake, Mom," I replied. "I just hope my cheering section returns!"

253

"Cheering section?" Mom looked at me funny as we left her classroom, locking it up for the night. We walked the hallway in silence, as I didn't want to say anything inside of the school building. "Nobody was supposed to be at the Citywide Spelling Bee except team members, coaches, and judges. How did you have a cheering section?" Mom inquired as we got into the car.

"I'm thinking that the usual spectator rules probably don't apply when someone is a specter."

"Oh?" Mom said, taken aback. "Wow, I didn't see that coming."

I giggled. "I guess most people, in general, don't exactly see *him* coming either."

"Good one, my Little Dragon," Mom praised, "very clever." I grinned triumphantly, and yes, I can spell "triumphantly" without any hesitation as well!

Bring on the Statewide Spelling Bee. I am ready.

chapter twenty-three

Embarrassing Moments

Do you have any idea how bizarre it is to have a ghost as one of your best friends? There were definitely some elements of this whole situation that I couldn't quite get used to. Like never knowing where or when he might pop up next. And let me tell you, there are moments in *all* of our lives that we would rather *not* have anyone else see! One time I was getting dressed for school, and I looked up and Seth was pointing and covering his mouth as if he was laughing... as I was standing there in my underwear! I told him to cover his eyes that instant, and he did, but I was so embarrassed! I still can't tell you if he went through walls, like you see in the movies, but one minute he wouldn't be there, and the next moment, there was Seth!

I'm certainly not complaining. There's not a chance that I would ever grouse about seeing that Seth was fine. Okay, he was a *ghost*, but he sure seemed like the same ol' excitable, quirky, carefree, happy, Seth I had always known and lov- I mean, cared about. Alright, him not being able to talk was a little strange, and apparently

I really was the only person who could see him, but in the grand scheme of the finale known as death, witnessing an encore of peaceful haunting provided me with a wonderful level of comfort.

On the Saturday after the Citywide Spelling Bee, I was sitting on a stool at the counter, eating a bowl of my favorite cereal while watching some Saturday morning cartoons on the little, portable TV in the kitchen. Sure, some folks think ten year olds are too old for such traditions, but I say if you're having fun and not hurting anyone, you never can be too old for kids' stuff. Dad was outside snowblowing the driveway, and I could hear Mom's slippers scuffing towards the kitchen, to signal that she was awake.

"Good morning, my Little Dragon," Mom announced with a yawn. "And good morning, Seth," she added.

I looked around the room, but I didn't see Seth anywhere. "Mom, do you *see* him?" I frantically asked, hoping she would be able to affirm that she did.

"No, Kiddo," she admitted with a sigh, "but I've never knowingly seen a human ghost in my life... only animals." She saw my look of disappointment. "I just assumed he's nearby, because he usually is, and I didn't want to not acknowledge him simply because I can't see him."

Just then one of the dishtowels inexplicably fell from the counter.

"Like I said, good morning, Seth." She smiled. I nearly choked on my mouthful of cereal.

"He's here?" I blurted, when I found my voice. "But I don't see him!"

256

"Just because you can't always see a ghost doesn't mean they're not there," Mom explained. "I've talked to ghosts for years, but I've never seen a human one."

"Are you like one of those guys on the TV that goes around looking for ghosts in all the haunted places?" I sat up, intrigued and amazed that someone I've known my whole life would not have already shared such cool information with me!

"Not at all," she denied. "The people on TV speak forcefully, to provoke a reaction from the ghost. I have found, for myself, it works much more effectively to just treat ghosts with respect and maintain a constant effort to listen through their actions to see if they're trying to communicate something to us."

"Well, how is Seth here now but I can't see him?" I asked, still confused.

"In order for a ghost to do something, it takes a lot of energy. For you to have knocked that dishtowel off the counter, you could have used one finger of your body. Ghosts don't have physical bodies. In order for them to move something, it takes a huge amount of effort, and the heavier the object, the more energy is required to move it. If he's manifesting so you can see him as an apparition, merely visually appearing takes a great deal of energy on his part." She paused, looked with trepidation around the room, and continued, "He's here, right now. Just neither of us can see him."

"Hi, Seth," I said nervously. The dishtowel flew back up to the countertop. "Whoa!" I exclaimed.

"Thanks, Seth, you can come over to help with the housework anytime," Mom teased.

257

"Why doesn't he talk to me?" I asked.

"Making sound requires energy as well," Mom explained. "I'm actually amazed that he was clapping at the spelling bee, but yeah, I guess speaking is more difficult than appearing," Mom hypothesized. "Or else Seth just knows that you'd believe seeing him more than you'd believe hearing him."

I pondered that for a moment. Then my mind had a much more panicked thought. "Oh my goodness, if Seth doesn't have to be visible to be in the same room as me, then how many times has he seen things *I* wouldn't want him to see? Like, you know, me in my underwear!?"

"Well, I am sure that Seth is always the gentleman who knows when to look away during your private moments in life, Persephone, isn't that right, Seth?" Mom suggested.

The dishtowel fell to the floor again. I took that as a "No." I put my cereal bowl on the counter and covered my face with both of my hands, utterly embarrassed as my mind raced with all the moments in the past month where the last thing I would've wanted was an audience.

"Young man, you hear me..." Mom threatened, "You behave yourself around my daughter!" I peeked through my fingers as she shook her finger in the air as if she was an old lady scolding a toddler. I couldn't help but laugh. The visual of Mom chewing out a ghost was just too funny for words!

"What on earth are you two up to?" Dad asked as he tracked snow into the kitchen.

I was laughing so hard that I could barely gasp out an explanation, "Mom was scolding Seth... for seeing me... in my underwear! She was literally... shaking her finger... at him!"

Dad looked uber confused, so Mom filled in the details. "Persephone didn't realize that Seth can be present without her seeing him, so he presumably could have caught her at some rather... personal moments."

"Like in the bathroom?" Dad suggested. I immediately stopped laughing, and my eyes went big as saucers and my face burned hotter than I can ever remember with an embarrassment so deep I couldn't breathe!

"Thanks, hun," Mom said to Dad, "it's not like I was trying to not let her think of *that* since it hadn't crossed her mind yet."

"I'm never taking a shower again!!" I screamed and ran to my bedroom, slamming the door and hiding under all the covers of my bed. The mere concept of anyone having full access to my every moment was suddenly, absolutely mortifying. I must've hid in bed for at least five minutes before poking my nose out to peek around my room.

Seth was sitting at my desk, waiting for me to emerge from my hiding spot. He jumped up when he saw that his wait had paid off.

"You've seen me in the shower?" I asked, horrified.

Seth frantically shook his head to say, "No," raising his right hand as if to take an oath and making a cross sign over his heart.

"You've seen me in the bathroom?" I asked.

Seth made a disgusted face that made me realize that nobody in their right mind, ghost or otherwise, would actually want to see someone using a toilet. He obviously shook his head, "No."

"But you *have* seen me in my underwear," I accused.

I didn't know ghosts could blush, but he definitely blushed. He looked down as his feet and then nodded. He looked around the room nervously but wouldn't look at me again.

"Uh, Seth, I'm over here," I summoned his attention. He slowly looked at me, seemingly braced for a scolding. "Ok, mister, here's the deal... the entire bathroom is strictly off-limits!" Seth mockingly squinted his eyes to mirror my serious expression and nodded once to show understanding and agreement, with a smirk emerging from his lips. "And if you *ever* again see that I am not properly attired for polite company, you are to avert your eyes immediately, do you understand?" He gave me a vacant look that made me realize I may have selected words that were not resonating with him. "I'm saying if you ever see me and I'm not appropriately dressed, cover your eyes immediately!" He covered and uncovered his eyes in a manner that looked like a grown-up playing peekaboo with a toddler, with a big smile to match the imagery. Then he winked and gave me the "OK!" hand gesture.

I heard Dad's rat-a-tat knock at my door. "Come in!" I yelled.

"Hey Squirt, would you like to call Jade and invite her over to play this afternoon?" Dad asked.

I realized I hadn't seen Jade in nearly a month. I hadn't been able to bring myself to calling her in weeks because at last check, all she did on the phone was cry hysterically. "Do you think she's up for visiting yet?" I asked.

"Mom called her mom already and did some investigating as to how Jade's doing," Dad admitted. "Her mom reports that she hasn't cried in two weeks, but that she is in need of some friend time."

I grabbed my cell phone and called Jade without further hesitation. Seth gave me a look of confusion. "Hey, she was *my* friend first," I said to him. Dad looked at me like I was crazy, as I must have appeared to be talking to myself.

"Oh, Seth's in here, too?" Dad asked aloud.

I nodded an affirmation to him as Jade answered my call.

"Hey Girl! Why you ain't been callin' me?" Jade accused without even a hello.

"Uh, well, I've been… busy…" I was taken aback.

"Oh stop your frettin', I'm just messin' with ya! I am in serious need of a makeover, you game?"

"I was actually calling to see if you wanted to come over this afternoon?"

"If we can do foofy girl stuff like face masques and hairstyling and funky nails, then yeah! I haven't done anything with my fingernails since your birthday! And you're like ten and a twelfth now! This orange junk on my nails has got to go!"

I remembered our trip to the manicurist for my birthday. I simultaneously recalled how jealous I felt that evening when I saw Jade's neon orange fingernails entwined with Seth's hand as they watched the movie on our loveseat. I suddenly felt a tremendous wave of pressure in my chest because I had been so foolish as to begrudge them that small moment of happiness. "Sounds perfect," I choked out. "Mom and I will be over to pick you up at 1:00?"

Jade agreed. "You're not gonna skimp on the junkfood, either, right?"

"Have you *ever* known us to skimp on the junkfood?" I asked lightheartedly, before quickly doing the math to figure out if I could eat chocolate yet.

"Now, that's what I'm talkin' about, Girl! See you when you get here!"

I closed my phone. "Jade wants to do makeovers and junkfood," I told Dad.

"Sounds like a good way to spend your afternoon, Squirt," Dad agreed. "One o'clock you said?"

"Yup," I confirmed.

"I'll go tell your mom, and in the meantime, you better get ready, as it's almost noon," Dad advised. He walked away from the door, leaving it open behind him.

I turned to Seth, "Now, remember our deal… bathrooms are *off-limits!*" He sat down at my desk, nodded, and proceeded to painstakingly twiddle his thumbs. As I hopped off of my bed and hurried to the door I added, "And you'll *still* be right here when I am done with my shower and dressed, right?" I saw him nod again as I rounded the doorframe out into the hall.

And indeed, he was.

Jade's visit was really nice. We didn't mention Seth at all. It was just a typical girls' get-together with makeup, hair products, skin stuff, music, and junkfood! I was shocked at how completely normal

262

the whole interaction was, considering the sadness we had endured only a month before. I really wanted to bring up the elephant in the room, but I couldn't. Jade was happy. I was happy. And I knew Seth was happy, too, even though I was the only person who had seen that.

As we dropped Jade off at her house later that evening, she thanked Mom and me for the day. "That was totally what I needed," she admitted. "Thanks for bringing me back to life again."

"Anytime," I agreed.

Our car pulled away and her words echoed in my head. Back to life again. I had to ask, "Mom, is it possible to *actually* bring someone back to life again?"

"Not once they're embalmed, my Little Dragon," Mom disclosed, reading the disappointment on my face. "I'm sorry, Persephone, I know you'd do anything to have him back, alive, and well, again."

"Yeah, Mom, I would," I admitted.

chapter twenty-four

Opalescence

The Statewide Spelling Bee was the following Saturday in Essex, Vermont. This time, parents and supporters were welcome to go and cheer the teams on, so I rode up with Mom and Dad. As Dad turned into the driveway, Mom reached over and touched his arm gently and said, "Oh, honey, I remember when I came here to see you in concert, so long ago…"

Dad chuckled and shook his head. Mom's excitement and panache for detailed recollections about life during his UR My QTπ days always seemed to amuse him. Meanwhile, he was focused on reading the signs to get us to the parking lot for today's event. When he had successfully parked the car he turned to Mom and said, "And dear, I remember the first time I took you on a date when you lived not very far from here, and the whole neighborhood came out of their homes to see who was in the limo that pulled up to your building."

"You had to sign autographs for everyone there just to allow us to get to dinner," Mom recounted with a smile. "My neighbors were worse than the paparazzi."

"Think fast, Squirt... paparazzi?" Dad quizzed.

"Uh, p-a-p-a-r-a-t-z-i?" I guessed.

"Close, two Zs, no T," Mom corrected.

"Got it," I agreed. I felt like kicking myself for missing one, but it wasn't during the competition, and I hadn't actually looked that one over.

"Well, then, let's do this," Dad encouraged. We got out of the car and walked to the building where the Statewide Spelling Bee was being held. I located Mr. Harper and the rest of my team. Most had traveled together in the thirteen passenger van, though their parents were there to cheer for us, as well.

"Why on earth would you ride with your parents?" Skye confronted me as I joined the group. "What are you, four?"

"Actually, Skye, I love my parents and enjoy hanging out with them. It's called a healthy relationship."

"Persephone's parents ROCK, Skye," Freddie defended.

"Oh, please, her mom's a teacher. Teachers are not cool," Skye argued. As if timed straight from a movie, Mr. Harper walked by her at that exact moment, clearing his throat in presumed non-agreement.

"You were saying, Ms. Stanley?" Mr. Harper inquired.

"Uh, I was saying, um," Skye stammered.

"I hope her foot tastes good in her mouth," Joey whispered to Freddie and me.

"Maybe you shouldn't be saying anything, if you can't say something nice, Ms. Stanley," Mr. Harper concluded.

We all gathered in Saint Bart's area on the stage. I looked at the huge audience and my stomach did a flip-flop. I focused on breathing... in... out... in... out... pause... I couldn't remember what came next. The idea came to me suddenly and I sucked in a big gulp of air before exhaling it slowly.

"You okay?" Joey mouthed to me. I nodded. I scanned the audience again. Finding Mom and Dad in that crowd would be like a needle in a haystack... that is, unless one's friend who is a ghost happens to be there to draw one's attention right to them. I waved right at Mom and Dad in the audience. They beamed with ear-to-ear smiles of pride and excitement, tickled pink that I had located them in the massive crowd. Joey followed my line of sight. "How did you find them out there?" he asked, waving to them, too.

"I had a little help," I whispered.

"Can your 'little help' help me find *my* parents out there?" Joey asked.

"I don't know," I truthfully admitted. I had no idea if Seth knew who Joey's parents were, or if he would be willing to become a parent locator, but before I could scan the crowd from left to right, I noticed him standing behind a family of familiar faces six rows from the front. "Aha, right there!" I pointed and Joey followed where I was pointing, jumping up and waving frantically at his family.

"You have eagle eyes!" Freddie jumped in. "Where's my mom?"

"I *don't* have eagle eyes. I simply have help," I admitted. I scanned the crowd from front to back and saw Seth waving from

266

near the right wall, halfway back. "Is that her over on the right?" I asked Freddie, pointing.

"Hot dog, it is! How'd you do it?" Freddie exclaimed, waving to his mom, too. I helped Danielle find her family, too, thanks to Seth's ability to flag them for me to see.

Then a girl from the school group sitting next to Saint Bart's leaned over and asked, "Can you help me find my parents out there?"

I looked at her. "I don't know what your parents look like," I admitted.

"I know," she responded, "but you're psychic, aren't you?"

"Not that I know of," I answered, confused.

"Oh, I'm sorry," she apologized, "I had been watching you find the kids' parents in the audience and you seemed to have an extraordinary ability and some pretty amazing powers."

I shrugged. "I'm just me," I explained, "and it's just how I am."

"Fascinating," she looked at me in awe. She put her hand out to shake mine. "I'm Misty Creek, from Williams School."

"Hi, Misty, I'm Persephone Smith from Saint Bart's School," I introduced as I noticed Seth waving for my attention, "and apparently your parents are right over there." I pointed at the smiling couple in front of Seth. They didn't look anything like Misty, so I was concerned that Seth was sorely mistaken, but the suffocating bear hug that she then gave me and the wave that she gave them alleviated all of my concerns.

"Amazing!" she said to me. She waved to them some more and blew kisses. "Please say you'll keep in touch with me outside of this spelling bee?"

"Um, sure?" I replied, not certain how *that* was going to occur.

"Okay, you sideshow freak," Skye approached with a tone of contempt. "Go ahead, find *my* parents out there."

"They're in the front row, Skye," I answered without moving my eyes from hers.

"That's right, because my parents love me more than your parents love you."

"Really, Skye? Really?" I stepped up to her. "Is that so?" I was so angry I wished I could punch her without getting in trouble. One pop, right to her nose. Pow. Just one. Nothing an ice pack wouldn't fix in time.

"You bet it is," Skye challenged, averting her eyes from me and blowing kisses to her parents. Mr. Harper walked over, sensing the brewing tension, and stood between us.

"Whatever," I said, returning to my seat.

At the state level, the rules were a bit different. The rounds were played much the same way, but if any speller missed two words, he or she was eliminated from the rest of the competition, and the other team members would consequently have to spell more often. If all of the spellers from a school were eliminated, that school would be out of the rest of the competition. I looked at Mr. Harper with a panicked look. He gestured with his hand to relax and it would be fine.

So the structure was four rounds with twenty words given to each school in the morning session, with a lunch break, and another four rounds with twenty words given to every non-eliminated school in the afternoon session. In the event of a tie, subsequent rounds would be played as needed, until the winners were crowned.

For the first two rounds, each speller was guaranteed to get a word, as it was mathematically impossible for anyone to be eliminated yet. As luck would have it, everyone was still in for the third round, but that round was when spellers started dropping like flies. Danielle missed "cemetery" and was out in the third round, so four Saint Bart's students remained in the competition, entering the final round of the morning. As I was the first member of my team to spell in the fourth round, I knew I'd take on a fifth word to end the morning.

"Paparazzi," the announcer requested.

I laughed. Then I breathed a big sigh of relief. I couldn't be a luckier girl than I was at that moment. "Paparazzi," I repeated. "P-a-p-a-r-a-z-" I heard Skye laugh behind me, but I continued, "z-i, paparazzi."

"Correct," the judge determined. The audience applauded and I turned and shot Skye a smug smirk.

"Wait, isn't there a 'T' in paparazzi?" Skye asked Joey.

"Apparently not," Freddie answered.

When the fourth round concluded, the four of us – Skye, Freddie, Joey, and myself – remained in the competition for Saint Bart's, but each of my teammates had missed a word. Most of the schools were down one or two spellers, going into the afternoon session, so it was really hard to determine which school was in the lead at this point.

269

"Way to go, Persephone!" Dad announced as I ran up to him with a hug.

"You were awesome, my Little Dragon," Mom agreed with an equally big hug.

"Can you believe my last word of the round was paparazzi?!" I exclaimed.

"I'm glad we reviewed that one in the car, Squirt," Dad acknowledged. I ate my lunch with my parents, because they treated me to the food that was available at the site. It wasn't the healthiest food, and it wasn't the tastiest, but I felt really good going into the afternoon after having those minutes of reprieve from the competition while eating greasy burgers and fries with my family.

Saint Bart's team successfully navigated round five, but Skye got knocked out in round six on "rutabagas" and Freddie led off round seven with a misspelling of "cephalothorax." That left Joey and I with nine words to go until the scheduled end of the competition.

Joey reached over and grabbed my hand, squeezing it for a moment before releasing it. I looked over at him. "Good luck," he whispered as he stood up and walked over to take the podium for his first word of the seventh round. His word was "oxymoron." "O-x-y-m-o-r-o-n, oxymoron," he spelled, correctly, receiving applause. He returned to his seat, shooting me a relieved look when his back was to the audience.

After the six remaining schools sent another student to the podium, it was my turn for Saint Bart's. When I stepped up, I closed my eyes and inhaled and exhaled a deep breath. My word was "exclusions." "E-x-c-l-u-s-i-o-n-s, exclusions," I spelled with ease. I

270

smiled graciously for the applause I received and returned to my seat.

Another school was knocked out before Saint Bart's next seventh round word went to Joey. "Chrysanthemums," the announcer announced. I closed my eyes and visualized the word, hoping Joey could read my mind.

"Chrysanthemums," Joey repeated before spelling, "c-h-r-y-s-a-n-t-h-a-m-u-m-s, chrysanthemums." My heart sank as soon as I heard the "a" that should have been an "e."

"Incorrect," the judge determined.

Joey turned to me. "I'm sorry," he mouthed, with a frown of visible disappointment.

"It's okay," I whispered back, "You did good." I faked a brave smile for him as I realized that the hopes of Saint Bart's to win the Statewide Spelling Bee now rested completely on my shoulders.

My final word of the seventh round was "haphazardly." "Haphazardly," I began, "h-a-p-a-z-a-r-d-l-y, haphazardly." The applause drowned out the judge's determination that I was correct.

They then announced that the coaches could take two minutes, literally, to pep talk their teams for the eighth, and final, scheduled round of the competition. Mr. Harper sprinted to me. "How you doin', Persephone?" he panted.

"Hangin' in there, Mr. Harper," I affirmed. "I can't fathom being more nervous, but it's only five more words worth just a total of 100 points towards our score," I futilely played it off nonchalantly.

"You'll be great!" Mr. Harper encouraged. "I can't think of a student better equipped to take on the final round on her own."

"I'm glad I didn't miss any words yet, Mr. Harper," I admitted. "It takes a little pressure off to know that if I miss one, I'll still be around."

"You can do it, Persephone," Mr. Harper cheered. "We're *all* rooting for you."

"Except Skye," I pointed out.

"Who cares what she thinks?"

"Not I," I admitted.

"So, show her who's best, once and for all!" Mr. Harper encouraged. He put his hand out like he thought we were still in a circle. I rolled my eyes at him, but when he shook his hand around, I figured he was serious and put my hand in, over his.

"Go Saint Bart's!" the two of us yelled.

"Come on, Persephone!!" I heard Dad yell, with a "Wooohooo!" at the end of it. I laughed and waved to him and Mom. I was determined to *not* let them down.

The eighth round was ugly for all remaining contestants. My words were "camaraderie," "syncopated," "infamously," and "gigantic." Okay, I confess, I did misspell "camaraderie," but in the meantime, other students and schools got eliminated leaving me and two other spellers, representing two other schools, to take on the fifth words of the eighth round.

"Opalescence," the judge requested of me.

"Opalescence," I repeated, "o-p-a-l-e-s-c-e-n-c-e, opalescence." The judge determined I was correct, and the audience gave a standing ovation to signify that they appreciated my representation of Saint Bart's through the final round of spelling.

272

That Misty girl was also still in the competition, representing Williams School. Her word was "anthology," which she spelled with no hesitation. I clapped for her when she got her standing ovation, too. She smiled, appreciatively, towards me.

Lastly, a boy named Paul was the lone remaining member of the team from Stuart School. His word was "magnanimously," which he looked to be guessing his way through, albeit somehow correctly. His efforts, too, brought the audience to their feet again, and Misty and I both joined in the applause for him.

"Ladies and gentlemen, we ask that all of the competitors rejoin us onstage in ten minutes for the announcement of the winner of the 2010 Statewide Spelling Bee! Congratulations to all of the spellers, it is a very close competition this year!"

My team ran up onstage and jumped around me giving hugs and high fives. "We made it all the way to the end!" Freddie exclaimed.

"That was awesome, Persephone," Danielle agreed.

"I missed one," I pouted, "and it cost us twenty points."

"You earned us a lot more than twenty points, Persephone," Mr. Harper reminded. "The other teams missed words, too. We still have a real chance at this!" We stood anxiously in a crowded mass together on the stage.

"Your attention please," the announcer's voice boomed. "At this time, we would like to announce the winner of the 2010 Statewide Spelling Bee." My teammates and I joined hands. I could feel the nervous energy running through our connected group. "In third place, with 256 points, Williams School!" I let go of the hands I was holding and clapped for Misty's school.

"Our top two teams this year are separated by only one point," the announcer revealed. "Just one point will make the difference between the team who will be on their way to represent Vermont in the New England competition next month in Salem, Massachusetts, and the team that came *so* close to winning the state title. So now, without further ado, the team that came in second place... congratulations to Stuart School, and that means that Saint Bart's School is the Statewide Spelling Bee Champion in 2010! Congratulations, Saint Bartholomew's School!"

We were so excited that the next few minutes became a complete blur to me! We jumped up and down, we hugged, we cried, we laughed, we cheered, we screamed, we danced, we waved, we smiled, we cried some more, and hugged some more! Mr. Harper held the trophy way up over his head and the audience celebrated with us. We then shook hands with the judges, the announcer, and with the other teams. The competition had been intense, and somehow we had been victorious. We were on cloud nine!

My parents pushed through the crowd to come to the stage to claim me. I ran to them and hugged them both at the same time.

"We are *so* proud of you, Persephone!" Mom announced.

"That's my girl!" Dad exclaimed at the same time.

"We did it!" I cheered, when I had stopped hugging them.

"Congratulations!" Mom said. The other kids ran up to hug Mom, too, since they all knew her from school. Even Skye wanted a hug from Mom. "You all did *so* well! I am so proud of all of our Saint Bart's kids!" Mom praised.

As the other parents came for their kids, I got hugs from most of the Saint Bart's families, as they appreciated my role in our victory.

"When do we get to get out of here and go have some celebratory dinner?" Dad suggested.

"Ooh, we're going out to dinner?" I asked.

"I should hope I can treat the star of the Statewide Spelling Bee Champion Team to a fancy dinner," Dad continued, "seeing that I am her proud papa!"

"Yay!" I cheered. "Mr. Harper, we're outta here!" I hugged Mr. Harper and ran over and grabbed Mom and Dad's hands. "See you Monday!"

"Bye, Joey," I called as we passed by Joey and his parents. He waved. I saw that Misty Creek girl across the parking lot so I waved to her, and she waved back. I climbed into our car. "I can't believe we won!" I said when we were finally away from the hubbub.

"We really are *SO* proud of you, Squirt," Dad said with a smile.

"I'm proud of me, too," I announced. "I just wish I hadn't missed that word."

"We never expect you to be perfect, my Little Dragon," Mom comforted. "We only ever want you to do your best, and you definitely did that today." And she was right, I had given my absolute best effort, and that was all I could ask of myself.

At least that's all I can do until the New England Spelling Bee next month...

chapter twenty-five
Green Hair Isn't THAT Bad

There is something about springtime in Vermont that makes a young lady even more boy crazy than usual, or at least that's always how it works for me. With the onset of April, everyone in my class was acting like love struck teenagers.

"Who are you going with to the Fifth Grade Dance?" Danielle whispered to me under the monkey bars at recess.

"I don't know," I responded, not having yet given it any thought. "Who are you going with?" I asked in return.

"Arnold asked me yesterday, so I'm going with him," she smiled, "I can't believe nobody has asked you yet." She skipped off to the swings where I saw her say something to Tisha and Deena before all three of them looked over at me. Then they all laughed.

"Girl, you have got to go to the Fifth Grade Dance with Joey," Jade announced as she climbed up on the monkey bars.

"Joey won't ask me," I blushed. I couldn't think of another boy I'd rather go to the Fifth Grade Dance with than Joey. But smart girls, like me, don't honestly get the guys they have crushes on, except in movies.

"Then ask him!"

"I can't do that," I turned a deeper shade of scarlet.

"Then I'm askin' him for you," she announced, racing over to Joey and Freddie.

"No, Jade, don't!" I pleaded, but I did not follow her. Instead, I sat down on the far side of the monkey bars, hoping the guys couldn't see me there. I hid my face in my hands.

I heard footsteps run to where I was hiding. "He said he'll go with you," Jade announced.

"What?" I looked up at her in disbelief.

She sat down next to me. "Joey said he will go to the Fifth Grade Dance with you!" she reiterated. "Isn't that exciting!?" she bubbled.

"He actually said, 'Yes,'" I repeated aloud in an effort to make it sink into my reality. I was going to the Fifth Grade Dance with my crush, Joey!?! Yeah, no, just saying it didn't make it sink in. This was completely incomprehensible for me.

"Of course he said yes, you dingy!" Jade looked at me in disbelief, "You truly didn't think he'd go with you, did you?" I shook my head. "But you wanted to go with him, right?" I nodded. "And now you two are *going* to the Fifth Grade Dance together!" Jade repeated, "So how about just thanking me and then we can get planning your big night out!"

"Thanks, Jade, for asking him, since it worked out," I relented.

"Yeah, yeah, if he had *said* no, I would've never heard the end of it, I know, I know," she giggled. "But I knew he'd agree to go, cuz he *likes* you."

I blushed. "I don't know about *that*, Jade."

"You didn't witness the boy saying yes when I asked him to go to the dance with you," Jade smiled. "I did. The boy likes you."

I giggled, "Stop it, Jade, you're embarrassing me!"

"Whatever, Girl! You *so* owe me for this one."

I gave her a hug. "Really, thanks Jade."

"Don't mention it," Jade grinned, "but if your boy, Freddie, is still going solo when dance time comes, send him my way, okay?"

I laughed. "You like Freddie?" I asked.

Jade shrugged. "He's your boyfriend's friend," she explained, "it's more convenience than anything."

"Joey isn't my boyfriend," I defended.

"Yeah, okay, whatever," Jade headed over to line up with her class. "Catch ya later!"

I exaggerate not when I say that less than thirty seconds later, Deena, Tisha, and Danielle ran over to me. "So you're going to the Fifth Grade Dance with Joey?" Deena asked.

"Seriously, girls, it's been all of five minutes since this news even occurred," I clarified.

"Yeah, yeah, yeah, it's all over the school already," Tisha confirmed.

"Rock on, Persephone," Danielle congratulated me. "You two will be super cute at the Fifth Grade Dance."

I suddenly missed my anonymity of being the dateless Miss Smarty Pants of our class, because gossip and rumor mills don't find the girls who aren't in the dating pool... but apparently my having a date to the Fifth Grade Dance thrust me to the forefront of attention. "Thanks," I giggled.

Our class was called to line up. I appreciated being saved from further embarrassment by returning to our classroom. I walked to the line, second to last in line. Joey lined up behind me. "Hey, Joey, thanks for agreeing to go to the Fifth Grade Dance with me," I said nervously.

"It'll be fun, Persephone," Joey stated, looking at his feet and blushing. I don't know if he looked up again cuz I looked at my feet and blushed, too.

"Miss Smith, the line is moving without you, apparently," Mrs. Larson nagged, catching my attention. She was substituting today for Mr. Harper who was away at a math conference.

"Sorry, Mrs. Larson," I apologized and hurried to catch up with the class.

"Maybe if you weren't all caught up in love world with Mr. Gardens you wouldn't *have* this problem," Mrs. Larson teased as I hurried by her, into the building.

Back in the classroom, we were working on a science worksheet in our small groups. Mrs. Larson moved from group to group to see how we were progressing. When she got to my grouping, she asked, "So, Freddie, are the lovebirds getting any work done or are you having to do it all for them?"

The nearby groups overheard her and started giggling and whispering. Joey stood his textbook up on his desk to hide behind it. I put my head down on my desk to hide my face. I heard the whispers turn into the rhymes we all knew too well. "K-I-S-S-I-N-G," the class chanted, with Mrs. Larson even louder than the kids' voices!

"You two are *so* cute!" Mrs. Larson teased. "I hope you grow up and get married!"

I don't know what possesses people to tease someone far beyond the point of funny – ha ha – oh, aren't they cute – giggle, giggle. Both Joey and I were not doing schoolwork because we were too busy hiding from the rest of the class's torment. I could hear Freddie defending us, even against Mrs. Larson, but it didn't slow any of them down a bit. I heard Joey's feet run to the bathroom. I heard the class laugh and "ooh" even louder. I covered my head with my arms in an effort to hide my face *and* block my ears from the sounds, but it didn't do a lot of good.

The tormenting only ceased due to the class leaving the room to go to physical education, continuing to hoot and holler things about "lovebirds" and "Joey and Persephone" as they departed. Mrs. Larson not only didn't stop them, she encouraged them the entire time. I was mortified and still didn't budge my head off of my desk.

When I realized the room was silent and still, I removed my arms from my head. Unable to hear any sounds, I lifted my head from my desk. The classroom was dark and empty. I breathed in a big breath. I was confident that I was all alone.

But I was wrong.

The bathroom door opened slowly and Joey poked his head out. Seeing only me, he emerged into the dark classroom. "Hey, Joey…" I greeted him.

"Hey, Persephone," he smiled back.

"I'm glad they're all gone," I admitted.

"Me too," he agreed. "So yeah, turns out I can't go to the Fifth Grade Dance with you."

My eyes filled with tears. "I understand," I accepted. My chest felt like it had snapped in two pieces. I supposed this was how a broken heart felt.

"No, wait," he started, looking upset at the look on my face. "I mean, I can't go because, you know, I have a family thing that day that I forgot all about," he fidgeted. "So I won't be able to go to the Fifth Grade Dance at all. I'm sorry, Persephone." He headed out the door towards the gym.

"Yeah, I get it," I said to the empty classroom. It felt like Joey was lying to me, because it sure seemed that he didn't have a previously scheduled family function on the day of Fifth Grade Dance when he agreed to go with me an hour earlier. No, I firmly believed that he couldn't deal with the level of teasing that he and I received due to our deciding to go to the dance together, and so to eliminate that teasing from his life, he broke off our date.

I was furiously mad, though I wasn't angry at Joey. I was hurt by Joey, yes, there's no denying that, but the emotion I felt engulfing my every molecule at that moment was rage. And that rage was directed solely at Mrs. Larson. Teachers are supposed to advocate for students and keep us safe, *not* be the ones to hurt us.

Losing Joey as my Fifth Grade Dance date was already sacrifice enough, so all that was left for me to do was to speak my words. I ran out the door and straight to the gymnasium, not slowing down in the halls as three different adults told me to walk. I didn't care if I was breaking the rules. I didn't care about anything in that moment except revenge. This evil woman needed to pay for the pain that she had caused. I ran past Joey and found my class in the gym.

Mrs. Larson immediately started in with the teasing. "Oh, so the lovebirds have decided to join us today for P.E., how nice!" I stormed to the middle of the gym and turned to her. The class was dead silent, a strange hush having overcome them when they saw that I was not going to passively sit with them and let this woman hurt me anymore.

I took a deep breath, instinctively pointed my left hand straight at Mrs. Larson's head and boomed, "May you have green hair and ugly blue warts on your face, you evil, wicked, pathetic, substitute teacher! Powers that be, grant me my revenge!" I noticed what could only be described as a force field shoot from the end of my finger towards Mrs. Larson. Then, I gasped in horror as I realized just what I had done, in front of everyone in my class.

Well, apparently not *everyone* in my class, as Joey appeared just *then* in the doorway. "Wow, you guys are quiet in here," he said aloud.

At that precise moment, the force field struck Mrs. Larson. Immediately, her hair sprawled out of her neat bun and into three-foot cascading ringlet curls of varying shades of green! As her mouth wrinkled into a horrified expression, she reached for her face, and I could see blue spots popping up on it!

Mrs. Larson ran from the gym towards the principal's office. The class burst into laughter. Joey looked confused so Freddie ran over to him and filled him in. "Dude, Persephone just did that to Mrs. Larson! Isn't that awesome?"

Joey grinned from ear to ear and laughed. "Yeah, that *is* awesome! But how did she do it?" Freddie provided a full description of what had happened as Mr. Jacobs appeared at the doorway.

"Persephone Smith! My office! *NOW!"* his voice boomed through the entire gym. The gym went silent. I momentarily drooped my head in embarrassment that I was being summoned to the principal's office, but then I realized I had no reason to hide – everyone had seen what I had done, and I would need proper punishment from the school for my actions. So I held my head high and walked proudly across that gym.

Tisha clapped first, with Deena and Danielle quickly joining her. Soon the entire class, including Skye, was clapping and I heard Curt yell, "Go Persephone!" I smiled at my classmates and they erupted in hoots and hollers again, but this time they felt supportive rather than hurtful.

Freddie and Joey were still standing by the door. Freddie said, "Go show 'em what you got, Persephone!" with a chuckle. Joey just smiled at me and clapped. I strutted right past them, past Mr. Jacobs, and straight to the principal's office. I was terrified for what I would be in for, but it was inevitable. Despite Mom's warnings to only ever say good things, I had knowingly and remorselessly spoken a purely bad outcome, with every pore and fiber of my body, for revenge. Karma would obviously need to deliver its threefold retribution, whatever that may be.

Yet, as I waited for Mr. Jacobs to dole out my punishment, I smiled. I knew it was the perfect time for a waterworks sob-fest, in an effort to get out of trouble, but I couldn't produce a tear. Mrs. Larson had gotten what she deserved, and I was relieved and beaming. I strategically placed my hand near my mouth so as to obscure my grin, as Mr. Jacobs handed me the longest suspension in Saint Bart's School history, effective immediately until the day before the New England Spelling Bee Championship. I had known all along that any punishment I received wouldn't impact my participation in the New England Spelling Bee, because Saint Bart's needed me to be there, so it was a sensible endpoint to my suspension. "And this, young lady, will go on your permanent record!" Mr. Jacobs exclaimed, in closing.

It should come as no surprise that Mom subsequently grounded me until the spelling bee team's trip to Salem. My enacting revenge on another person, even though Mrs. Larson's behavior completely justified it, was a clear-cut act of disobedience and a blatant misuse of my powers, as Mom had emphasized to *always* only say good things. Mom would have let me out of being grounded, if I agreed to fix Mrs. Larson, but I refused. That evil demon was the catalyst for my broken heart, and I believed she deserved her punishment as much as I consequently deserved mine. I certainly wasn't sorry for my actions.

So, in one afternoon, I had lost my date to the Fifth Grade Dance, was enduring a broken heart, was suspended from school for a week, and was grounded. Yeah, it's really ugly to be on the retribution end of Karma! For the next seven days, I would be stuck at home with no school, no TV, no computer access, no cell phone, no friends visiting, and no junkfood, but I *would* have an abundance of extra time to hang out with my ghost buddy, Seth. Hmm… on second thought, maybe threefold isn't always so dreadfully horrible after all.

chapter twenty-six
Chit-Chatting With Ghosts

In actuality, the suspension and grounding would be, in all, merely a total of one week. In kid time though, one week feels like an eternity! I had no way of knowing what was going on at school. I couldn't find out what things were being said about me, if my classmates were now scared of me, if... if... if Joey now hated me.

I rolled over on my bed and looked at the clock. I had been sent home from school three hours ago. I knew I still had another seven full days of my sentence. I heard Dad's rat-a-tat on my door. He came in without waiting for me to invite him.

"So, did you really turn the substitute's hair green and give her blue warts as revenge for her teasing you about Joey?" he asked excitedly, coming over and sitting on my bed.

"Guilty," I pleaded.

"That's my girl!" Dad grinned. "I'm glad you did it so I wouldn't have to dole out my own revenge on that evil substitute."

"On top of that, I'm suspended, grounded, and oh yeah, Joey broke our date to the Fifth Grade Dance. It's been a stellar day, Dad."

"But I heard Joey broke off your date *before* your little outburst."

"Yeah, but it still hurt, Dad."

"Well, you're stuck with me here at the house all week, so quit this feeling sorry for yourself stuff."

"*You* are staying home with me?"

"Ayup."

"So, TV? Junkfood?"

"What Mom doesn't know doesn't hurt her, right?"

"But you and Mom don't keep secrets from each other."

"Yeah, I know…" Dad hedged, "and okay, she's already fully aware that your suspension and grounding are going to feel more like a vacation, but she had to at least make it *look*, at school, like she was punishing you, now, right? She's actually super proud of you, Squirt, for standing up for yourself and not letting that substitute teacher get away with hurting you."

"Is it safe for me to come in now?" Mom asked at the door.

"Hi, Mom," I sat up on the bed.

"You're still grounded, my Little Dragon."

"It's okay, Mom, I get it."

"You can't go around using your powers to do bad things to people. You know that."

"She deserved it."

"You have to let Karma do its thing on people who deserve it. It's not your job to enact revenge on those who have wronged you."

"Dad would've gotten revenge on her if I hadn't," I pointed out.

"Hun, when are you going to learn that there are *some* things you don't need to tell your daughter?" Mom shook her head. "What am I going to do with the two of you?"

"I think you'll keep us, Mom," I suggested. Dad nodded in agreement.

Mom sighed. "I don't really have much of a choice, do I?" She laughed. "Hun, let's go make dinner, and *you*, Miss Troublemaker, you stay here."

They exited my room. I lay back down and rolled over on my bed. I saw Seth standing on the far side of my room. "Hey stranger," I said to him. He waved. "Where have you been hiding lately?" I asked, but of course he couldn't answer. "I wish you could talk to me, without using too much energy," I sighed and just stared at him, trying to think of a way for Seth to communicate with me.

I schemed until dinner, and ate without a word, my mind abuzz about solving my dilemma. Mom asked me what I was thinking about, so I told her. "I want to be able to hear what Seth wants to tell me," I admitted.

"There are tools through which ghosts can communicate, Squirt," Dad suggested.

"And are they cheap?" I asked.

"Yeah, not exactly," he admitted. "Hey, didn't you have a way of swinging your keys in college to talk to spirits, dear?" he asked Mom.

"I could never prove that I was actually talking to real ghosts, hun," Mom dismissed and glared at Dad with a look that suggested he should drop the idea.

Dad completely missed Mom's subtle hint. "Do you still have your keys, dear?"

"I'm sure I don't still have my keys from college, hun," Mom replied.

"Do you think you could tell Persephone what to do, though?"

"No, I don't think I can," Mom answered, raising her voice. "If she figures it out herself, that's one thing, but I'm not just going to hand over a free pass to my ten year old daughter to communicate with all the spirits that wander the earth." Mom calmed herself and turned to me. "I know you would like to hear from Seth, but I fear you're too young to handle all the responsibility of talking with the spirit world."

"Fine, whatever," I dismissed. I was not happy. Mom knew a way that I could talk with Seth and she wouldn't tell me how to do it!

"I figured it out on my own in college, so I'm sure you can figure it out on your own if you want to, badly enough," Mom encouraged, "but if you find yourself talking to someone harmful, you must break that connection. Do you understand?"

"I only want to talk with Seth, Mom," I admitted.

"That's what I'm telling you, my Little Dragon," Mom stated. "There's no way to control with whom you're talking when you are talking to spirits, Kiddo. So, if you ever find yourself talking with someone who scares you, you need to say 'In the name of God, be gone!' to force them away and protect yourself."

"Um, okay, but I only want to talk to Seth, and if I can see Seth, then won't I be talking to him?"

"Presumably, but you never know," Mom cautioned. "I really think you're too young to handle communicating with spirits."

"Mom, you always think I'm too young for everything," I huffed as I stormed off from the dinner table.

"You know she's going to figure it out," Dad said to Mom.

"That's why I gave her the way to ward off evil spirits," Mom replied, as I stomped up the stairs.

I slammed my door and snatched up my key ring and keys when I got into my room. I flopped onto my bed and held the keys in every configuration I could fathom. I held them up by the key ring. I put the metal ring around my finger and dangled them under my hand. I held onto one of the keys and dangled the rest below. I held onto everything and dangled only one key below. I noticed that the key could swing freely when it was hanging by itself.

At that moment, I remembered when Seth had knocked the dishtowel off the kitchen counter and I had seen, firsthand, that ghosts were capable of a short burst of energy to move an object. "Seth, can you move the key?" I asked aloud. The key moved, but I wasn't sure if it was Seth or if it was because I was having a hard time holding my hand still in that position.

I tried to recall exactly how Dad had described Mom's communication with the spirits using her keys. "A way of swinging your keys," he had said. I tried to swing the keys, but they didn't really swing. They would need to be hanging on something in order to truly swing. I looked around my room to find something that could be used to dangle the keys.

Being a packrat, I found a piece of curling ribbon that I had saved from way back at my birthday. I knotted one end of the ribbon to one of the metal rings of the key ring. I sat down on the floor, holding up the other end of the ribbon and the keys hung in the air. I gave them a swing and the knot slid apart and the keys flew through the air, landing a few feet away from me. I looked over and saw Seth laughing at me. "Yeah, okay, I'm lucky they didn't land in my eye, aren't I?" I said to him. He nodded in agreement. "Hey, I'm doing this for you," I argued, "You *could* make this a little easier on me."

Seth moved over to my bureau. He pointed to my jewelry box. "Oh, so *now* you want the ring back, I see," I accused. Seth shook his head to indicate he was trying to say something else, but I had already started my tirade, "It's not *IN* my jewelry box anymore, Seth! I wear it on a chain around my neck every stinking day, okay?"

Seth stopped pointing at the jewelry box and looked at me with a look of shock. I quickly covered my mouth with my hand, because I had never intended for *anyone* to *EVER* find out that I had been wearing Seth's ring as a necklace. Honestly, I've worn it nonstop ever since I put the ring on a chain after removing it from my right hand just before I went to bed on my tenth birthday. So, yes, I was wearing it when I had the nightmarish vision, and I was wearing it at his funeral, at the spelling bees, and of course today when I made Mrs. Larson's hair green.

I clutched the ring on the chain around my neck. "I'm sorry, Seth, I don't mean to yell at you," I sighed. "I'm not actually mad at you; I'm just frustrated that I can't figure out how to know what you are trying to tell me."

Seth disappeared. One of my necklaces fell off my bureau and onto the plush carpeting on the floor. I crawled over to it and picked it up by the chain, letting the pendant dangle heavily below. I moved my hand back and forth a little and noticed it swung freely, although it didn't swing in any sort of logical pattern. I looped the chain on my finger, dangling the pendant again. I moved my hand in a circular motion and noticed that the pendant followed suit in a circle, even long after I had stopped moving my hand. Suddenly, without slowing or any warning, it stopped perfectly still!

"Seth, was that you?" I asked. The pendant remained still. Seth reappeared and smiled at me. "Aha! It was you!" He nodded. I swung the pendant again. "It's too heavy," I said. "It's not easy for you to stop something that heavy, is it?" Seth shook his head. "So I need a lightweight pendant," I thought aloud. I toyed with the ring on the chain around my neck. That's when the idea struck me!

That ring would be the perfect weight! Although I hadn't taken it off since my birthday, I believed it would be safe enough if I just held it here in my bedroom. I unclasped the chain, removed it from my neck, and holding it in front of me, refastened the clasp. "It's much lighter than that other pendant," I admitted, looping the chain on my finger and dangling the ring below. I barely moved my hand in a circle and it was able to swing with such ease it was as though it was always meant solely for swinging.

Seth disappeared again. "Are you there, Seth?" I asked, with the ring still swinging. At once the ring stopped the circular motion and rocked back and forth. The resulting movement reminded me of nodding. I sent the ring circling again. "Is that how the swing for the

292

answer 'yes' looks?" I asked. The ring stopped and rocked back and forth in the same manner.

I paused for a moment, trying to construct the perfect question. If I asked, "Could you show me what 'no' looks like?" he might answer "Yes" because he could show me, and I wouldn't get to see "No." I circled the ring again. "Seth, please show me what 'no' looks like." The ring stopped, rocking from side to side, much like if someone shakes their head to say, "No."

As tempting as it was to just sit there and ask like a hundred yes or no questions about anything that crossed my mind, I already was able to get "yes" and "no" answers from Seth whenever he appeared visually to me, as he was capable of nodding and shaking his head. I wanted more. I wanted to know what was on his mind. I needed words.

"I'm gonna try something, Seth," I suggested. "I am going to spin the circular motion, and then I am going to start saying the letters of the alphabet. When I say the letter you want me to stop at, stop me. Then I'll repeat the circular motion and start again with the alphabet. The letters you stop me on will spell something, so make it something you want to say to me!" I circled my hand and asked, "Do you understand?" The ring rocked back and forth to signal, "Yes."

"Great, hold on, I'm going to get something to write on!" I jumped up and grabbed a notepad and pen from my desk. I rushed back to sit on the floor again. "Okay, I'm ready," I announced. "Now, to make sure I'm talking to the right spirit, what is your name?" I sent the ring spinning in circles, as I set to work saying the alphabet. "A- B- C- D- E- F- G- H- I- J- K- L- M- N- O- P- Q- R- S-" the circular motion stopped suddenly when I said "S" and the ring rocked back and forth in the "Yes" motion. I wrote down "S" on my notepad. "Okay, next letter," I announced, repeating the process, "A- B- C- D- E-" the circular motion stopped me on "E," and I added the "E" next to the "S" on my notepad. Predictably enough, the ring stopped on "T" and "H" for the next two letters. I spun the ring again. "So your name is 'S-E-T-H,' correct?" I asked, and the ring responded affirmatively. "Hi, Seth," I giggled.

"So, what's my name?" I asked, just to make sure I didn't have an imposter on my hands. I tried not to think about what letters were coming up, in case there was a way I could influence the ring's answers. I tried to focus only on being fair to this process. I wrote the letters down on my notepad without really looking. When I spun the ring and got through the entire alphabet without it stopping, I wondered if I had reached the end of the word, and so I looked at my notepad. "P-R-I-N-C-E-S-S" was what had been spelled.

I smiled and burst into tears at precisely the same time. I didn't know such a range of emotions was simultaneously possible, but believe me, it evidently is. I didn't ask any more questions that night. I continued to bawl my eyes out, and hours later, when I had cried every tear I could find, I remained curled up on the floor, still clutching the ring and the chain in my hand.

I heard Dad's rat-a-tat on the door. "Time for bed," he began to announce as he walked in and found me. He didn't finish his thought, he simply scooped me up and tucked me into bed. "Good night, Persephone. Sweet dreams." I heard him outside my room, trying to assure Mom that I was fine, but she wasn't sufficiently convinced.

"How's my Little Dragon?" she asked, entering my room. I couldn't reply. She pried my necklace from my grasp, carefully fastening it around my neck again. "You don't want to lose this," she said to me, kissing me on the forehead. "Sleep tight."

I heard Mom's voice outside my door. "Yup, she figured it out herself. Using the ring was a clever maneuver. I don't know that I would've thought of that."

"Well, she is *our* daughter, dear," Dad bragged. "The poor kid's got twice our clever, twice our ingenuity, twice our good looks and charm..."

"And apparently, whether we like it or not, twice our powers."

chapter twenty-seven

Back To Normal

All in all, my week of suspension wasn't so bad. I spent oodles of quality time with Dad, and I got to talk with Seth a whole lot. I even stayed caught up on my schoolwork, though Mr. Harper doubled the assignments because I had, indeed, wound up back in the principal's office and his note revealed that he was none too happy with me. Honestly, even the extra work felt like a vacation, and well, I may as well have been enjoying myself because my suspension would be forever noted on my permanent record.

Mom told me that permanent records don't really matter, but I don't fully believe that colleges are truly going to grant a troublemaker, who got suspended in fifth grade for behaving inappropriately towards a teacher, admission at their schools. So, yes, I had actually learned my lesson in all this, too. Even if someone truly, richly, thoroughly deserves it, never ever use my powers to do bad things at school.

I know Mom wants me to say "anywhere" or "under any circumstances" instead of "at school," but given the meanness of those counselors at Birch Bog Camp last summer, I am not fully convinced that there are not true badguys out there who wouldn't think twice about genuinely harming me. In such instances I reserve the right to cause them just as much harm as I can think of.

Dad tells me not to worry about badguys, and honestly, I don't. I simply will promise not to use my powers to do negative things to people at school anymore, no matter how much they deserve it. Is it horrible that I still smile *every* time I think of Mrs. Larson and her green hair and blue warts? Yes, yes, it actually *is* bad that I derive such pleasure, but I can accept that I'm just not the nicest person on the planet. And yes, I confess, I *am* even smiling right now.

In case it's not obvious, today is my first day back to school since I was suspended last week. I've already been awake for hours. Okay, not actual hours – it only seems that way. But I woke up just before 6:00 and I don't usually get up for school until 6:30, so not being a morning person, I'm not so psyched that my dread of returning to school had such a detrimental impact on my beauty sleep.

I tossed and turned again. 6:12. I did not want to go back to school. Yeah, I loved school, and Mr. Harper was awesome, but I had no desire whatsoever to face anyone at Saint Bart's again.

What did my classmates think happened? What had they been saying when I wasn't there? I can't even begin to speculate at the gossip.

I know I tried to disappear on my birthday, and I think I now know exactly why it didn't work. You see, I didn't *truly* want it badly enough. It would've been nice to escape that situation, but it doesn't begin to compare to how completely I wanted to vanish now! To not return to school would be perfect! Returning was punishment far worse than the actual suspension. Life in my class had continued for a week without me. Goodness only knows what stories were meanwhile concocted about me.

And all this panic was before I even considered the most horrible thought of all back at school... Joey! I had crushed on Joey since fourth grade. He was absolutely my best friend in my class. And he had agreed to go to the Fifth Grade Dance with me... so part of me definitely wondered if he liked me... but then he broke off the date because of all the teasing we got in school. So now I'm thinking he didn't like me. Yeah, I know, he said he has a family function that day, but how am I supposed to buy that? Do you believe him? I know I'm supposed to believe my friends, but I can't shake the idea that he's just trying to be nice and not hurt my feelings.

6:18. Seriously? That's all? This is going to be the longest day ever. And as if seeing people at school today isn't bad enough, tomorrow kicks off the weekend of the New England Spelling Bee in Salem. The mere concept of such a huge spelling bee makes me want to disappear, too. Compound the nerves with knowing I have to spend all weekend with Joey – from whom I definitely would like to disappear - and I just don't know how I'm going to make it through the next seventy-two hours!

Okay, I confess… he totally broke my heart! I don't care if he's busy with other plans or if he couldn't take the teasing! Bottom line – we had made plans to go to the Fifth Grade Dance and he broke off our plans. It hurt. It hurt me last week. It hurt me every day I've been home. It hurts now, and it'll hurt to see him at school today. It'll hurt to see him in Salem tomorrow… and Sunday… and on Monday it'll hurt to see him at school again.

I didn't know what he thought of me anymore. I was okay with us just being tight friends, but now he knew I liked him liked him. And he didn't like me back. And I was embarrassed. And then I went and used my powers in front of him like some kind of freak? I'm mortified at the concept of ever seeing him again.

6:23. Really? Ugh. Longest. Day. Ever. I pulled my blankets over my head in a desperate attempt to hide from the world.

"Squirt, you're not up yet?" Dad's voice jostled me.

"Been up for hours, Dad," I answered groggily.

"Um, Mom's ready to leave for school and you're not dressed yet."

"What time is it?"

"7:30."

"What? It was just 6:23!" I realized I must have fallen back to sleep when I covered my head.

"I'll bring you to school," Dad offered, "so you just take your time and get ready."

I jumped out of bed. "Thanks, Dad!"

"Don't mention it."

Going to school with Dad was awesome because I wouldn't have to deal with being the first kid there today. Don't get me wrong, I love being the kid to know everything first and to have all the special privileges, but when returning from a week of suspension, I'd much rather just blend in as much as I can.

At 8:00 I showed my ready-for-school face in the kitchen. "Is a chocolate chip muffin a breakfast that'll work for you, Squirt?" Dad offered.

"My favorite!" I couldn't figure out why Dad was being such the perfect dad! I mean, yeah, he rocks, but bringing me to school separate from Mom *and* preparing my favorite breakfast? Maybe I needed to be suspended more often! Okay... maybe *not*!

The schoolyard was filled with Saint Bart's students when we pulled up. I felt my stomach churn into a huge knot. "Can I just stay in here until they line up?" I hopelessly inquired.

"Sure," Dad replied.

Sure? Sure? Maybe Dad wasn't feeling well. Prime lecture opportunity about facing fears and it won't be so bad, Squirt, but no, I was getting permission to hide in the car until the kids lined up? This could only mean one thing... going back to school was going to be way worse than my darkest expectations!

8:30. The kids lined up. "Okay, Squirt, let's do this," Dad encouraged. "There's nothing to worry about. It's just another day at Saint Bart's."

"Good point, Dad," I interrupted, "In less than two months I won't go to Saint Bart's anymore."

"Hey, Squirt, that's true," Dad jumped on my idea, "and then comes summer and then middle school." Dad's smile faded after he said "middle school."

"Dad, what's wrong with middle school?" I inquired.

"Uh... nothing..."

"I'm not convinced," I cautioned.

"We'll talk about it later, for now you're at Saint Bart's and I see Mom's class heading inside."

"Oh man, I'm late!" I exclaimed. I hurried out of the car, grabbing my things.

"Don't worry, it's just another thing to go on your permanent record," Dad chuckled.

"I love you, Dad," I said, ready to close the door.

"Love you too, Squirt."

I ran in a tiptoe to join the back of Mr. Harper's line, hoping to remain unnoticed. Just my luck, Joey was at the end! He turned and saw me sneak up.

"Welcome back, Persephone," he whispered, "I thought you were already inside!"

"Thanks, Joey, naah, Dad dropped me off today," I said nonchalantly. I truly didn't feel my usual blushing when talking to Joey this time. It was very peculiar. He was being super-duper sweet and yet I felt... numb.

My class filed into the building and headed down the hallway to our classroom. Mr. Harper stopped us at our door. He turned and addressed us, "Ladies and gentlemen, it is with great honor that I present to you a local legend."

I looked around. I didn't see anyone.

"Is she already in the classroom?" Deena asked.

"No," Mr. Harper answered. "Not only is this young lady poised to help Saint Bart's represent at the New England Spelling Bee this weekend, but she also can turn your hair green if you make her angry."

"Don't forget the nasty blue warts," Skye suggested with a cringe.

"So I would advise you all to stay on her good side," Mr. Harper cautioned.

"But isn't she already inside the room?" Danielle pressed.

"No!" Mr. Harper responded, clearly annoyed. "So without *further* interruption, Persephone Smith, could you please step forward and receive the honorary key to the classroom?"

I hung my head down ready for sneers and jeers and mockery. I walked over to Mr. Harper who handed me a decorated, oversized manila key, signed by all my classmates. I didn't hear anything, so I looked up. The kids were smiling. "Wait, you guys don't hate me?" I realized.

"Hate you?" Mr. Harper asked with a chuckle. "Well, we have a ton of questions for you, but hate has never even been suggested." Then he leaned in and whispered, "Well, I won't speak for Skye, because she's seemed to despise you all year."

I giggled. "She'd look good with green hair," I whispered back.

"Hey, hey, none of that now," Mr. Harper said. "So, we're itching for you to use your key and lead us into the classroom." I heard the students whispering and giggling.

I held my key up in the air and... turned the door handle with my free hand. The lights were off so I flipped on the switch.

A big banner hung across the classroom reading, "Welcome back, Persephone!" with artwork and notes clearly from my classmates. The desks had been rearranged into a circle, and my desk was decorated in construction paper creations.

I walked into the classroom to get a closer look at the festive changes.

Mr. Harper cleared his throat. I turned around and saw my class standing there, still holding their backpacks. "Class, what do you want to say to Persephone?"

"We're sorry that we made fun of you last week," all but Joey and Freddie chimed, in unison.

"Thanks guys," I accepted. "Did you already apologize to Joey?" I inquired.

"Yeah, but he didn't get a key to the classroom," Freddie admitted.

"We are glad you're back," Mr. Harper added, "but there are a ton of questions and I really don't have the answers."

"Can we hang up our backpacks yet?" Curt asked.

"Good plan," Mr. Harper agreed. We all started putting our stuff away. "When you're done, take your seats and we'll get started on our class meeting."

When we were all seated, I began to get nervous. All eyes were on me. I soon realized this class meeting was going to be about *me*.

"Let me explain the rules of the class meeting," Mr. Harper began. "It's easy. If you have the talking ruler, you can talk. If you don't, you stay quiet. I'm making a couple of exceptions today... first, since I am the teacher, I'll reserve the right to talk to facilitate the meeting and make sure it doesn't get out of hand, and for today, the key to the classroom gives Persephone free access to talk as long as she's not casting spells on us. Agreed?"

We all agreed. Then I held up my key and added, "But that wasn't a spell, Mr. Harper, as I'm not a witch. Witches cast spells, not me."

"All of us saw you turn Mrs. Larson's hair green after saying, 'May you have green hair,'" Katie began, holding up the talking ruler. "If that's not casting a spell, what is it?"

"I was just using my powers," I explained. "We all have them."

"Class, let me remind you that you go to parochial school so your parents won't be hip to the idea that you have supernatural, paranormal, or magical powers," Mr. Harper interrupted.

"Using our given powers is the same as using our natural talents, Mr. Harper," I defended.

"Parents and parishioners will not see turning someone's hair green as the same as, say, playing a piano," he cautioned.

"But they're exactly the same," I countered.

"No, one is evil and one is good," he judged.

"I wouldn't call playing the piano 'evil,' Mr. Harper," I responded, raising an eyebrow at him. The class laughed.

"I wasn't suggesting *that*," he defended.

"No, you were clearly inferring that because I have powers, I am evil. I am *not* evil, Mr. Harper."

"I simply meant that the public perceives casting spells as evil," he rationalized.

"Well, I don't even think casting spells is always evil, but it's a moot point, as I don't even cast spells."

"No, but you say things that come true," he continued. "People will consider that casting spells."

"I can't help that people are ignorant," I suggested.

"Can I talk? I have the talking ruler still," Katie said.

"Of course, Katie," Mr. Harper agreed.

"How do you do it?" Katie asked.

"Well, first of all, I have to want something more than anything, and then, I have to sacrifice something," I started.

"Eeeewwww! You kill animals?" Katie gasped.

"No, sacrifice like where I have to give up something, not kill animals!" I explained. "Eeewww, gross!" I added, chilled by the concept of harming critters.

"Remember kids, your parents don't actually want you using powers, so don't worry about sacrifices," Mr. Harper cautioned.

Freddie grabbed the ruler from Katie. "Sorry, Katie, but I gotta say, Mr. Harper, stop treating Persephone like there's something wrong with her!" Much to my surprise, the class applauded.

"I didn't say there was anything wrong with her," Mr. Harper defended.

"Well, you're acting like there is, but there's not," Freddie continued. "We've always known she's special. Things always go her way. She knows stuff that kids our age don't. She's awesome. We don't want her to change."

"I didn't say she sh-"

"I'm still talking," Freddie continued. "We're not gonna run home and turn into witches and cast evil spells upon the world! We just wanna know how she does it and when she started doing it and stuff like that."

"But I just – "

"So stop being mean and just let her talk!" Freddie concluded. The class clapped again.

"Well, obviously this class isn't mature enough for a class meeting," Mr. Harper deduced, reaching for the talking ruler as Skye snagged it away.

"Or YOU are not mature enough for this class's dialogue, Mr. Harper," Skye stated. I smiled. Too bad that statement went over the heads of my classmates cuz it was a good zinger. "So, Witchy Poo, was that the first time you've used your powers for evil?"

"Yeah, it was," I admitted, not caring if Skye believed I was a witch.

"And are you gonna use your powers to win the spelling bee this weekend just like all the other times?" she pressed.

"I don't cheat. I haven't before, and I won't this weekend. It never even crossed my mind." Mr. Harper almost had the talking ruler when Deena snagged it away.

"So, did you use your powers to get Joey to go to the Fifth Grade Dance with you?" Deena asked.

"Knock it off!" Freddie blurted out.

"You don't have the talking ruler," Deena pointed out, "so you can't talk." She stuck her tongue out at him.

306

"Thank you, Deena!" Mr. Harper said, snagging the talking ruler from her. "Now, nobody can talk because the meeting is over."

But the previous question remained unanswered. But what answer would be the right one to say? I did *not* use my powers to make Joey go with me, but if I said that, everyone would think he liked me and he'd be teased again. I couldn't lie and say I did use my powers, cuz I don't lie. So I said what only I would say, "Well, we're not actually going to the Fifth Grade Dance together so you go ahead and believe what you want to believe."

Later that morning, Joey caught up with me at recess. "You did *not* use magic because I really wanted to go with you," he confessed.

"Really?" I asked in shock.

"Did you *think* you used your powers to make me say I'd go?"

"No," I admitted, "my powers never even crossed my mind."

"So, can you *use* your powers to get me out of my family thing so I actually can go to the Fifth Grade Dance with you?" he asked.

"That's funny, Joey, but it doesn't work like that," I giggled.

"Guess I'll have to try to get in touch with *my* powers, then," Joey chuckled back.

"What are you two up to?" Freddie asked, catching up with us.

"Can you use *your* powers, Freddie, to get me out of my family thing?" Joey asked.

"I knew it! I knew you didn't use your powers, Persephone," Freddie admitted, "and no, bro, I can't."

With all things supernatural behind us, we resumed playing like usual. We talked excitedly about the weekend on the horizon.

"You've been to Salem before, right?" Joey asked me.

"Yeah, last Halloween," I responded.

"What's it like?" Freddie inquired.

"It's a quaint New England town, on the ocean, filled with witches and witchy stuff," I described.

"So, it's your home away from home?" Freddie teased.

"You are so gonna get it!" I playfully threatened, striking the "ready for a chase" stance.

"Can't catch me!" Freddie announced, running away. Joey ran with him and I chased them around the playground for the rest of recess.

Running after the boys and laughing was certainly the perfect remedy to all the tension I had been feeling lately. I wasn't a witch in their eyes, I was just same ol' me. And I didn't feel my broken heart at the moment because I was clearly having way too much fun as just friends with Joey. And I wasn't stressing about the New England Spelling Bee, because well, Vermont never wins these things. I mean, have you ever seen Vermont represented as a finalist in any contest ever? No, cuz we're just not raised to be competitive in Vermont. We're raised to be nice and generous towards others. Vermonters don't rush and our laid back way of life transcends to a general blaséness about all things competitive. And well, I suppose I was as ready as I'd ever be to head back to Salem... location of the infamous lightning bolt that, once and for all, ended my friendship with Coral.

Life was perfectly back to normal.

chapter twenty-eight
Saturday Morning in Salem

Our plan was to head for Salem very early on Saturday morning. When I say "very early," I mean ridiculously early! Dad, Mom, and I were going to leave at five o'clock! Obviously I would be sleeping for much of the trip!

My Saint Bart's teammates left right after school on Friday in the thirteen passenger van. Apparently Mr. Harper's sister lives in Salem, so the rest of the team, Mr. Harper, and some of the kids' parents were going to crash at her house on Friday night. If they deemed the weather warm enough they were going to camp out in tents in the backyard and eat s'mores.

Predictably, I was perfectly content with missing out on the camping and instead heading down with Dad and Mom on Saturday morning, even if it was way too early. I still had never had a s'more, but the mere word triggered shudders as it reminded me of that wretched night at Birch Bog Camp. Besides, Mom and Dad and I would stay at a hotel, and that made the weekend technically a mini-vacation!

When I opened my eyes on Saturday morning, I didn't recognize my surroundings one iota. I tried to jump up but realized something was holding me in place.

"Where am I?" my voice cracked.

"Good morning, my Little Dragon," Mom greeted. I looked towards her voice and got a faceful of sunshine. "We're almost there!"

"Wait, we're not at home?"

Dad flexed his arm playfully, in the driver's seat. "Muscles. Good for moving sleeping ten year old children."

I looked at myself. "Mom! I'm still in my PJs!"

"It's okay, Persephone, you have time to change at the hotel," Mom reassured.

"But I have to walk from the car to the hotel in front of everyone in my PJs!" I pointed out.

"See, hun," Mom said to Dad, "that's why I said we had to wear our PJs, too."

The only thing more humiliating than wearing PJs to the New England Spelling Bee was having my parents show up in their PJs, too. "Mom, tell me you're kidding."

Mom smiled at Dad. "Would I really wear my PJs to Salem?" she asked playfully.

"Yes, yes you would," I admitted.

"Yeah, actually you would do that, dear," Dad agreed. We all laughed because we knew it was the truth. "How are the nerves today, Squirt?"

"I'm fine. I've already accepted that we're not going to win, so I am just aiming to do my best."

"Hey, hey, what do you mean you're not going to win?" Dad asked.

"We're Saint Bart's from Vermont, Dad," I stated.

"So?"

"Vermont doesn't ever win big competitions," I explained.

"You can't go into it thinking you won't win, Squirt."

"I can't go into it with my hopes up, Dad."

"Worst case scenario, you come in sixth, Kiddo," Mom piped in. Mom has always been Queen of the Reality Check.

"Thanks, Mom. It helps to know my parents are cool with last place."

"Not last place, Squirt... sixth place," Dad explained.

"Sixth place in all of New England is very good," Mom stated.

"We're proud of you no matter what," Dad admitted. We pulled into the parking lot of the hotel. "Throw your hoodie on and you'll just look casual," Dad suggested. "Nobody will know it's your PJs."

"I think they'll notice you and Mom in your pajamas!"

"Okay, fine, we'll be fully dressed," Mom consented. "Take away all our fun."

"Thanks guys," I breathed a sigh of relief that my parents weren't actually scheming my humiliation by wearing their pajamas to Salem.

Our hotel was attached to the conference center that housed the New England Spelling Bee. It certainly wasn't the fanciest place I had stayed, but it had big, dramatic, chandeliers in the lobby. I saw the signs for the spelling bee as I dragged my wheeled suitcase behind me. The floor's beige tiles made the wheels of my suitcase click as they rolled on the grout.

"Reservation for Wallingford Smith," my dad said at the front desk. I left my suitcase near Dad and wandered around the lobby to see what I could see.

Apparently there were two restaurants on site, and I found the computer room and gift shop, too. Towards the stairs I could smell the indoor pool and saw the sign for the gym but I didn't explore any further. I headed back to my parents.

"Ready to go up to the room, Squirt?" Dad asked, pulling my suitcase towards me and the elevator.

"Yup!" I announced, grabbing my suitcase from him.

We rode the elevator to the third floor and trotted down the corridor. We picked up the newspaper outside our door and went in.

"Alright Persephone, showered and dressed in a half hour, okay?" Mom challenged.

"What do you want for breakfast?" Dad yelled as I hustled into the bathroom.

"Um, food, Dad," I shouted from inside the bathroom, running the water to warm the shower. I was clean and dressed in my school uniform in less than twenty minutes, so Mom French braided my hair while we waited for Dad to return with breakfast.

Dad appeared with muffins and orange juice as Mom put a teal ribbon in my hair. "Voilà, chocolate chip muffin and OJ, breakfast of our champion speller," Dad announced as he presented my meal.

"Thanks, Dad," I giggled and wolfed down my muffin, chasing it with a guzzle of orange juice.

"Take it easy, my Little Dragon. We're meeting up with your team in fifteen minutes. You can chew and swallow between bites."

"Can't be late," I attempted to mumble, mid-mouthful.

"Um, manners?" Mom encouraged. I paused long enough to shrug at her before polishing off the rest of my breakfast. "Now, any good luck charms or superstitions you need for this?" she asked.

Without responding, I touched my necklace through the neckline of my blouse. "Ooh wait, my fluorite!" I exclaimed. I ran to my suitcase and grabbed my fluorite crystal tucking it into my pocket. "Okay, let's do this!" I cheered.

We rode the elevator to the lobby and quickly spotted the rest of my team accompanied by Mr. Harper, Skye's mom, Freddie's dad, and Joey's dad. "You're here!" Freddie exclaimed as he ran across the lobby to greet me. "We were wondering if you were coming!"

"Why would you wonder that?" I asked. "I'm not even late!"

"Well, the rest of us did the overnight last night, so we just didn't want to be a man down for the New England Spelling Bee," Freddie explained.

"Relax," I reassured, "I'm here."

"Saint Bart's families, it's time to go take your seats," Mr. Harper encouraged. "We'll meet you back here at the lunch break."

Mom and Dad initiated a group hug between the three of us. "Good luck, Persephone," Mom said, "and remember we're proud of you no matter what."

"I know, Mom."

"You've studied hard, and don't forget you're as smart as any other student on that stage," Dad encouraged.

"I know, Dad."

"You nervous yet?" Mom asked.

"Nope," I answered, "cuz with low expectations, it shouldn't be hard to surpass them."

"We just expect your best," Dad reminded.

"That, I can do."

"We love you!" Mom hugged a little harder. "You'll do great!"

"I love you, too!" I exclaimed, hugging them harder.

"Okay, we better get to our seats," Dad encouraged. He kissed me on my cheek. "I love you, Persephone."

I kissed him back. "I love you, too, Dad."

Then Mom kissed me, "Love you, my Little Dragon."

I kissed her on her cheek, too. "Love you, too, Mom." They went into the ballroom, waving from just inside the door. I waved back and watched them disappear inside. Then, I turned back to my team, but they weren't there! They had apparently left without me! I looked around the lobby but found no trace of my team or of any of the other teams!

I knew they hadn't gone into the audience entrance, but I didn't see any clearly marked competitor entrances, so I had no clue where to go! I sat down on the couch that was next to where we had been gathered. Obviously Mr. Harper would return for me when he realized I wasn't with the group.

"Persephone!" a voice called. I turned around and saw Coral waving near the audience entrance.

"Coral?" I asked, with complete confusion as to why she'd be at the New England Spelling Bee. "What are you doing here?"

"Didn't Charles and Drew tell you in an email?" I shook my head no, as I still hadn't gotten around to getting an email address. "Drew's school is representing Massachusetts," Coral explained.

"You and Charles are still together then?" I asked.

"Why? You still jealous?"

"Not jealous, just shocked."

"I miss you, Persephone," Coral revealed. "It's been a long time. Can't we be friends again?"

"I never wasn't your friend, Coral," I countered. "We just haven't been speaking."

"Did you like your birthday present?" Coral asked. "I knew Mom and Erica had burned the set that you left at Erica's house on Halloween, so Charles thought you oughta have a new set."

"Why did they burn my other tarot cards?" I asked, confused.

"I don't know," Coral shrugged, "So, did you like them? Charles said you liked the unicorn pictures when you were in Mrs. Hammock's shop."

"That is the coolest deck of tarot cards, *ever*! Could you please thank Charles when you see him?" I requested.

"How about we meet up here later and you can tell him yourself?" Coral offered.

315

"I suppose that works," I agreed.

"So, lunchtime?" Coral suggested. I remembered that my parents would be back at lunch, so that seemed like a fine idea.

"Okay," I consented.

"I gotta go find Charles inside and sit down," Coral announced. "You better catch up with your team," she called, waving, as she entered the audience entrance.

That reminded me. Where was my team? Why hadn't Mr. Harper returned for me yet? Wasn't the spelling bee about to start? What was going on? I got a nervous feeling that I wasn't going to actually make the New England Spelling Bee. I began to pace back and forth.

I looked at my watch. 9:58. The spelling bee would start in two minutes. I decided to go find my parents. I stomped off towards the audience entrance.

"Persephone Smith!" I heard a voice shout behind me. I turned.

"Erica?" I recognized.

"Come on, you're gonna be late!" she urged.

"What are you doing here?" I asked.

"Didn't John tell you?" she inquired, hurrying to me.

"John?" I repeated.

"Oh, right," Erica conceded, "I mean, Mr. Harper."

"You know Mr. Harper?" I asked, stunned.

"He's my brother," she admitted.

"Wow, I had no idea that *you* were his sister," I confessed.

"Yeah, anyways, he's been blowing up my phone because he's frantic for you to catch up with the team, and the judges won't let him leave the backstage area without forfeiting."

"Won't he forfeit without me?" I asked.

"Thus why he sent me out to look for you," Erica encouraged. "Come on!" She grabbed my hand and pulled me to follow her away from the audience entrance and towards what seemed to be the direction of the backstage area.

We hurried down a hallway and rounded a corner. The fancy décor was suddenly nowhere to be found and we were standing in a hallway that seemed like a service access. "John said to just go through that door down there!" she pointed to the door at the end of the hallway. "You better run, it's starting any second now," she encouraged. "I gotta get back to the audience. Now go!"

I bolted down the hallway, slamming against the crashbar of the door with my full force. My speed carried me through the door and I quickly noticed I was outside. I caught my balance and reached for the door but it snapped closed behind me.

"Noooo!" I called out, simultaneously realizing I had misunderstood what door Erica had indicated. I pulled frantically at the doorknob. It didn't budge. I smacked the door with the palm of my hand, hoping someone might hear me, but the door didn't open.

I looked at my watch. 10:01. The New England Spelling Bee had certainly begun. I looked left and right to gauge which way seemed like it would most directly lead to the front of the hotel and started walking around the exterior of the building.

I had only taken a handful of steps when I sensed someone come up behind me. Before I could even turn around to see who it was, something covered my mouth and nose. I gasped for a breath, only to find myself inhaling a putrid odor.

At once, I felt dizzy and wobbled on my feet. My hearing went silent and my vision darkened around the edges, continually narrowing, like a tunnel. I realized I was passing out again. I sensed I was falling and felt hands catch me as everything went dark.

chapter twenty-nine
Kidnapped

W hen my eyes opened, the darkness continued to envelope me, but I could tell that I was not blindfolded. The room I was in was simply dark. I knew I was laying on something hard and flat. The room seemed to expand upward from where I was situated, so I presumed I was on the floor.

"Hello?" I spoke softly, with a frog in my throat that felt like I hadn't spoken in hours. Getting no response, I believed I was alone, so I sat up, cautiously.

Despite being unable to hear or see anything, I was confident that my senses were working just fine. I could not determine the time of day and whether the darkness was due to nighttime or simply a lack of windows and lamps. I attempted to press the light on my watch, but it was no longer on my wrist. I had no guess as to where I was. The last thing I could remember was being in Salem, Massachusetts, just outside a back door at the hotel where the New England Spelling Bee was about to begin.

Hoping that maybe I was just in a nearby janitor's closet, I stood up and felt around to get my bearings. I scuffed my feet carefully so I wouldn't stub my toes, but with hopes that I would bump into something to give me a reference point in the room. I soon realized that the room was not a janitor's closet, as I moved for what felt like forever to reach the bare cement wall. As I walked along the entire perimeter of the room, I realized there was no trace of windows, doors, or anything other than the solid, imprisoning, cold walls.

I began to panic. How did I get into this room? How would I get out? If there were no windows or doors, how would anyone get in to find me, to save me, to feed me? My mind and heart began to race. My legs felt suddenly weak and tired and my spirits sank fast. I sat down to conserve my energy and brainstorm a way out of this.

I decided I had about three options. I could sit and wait. I could feel every inch of the floor for a trap door. Or I could try to figure out the ceiling, although I was too short to reach it. As I was unsure of who put me here or if they had *any* intention of returning, doing nothing was clearly not my best option at the moment. I concluded that if I flailed my hands over my head while sliding my feet on the floor, I could simultaneously accomplish both of my other options.

Although my feet continually detected only the same hard cement, when I was near the middle of the room, my idea to wave my arms over my head paid off, as my hand hit a string that hung from the ceiling! It swung in the air and I grabbed at where I thought it should be. But I just couldn't catch it! I took a deep breath and moved my hands slowly in the area where the string had been.

Suddenly, I felt it on the back of my right hand. I then kept my right hand still and reached over with my left hand to grab the string. Holding the string in my left hand, I had two choices... to pull or not to pull?

I knew I had to pull the string. I wasn't sure what would happen if I pulled it, but it was the only non-cement thing my hands had felt in this room yet. Maybe it would signal someone that I was awake. Maybe it was an overlooked detail of my holding pen. Maybe nothing whatsoever would happen. The only certainty was that I needed to know, so I tugged on the string. A bare light bulb turned on overhead.

When my eyes adjusted to the brightness, I could see that I was in a cellar. The floor and walls were, indeed, bare cement. The ceiling was unfinished with visible insulation. I saw a gap in the insulation so I walked over to get a better look. In the gap, I noticed hinges and a trap door. I was immensely relieved that there was a way out, even if I wasn't tall enough to reach it. Just knowing that I wasn't permanently enclosed gave me tremendous peace of mind.

I stood under the trap door and then stepping heel-to-toe, counted off how many steps it took for me to get to the light. Twenty-two. I knew whoever had put me here would assume I hadn't found the light, so I needed to shut it off to perpetuate that assumption. I pulled the string and turned around 180 degrees, returning via twenty-two heel-to-toe steps and sat down, presumably under the trap door, just waiting. I knew in my heart that whoever had left me in this cellar would come back, for if they hadn't planned to return, I wouldn't be alive right now.

I didn't know why they put me here. Who hated me so much that they would take me away from Mom and Dad? Maybe they were trying to hurt Mom and Dad by scaring them? It didn't make sense. Who leaves a ten year old girl in a dark cellar? I sat, staring up at the darkness, in the direction of the trap door. After awhile, I found it easier to lay down to keep an eye on it.

I opened my eyes when something thudded next to me. I caught a glimpse of light in the ceiling as the trap door snapped shut. I heard footsteps move across the ceiling, away from the trap door. I stood up and walked twenty-two steps in the direction I remembered the light to be. I carefully moved my hands over my head, in a successful attempt to find the string. A tug of the string exposed that a cloth bag had been dropped into the cellar.

I scurried to the bag and opened it. Inside there was a grinder, a bottle of water, and a cell phone. I immediately dialed Mom. "Hello?" Mom answered.

"Mom!" I squeaked into the phone. Her voice sounded more beautiful and comforting than it had ever seemed before.

"Persephone?" she panicked.

"I'm in a cellar, I don't know where or why!" I was resolved to keep my side of the conversation short, in case my captors didn't plan to allow me much chatting time.

"Can you get out?"

"There's a trap door in the ceiling, but I can't reach it. They just tossed down a bag with a grinder, water, and this cell phone."

"Who?" Mom inquired.

"I don't know," I confessed.

322

"What do you remember, Persephone?" Mom pressed.

"You guys went in to sit, but when I turned to follow my teammates, they were already gone. I waited in the lobby for them to come back, but they didn't. Coral saw me, so I talked to her. Then Erica came along and said she's Mr. Harper's sister and that he told her to bring me backstage."

"You went with Erica?" Mom said with a tone of well-deserved suspicion.

"She pointed to a door at the end of the hallway and told me that Mr. Harper said to go through that door. I did and wound up outside. The door closed and locked behind me, and I couldn't get back in. When I was outside, I thought I was all alone, but someone was following me."

"Who?"

"I don't know. I blacked out and woke up here."

"We are looking for you, Persephone. We're never gonna stop. We love you."

"I love you, too." The phone beeped. I noticed that not only was the battery low and blinking, but the call waiting had sounded. "Mom, it's call waiting."

"Take the call. Agree to anything to stay safe. We'll find you. We love you!"

"I love you, too!" I clicked to the other call. "Hello?"

"Persephone Smith?" an unidentifiable and seemingly altered voice said.

"What do you want from me?" I questioned in an accusing and screechy tone.

"How do you like your room?" the voice taunted.

"Let me out of here!" I demanded.

"Didn't that mother of yours teach you any manners, Persephone?" Did every grown-up on the planet care more about manners than anything else? It was bad enough when my mom would remind me to mind my manners, but to be chastised by an unidentified kidnapper really took the cake.

"*PLEASE* let me out of here?" I pleaded.

"All things in time... first, we have business to attend to."

"What do you want from me?" I whined.

"You called your parents, right?" the voice questioned.

"Of course I called them."

"Just so you know, the phone is untraceable, Persephone. They only know whatever information you told them."

"They are fully aware that you have me, Erica," I accused.

"So, they think Erica is responsible?" the voice reiterated. "Perfect."

My heart fluttered at the apparent incorrect conclusion I had drawn. If Erica didn't have me, who did? "What is it that you want?" I pressed.

"Your powers."

"My powers? I can't give those away," I tried to explain. "They're just part of me."

"Join my coven."

"Coven?" I was quickly realizing that my kidnapper was a witch. I couldn't help but recall when Erica had made the comment that witches had use for *my* powers, even if I didn't have use for witches.

"We need a powerful third," the voice explained. "With your natural abilities and powers, you have been chosen."

"I'm not a witch," I argued.

"You will join our coven or you will remain in the cellar forever," the voice threatened.

At that moment, the battery shut the phone off, thus ending the call. I contemplated attempting to call Mom back but with the battery shutting the phone down, I thought my best bet would be to call emergency and hope that they could track the call before the battery lost all of its charge. I turned the phone on and dialed.

"Emergency," the dispatcher answered.

"I've been kidnapped and I'm being held in a cellar against my will. I don't know where I am, so trace this call and find me!"

"Stay calm," the voice urged.

"The battery on this phone is dead, I don't know how long it will work!"

"You said you've been kidnapped?"

"Yes! Please send someone to where I am!"

"How do you have a cell phone?"

"The kidnappers gave it to me so they could call me. They just did and told me I have to join their coven or remain here forever."

"What's your name?"

"Persephone Smith. Please hurry!"

"Persephone, it appears that the tracking has been disabled on the phone you're calling on so we don't know where you are."

"You what? Whaddaya mean you can't track the call? You're Emergency!"

"Can you look out the window and describe the view?"

"I'm in a cellar. There are no windows."

"Persephone, unless you give us more information, we won't be able to help you."

"Like what? This phone is gonna die! What do you need to know?" I snapped.

"Where are you, Persephone?"

"I don't know! In a cellar! There's a trap door on the ceiling. The kidnappers threw down a grinder, a bottle of water, and apparently an untraceable cell phone!"

"What kind of sub?"

"What? How should I know?"

"Persephone, look at the sub and describe it!" the dispatcher demanded.

"It's an Italian sub."

"Describe the *wrapping*, Persephone!"

"It's wrapped in clear plastic cellophane, and there's a sticker with ingredients and wait a minute-" I stopped fast, realizing that the sticker also revealed the store from which it was purchased.

"What grocery store is it from?" the dispatcher prompted.

"Galeway Grocers, 459 Galeway Street," I read. "I have no idea where that is."

"*We* can figure that out. How big is the cellar you're in?"

326

"It's smaller than a regular house basement. I don't know... like maybe forty by thirty?" I guessed. "I don't really measure rooms, you know!"

"Okay, who was the last person you remember seeing? You can name them or describe them."

"Erica," I calmly stated.

"Erica who?"

"I don't know!" I was becoming increasingly frustrated that I didn't have answers for the dispatcher's questions. "She is friends with Coral and Marina Jones and is the sister of my teacher, John Harper. So maybe her last name is Harper? Erica Harper?"

"Are you sure?"

"That's what she claimed."

And with that, the phone died. This time, I couldn't get it to power on again.

I could only wait helplessly until either my kidnappers returned or help arrived.

I fiddled nervously with the ring on the chain around my neck. Then, I suddenly had a realization. I had been so caught up in the situation that I had completely spaced on the one method of escape I always had with me... my powers!

I grabbed the fluorite crystal from my pocket and held it firmly, with both hands, high in the air. I began chanting things I didn't fully understand, but I said whatever words entered my mind, completely trusting my natural powers to lead me in the right direction.

"May the power within me magnify and manifest through the power of this fluorite to call the white light to bestow upon me a circle of protection and may that circle enrobe Mom, Dad, and all those searching for me with a white light of peace, calm, and clarity as to my whereabouts and wellbeing." I found myself spinning in a circle as I spoke, and I noticed that the fluorite began to glow. At the same time, the circular area around me became brightly illuminated in a white light.

I felt I had more to say, so I continued, "Let my kidnappers and everyone who knowingly aided in my abduction receive full Karmic retribution for all the wrong that they have done and will do in their lives. Forever there will be, in one the power of three."

I paused, completely not understanding that last part. I put the fluorite back in my pocket, and then I grabbed the cloth bag, stuffing the sub and spent cell phone inside. "I offer this bag and its contents as my sacrifice to ensure that I shall be safely reunited with Mom and Dad and that my kidnappers will receive due punishment."

I felt the urge for a tag line... some way to close the chanting... the casting, as some would surely choose to call it. Only that strange phrase filled my head. So I said it again, though slightly altered, "Forevermore let there be, in one the power of three."

My mind felt cleansed and I was completely confident that there was nothing more to say. I carried the cloth bag to the far corner of the cellar and placed it there, as a sign that it would not be consumed or used anymore. I walked back to pick up the water bottle, and I carried it over to the string that controlled the light bulb.

I pulled the string to shut the light off again, but the room stayed lit. I looked at the bulb, but it was off. I then noticed that the light was glowing around *me*! I laughed and moved quickly around the room watching the glow move with me wherever I went!

That cellar was not a scary place when it was always illuminated. I knew I'd no longer have the element of surprise on my side, but I felt completely confident that my words had worked. Consequently, I would be safe, Mom and Dad would find me, and until that time, they'd be reassured that I was okay. Then I smiled even more as I remembered the other part of my spiel... that my captors and all their accomplices would receive the punishments they deserved.

I threw back my head and cackled the most guttural laugh I've ever heard. And then I threw my head back for a second laugh, as the most terrifying and evil laugh I had heard in my life had just come *from* me! Twice even! And I liked it!

As hours seemed to pass, I realized what was taking so long... I had given no timeframe in my commands! Oh, what I wouldn't give to rewind time and say, "within an hour!" in the midst of the chanting! But my resolve was strong and I knew I could wait however long was necessary, as I was encircled in a protective white light through which no one could harm me! My parents and I *would* be reunited, I just didn't know exactly when.

I became so accustomed to the light that surrounded me that I stopped noticing it after awhile. It was certainly there, as I could see perfectly in the dark cellar, but it wasn't distracting me like it had at its onset. I sat down near a wall and leaned against it. Boredom was quickly setting in. I fidgeted with my necklace again. Then, I had an idea. I unclasped the necklace and looped it on my finger, dangling the ring below. I sent the ring spinning.

"Is anyone here?"

"Yes," the ring swung back and forth.

"Do I know you?"

"Yes," the ring swung again.

"Is it Seth?"

"Yes," the ring replied.

"Seth, I'm so glad you're here! I was so bored and lonely! Am I getting out of here okay?"

"Yes," the ring agreed.

"Who did this?"

"E-R-I-C-A," Seth spelled using the ring.

"Who else?" I inquired, anticipating that Erica hadn't pulled off this entire scheme alone, but not having any idea as to who assisted her to make it happen.

"H-A-R-P-E-R," Seth claimed.

"Wait, my teacher?" I shouted in shock. My stomach turned into a knot. Handsome Mr. Harper was a kidnapper in disguise? There had to be a mistake!

"Yes," the ring swung, confirming my horrible thought.

"Anyone else?" I asked. As scared as I was to find out anything more, I needed to know.

"Yes."

"Who?"

"M-A-R-I-N-A," Seth claimed.

"What?   Marina?" I exclaimed, blown away by this development. Marina was my mother's longtime best friend! Sure, she had proven that she obnoxiously liked to pick fights with me, but to actually be a part of kidnapping me? To hurt my mother like that? It seemed like an insane notion! "Why?" I asked.

"P-O-W-E-R."

"That is really what it comes down to, isn't it? They want my powers and will do anything to get me in their coven," I spoke aloud but didn't swing the ring as I didn't need an answer.

"Thanks for being here for me, Seth," I added. I spun the ring in case he still wanted to talk.

"N-E-T-I-M-E-P-R-I-N-C-E-S-S."

I put my necklace on again and curled up on the uncomfortable cement floor and fell asleep.

chapter thirty
Cauldrons and Culminations

I was dressed in a black dress that had a jagged, layered, flowing bottom hemline, and atop that I wore a black velvet cloak and had a witches' hat on. Two other cloaked witches were with me, and we were holding hands and dancing and chanting around a marble table that held a silver cauldron. I focused on their faces, but I couldn't see them, so I couldn't identify who donned the other witch clothes.

And then I woke up.

Opening my eyes, I was blinded by the intense brightness. It scared me until my eyes adjusted and I remembered where I was and that the light was a symbolic reminder of my protection.

Then, I remembered the nightmare that had just woken me up. In the dream, I wasn't glowing! Maybe I wouldn't be saved from life as a witch! The thought of being in some awful coven for the rest of my life was terrifying! I recalled that I looked no older in the dream than I did the last time I saw a mirror. My hair was even the same length! I feared that the cauldron thing would happen *soon* and that apparently my circle of protection would expire even sooner.

When my eyes had fully adjusted, I could see a rope ladder hanging from the trap door. A book light was clipped to the top of it to light the ladder. I wasn't sure why they placed the light on it, as I lit up a significant portion of the cellar, but I jumped up and ran to the ladder anyways. I pulled on it, but it was securely attached at the top. I stepped cautiously onto the first rung. The ladder held. I went up to the second rung. The ladder didn't budge. I ascended to the third then the fourth rungs. The trap door was nearly within reach. I climbed to the fifth rung and reached up. I could touch the trap door with my fingertips. I went up another rung and knocked.

The trap door swung open. I climbed up another rung and peeked up through the opening. Daylight lit up what appeared to be a living room.

"Hello?" I spoke with a groggy voice that seemed as though it hadn't been used in a few hours.

"It's about time you joined us, Persephone," the disguised voice that spoke to me on the phone beckoned. "Come in, and make yourself at home."

"It's okay to come up?" I asked, shocked.

"Of course, Persephone," the voice welcomed. "We have been expecting you."

Rather than retreat into the dungeon, I pulled myself up the final few rungs and emerged into the small living room. It opened directly into a kitchen and a set of stairs went upstairs along the wall. The visible floor space matched the size of the cellar.

I scrambled to the nearest cushioned chair and sat down. The cushions felt like clouds given how I had been sitting and laying on cement for goodness knows how long. "What day is it?" I inquired.

"It is Saturday," the voice, seemingly attached to a person completely shrouded in layers of black witchy clothing, acknowledged. The person closed the trap door, locked it, covered it with a throw rug, and moved a coffee table atop it, camouflaging it completely. "Seriously, Persephone, think of this cottage as your new home," the voice encouraged. "The bedroom and bathroom are upstairs."

I immediately dashed upstairs to check out the bathroom. Then I entered the bedroom which was an immaculate summer cottage bedroom that one would see in interior design or home decorating magazines. Breathtakingly beautiful! I touched the patchwork quilt on the white wooden framed canopy bed. Then I ran my fingers over the cedar hope chest at the foot of the bed.

The bedroom door closed behind me. I snapped my attention to the door to hear a padlock being fastened on the outside. I hustled over to try the knob, but to no avail.

"Persephone, dinner will be served soon," the voice called through the door.

I released the doorknob and turned to admire the view from the windows. The sun was clearly setting and the sky was afire in bright pink, magenta, orange, and purple clouds contrasting vibrantly with the brilliant blue darkening sky. In the distance I could see the sea. It looked many miles away. There were hundreds of trees between the sea and where things became detailed and clear in my view.

The driveway below was white pebbles. The cottage was atop a hill. I could see the treetops of the forest below me through the sea-view window, but the other two windows were level with thick trees and provided no view other than branches, buds, young leaves, and pine needles.

The shadows quickly crept over the yard below hindering my ability to memorize its layout. My room darkened, too, with the exception of my glowing circle of protection. I lay on the bed in the darkness. The softness of the mattress and pillows felt like utter bliss in comparison to the awful memories of having lounged on that cold, hard, cellar floor earlier in the day.

I heard the rumble of pebbles in the driveway and hopped up to peer out the window. I saw headlights shining up the driveway. I waved in the window in hopes of getting the car's attention, just as I heard someone at the bedroom door. Suddenly, I was grabbed from behind, brought down to the floor, and held in a full body restraint that did not allow me to move an inch. A strong manly hand covered my mouth as to stop all sound.

"Make a sound and you will never see anyone again," the man threatened. He pressed harder against every bit of my body that was held tightly and uncomfortably in his restraint, in a way that made me absolutely believe him.

I heard a knock on the door downstairs.

"Not a sound, Persephone," the man warned.

I noticed my glow was intact and couldn't understand how this man was able to restrain me completely when my circle of protection was still in place. But then I realized I wasn't in any pain. I wasn't exactly comfortable, but I certainly wasn't hurting.

I heard voices downstairs. I could've sworn it sounded like Mom and Dad. I wiggled in my captor's grasp. I needed to break free from him. I would give anything, anything at all, for the ability to speak words right now and free myself.

"Dream on, Persephone," the man whispered. "You are not getting to them."

I heard the cottage door open and close downstairs, followed by the sound of car doors opening and closing. The ignition turned on and I heard the white pebbles again as the car drove away down the driveway. When silence had resumed and my opportunity to escape had passed, the man released his grasp on me. I turned quickly, and in my glowing circle of protection, I could clearly see his face.

"Mr. Harper!?" I scooted backwards away from him.

"Little girl, it is pitch black in here," Mr. Harper whispered, probably so I wouldn't hear his familiar voice. "Obviously you cannot *see* anything because your teacher would not have any involvement whatsoever in your abduction from a spelling bee."

"But Mr. Harper, I see you perfectly," I confessed.

"You cannot see in pitch blackness, little girl, and you are mistaken regarding my identity," he claimed.

My glowing light revealed that Erica had appeared in the doorway. "Alright you two, time for some dinner now that those two left."

"Did they suspect anything?" Mr. Harper whispered.

"Nope," Erica said confidently. "Her mom said something about security cameras at the hotel and I guess someone back in Salem said I had a cottage up here, so they came up to check it out.'"

"Erica, Mom and Dad were here?" I inquired.

"Did *you* tell her who I am?" Erica asked Mr. Harper.

"Of course not, but she thinks she has us both figured out," Mr. Harper explained.

"Anyways, they won't be coming back," Erica claimed with an air of certainty that concerned me.

"What'd you do to them?" I asked, scared by her tone.

"I straight up lied to them. I told them I didn't know where you were but that you had said something about you being tired of your school treating you like a witch and that you were running away, once and for all. Of course I added that I *hoped* they found you."

"They believed that lie?"

"Your dad actually said, 'Well, that sure explains why she ran out the door!'"

"No! It's not what happened!"

"It is time you learn that the truth doesn't actually matter, Persephone. All that matters is what people believe," Mr. Harper said.

"You forgot to whisper when you talked that time, Mr. Harper," I pointed out. Then Mr. Harper used language that I won't repeat, but trust me, there were definitely words that warranted a bar of soap in his mouth. He certainly didn't whisper *that* time either.

"Good goin', John," Erica ribbed. "So much for you keeping your teaching job."

337

"I only lose my job if they find her and if they find evidence that I was involved in a crime."

"Mr. Harper, you kidnapped me! You were most definitely involved in a crime!"

"Only if they find you... and *only* if you're capable of telling them about me, if they do."

"Did you just threaten her?" Erica asked. "You *don't* threaten her, do you understand?"

"I am *NOT* going to jail because of some little girl," Mr. Harper insisted.

"She's my third in my coven," Erica argued. "If you hurt her, I will wage my wrath on you, John."

"Do I look scared of you, Erica?" Mr. Harper asked.

"Well, you better be."

"I'm not. Not afraid of you, not afraid of little witchy girl, and not afraid of your coven."

"Leave, John," Erica demanded.

"Gladly," Mr. Harper defended. "Good luck controlling the little witch without me." He stormed past Erica at the door.

"Persephone, can you put on the garments that are in the hope chest and meet me downstairs for dinner?"

"Sure, Erica," I agreed, remembering Mom's words to do whatever my kidnappers asked of me.

She ran downstairs. "John, wait!" she exclaimed, chasing him.

I opened the trunk and from the glow of my circle of white light I could see the dark witch clothes and pointed hat that I had worn in my dream. I put them on and went downstairs.

"Persephone, you can turn on a light so you can see something," Erica called when she heard me on the stairs.

"I'm good, Erica," I answered. I was beginning to suspect that I was the only person who could *see* the circle of protection around me, because everyone else seemed preoccupied with the darkness that wasn't impacting me at all! At the bottom of the stairs I saw Erica and Mr. Harper in layers of dark flowing clothing. A marble table sat in the middle of the kitchen with three place settings and three chairs around it.

"Do you like macaroni and cheese?" Erica asked.

"Sure," I answered.

Erica portioned out the macaroni and cheese and we sat down to eat. We didn't converse. It was just shoveling quickly as if we had better things to do.

At the conclusion of the meal, Erica cleared the table while Mr. Harper excused himself to go outside. He returned with a silver cauldron that he placed in the center of the table. Then he and Erica covered their faces with black fabric and he went back outside. Erica shut the lights off. A fully cloaked witchy figure, dressed exactly like Mr. Harper, but who wasn't as tall as Mr. Harper, returned with a big bag of supplies.

I simply sat at the table, watching. Erica removed candles from the bag and placed them around the room. The other witch lit them, using the voice disguiser to chant as he or she lit the candles. Then they took the chairs away, so the three of us wound up standing in a circle around the table.

"Let us join hands and repeat after me," Erica directed. "Tonight let there be…"

"Tonight let there be…" we repeated.

"This coven's true power of three."

"This coven's true power of three," we replied.

Then we danced around the silver cauldron, with our hands still joined. I recognized the moment from my dream, except now I knew I was still protected by the white light. The other two began chanting words I didn't understand as they added ingredients to the cauldron. As opposed as I am to doing anything witchy, I just went along it, as I lacked an exit strategy. I took comfort in remembering that Dad had said that witchcraft couldn't hurt me if I didn't believe in it, and watching these two fools wildly dance and chant, I doubted their natural powers. As much as I don't want to admit it, Charles was evidently insightful when he suggested Marina and Erica were not true witches but merely costume-wearing demons.

With no warning, blue, strobing lights illuminated the room. I instantly and instinctively ran for the door. Their hands grabbed towards me. "Stop! No!" the disguised voice screamed, "The spell isn't done! We haven't taken all of her powers yet!"

"Persephone! No!" Erica called.

I threw the exterior door open and ran outside with my hands up. I heard my captors scamper out the door behind me. I didn't look for them. I focused on the police cruisers that were driving up the driveway. Officers jumped out, weapons drawn, and pursued the fleeing kidnappers. I stood in the yard with my hands still over my head.

I noticed that the last few cars coming up the driveway didn't have blue lights. As soon as the first non-police car had gotten into the yard, the passenger's door flew open. I immediately recognized the silhouette amid a strange glowing orb and ran straight towards Mom, arms extended. "Mom!" I shrieked.

"Persephone!" Mom screamed, rushing to me.

At the same time, Dad put the car in park, and leaving the driver's door wide open, he jumped out and ran to me. I saw that he, too, was encased in a glowing sphere.

The hug that ensued between the three of us was the best hug of my entire life. The circle of white light glowed at least three times as bright when we came together, before fading out completely. I knew the horrific ordeal was over and I was safe, reunited with my family.

"Are you okay?" Mom asked. I noticed a bunch of reporters stood very near us, cameras pointed at our reunion.

"I made a circle of protection, Mom," I explained. Mom looked impressed. "They couldn't hurt me if they wanted to!"

"How did you know to do that?" Dad asked.

"I let my mouth go on autopilot and said whatever crossed my mind." I explained, "Totally my natural abilities."

"I'm glad it worked," Dad accepted. The reporters started shouting tons of questions at me.

"Are you ready to talk to the police, Persephone?" Mom encouraged.

"Yep," I consented. They introduced me to two detectives who took my statements.

341

In the meantime, I saw police come out of the woods with Erica in handcuffs. The news crews shouted questions at her but she wasn't talking.

"We got your kidnapper," the younger detective said.

"There are two more," I challenged. The reporters went wild.

"Really?" the other detective asked.

"Yes, Mr. Harper restrained me in the cottage," I recalled.

"Who else?" the older detective asked.

"I suspect Marina Jones was wearing a voice disguiser thing," I hypothesized.

"We'll look into that," the young, dimpled, brown-haired, detective reassured with a notation to his notepad.

The police led out another person from the woods. "Mr. Harper?" I asked aloud. I heard the reporters saying in a jumbled unison that he was my teacher and coach of my spelling bee team.

"Yes," the officer confirmed.

"Does he have a voice disguiser? Check him for a voice disguiser!" I insisted.

"Nope, nothing," the officer admitted.

"Then there's one more person out there! One was using a voice disguising thing!" I insisted. The reporters continued their clattering, chattering frenzy.

Moments later different officers returned from the woods with a witch outfit with a voice altering device. "You were right, young lady. Someone was wearing this."

They marked it as evidence, but they didn't find who had been wearing it. I talked to the detectives for hours, but eventually I answered every question they had and stated every detail of the ordeal I could recall. They requested I give them my witch clothes as evidence, trading me a police t-shirt and shorts in exchange. I only too happily obliged to get out of those dreadful witch duds.

With two suspects in custody and all of the DNA and other evidence they needed from me, the police released me to my parents. The reporters wanted interviews but Dad strongly insisted we had no comment other than thanking everyone who helped bring me home. I got in the car, and Mom climbed in the backseat with me, hugging me and not letting me go. I thought we were heading home, but instead Dad drove us to Boston. The police had suggested that I receive medical attention, so we spent the night at the hospital, so the doctors could do whatever they needed to do, and observe whatever they were looking for.

Now, maybe I was supposed to be quiet at the hospital, but I had been quiet long enough that day. I spent the whole time talking, asking questions, and learning all sorts of things I didn't know about what we had just endured.

I rewound to the beginning, telling Mom and Dad more details about my conversations in the hotel lobby and of leaving the hotel out the back door. "At the time I thought I had misunderstood Erica, but now I know she was just lying to get me outside." That was when my parents told me about the hotel's surveillance system and how they had watched tapes of everything I had told them about. "So, who grabbed me outside?" I asked.

"A man, but we couldn't see his face," Dad said, sounding furious just talking about it.

"Mr. Harper would've been inside at the spelling bee," I recalled.

"Well see, that's part of the problem," Mom admitted. "When the teams took the stage, Vermont's coach was nowhere to be found."

"Neither were you," Dad added. "The officials announced that Vermont's coach was out in the hotel trying to find the lost fifth member of the team, but that the spelling bee would commence."

"That's when we knew something was wrong and bolted for the lobby," Mom explained. "Coral and Marina were right behind us, offering to help."

"But Marina was in on the whole thing, Mom," I insisted.

"That doesn't make sense, Persephone. We found you *because* of her help," Mom defended.

"Marina told us about Erica's cottage," Dad explained.

"Where she knew I was being held!" I insisted.

"But you never saw her face during the kidnapping?" Mom quizzed.

"No, but the person with the voice disguiser was preoccupied with my powers and insisting I join their coven. Aren't Erica and Marina in a coven together? If the push was for me to be in Erica's coven, that'd be Marina's coven, too! When the police drove up to the cottage, we were doing witchcraft as a 'coven of three.' Who else other than Marina would be in Erica's coven?"

"Marina has an alibi, Persephone," Mom admitted. "Coral insists she's been with her all day."

"Coral is known to be a liar," I snapped. "Why don't you believe me about Marina?" I asked. I couldn't understand why Mom was being so defensive of Marina. So, she had told them about the cottage? So what? That evil monster picked fights with me on our getaway to Salem last October, so the concept that she was capable of organizing my kidnapping didn't seem as far out of character and implausible as it really should! "She's been mean to me before. We saw what she did to *you* on Halloween. You know how envious she is of my powers. Why are you defending her so?"

"Not exactly defending, my Little Dragon. I was just trying to see if we could further help the police with more information than we've already provided."

"What made you first suspect Marina in your kidnapping, Squirt?" Dad asked.

"Well, it was when Seth told me," I started.

"You talked with Seth?" Mom inquired.

"Yeah, I was wearing the ring on the chain around my neck, and being bored in the cellar, I asked him a few things. I was shocked when he named Marina as my third kidnapper!"

"You do know that wouldn't be admissible in court, right?" Mom revealed.

"Yeah, but Seth doesn't lie to me."

"No, he doesn't," Mom admitted, "but it makes no sense that Marina would point us to the place where you were being held if she were in on the kidnapping."

"Why *did* you come back with the police?" I asked.

"How do you know we were there before?" Mom inquired.

"I saw you from the bedroom window," I explained. "But Mr. Harper restrained me and threatened me so I couldn't get to you. I

345

would have risked the threats he made though, because I had my glowing circle of protection, but I just couldn't physically get away from him."

"You have been through *way* too much, Squirt," Dad added.

"But how did you know to come back? Erica told you I had run away, right?" I pressed.

"Persephone, we knew she was lying. You wouldn't run away from us no matter how bad life at school had gotten," Mom said confidently. "And when I was in her kitchen, a dishtowel fell off the counter to the floor without any physical reason."

"Seth!!" I exclaimed.

"Yep, just like the day when he was knocking the dishtowel off our counter. I knew he was sending us a sign that you were there."

"So Marina never *actually* intended for you to find me there," I deduced. "Although she told you how to get to the cottage, she expected Erica to tell a good lie and that you'd leave me there and not ever come back."

"Or she had a change of heart and figured we'd catch Erica and Mr. Harper red-handed and never know she was involved," Mom hypothesized.

"Maybe she believed she'd have enough time to steal my powers *before* you found me," I guessed.

"Well, I believe Seth," Dad suddenly confessed. "He might be a ghost, and I might not be able to see him, talk to him, or know he's there, but I think Marina masterminded the whole thing."

"Honestly, I really do, too," Mom agreed. "I just wish we could prove it."

"Maybe Coral will slip up and admit that Marina wasn't with her the whole day," I suggested.

"But who would have been with her if Marina wasn't?" Dad asked.

I sat up straight in the hospital bed because I knew exactly who I needed to talk to. The one who pledged to keep me safe, whether I wanted the protection or not. The one who was now dating my former best friend, who was also the daughter of the accused. My shield. My protector. "Charles!" I announced.

"Guess you'll be making a phone call in the morning," Dad chuckled.

"Unfortunately, I only have his email address. So I'll have to call Coral to get Charles's number."

"Won't that tip her off, Squirt?"

"Nope," I answered confidently. "We were all supposed to meet up at lunchtime so I could thank him for my birthday present. Besides, shouldn't I be thanking Coral for all her help in finding me?"

"You sure are a sneaky Little Dragon, aren't you?" Mom said proudly.

"I've learned from the best that it's always good to keep your friends close, and enemies closer, Mom," I said with a grin as my mind raced with possible outcomes from my phone calls.

"She's definitely your daughter," Dad said to Mom.

"Funny, I was just going to say the same thing to you," Mom agreed, smiling and reaching over to touch Dad's arm lovingly.

The happiness and love within that room that night made me suspect it could be, literally, a glowing sphere, even though we were no longer subject to an official circle of protection. Perhaps the white light that kept me safe all day didn't actually originate from the fluorite but was simply the love shared by my parents and myself.

I quickly pushed that thought away though, as there was definitely something inexplicable and extraordinary about those glowing orbs that had surrounded each of us. I wondered if I should trust myself more often to chant or say things that ordinarily seemed nonsensical to me, but that came naturally to my uninhibited mind. Perhaps my natural powers truly *were* greater than I had previously considered. Or maybe they have always been completely contingent on the strongest power of all… unconditional love.

chapter thirty-one
A Couple of Phone Calls

"Hello?" Coral's voice answered with a high degree of anxiety. My pulse raced, too, as I didn't want to say the wrong thing and ruin my chances of getting Charles's phone number. I took a deep breath.

"Hi, Coral!" I mustered shameful levels of fake enthusiasm. I was counting on Coral's tendency to not pick up on subtlety, as anyone with a healthy level of interpersonal skills would see through my bubblingly chipper salutation.

"Persephone! You're okay?" Coral asked.

"Safe and sound, Coral, but wow, that was a scary experience I never want to go through again!" I was determined to keep the whole kidnapping ordeal as removed from the conversation as possible, so I figured it would be best to use obvious, yet vague, comments, as needed.

I heard Marina's voice in the background asking if it was me on the phone. Coral covered the mouthpiece and told her that it was. Then Marina said to tell me how happy she was that I was okay and how responsible she felt for what Erica did. "Mom says she's happy you're okay and that she feels bad for what Erica did," Coral repeated back. "Wait, Erica was the kidnapper?"

"Yep," I admitted. "She had help from my teacher, Mr. Harper."

"Mom, Erica was the kidnapper and Persephone's teacher, Mr. Harper, was in on it, too!" Coral announced to Marina.

"I know," Marina's voice said in the background, "I saw it in the newspaper this morning. How awful!"

"It was in the newspaper, Persephone," Coral relayed. I couldn't tolerate any more of this back and forth conversing with Marina through Coral stuff, so I decided to push onward to the real reason for my morning phone call.

"Hey, Coral, could you give me Charles's phone number?"

"He's *my* boyfriend, Persephone," Coral jealously snapped.

"Wait, I don't want it because I want to be his girlfriend, Coral! Blech! No way! I just figured I would thank him for those tarot cards that he gave me for my birthday, because I didn't get to meet up with you two at lunch yesterday."

"Yeah, you were kinda kidnapped at lunchtime yesterday, Persephone," Coral recalled.

"So, is it okay if I have his number?" I pressed.

"Sure. I know he'd really like to hear from you. He was wicked worried that something bad had happened to you."

"Something bad *did* happen, Coral," I clarified. I couldn't believe that due to the happy outcome, the gravity of the actual kidnapping had apparently been completely obliterated from Coral's grasp on reality.

"Yeah, I guess it really did. Wow, I didn't know bad things really happened to people," Coral said, far too innocently. "I always thought bad things only happened in books and on TV!" I was grateful to be on the phone so I could roll my eyes without insulting her. Coral gave me Charles's phone number with explicit directive that I had to promise to not be using it to become his girlfriend.

"Coral, I would never ever date Charles, no matter what! Blech! No, thank you! I'm so not interested in him like that!" I truthfully responded. I shuddered as my skin felt as though it was crawling at the mere idea of romance with Charles. He might be my "shield" and my "protector," but there was no way, no how, that I would ever pursue Charles as a boyfriend.

"Good! Then call him 'til your heart's content, Persephone!" she consented.

"Cool, I gotta go, Coral," I said, plotting my escape. "Thanks for all your help in finding me yesterday... and to your mom, too!"

"Of course we'd help find you, Persephone! You're my best friend!" Coral announced.

"Yeah, thanks again," I tried to close the call. "I'll talk to you later." And with an exchange of goodbyes, I closed my phone.

"How'd you make out?" Dad asked.

"I got Charles's number," I smiled proudly. I took a deep breath and dialed.

"Greetings, mere mortal, what reason have you to disturb my existence?" Charles's voice answered.

"Hi, Charles, it's Persephone," I spoke while smiling so I would sound like the picture of sweetness and innocence. I sounded so chipper I almost made myself want to puke.

"M'lady!! Oh, M'lady, please accept my deepest heartfelt apologies for my informal and completely inappropriate phone greeting." Yup, Charles certainly hadn't changed an iota since Halloween. "I had no idea you would be on the line when I answered the call."

"Yeah, yeah, yeah, no problem, Charles," I placated him.

"M'lady, you have safely escaped the clutches of the evil poser witches who held you for your powers? I'm not attempting to say that I gave you forewarning as to the pure evilness of the intentions of those witch imposters with whom you shopped in Mom's tarot card store, but I completely gave you clear, dire, forewarning to stay away from them."

"Charles, I think I'd prefer you simply say, 'I told you so.'"

"M'lady, someone as spectacular and powerful as yourself should never be relegated to such pedestrian expressions as 'I told you so.'" I rolled my eyes. Maybe I shouldn't have called, because I wasn't sure I could muster up sufficient willpower to not puke at Charles's pure smarminess.

"So, how are things with you and Coral?" I asked without building up to it.

"Coral Reef? My mesmerizing Priestess? I owe you an abundance of gratitude for introducing us, M'lady. Of course she holds no candle to your powers, but she's amazing in her own ways."

"Did you get to hang out with her this weekend?" I asked, knowing there would be some level of affirmation there.

"We joined the festivities at Erica's house on Friday evening, welcoming your Saint Bart's spelling bee team to Salem. I had attended with high hopes that M'lady would bless us with her presence, but you were nowhere to be found. I did meet Erica's brother, John, and your teammates Danielle, Skye, Joey, and Freddie. Those boys are psychotically protective of you, M'lady."

"I'm in good hands around those two," I admitted.

"They surely highlight that I need to up my game if you shall ever be mine," Charles revealed.

"Charles, you're a great friend to me, but we're not going to have a romantic relationship," I dismissed, conveniently keeping my pledge to Coral.

"M'lady, you know I will fulfill any request of me you bequeath."

"I want to know more about your weekend."

"You want to know if I have any information that can help the police, don't you, M'lady?"

"Obviously if you know something that can help in punishing the people who kidnapped me, I would hope that you would tell the proper authorities, Charles," I pleaded.

"From your lips to my ears, M'lady," Charles obliged. "With complete frankness, my family had predetermined that we would travel to the police station and converse with the detectives and officers involved in the investigation, within this hour."

"You all know something?"

"My Priestess wasn't telling the complete truth," Charles revealed. "Her presence was requested and fulfilled at the Hammocks' family dinner last night, but her mother did not attend with her."

"So, Marina doesn't have an alibi for dinnertime?"

"No, M'lady, she does not. Or at very least, her alibi is not the fair Coral."

"I appreciate you and your family telling the investigators this information, Charles."

"We do not aid criminals, M'lady. The truth must prevail."

"Thanks, Charles."

"I pledged to you to be your shield and to protect you from the evil forces, and I failed miserably, M'lady. Helping lead the justice to rectify the situation is the least energy I can extend to make amends for my shortcomings as your protector."

"I'm alright, Charles. It was scary, but I was not physically harmed."

"I will never forgive myself for not keeping you safe from them."

"I forgive you, Charles."

"M'lady, I am so undeserving of you."

"Yeah, I know, but I'm forgiving you anyways. Oh, and while I'm talking to you, thank you for the unicorn tarot cards for my birthday!"

"M'lady, I beg of you to get an email address. I had been concerned that you did not receive them."

"I'm sorry I didn't send a 'Thank You' note, but manners aren't exactly my forté and well, it's been a crazy few months. I appreciate that you got me a new deck of those beautiful unicorns."

"M'lady, have you used them yet?"

"Not yet. I was planning to study them this summer, when I have free time."

"M'lady, my family requests that at this time I release you from this telephone conversation so I can attend with them on the journey to the police station."

"Thanks, Charles," I said. "Call me sometime and update me on life and stuff, okay?"

"M'lady, it would be my honor to telephone with you again."

"Bye, Charles," I laughed.

"The pleasure has been all mine, M'lady, and I will fondly recall this time until the next time we speak."

I closed the phone and rolled my eyes. Dad asked me how that went.

"Well, apparently Charles and his family are heading to the police to tell them their side of the story."

"They have a side to the story?" Mom asked.

"Yeah, Coral was their guest at dinner last night, but Marina didn't go with them."

"So, Marina has no alibi for yesterday evening?" Mom gasped.

"Precisely."

chapter thirty-two

Paparazzi

Monday brought about huge developments in my kidnapping case. Erica and Mr. Harper were arraigned and pled 'not guilty,' and now, they're locked up, awaiting their trials. Surprisingly, it was also the day when Marina was arrested for *her* role in my kidnapping.

"They got evidence?" I asked Mom, excitedly.

"Yeah, the DNA on the voice disguiser thing matched hers *and* her alibi didn't pan out, as several eyewitnesses gave statements that Coral wasn't with her on Saturday evening."

"Charles and his family," I smiled. Mom nodded. "And I'm not surprised that Erica and Mr. Harper pled not guilty. It's not like they're going to admit that they did it."

Within a few days, I knew that my life needed to feel normal again, and I desperately wanted to see my friends and finish up fifth grade. Given my abysmal track record with some of Saint Bart's esteemed professionals, my parents were no longer willing to blindly trust my safety to Mr. Jacobs's judgment, so until the end of the school year, they insisted on hiring a bodyguard to keep an eye on me at school. I'm really not so sure about this whole bodyguard thing, because I'm extremely concerned he might interfere with the normalcy I have with my friends, and I don't need any more drama in my life. I hung out in Mom's classroom until it was time to join the kids on the playground. For obvious reasons, I didn't want to go to Mr. Harper's room unless I absolutely had to be there, and I certainly didn't need to be there before the school day began.

It wasn't until I was outside waiting for my friends to arrive that the realization struck me that Mr. Harper wouldn't be my teacher anymore! I mean, I knew he had been arrested, and I knew he wasn't the awesome person I had thought he was, but it hadn't sunk in that I suddenly would have a different teacher! I ran over to Mom. "Mom, who's gonna be my teacher?"

"I'm sure Mr. Jacobs has found a substitute," Mom reassured.

"Oh, I hope it isn't Mrs. Larson," I revealed.

"That would be horrific for you, my Little Dragon," Mom agreed.

I went back to playing on the monkey bars. "Oh, so, you're not dead?" Skye asked, running over. My bodyguard growled at her. She looked slightly rattled but continued, "My parents told me they thought you'd be dead."

"No, Skye, I'm very much alive," I admitted. "Sorry to ruin your day," I snickered.

"That's too bad," Skye said, running off to play on the swings.

"Wow," I said aloud. "I'm feelin' the love."

"Skye loves you?" Freddie exclaimed, arriving on the playground, dropping his backpack, and immediately climbing to the top of the monkey bars.

"No, she's disappointed that I'm alive," I recounted. I shook my head in utter disbelief that Skye could be so heartlessly callous to me after I had endured what I had been through over the weekend.

Freddie did a flip off the top bar and landed like a gymnast. He then hustled over to me. "*I'm* glad you're alive, Persephone!" He gave me a big hug and said, "So I'm smarter than Skye."

Jade interrupted the way-too-long hug. "So, Girl, you went and got yourself kidnapped this weekend and didn't even call me to say you were fine?"

"I didn't know you even knew!" I admitted.

"Girl, *everyone* knows! It's on the news, you know... or did you totally miss that row of television crews in front of our school?"

"Reporters are here?" I asked, in a daze. I hadn't seen anything out of the ordinary when Mom had driven into the parking lot this morning.

"Oh yeah, they are," Jade reassured.

Freddie nodded, adding, "Mr. Jacobs said they have to stay in front of the school, so we've been out back here a lot this week."

Joey ran up to join us. "Hey guys! I didn't think I'd *ever* get here with all those reporters in the way!"

"Did they interview you, too?" Freddie asked.

"Interview? Is that what that was? They kept hounding me with questions, but I didn't feel like it was an interview. Where was my fancy coffee mug and cool leather couch?" Joey asked. We all laughed. I hadn't realized what an impact my kidnapping would have on my friends. I felt badly that their lives had gotten so crazy.

"So, does anyone know who our teacher will be?" I asked. My friends said nothing. Coincidentally, we were all summoned to line up at that exact moment.

In line, I got my answer as Mrs. Larson walked up to me. "So, Persephone, looks like I get to make your life miserable for the remainder of the school year!" she threatened, before cackling. "It's time for a little payback, honey!"

Junior, my bodyguard, stepped up to her. "Not so fast ma'am," he uttered, putting his large, scary body, between Mrs. Larson and myself. He picked her up and slammed her against the nearest wall. "There will be no threats or harm to Miss Smith on *my* watch." He turned and grinned at me over his shoulder. Maybe I *was* too judgmental of this whole bodyguard thing. After careful consideration, I daresay Junior just might be a welcome addition to my fifth grade classroom, after all!

I decided that it would be in everyone's best interest if I did not say one word in class that day. If Mrs. Larson dared to tease me – and I believed she would certainly do so – she'd have Junior to face. I would sit there and take anything she could dole out, not uttering a word, crying, or hiding. If I could endure a kidnapping, I could certainly survive a day with Mrs. Larson, particularly with Junior to back me up.

And somehow it worked! I got through the whole day without talking in the classroom at all! I got some strange looks because I was just *so* quiet, but I didn't care. I had survived the day in one piece

359

without agitating the green haired substitute teacher, who wore way too much makeup, *and* without having to rely on my bodyguard to save me. I talked to Joey and Freddie at recess, sure, but no talking *in* the classroom. Boy oh boy, I was so relieved for the sound of that end-of-the-day bell.

I ran to Mom's room, not caring if I got in trouble for running in the halls. "Mom! Mrs. Larson was the substitute!" I announced.

"I heard! Was it dreadful?" Mom asked.

"Yes!" I admitted. "But I didn't say anything and I didn't get in any trouble."

"Are you ready for the news crews getting in our faces as we make our way home?" Mom asked.

"Seriously, Mom?" I had almost forgotten all about my sudden rise to fame. "What do they want?"

"They want a statement, Persephone," Mom urged.

"If I survived a kidnapping, I can surely give a statement to the reporters," I boasted. We walked out the front door of the school. Junior stayed between me and the paparazzi. There were so many flashes, and it instantaneously got so loud with questions being hurled my way. I held up my hand in an effort to quiet the crowd. They followed my cue.

"I would like to thank you all for your coverage of my kidnapping and I would like to thank everyone who has helped out in any way. I also want to say that I believe justice *will* prevail and that I am confident that the investigation will lead to the people who did this to me being punished. Now, please leave my friends and family and myself alone so we can get back to our normal lives.

Thank you." Junior parted the press to allow me a path to our car, and Mom and I got in and drove away. Undoubtedly the cameras were still rolling, but I was hopeful that they would give us privacy.

I was wrong. More camera crews greeted us at home. When I got out of the car and was besieged by questions, I simply shoved by and said, "People, I'm old news now, or did you miss the statement that I *already* gave at school?" Somehow, Mom and I navigated the crowd, got inside our house, and found Dad making dinner in the kitchen. Within minutes, we saw cell phones being whipped out and the news crews dissipated. "See, guys, I *am* old news," I grinned.

"Well done, my Little Dragon," Mom praised.

"Eh, ya get kidnapped, ya get a little tougher in life," I noted with a shrug. "I guess it happens to the best of us."

"Squirt, kidnapping is *not* wicked normal," Dad reminded.

"No, but growing up is," I determined with a smile.

chapter thirty-two
The Fifth Grade Dance

Without warning, the month of May had passed by, and we had reached the night of the Fifth Grade Dance. Mom and Dad insisted that I should go, even without a date. So the weekend before the dance, Mom had bought me a really pretty pink floral dress with pearl buttons, faux pearl clip-on earrings, new sandals, and a new hair barrette that was a mix of lace, beads, and ribbons. The night of the dance, I donned my new dress and accessories and admired myself in the mirror.

"Well, Squirt?" Dad asked, looking proudly at me.

"I look good, Dad," I confidently admitted.

"You look beautiful, Squirt."

"I have a little surprise for you, Persephone," Mom said, holding something behind her back.

I closed my eyes and held my hands out in front of me. She put something in them. I opened my eyes and saw a package with a tube of pink, sparkly lipstick in it. "Mom? I can wear lipstick?"

"Well, you are ten now, so yes, but for special occasions only, my Little Dragon," Mom explained, winking. "Can I help you put it on?" she offered. Having not worn real lipstick properly before, I thought it would look better if Mom helped me out with it this time. When she finished, I noticed it was the perfect final touch.

"Wow, I do look beautiful," I said, gazing proudly at myself in the mirror.

"Told you so," Dad agreed.

As my 'Rents were helping to chaperone the Fifth Grade Dance, they gave Junior the night off. When the three of us arrived at Saint Bart's, we noticed that the school gym was decorated with twinkle lights and tulle and streamers. It looked like a fantasy land! A DJ was playing good pop tunes, but the dance floor was empty. The kids were all sitting at the tables. Freddie jumped up and ran over when he saw me.

"Persephone! You look beautiful!" Freddie exclaimed.

"Thanks, Freddie!" I blushed. "You're wearing a suit?" I giggled. "You look so grown up!"

"It's just a clip on tie, Persephone," he said, demonstrating the ease with which it went on and off. "So, are you ready to dance or what?"

"The purpose of a dance *is* to dance, Freddie," I agreed. I ran over to the DJ to request a surefire floorfiller as Freddie hurried over to the other kids to encourage them to hit the dance floor. When the song that I requested started, I squealed with delight! I rushed over to Mom and Dad, grabbed their hands, and pulled them out onto the floor to dance with me. Freddie and the other kids joined us.

"Hey, it worked!" Freddie exclaimed towards me, when we reconvened on the dance floor. "Everyone's dancing!"

"Yay!" I cheered. With the students and chaperones all dancing, people didn't care whether or not they could dance well, so we were all just having a good time. The jammin' dance tunes kept cranking and we kept dancing for probably an hour!

And then the DJ played a slow song. I headed off the dance floor, as I didn't have a date to this shindig. Mom and Dad danced with each other though, as did all the couples that had gone to the dance together. I was actually the only student sitting out for the love ballad. I wished Joey was there, cuz then I'd have an excuse to insist that he danced with me, so that we wouldn't be the only two kids sitting out.

The DJ followed up that slow song with another slow song. And another. And a fourth. I walked over to the refreshment table and got a cup of punch. I looked back at the dance floor and saw that all the couples were *still* dancing, so I took my punch outside for some fresh air. The front entryway was impressively decorated with twinkle lights, too, so that even when getting some air we still felt within the fantasy world created inside. I looked up into the sky and saw a star. So I made a wish. I took a big breath and tried to look for constellations, but there was only the one star in the sky.

"Persephone!" a familiar voice called. I looked down from my celestial search.

"Joey?" I said, smiling. Joey ran up to me, from the parking lot. He turned and waved to his car, and it pulled away. His cheeks were rosy, his blue eyes twinkled, and his dimples were so pronounced due to his smile being wider than ever. He was wearing a yellow shirt, blue tie, and khaki pants. I've never seen him look so cute!

"The family function got done a little early and I got to come to the end of the Fifth Grade Dance!" he exclaimed. "I guess the magic worked!" he grinned. "I brought you something," he said, handing me a white cardboard box. "Open it!"

I opened the box and inside was a wrist corsage with pink roses, white carnations, and teal ribbons! "Joey! It's beautiful!" I exclaimed, slipping it on my wrist. "Thank you!"

"You're welcome, Persephone!" Joey blushed, looking down.

"Did you really use magic to get here?" I asked, remembering what he had said.

"Oh, I thought you had used *your* magic to get me here!" he exclaimed. "I didn't think the family thing could possibly be done this soon, so I thought you had given it a nudge."

"It wasn't me, but I'm just glad you're here, Joey," I admitted, not wanting to discuss that I never believed that he actually had a family function anyways.

"Are you ready to make a splash, Persephone?" Joey asked, holding his arm out for me to take.

"Yes, let's do this!" I said, taking his arm. We walked in and the DJ had resumed playing good pop dance tunes again. We joined everyone else on the dance floor, happily laughing and dancing up a storm for what seemed to be another hour.

Then the DJ announced he was playing the last song, and in accordance to tradition, it was a slow song. "Persephone, wanna dance with me?" Joey asked, nervously. I nodded and we faced each other. I put my hands on Joey's shoulders and he put his hands on my waist. He looked down and blushed and I couldn't help but giggle, but somehow we managed to dance, stepping back and forth and turning slowly to the music. We each struggled with looking at each other while dancing, but we stole a few glances while primarily watching our feet.

Then the song ended. "Thank you, Joey," I said, dropping my hands off his shoulders as he dropped his hands off my waist.

"No problem, Persephone," he smiled at me. Everyone started filing out to the front entryway area to wait for their rides. Of course my ride was already at the dance, as they were chaperoning.

"Do you have a ride home?" I asked.

"Yeah, Mom's coming back at nine o'clock," he revealed. We both looked at the clock. "Which would be about now," he said, as I thought the same thing.

"I can walk outside with you to wait for your mom," I offered.

"Okay, that works," he agreed with a smile. We walked outside. Our classmates were taking advantage of the ambiance of the entryway, so yeah, that wasn't a very comfortable scene. All the couples were holding hands or kissing goodbye and stuff. It was really mushy out there.

"Thank goodness you two are out here now," Freddie revealed as he ran up to us. I was honestly grateful that Freddie joined us, because it took that awkwardness of whether or not kissing would be appropriate completely away. "With everyone else like kissing, there wasn't anyone to talk to!"

"You've got us," I sighed with relief.

"Yeah," Joey agreed. "Hey, Mom's right over there," he said, pointing to his car. "Persephone, I had a really nice time. You look awesome tonight." He fidgeted a little, uncomfortably.

"Thanks, Joey," I tried to help with the awkwardness of the moment. "You look so cute!" I confessed. That just made him blush and look more uncomfortable. "Thanks for the corsage!" I added, feeling as though I wasn't helping the situation at all.

Joey looked at his car and then looked at me. Then he looked back at the car, sighed and hurriedly hugged me. "Bye, Persephone," he blurted out, rushing off to his car.

Freddie and I watched his car pull away. "Dude, he so wanted to kiss you," Freddie teased.

"Nuh-uh," I disagreed.

"How did you miss that?" Freddie continued. "If I wasn't here, and if his mom wasn't right there in the car, he so would've smooched you!"

"You are so gonna get it!" I threatened Freddie with my "ready to chase" stance.

"You don't scare me, Persephone!" Freddie challenged, ready to run. "Oh, wait, Dad's here! I'll see ya Monday!" he said, running to his car. I found an empty bench and sat on it. One by one, everyone's rides came and in a few minutes, I had the twinkling entrance all to myself.

"You ready, Persephone?" Dad asked when he and Mom came outside, after all the other students had left.

"Yup," I said, getting up and joining them.

"Well, that was a nice evening, wasn't it?" Mom asked. "How's Joey?"

"Mom!" I blushed.

"He brought you a wrist corsage?" Dad asked, noticing the flowers. "He must really like you."

"Did he kiss you?" Mom inquired.

"Mom!" I hid my face.

"Ooh, I think that's a yes!" Dad teased.

"No, he didn't," I admitted. "Freddie said he thought Joey wanted to kiss me, but he didn't kiss me."

"So he's a gentleman," Dad concluded. "I like this Joey guy. He might actually wait until you're thirty-four to date you."

"Dad!" I blushed some more. "We're friends!"

"Friends don't usually drop everything to get out of family plans, bring corsages, and slow dance to the last song of the night, Persephone," Mom pointed out.

I giggled. Okay, so Joey apparently liked me. This was a good thing. After all, I liked Joey again, too. At home, I put my corsage in the refrigerator to keep it nice as long as possible. Then, I smiled nonstop until I fell asleep, continually thinking of Joey, of the Fifth Grade Dance, and of all the possibilities. The world seemed limitless, and I was perfectly happy.

chapter thirty-three

Summer

P erhaps for some people, graduation from elementary school was a big deal, but at Saint Bart's, it really wasn't. We didn't have a ceremony. We just completed our year, got our report cards, and tore out of the classroom shrieking that there was no more school. We knew that most of us would see each other again in September when we wound up together for sixth grade at the public middle school.

Unfortunately, Joey won't be there. On the last day of school, he confessed to me that he was moving to northern Vermont at the end of June. As it turns out, his family thing on the day of the Fifth Grade Dance was something related to the move, and that's why he hadn't gone into detail about it. I was devastatedly sad that I wouldn't get to see him anymore, because let's face it, ever since the Fifth Grade Dance my crush on him had become colossal, *and* he was absolutely one of my best friends! So yeah, *total* bummer! We promised to keep in touch, but I don't have his address. Cue big, dramatic sigh.

Speaking of keeping in touch, Mom and Dad actually let me get an email address, and I heard from Charles and Drew a few times over the summer. I did not hear from Coral, and I made no attempt to contact her as I wasn't sure of the legal ramifications if I did. In one email, Charles revealed that Coral was having difficulty dealing with her mom being in jail, blaming me for it. I tried to argue with him that at no point did I *ask* Marina to kidnap me. He agreed and also lacked understanding as to why Coral's anger was directed at *me* and not at him, when it was *he* and his family who told the police about Marina's lack of an alibi. In every correspondence, he reaffirmed that he was still my "shield" and vowed to continue being my protector, but frankly, I just hoped I never needed saving again.

While we're sort of on the topic of bodyguards, my 'Rents said that Junior had the summer off *and* would only be called upon to keep me safe in middle school *if* I needed such help. Although I actually don't mind having Junior around, I think I'll cause less of a scene at my new school if I *don't* have a bodyguard with me, so I certainly have sufficient incentive to stay safe. And for the record, I tried and tried all summer to get Mom and Dad to explain why Dad had made that face when I mentioned middle school, but they *still* weren't talking about it. Call me psychic if you must, but I sense I won't be a big fan of middle school, and that I probably shouldn't be surprised if Junior returns to keep an eye on me again in sixth grade.

Jade and I kept busy with lots of swimming adventures and riding bikes and playing basketball at the nearby public school yard. She kept going on and on about her new boyfriend, Danny. Danny was a boy she met when her family went on vacation to Maine for a week at the end of June. As luck would have it, he lives one town over from where we live and would go to our high school in a few years. Apparently, Danny made Jade very happy, and it sure was good to see her back to her usual impish self.

In July, my family and I went on our annual vacation to Maine. We rented a cottage by the ocean for a week. One of the other families, who had also rented a cottage, had a boy who looked to be about twelve. Blonde hair and blue eyes and *cute!* I heard them call him "Ricky." Ooh, it was crush at first sight! Okay, I never did actually talk to him, but I looked at him a lot that week.

Now, it might not be necessary to say, but I never became a CIT at Birch Bog Camp. Honestly, it was still closed after the scandal that erupted on account of me last summer! No, I didn't go to *any* camp, and I didn't miss it one bit. And I still haven't had a s'more, and I'm okay with that.

On August 7, 2010, I celebrated my 10 ½ Birthday! Some people don't celebrate half birthdays, but with the exception of last year, I do! "Dad, I've been ten for six months and yet my room is still not painted," I mentioned. "When were you planning on actually getting around to it?"

"Squirt, could you tell me when in the last six months I was supposed to find time to give your room a makeover?" Dad asked. "Should it have been when Seth died? Or maybe in the midst of not one, not two, but three spelling bees? Oh, perhaps when you were suspended from school? Oh no, wait, I know, maybe when I was dealing with you being kidnapped?"

371

"Okay, okay, it's been a crazy year, Dad," I admitted, obviously interrupting his tirade.

"We'll get to it, Persephone," Mom encouraged. "Someday."

"Someday," I repeated absentmindedly, wandering to my plain old bedroom.

But Dad *had* reminded me that my birthday wasn't the only thing that happened six months ago today. Today was also the six month anniversary of Seth's death. I hadn't seen or heard anything from Seth since my kidnapping. I had always suspected that he was "haunting" me for a purpose, and apparently it was to help save me from my kidnappers, because there was no sign of him afterwards. I missed him. I toyed with the ring on the chain around my neck.

SNAP! Without warning, the chain fell from the back of my neck. I held onto the ring as the chain slipped off, hanging limply from the ring. I confirmed the chain had broken, clearly beyond repair. I slipped the ring onto my right ring finger and brought the chain to Mom. "Mom, is this chain real silver?" I inquired.

Mom studied the chain. "No, Kiddo, it's just cheap garbage." She threw the broken chain away. Then she looked at me with wide eyes that looked panicked. "Did you lose the ring?"

"No, I still have it," I admitted. Mom smiled, comfortingly. "Mom, would you let me light a candle in Seth's honor tonight?"

"Wow, today's the six month anniversary of –," she stopped herself. "Persephone, you know how I feel about children and fire."

"One votive candle in a candleholder, outside on the end of the concrete sidewalk where I last saw him, no flammable stuff

372

anywhere near me, *and* a jug of water right there," I offered, "please?"

"It sounds controlled and reasonable," Dad admitted.

"She's ten, she shouldn't play with matches," Mom argued.

"She's lighting one candle, it's not playing with matches," Dad countered.

"Your father is too soft. Guess I'm overruled." Mom let me look through her votives to find the perfect color and scent for my memorial. Dad stretched the hose out to be next to the end of the sidewalk, just in case things got out of hand, and he brought two open, uncapped gallon jugs of water to place next to where I would be on the sidewalk. Dad demonstrated how to light a match without getting burned, and then how to light a candle successfully without getting burned. Mom suggested I should just learn how to cast fire on wicks, because it'd be safer than me lighting matches. After that, I just waited for darkness.

At dusk, I carried a blue votive candle, which smelled like the ocean, in a clear glass votive holder, carefully, to the end of the sidewalk. I set it down gently and sat down, crossed-legged. I took a deep breath, because as much as I knew I needed to do this, in memory of Seth, I was still very nervous about actually lighting a match and a candle.

I pulled the fluorite crystal from my pocket. "By the power within this fluorite, let me remain in a circle of protection, safe from fire and all things evil, this evening." I laid the crystal next to the candleholder on the right side. I took out my clear quartz crystal and held it up. "May the power of the quartz cleanse this candle of all impurities and allow the candle to burn solely in the memory of Seth Totter, who lost his life six months ago tonight." I placed the quartz to the left of the candleholder. I reached into my pocket and pulled out my rose quartz. I held up the rose quartz and said, "And may everyone in the world know the power of true love." I placed that crystal directly in front of me.

I took another deep breath and exhaled it slowly. I removed the box of matches from my pocket. "Please don't let me get burned," I whispered as I pulled out a match. I held it between my fingers and began to speak words I had not planned, but that felt like they needed to be said. "Six months ago today, Seth Totter, age ten, drowned unexpectedly in Elk Pond. May Seth and all who cared about him find peace and comfort wherever they may be. In Seth's memory, I honor him on this anniversary with a candle that burns with a light as bright as the light he brought to all those who knew him. I miss you, Seth." I felt tears forming in my eyes, so I lit the match, without difficulty, and quickly lit the candle before blowing the match out and placing it in one of the jugs of water.

I closed my eyes to fight back the tears. "Seth, I want you to be alive," I whispered, struggling with remaining composed. "I'd give anything for you to be alive and well again."

"What would you do if you could rewind time?" a voice I knew too well, but hadn't heard in six months, asked.

I smiled, keeping my eyes closed. "I would stop myself from breaking up with you because you splashed mud on me that Easter, and I would have run out here, in the cold, on my birthday, to stop you from going up to the pond." I felt the tears running on my cheeks, but I was smiling. I hadn't heard Seth's voice since my birthday, but it sounded like music to my ears. I knew it must be taking a great deal of energy for him to talk to me, but I felt such a sense of peace in hearing him. It was like he was right there again.

"Really? You would've stopped me?"

"I want you to be alive more than anything else in the world, Seth," I admitted. "If I could change something, anything at all, that would be it."

"Open your eyes, Princess," Seth directed.

I opened my eyes, and Seth stood there, cuter than ever! He looked so real! I jumped to my feet in shock! It seemed as though I could reach out and touch him! "I've missed you, Seth!" I admitted with a goofy grin on my face.

"Nice ring, Princess," Seth commented. I instinctively put my right hand behind my back. "Um, it's on your *other* left hand," he teased.

I looked at my left ring finger, where Seth's ring sparkled brilliantly. "But I swear I put it on my right hand when the chain broke!" I stated. I was so confused. I couldn't find words. Seth took my hand in his and looked at the ring as well. I couldn't understand how he was touching me! Since he died, every time he had tried to touch me, he passed through me and I felt nauseated. Yet, here he was holding onto my hand and my stomach felt great!

"It's definitely on your left hand now," Seth pointed out. He then let go of my hand and took a step back to look at me. "Oh no, you're freaking out. I think you need a hug," he suggested. I looked at him like he was crazy. I did *want* to hug him at that moment more than anything, but the memory of that hug in February where I had passed right through him haunted me. But he just looked so real that I *had* to hug him. I reached out my arms... and I hugged him!

My arms didn't flail in the air or go through him. No, I felt him in my arms, and he felt just as real as could be! I hugged him tighter and for an extra long time because I couldn't understand how it could be that a ghost could feel *SO* real! "How is this possible?" I asked aloud.

Seth released me from his hug and took a step back, looking at me with an incredulous look that suggested he believed I was missing something obvious, but I honestly had no clue what it could be. I desperately hoped for an explanation, but he just smiled sweetly and shook his head in disbelief as he cryptically announced, "Wow, Princess, you really do have *no* idea how wicked powerful you truly are!"

Made in the USA
Charleston, SC
05 March 2013